MacG
McGlothin, Victor.
Every sistah wants it

$22.95

1st ed.   ocm55534807

Every Sistah Wants It

Also by Victor McGlothin

What's a Woman to Do?
Autumn Leaves

Every Sistah Wants It

VICTOR McGLOTHIN

St. Martin's Press ❧ New York

www.stmartins.com

Library of Congress Cataloging-in-Publication Data

McGlothin, Victor.
    Every sistah wants it / Victor McGlothin.—1st ed.
        p. cm.
    ISBN 0-312-32197-X
    EAN 978-0312-32197-0
    1. African American women—Fiction. 2. Triangles (Interpersonal relations)—Fiction. 3. Radio producers and directors—Fiction. 4. Rejection (Psychology)—Fiction. 5. Rap musicians—Fiction. 6. Dallas (Tex.)—Fiction. I. Title.

PS3613.C484E94 2004
813'.6—dc22

                                                                            2004050812

First Edition: December 2004

10   9   8   7   6   5   4   3   2   1

For Terre, my beautiful wife, who is the end all to be all . . . amen

Acknowledgments

Kings and Queens of the Airwaves

Special Thanks
To ABC Radio's Hollywood Hernandez with Dietra Miles, for suggesting that I write a book about deejays' private lives, and to K104's Cletus, for the insight I needed into the life behind the microphone.

The Tom Joyner Morning Show with Sybil Wilkes, *The Doug Banks Show* with DeDe McGuire and CoCo Budda, *The Russ Parr Show* with Olivia Fox, and *Steve Harvey's Morning Show* with Shirley Strawberry.

Dallas Radio—K104: Skip Murphy and the Morning Team, Skip Cheatham, Mel The Mack, Cat Daddy, Nate Quick, and Greg Street; KKDA 730 AM: Cheryl Smith; 97.9 The Beat's Big Bink, HeadKrack, Axion Jaxion, Super K, and Key Note; LA Radio—100.3 The Beat's PJ Butta, A-One, Spinderella, DJ Mo'Dav, Eric Cubiche & K-Sky, Corn Dogg Nautica de la Cruz, Angie B., and Eddie G.; Houston's Magic 102: Kandi Eastman, Dana Jackson, and Jeff Harrison; 97.9 The Box: Madd Hatta, Carmen Cantreras, DJ Aggravated, and Def Jam Blaster; New York—Hot 97: Sunny, Angie Martinez, FunkMaster Flex, and Fatman Scoop; Atlanta—Hot 107.9: *Ryan Cameron's Morning Show*; 97.1

Acknowledgments

JAMZ: JumpOff Crew's Tariq, Baby Boy, Mixxmaster Mitch, Big Mike, Skye, Jazzy J., Rise, and B-Rocka; Kiss 104.1: Stacy D., Sasha, Mitch Faulkner, and Cynthia Young; D.C. Area's WPGC: *The Donnie Simpson Morning Show*, Justine Love, Michel Wright, Rane, and EZ Street; Virginia Beach's 95.7 R&B: Sunny & Marie, Karen Parker-Chesson, Theresa Brown, and Charles Black.

And to all the Radio One and ABC affiliates that I'll meet on this tour, "If it ain't live, it ain't me, neither."

Every Sistah Wants It

1

Young Dogs, New Tricks

Five-thirty P.M. had the avenues of Dallas on lockdown. Typical Friday-evening traffic ground to an excruciating halt for the motorists who figured they'd get ahead of the game by leaving the office a few minutes early, only to be stuck in with the masses who'd figured the same. Interstate 635 sent its usual regrets. The twelve-year ongoing construction of I-75 was four years behind schedule, and the Tollway burst at the seams. Despite suffering the inconvenience of being held up, everyone was happy as hell. It was Friday, after all.

"Y'all gotta be giggling yourselves silly right now cause I'm still at work and you're not," spouted a familiar voice over the radio. "But that's alright cause Alphonzo the radio gigolo's gonna get his tonight. And if you're between paychecks, bounce over to Club Fix and have a drink on me. Tell Big Mike at the door that I said it and if he don't like it he can kiss my—hold on, hold on. Who? Big Mike's on the phone? For me?" There was a brief pause as the festive after-five head-bobbing drive-time beats flowed over the airwaves. "Hey y'all, uh . . . scratch that drink-on-me thing. Big Mike said he ran my credit and he's gonna pray for me. But you know where my heart is, the same place I live. Here on the Hot 100, the Monster Beats."

Inside the Hot 100 radio station, Alphonzo thumbed through a stack of CDs, then hooked the next song to play. As soon as the intro began, he snatched off his headset and darted out of the studio door to chase down Octavia before she could leave for the weekend. "'Tavia, bay-bee. Glad I caught you. What do you say to me and you gettin' to the good part, after I close the show tonight? You know I'm due." He thought back on the first time he had seen her at the station, three years ago. Her dark brown flawless skin and slight frame still sang to him just like it had then. "Come on now, give me the time of day and I'll make it worth your while. I ain't never been with no real Indian and them high cheekbones and narrow hips do it for me. I can't even lie about it." He continued to eye the way her tight blue jeans hugged her even tighter size-six behind and flared over a brown pair of narrow leather ankle boots.

Octavia Longbow tossed her shiny black shoulder-length hair back in Alphonzo's direction as he licked his lips like a starving dog, awaiting her reply. Even though he'd been shot down a minimum of thirty-nine times, he still went back for more abuse from the attractive junior producer. While Alphonzo salivated over a woman who was out of his league, Octavia returned his sly smile with one of her own, then let her head fall to the side. "'Zo, I'm only half *Native American*, and if that's why you've been spending time trying to get with me, you've wasted a lot of tired lines in the process. Besides, you know I love you like a play-cuzzin and we could never be more than what we are now: friends. Everybody knows the kinds of things you're into and I wants no parts of that. Bottom line is you're nasty and the hoochies you get with are nasty . . . so I guess that means I'll have to pass, yet again."

"'Tavia, don't do this. You know I need you in my world. Please think about it and get back to me. It's good," he added suggestively, wagging his tongue. "How's about a headboard pressed against your face and you sucking on my pillowcase? You know I got skills. You'll be sliding yo' feet against my ears and pleading me to let you pay for it." Octavia's eyes widened as the radio bad boy continued. "Come on girl, let me top that off for you. I'll make you breakfast in bed," he added, sweetening the pot. "Now, I can't cook worth a damn, but for you I'll learn. Baby I can learn."

"First of all, begging is very unbecoming. And secondly, you are not my type." She paused a brief moment to look him over thoroughly. "That bad-boy goatee and cornrow braids do suit you fine, but they don't suit me."

Alphonzo was a good-looking man, but the word was out on him. He had more women than a homeless dog has fleas and the simple truth was, Alphonzo the Radio Ho' didn't seem to mind the fleas. Slowly he backed away toward the booth but refused to give up. "Hey 'Tavia, that's the first time you ever called me 'Zo. I'm getting close. I can feel it, like you'll be feeling me . . . and soon."

Octavia threw him a just-this-side-of-flirtatious grin, then puckered her thin lips into a kiss. She smacked them softly. "There you go, Alphonzo. Put that where you want it."

"Yeah, I'll do that until you come to your senses."

"Uh-huh, whatever. Oh, by the way, your song ended fifteen seconds ago."

Cee-Cee Lovely stepped around the corner to investigate the silence coming out of the radio on her desk, which was always set to Hot 100. "Alphonzo, you'd better get your butt back to work before PMS gets wind of this. You know your luck is about to run out."

Before Cee-Cee, the former-Miss-Texas-turned lady deejay, could give him further advice, Alphonzo made a mad dash for the studio to do what he was paid to do—spin records. Patricia Maria Stapleton, who was also referred to as PMS, was all business all the time and had one thing on her mind as program director—maintaining her long run at the number-one spot in the Dallas market. No way she was willing to let Alphonzo's antics or his well-known weakness for women come between her and her place at the top. She'd spent twenty years getting there and would just as soon show him the street before she'd risk relinquishing her reign as queen.

"That brotha is a hot minute away from being tied to a plastic chair with his name on it at the unemployment office." Cee-Cee commented, her arms folded like Octavia's. "I'll bet he was out here wasting his time trying to weasel his way in your pants, huh?"

"You know it. Some things never change."

"What's that make, his thirty-fourth . . . thirty-fifth attempt at the impossible?"

"Not that I'm keeping count, but I do believe that was the big four-o. It's just a game to him. He likes the chase. Just being a typical man, wanting what he knows he can't have."

Cee-Cee bit her bottom lip in a sexy and playful manner. "Truth be told, from what I hear, Alphonzo is packing and I ain't talking about groceries. My neighbor Shay says he's hung like the moon." Octavia flashed an "I know you are not considering getting with him" sideways smirk, and Cee-Cee began her backpedal. "Did you think I was talking about me? Oh, hell no!" Her adamant protest was almost believable. Almost.

"Uhhh-huh. You'd better watch your step, Cee-Cee. You seem a little bit too curious, and I remember the last time you wanted to see if a certain brotha's package had its own zip code. You've had nothing but woman problems ever since."

After Cee-Cee's eyes lit up like a roman candle, she humbly agreed. "You gotta point. It's been six months and ma' girl still ain't right. I'm just like my momma, though. She had a thing for men overly blessed in that department, too."

"Yeah, but Alphonzo can save his blessing for a sistah who doesn't mind spending months at the doctor trying to get her goodies pieced back together. I'm not down for all that jump-right-to-it bumping and grinding like I used to be. Now I like to be held." Octavia wrapped her arms around her waist sensually.

"Well, I rather enjoy a good bumping-and-grinding escapade. Having my back twisted just right is my idea of time well spent—then I like to be held. Can I help it that I love a challenge in the sack, even if I have to see the doctor to put everything back in its proper place? Like I said, I'm my momma's daughter, and speaking of time well spent, we'd better get going before we get locked out of The Chat."

Just outside the radio station, Octavia climbed into Cee-Cee's brand-new silver Mercedes C Class sedan in the employee parking lot. "Cee-Cee, I really like this Benz, and that new-car smell. You know how I feel about leather. How can you afford all this on what the station pays you?" As soon as the words left Octavia's lips she wished that she could pull them back, but it was too late. The insult had already been launched.

Cee-Cee stopped rummaging through her cluttered purse when the words slapped her like an open hand. "And just how would you know what the station pays me?"

"Uh, I'm sorry. It's just that last month I received your paycheck by mistake and opened it before I realized that it wasn't mine." Octavia was overwhelmingly surprised that an on-air personality made less than she did. It never occurred to her it was why so many of them did odd jobs or made appearances at nightclubs when they were dog-tired from working all day. The "Pimpin' Paper," those gigs typically paid under the table in cash, came in handy. If deejays showed some real initiative, they could make an additional twenty to thirty grand a year by giving up all their private time to be in the public eye.

"Forget about it," Cee-Cee said eventually. "Everybody gets pimped, played, pushed, and pulled in this business at one time or another. It sure beats working part-time jobs to make ends meet. Some of the guys at other stations don't have it so good."

Silence stood between them. Octavia was busy wishing that she could have been any other place than where she was.

"I didn't mean to go there on you Cee-Cee, but I must admit I was taken aback when I . . . uh, saw it. Y'all make the station so much money in advertising, I just assumed that the profit-sharing end of it was more beneficial."

"That makes two of us." Cee-Cee felt too deep into a conversation that made her feel less than what she was, a beautiful young woman whose face was more suitable for television than radio. Some of the local talent didn't have a choice. In the beginning, Cee-Cee was like most newbies fresh out of broadcasting school. She had been taken in by the grandiose outer appearance of radio but after experiencing life from the other side of the microphone, she wasn't too sure if the pageantry and fame from her yesterdays hadn't been holding her hostage by dangling minor celebrity status. In either case, she spun hits for a living and shared her personal thoughts with hundreds of thousands of attentive listeners every day, for a lot less money than she thought she was worth.

When Cee-Cee turned the key to start her car, Alphonzo's light-hearted voice broke the spell of the awkward moment: "I just wanted to say good evening to two visions of utter perfection although they're trying to ignore me. Y'all know you hear me cause I'm looking right at'cha." Suddenly the ladies peered up at the bay window of the studio booth. Alphonzo was leering and waving like a man who was up to no good.

Well aware of Alphonzo's propensity for practical jokes, Cee-Cee had a bad feeling about it. "Uh-uh 'Tavia. 'Zo's up to something."

Still somewhat perplexed, Octavia had not caught on. "What do you mean?"

Cee-Cee began waving her fist, warning Alphonzo to let go of whatever stunt he had up his sleeve, but his smile was unrelenting as were his intentions. He discovered that Octavia had given too many good years to I. Rome, last year's double-platinum R&B singing sensation, only to have her love along with those good years shelved.

Returning to the microphone, Alphonzo served up a nasty dose of love the one you're with or at least love the one who's been begging for it. "I see you down there. Our very own Cee-Cee Lovely, the glamour girl of the Hot 100 world, and of course her partner in crime, the dope-producer Ms. Octavia Longbow. And just for her, here's a little something from me. This is the latest joint from Dallas's own, I. Rome, "I want U 4 myself." I'm taking the *fortieth* caller, that's the *fortieth* caller for the sold-out I. Rome concert tickets. That's right, you heard me. Number four-zero is the lucky number of the day."

As the jazzy beat hit the speakers in Cee-Cee's car, Octavia moved to pry open the passenger door and race back up to the building to get in Alphonzo's face for showing his behind at her expense, although it was an inside joke. "Oh hell no! I know he didn't just put me out there like that."

"Yeah, he did too, but 'Tavia, don't let him get next to you. That's just another of his little ghetto tricks to knock you off balance. He thinks if he can catch you slippin', you might do something to swing momentum his way. I've seen that tactic before, so calm down. He almost got me with it last year. I wasn't sure whether I wanted to choke him or stroke him."

"Cee-Cee, how does big mouth Alphonzo know about me and I. Rome?"

"Don't look at me. I didn't tell him. You know that is not my style. Besides, I don't know enough about your personal business to share it with someone else. You're always so guarded about stuff like that."

"Dammit Cee-Cee, if 'Zo knows, everybody knows. He's like a gossiping woman." Octavia stormed out of the car. When Alphonzo saw her heading toward the building, he scampered away from the window, fearing retribution. "You'd better run, punk!" she barked loudly toward the window Alphonzo had abandoned.

Once Octavia was back in the passenger seat, chest heaving rapidly, she let her frustrations fly. "I can't stand it when brothas try to get into your business after they realize ain't no getting in anything else."

Cee-Cee flashed a grin. "Just look at you. In a strange sort of way, you're a lil' turned on, huh?"

Octavia made a quick assessment of her semienraged state. She opened her mouth to deny it but couldn't. "Yeah, I do feel . . . kinda stimulated right now. How'd you know?"

"Because 'Zo has figured out in that twisted mind of his that adequately pissing off a woman by using a man who she feels strongly about, some of the juices that get to flowing in the process just might end up on him." Cee-Cee cut her eyes sharply at her passenger. "Uh-huh, you'd better watch *your* step."

While they inched forward on the freeway, Octavia turned down the volume on the car stereo so low that it was barely audible, but only Cee-Cee cared to hear it. She couldn't stave off the desire to get to the bottom of why the double platinum artist's music was forbidden to be played above a whisper in her own car. "Octavia, we've been friends for a few years now, and although we would probably be much tighter if you haven't been in night school working on your master's degree for the past twenty-four months, I know a little about your love life or lack thereof. We've shared some things about each other's men problems from time to time, but you've never once told me what went wrong between you and I. Rome. It couldn't have been that bad. I mean, the man *was* voted *Essence* magazine's Finest Man on the Planet. The Finest Man had to have some good days. So what gives? Why didn't you two make it work, for keeps?"

Reminiscing back on some of the best and worse times of her life, Octavia let a smile dance on the corners of her mouth. "Maybe it wasn't supposed to work out for us. Sure, he's a superstar millionaire now with the homes, cars, and mountains of things to go with it, but I knew him when he was a fifth-year student at the University of Texas Consolidated with just about enough credits to be a first-semester junior. It wasn't that he didn't have what it took to breeze right on through. He was extremely bright but he had no direction."

"So, you met him in college? Was he singing then?"

"It's funny now—sometimes I laugh when I think about it—but his career began when he was trying to get with this thick chick from Louisiana, Heretta Malveaux. She had all those young brothas doing cartwheels. Rome was digging her, too, but she had it bad for Marshall Coates, the campus jock."

Cee-Cee squinted her eyes to help her peruse her memory. "Marshall Coates, the Atlanta Falcon's football player?"

"One in the same. That whole year was a real trip. Marshall was getting with some rich white girl, Shauni Woodbridge, until he discovered she might have AIDS. Rorey Garland, the star quarterback, killed himself and all hell broke loose on the campus after that. I was only a sophomore then, nineteen years old and with no business being off the Oklahoma reservation or on a college yard with thirty thousand other students trying to find themselves. Rome was just as lost as any of us until he entered a karaoke contest to impress Heretta and ended up winning the damned thing. Although she turned him down cold, there was no stopping him on the music front after that. He dropped out of school, worked three jobs, and paid for voice and piano lessons. I was just one of his many "friends," as he put it. Sprung, too, just like all his other so-called friends who knew about me."

"I. Rome had it going on back then, too?" Cee-Cee agreed with the magazine's assessment of the entertainer's style and appeal.

"No doubt, with or without money, Isaiah Rome is simply too much man for one woman, and that has always been his downfall."

"Isaiah? That's what 'I' stands for? I thought it was something cool, more street."

"Sounds kinda corny, I know, and he was so down-to-earth in the beginning. He would write music and sing to me while I studied. Said I was his muse, his hip and his hop, then one day I caught him in my bed with my dorm mate from down the hall. He was busy giving her the hip hop that I supposedly inspired."

"Ohh, that's so sad. What did you do about it?"

"I cried a river after my dorm mate gathered her clothes and left my room, although the damage had already been done. The private pedestal I created for him was too high. Each time he'd fall off it, the harder I'd hit bottom. He didn't care, though. The man just dusted himself off and went on about his business as if nothing ever happened. Make no mistake, the pain was mine and mine alone."

Like a trained stunt driver, Cee-Cee skillfully maneuvered the car across two busy lanes of freewheeling motorists while listening in. "Hmm, I thought you were seeing him after you finished undergrad and moved to Dallas."

"Embarrassed as I am to say, I never stopped. I was always there no matter what. He began to do more local singing gigs, then traveled from state to state. All the while, I waited. I waited through the drama resulting from several drug allegations, two bad marriages including the one he's currently in, his baby-mama drama, and too many paternity suits to count. Humph, after the first scandal I felt sorry for him and wondered if I would have been able to stick it out had I been his first wife. After lightening struck again, I was counting my lucky stars that I wasn't." Octavia gazed out of the window, reflecting on what she'd spent just as much time worrying about as she had trying to forget. "My mama always told me, if you want to see the end of a relationship with a man just look at the beginning. The future is always there, in plain view."

Somewhat at a loss for words, Cee-Cee made her point without wasting any. "Why, 'Tavia? Why does he have a hold over you? Is it a physical thing?"

"The sex is something to behold, I'll grant him that, but it goes deeper for me. I had just turned twenty and it was the first time a man ever told me that he loved me, *while my legs were closed*. And I thought I was the only one he loved—the one who mattered."

"Did you believe him?" Cee-Cee asked, really wanting to know.

"Don't matter, he said it," Octavia replied without hesitation. "That's the only thing I could think about two years later when I read in *Jet* magazine that he'd gotten married to someone else, just three days after he'd spent the weekend with me. I don't expect you to understand why I'm still wrapped up him. It's just so hard to let go of something you feel you never got the chance to finish. I guess there's a sucker born every minute, huh?"

In the years since then, Octavia had not invited any other men into the space she'd reserved for the man who had given her the biggest little piece of his love that she was ever going to get. What Octavia didn't want to discuss any deeper, and was glad that Cee-Cee didn't push, concerned her current involvement with the troubled married man. Regardless of whether she thought he should have been hers, it was a touchy subject. Conversation over another woman's man always is.

2

Hat Chat

When Cee-Cee pulled over next to the curb at Sylvia Everheart's half-million-dollar home on Allegany Way, she wanted to dig a bit deeper into Octavia's personal business but knew that the envelope had been pushed as far as their friendship would allow. "You ready to do this?" Cee-Cee asked instead, before making her way up the walk to the five-bedroom red brick that Sylvia Everheart was awarded in a legal separation agreement after her husband Devin walked out on her and the I do's he had vowed in front of God and the four hundred guests.

"Yep," Octavia sighed eventually. "I hope that she's not tripping like the last time we had The Chat here. I am not in the mood for a pity party tonight."

"I never am," Cee-Cee replied.

The women rang the bell. Cee-Cee cleared her throat as if she wanted to make one last comment before their business would become common knowledge for the entire room full of women to digest openly. Sylvia opened the door instead and the opportunity to drop a tidbit of knowledge about Octavia's longtime, part-time, significantly-someone-else's-other was gone.

"Hey y'all," Sylvia greeted, louder than necessary. She held a slender flute of champagne like she planned on making love to it later.

"Cee-Cee, you are as beautiful as ever and Octavia, I don't even have to tell you how jealous I am that you never have a hair out of place. Glad you two could make it. I feel some serious issues just around the corner. Come on in, we're just about to get started."

Octavia passed a look to Cee-Cee from the corner of her eye that hollered, "If she's already sippin' it won't be long before she starts trippin'." Cee-Cee cleared her throat again, this time as a gesture of agreement. Both of them surmised silently that the girl-talk session would have an abbreviated shelf life. Dealing with Sylvia's emotional rollercoaster separation with her husband had become too labor intensive for most of the members in her inner circle.

Inside the spacious home, seven women were grazing among neatly decorated tables holding finger foods on elegant silver-plated serving trays, trading small talk while sampling the party fare. In the kitchen area, three blenders stood at attention for daiquiri duty for the countless Cosmopolitans that would ease the flow once the party got started. Since it was customary to begin on time, the ladies checked their watches to ensure they were comfortable and prepared.

Hat Chat was serious as a heart attack for all the women who gave up a Friday night once a month to get down and dirty with the philosophical, analytical, sexual, financial, and mental-health needs of their contemporaries. Two things were guaranteed each time the women met—the gloves came off, and discussion of the business at hand was forbidden outside outside the room.

Sylvia held up her freshly refilled glass and began tapping a teaspoon against it. The designer silverware no doubt belonged to a very elaborate table setting, part of the spoils from her wedding. "Attention ladies, I do believe that the hour has arrived. Could someone please lock the door so we can get this thing started right."

As one of the guests quickly made her way over to the front door, someone knocked on it from the outside. "Yeah. Go ahead," Sylvia said, annoyed, waving in the woman's direction as if she were a queen bestowing a royal pardon.

"Whoo-wee! Hey girls," the latest visitor hailed energetically. It was Truest Muldoon, decked out in a fitted black denim outfit and designer Gucci flats to match. "I was almost late and I've been waiting all month for this. You know I gots to get my chat on." Truest was considered more attractive than pretty. She had the appearance of a strange and rare bird, a ghetto-raised bad girl with fair skin and hazel eyes, pale blue and green, depending on what she wore and how the light glinted off them. Because Truest had a body to die for, most women who made her acquaintance admired her shapely frame while simultaneously envying her genetic good fortune. A master at manipulation of both sexes, she was a confident woman's ally and an utter nightmare for those who didn't have their self-esteem in check. It didn't take long for new members to discover which side of the line they fell on. In either case, Truest was going to get her way, by hook and by crook if necessary. She carried that confidence around as if it were a winning lotto ticket.

"Come on in, Truest," said Sylvia rudely. "We almost lost you this time." Sylvia couldn't stand being upstaged in her own home by anyone, but keeping up with Truest required more raw energy and street intellect than she was anointed with, so she had to allow the tardy trespasser the latitude to do her thing.

As the ladies jockeyed for seats in the living room, Truest wiggled her hips in between Cee-Cee and Octavia on the loveseat. "Hey y'all. Cee, 'Tavia. I thought somebody was supposed to remind me where this month's meeting was."

"Actually, I forgot. My bad, Tru," Octavia apologized.

"I did too. Bad week at the office but hey—" Cee-Cee stopped in midsentence to angle her face away from Octavia while smothering her own voice. "We need to talk." Her tone was confined to a labored judgmental whisper. Since there hadn't been any secrets previously kept between the three women, Truest was at a loss as to what Cee-Cee could have been trying to keep from Octavia.

Before Truest had a chance to inquire about all the sneaky-speak, Sylvia began lighting candles scented with exotic fragrances. Then she methodically stretched out the group's sacred scroll and recited the creed that members had to submit to before a meeting could officially commence. "Good evening, ladies, and welcome. The Hat Chat Proclamation reads as follows: 'This is a circle of sisters, not one of friends, because sisterhood is constant and never ends. What's revealed here is concealed here for obvious reasons. The love we openly share sustains through all seasons. With our mouths we offer gifts worth more than gold and with our ears we receive insight from stories told. From this moment hence-forth let not our sisterly bond be broken nor the intent of this gathering, of which I have spoken.'"

As Sylvia concluded, a nervous calm subdued the room. "Let all who submit to the proclamation say 'I will'." All the women present seemed circumspect while agreeing to the edict that was read with the degree of sincerity they found adequate for the occasion. "Now then, for those of you who are new to Hat Chat, let me tell you what's expected. Everyone will participate and offer assistance, with a loving spirit." She paused and cast a nasty expression at Truest. "And give twice as much as you want to receive."

"Don't be looking at me like that," Truest spat back. "I'm a veteran at this. You need to finish what you've got to say so we can get on with it."

"Hey ladies, ladies. Calm down," Cee-Cee interjected. "This is supposed to be our time to share each other's views, not one another's attitudes."

Sylvia pursed her lips tightly then perked up as if nothing had happened. "Like I was saying, you'll get one three-by-three card each to write any issue that's heavy on your heart, or whatever you feel a need to seek a second opinion on. Don't fret, the cards are identical and will be tossed in the hat, which will be passed among us to be discussed in, and I quote . . . full detail. All issues will remain anonymous so feel free to submit the topic of your whim and we will share in it accordingly."

"That's right, ladies," Chanteau agreed. "We'll cover everything from good soup to good sex." She was always ready to signify with some juicy horizontal tell-me-more-about-it.

"Now that's what I'm talking about, serving up great cake and great coochie!" said Kris, well known for her unrestricted candor. "What? Y'all act like we don't get raw up in here. Humph, that's why I keep coming back! Truth be told, I'm addicted."

"Me too," Davne Dobbs added. Her two cents' worth was barely audible as she seconded Kris's motion in her typical shy manner.

"I'm sayin'," Tracey threw in. "Don't trip. My soaps don't have anything on the chat, okaaaay."

Sylvia handed out the small squares of yellow paper and identical blue-ink pens. "Oh yeah, before I forget, for those of you with long deep-seated issues and you don't have enough room on the card, you might need to seek some professional help and we can refer you to a good therapist."

Octavia laughed louder than she had intended, once she finally loosened up, having relived some of the topics discussed at the previous meetings. "Mmm-hmm! You can say that again."

"Before the night's over, I'm sure I will," Sylvia declared evenly.

Cee-Cee quickly scribbled her topic on the card as if it pained her to do so, sighed, then folded it before dropping the paper in a wide-brimmed crimson-colored hat that Sylvia took around the room. Nearly all of the members had completed the task and dropped their cards into the hat, but Octavia held hers close until Sylvia nudged her while making her final round. Reluctantly she dangled it above the cards resting inside the crown of the hat as the others looked on in suspicion. She felt compelled to drop it in, although her stomach twisted into thick knots of trepidation.

It appeared as though Octavia was giving up her last dime instead of relinquishing a troubled point of concern to be discussed. Cee-Cee had a pretty good idea why her friend had second thoughts. There would be a full debate on every topic pulled out of that hat and unfortunately, the final word wasn't always what the initiator wanted to hear.

Sylvia placed the hat on a coffee table in the center of the group. Now that everyone was in, there would be no turning back. Truest returned from the kitchen with a Cosmopolitan in a tall water glass and reclaimed her snug fit between two of her favorite people. She handed Cee-Cee a napkin covered with snacks from the dessert tray, then casually looked at Sylvia who had been vying for her attention, knowing that she might have something to say about the ten-ounce cocktails she had poured herself.

Truest's smile was wide and toothy like a child who'd found a bag full of candy as Chanteau retrieved the first card from the cloth pot, looked over the note, then read it aloud. "Ooh, this ain't a bad place to start if I do say so myself. The issue is: 'My man really likes oral sex and complains that I'm not doing it right. I can't help it that I can't get all that in my mouth.'"

"Ooh, what's your man's name?" Kris asked in jest.

"Forget that," Chanteau argued likewise. "What's his number?"

"Awwwe-right. We are here to lend a hand." Sylvia the good hostess was being true to form.

"Indeed. I have two . . . free . . . hands," mumbled Cee-Cee, shoving all the remaining treats between her lips. When she realized there were too many snacks to manage, she began to gag and cough out cookie crumbs. Octavia patted her on the back, laughing at the ironic sequence of events.

"See, that's why you have to watch how much you put in yo' mouth," Octavia teased as the room erupted with riotous clamor.

A tiny woman seated across the room came over to give Octavia a high-five for the timely comment. Before the woman could return to her seat, Truest pulled at the hem of her blouse. "Hey sistah, see me after this meeting. I'll show you a couple'a tricks that'll wind his clock right." Truest assumed the small member had to be the one who had submitted the card, and her assumption proved correct when the woman admitted she was more than open to suggestions.

"Obviously some of us often bite off more than we can chew," Sylvia surmised. She handed her champagne glass to Cee-Cee with hopes of aiding her in washing down the stubborn crumbs stuck in her throat. "I think that Truest has offered her assistance to everyone interested in additional ways to thoroughly degrade herself for the sake of obliging a man. And since it's common knowledge that our local sexpert is well versed on the tools of the trade, that conversation could take all night, so we'll move right long and pass the hat." Sylvia intended for the backhanded compliment to sting, but Truest didn't even flinch. She knew the real reason why Sylvia's husband ran away from home and the first stop he made when he did.

The hat now rested on Octavia's lap. She peered into it nervously, praying silently that she wouldn't select her own card, which did happen on occasion. Her chest tightened from an overdose of anxiety, but she forged on with all eyes glued on her. "Okay, let's see what we have here." She unfolded the card apprehensively, relieved to find the handwriting wasn't hers. "The issue is: 'I'm not good at pillow talk. Sistahs, can you help me out with this one?'"

"Just call him daddy," Kris said evenly. "Men like that."

"You could tell any man that his lovin' is the end-all-be-all and he'll take that to the bank." Tracey spoke with utmost certainty.

"What if it isn't?" someone shouted.

"Unfortunately, that's usually the case," Sylvia chimed in.

Davne, the most reserved member of the group, was bursting with exuberance. "Let me see if I can tackle this one. If all else fails, try this." She slurped down half a glass of wine in a fast gulp then threw her head back to work out the kinks in her neck. With everyone looking on, she began breathing in and out, deep in the throes of passion style. "Ohhh . . . ohhh!" she moaned wildly. "You're the best! You're the best! I can't take it . . . it's too good! Dayyy-um baby! Uh-uh-uh-uh-ohhhh-ohhhh! That's it daddy, that's it . . . don't stop, don't stop, don't stop, ohhhhhh!" Suddenly she was silent and motionless, then calmly finger-combed her hair back into place. "That usually works," she stated matter-of-factly when her impromptu presentation was complete. All the other women in the room were amazed. There was no way any of them could have imagined such a grand spectacle from Davne, of all people.

"Well I'll be," Cee-Cee uttered softly. "In wine there is truth."

"Uh-huh, let the liquor tell it. It's the quiet ones you gotta watch," Octavia consented.

"Funny, that didn't sound all that quiet to me." Sylvia twisted her lips, apparently offended to no end, and Truest enjoyed a private laugh of her own at Sylvia's expense. Perhaps she'd still have a man if she didn't think it was beneath her to stroke her husband's ego every now and then, as well as other things that needed stroking from time to time.

Kris was shaking her head in disbelief. "I've known this woman for seven years and had no idea she had skills like that. I'm not worthy. All hail the queen."

All the ladies except Sylvia hailed in unison, "Daaavne! Do yo' thang, girl."

When the room quieted down to a manageable roar, Cee-Cee pulled a card and read it aloud. "My man won't pick up after himself."

Tracey raised her right hand in the customary testifying position. "Just do that Davne thang and your man will do whut-ever you want him to—pick up his clothes, the laundry, the kids from school."

"I know mine would. I'm going home and trying it out tonight." Kris was still in disbelief, shaking her head. "Pass me that hat and let's see what else is going on." She eagerly accepted the hat from Cee-Cee.

"This one says the issue is: 'I'm in love with a married man and I can't help myself. How can I be expected to forsake my own happiness for some other woman's?' "

Silence fell over the lounging area. A few of the chatterers in attendance were married, and Sylvia's rocky relationship was front-page news, mainly because she'd bad-mouthed her husband to anyone who stood still long enough to listen. As luck would have it, word had traveled back to Devin, who wasn't the sort of man to stand for his woman running his name down in the streets. He was interested in making their marriage work, but Sylvia's idea of love was her controlling the household finances and rationing the booty in order to keep him on a short leash. Eventually he inched closer to becoming the sort of dog who refused to be leashed at all.

Sylvia's eyes surveyed the room, wondering who had entered the submission and if she had covertly crept in her back door only to dangle it in front of her now. "I'll just say this and be done with it." Her words came across harshly. Because her pride was riding high, she couldn't get out of her own way if she tried. "No matter what a married man and his wife are going through, they need to go through it together . . . with each other." She stood up slowly, clenched her teeth, then locked eyes with Truest. "A woman with any real self-respect wouldn't go after somebody's husband and break up an already struggling relationship. Any home-wrecker who stoops that low needs to have her ass whipped." This was a stretch for Sylvia, always standing on the premise of staunch Christian righteousness.

Truest did not appreciate the way Sylvia's accusations were hurled in her direction, nor was she about to let the lady of the house get away with it. "Sylvia, I know you are not in my face suggesting that I'm the reason your man left you. If you were half the woman you pretended to be, maybe he'd still be here. In any case, don't you go blaming me and pointing your fingers at anyone who don't live in this here house. I've known Devin longer than you have and if I wanted him," she cocked her head to the side for emphases sake, "*If* I wanted him, he would have been mine a long time ago. And you might want to watch yourself before you go acting like you're better than me, or the person's ass getting whipped will be yours, regardless of whose house I'm standing in at the time."

Before the situation could get any more out of hand, Cee-Cee found herself wedged between the two while the others seemed paralyzed to stave off the inevitable. "That's it!" Cee-Cee shouted. " 'Tavia, get Tru's purse. Truest, you need to apologize to Sylvia for disrespecting her in her own home."

"Cee-Cee, you must be out yo' mind thinkin' I'm gonna say I'm sorry when I'm not. I don't even roll like that."

"Yeah, you're sorry, all right!" Sylvia retaliated. Her gaze was dark and haunting. "You're sorry and you'll always be sloppy seconds, tramping behind leftovers."

"Awwww, hell naw!" Truest felt a raging spirit overtaking her.

In the time it took to blink, Truest doused Sylvia with the Cosmopolitan she'd been enjoying. Sylvia screamed, looking down at her new outfit in ruins. Then, in a blind rage she slung back her hand, slapping Truest so hard that it sounded off the walls.

"Hey-Hey!" Cee-Cee shouted, wrestling with both women as the other members found themselves at the crossroads of breaking up the skirmish and reveling over the drama from their ringside seats.

Suddenly Truest balled her fist and cocked it back like she was in the middle of a long yawn. Cee-Cee saw it coming and ducked. Sylvia's arms flailed and her feet came off the ground with the force of the stinging slug to her jaw. Octavia dashed in with Truest's purse in hand, searching for the source of the disturbance. Her eyes found Sylvia stretched out flat on her back in her own living room, attended to by other guests. Cee-Cee motioned toward the other side of the room in answer to Octavia's puzzled expression. It was one of the most peculiar things she'd ever seen. After knocking Sylvia out cold, in her own house no less, Truest had the nerve to be mixing herself another cocktail in the unconscious woman's blender.

"Truest, what are you doing?" Octavia challenged her. "I know you are not making yourself another drink after what you just did."

" 'Tavia, this ain't the time and I ain't the one. Besides, I'm still thirsty." Truest was so upset that she didn't know what to do next. "Don't worry about ol' Sleepy Head over there. I'll be gone by the time she comes to." As if that wasn't bizarre enough, Truest took her own sweet time sipping on a peach-flavored daiquiri.

From the outset, the evening was meant to bomb, and it did live up to Cee-Cee and Octavia's expectations. Sylvia and Truest were both loyal to their respective natures, but they were like oil and water in the same bottle. No matter how many times you shake the bottle, they won't stay mixed.

3

Ghetto Booties and Whatnots

During the drive back to the radio station parking lot, Octavia sat quietly for most of the trek, sullen, as if the world was on her shoulders. Thoughts of Sylvia lying heels up on the floor in her own living room and the ramifications of a marriage gone awry weighed heavily, not to mention that it finally occurred to Octavia how much she actually had in common with Truest. Men had come and gone from her life like whispers in the dark as well. She had wasted too many nights with men she didn't love, and it seemed they never wanted more from her than how she made them feel. Not one of them asked for more than that.

"You alright, Tavia?" Cee-Cee asked eventually.

"Yeah, I guess so."

"Then why the long face? You look as pitiful as Sylvia probably feels right about now."

Staring out of the window on the passenger side, Octavia huffed out a slow steady sigh before sharing what had her so dismayed. "I just don't know sometime, Cee-Cee. It's like one day everything on the planet is cool with me then suddenly I feel as though I've been living my life on the edge of a lie. A perfectly good lie that I've convinced myself is close enough to the truth, so I just let it ride."

Cee-Cee turned the radio down so she could ease into her

girlfriend-confidante-psychologist mode. "Hold on now. What's all this talk about lying and whatnot? You're probably the most honest person I know."

"See there, got you convinced too. I told you it was a perfectly good lie."

"Okay, let's begin at the beginning." Cee-Cee prided herself on being able to skillfully psychoanalyze other people's issues by digging deep enough into their woes to get to the root of them. She was quite adept at helping others turn corners in their lives, but didn't have a clue how to make things happen for herself. But that didn't stop her from jumping in with two feet at Octavia's moment of despair. "You have a good job that you seem to like and you're a wonderful catch if a man was in the right frame of mind to notice. Now that's from the outside looking in, I must admit, but from where I sit, it's all good."

"Looks can be deceiving. So deceiving. Since I hit puberty, I've been trying to find myself, define myself and measure things that happen to me against what everyone around me was going through. It's seems just like yesterday that I was a skinny teenager growing up on a red-clay reservation in Oklahoma. Not quite feeling adequately Native American and constantly reminded that I wasn't black enough to fit in with the cool crowd, either. I was about thirteen when I fell in to a blue funk, knowing that it wouldn't be easy being me but smart enough to know it would be twice as hard trying to be someone else."

Octavia thought back to those early adolescent years, then heaved another deep sigh, reliving the difficulties of her youth. A mixed heritage offered as many drawbacks as it did benefits and it was those drawbacks that stayed with her long after the benefits had been forgotten. Her soft features, bone-straight black hair, and virtually curve-free hips served quite well depending on the situation at hand. "When the rest of the black girls began to develop and started filling out like young black women, strutting around all proud like they were on parade, I watched them and enjoyed their first conversations about training bras and mannish little boys trying to cop a feel. You know, the usual stuff."

Cee-Cee nodded. "Yeah, I remember those awkward days of budding breasts and watching something happen to my body that I couldn't explain, but I also remember how all of a sudden those mannish little boys I couldn't stand until then started looking real good to me."

A smile danced around Octavia's lips. "Righhht-righhht. That's what I'm talking about. I watched them checking out girls like you all day at school, then cried my eyes out at night because they lost interest in the half-breed-mixed girl who they thought was so cute the year before. My mother, being the wise black woman that she is, broke it down for me, though, and it helped me take it on the chin a bit easier from then on. She told me that a black woman's body is a blessing as well as a curse because a man will do just about anything to get a piece of it, but rarely wanted the whole thing for the duration."

"Humph, sounds like moms was on to something. I know too many sistahs caught up in the middle of that ridiculous situation right now, present company included." Cee-Cee was mentally and emotionally attached to a man who more than adequately proved that premise to be correct. She'd been involved in an on-again, off-again love affair for more years than she cared to admit. "If it weren't for Tae-Bo and that fine chocolate thang, Billy Blanks, my blessing would be a bigger curse today."

"Tell me about it. But despite all of that, back in the day, I would have given anything to be cursed with a body like my mama's. Even at the grocery store, men checked her out like it was their first time laying eyes on a grown woman's behind. My hips wouldn't grow and my hair couldn't afro, but oh how I dreamed of just once having the stereotypical ghetto booty. I wanted so badly to know what it felt like to have a brotha run to go get a friend and drag him back so he could one of the finest asses ever made." Octavia laughed out loud when she realized how silly her girlish fantasies had been, and Cee-Cee cackled so hard that her eyes watered.

"'Tavia, you crazy. Why you're frontin', I still dream of stuff like that now and I'm way older than thirteen." After howling at the top of her lungs again, she wiped the tears away. "You're gonna make me wreck this car and I haven't even made the first payment yet. Ooh, ghetto booties. Sounds to me, you'd love to be Truest for a day."

"See, now you're feeling me. That sistah has grown men losing their minds over what her mama give her. In spite of her drama-queen-supreme lifestyle, she does have it so easy when it comes to attracting men. Gotta give her props on that."

Suddenly Cee-Cee stopped laughing altogether. There was something in what Octavia said that halted all the good feelings they'd shared. Truest was renowned for getting any man she wanted, even if he happened to belong to someone else. The thought of that stifled Cee-Cee's joy. "Hey, I thought we were talking about your issues and not the inexplicable Lady Tru." The mere mention of Truest's aptitude for luring the opposite sex had altered Cee-Cee's previously ebullient state of mind and it did not go overlooked, but Octavia simply chalked it up to petty jealousy among friends.

When they arrived at the station, Cee-Cee swerved into an open parking space in the nearly abandoned lot. "Come on up with me for a sec," she offered. "I have to run up and grab my bag and my pay-check—that I'm not even interested in discussing further—but I'm still not finished getting to the bottom of what's got you all washed out."

Although Octavia contemplated calling it a night, she felt good about delving into her past and perhaps coming away with a second opinion on life as she saw it. "I guess I could come on up for a minute. Got nothing better to do," was her stoic reply.

Once they reached the second floor, Octavia plopped down at Cee-Cee's desk, which was nothing more that a cluttered office cubicle.

"You really need to do something about this mess. How can you get any work done with mountains of paper everywhere?"

"It's my mess," Cee-Cee answered flatly, flipping through envelopes stacked in her mail tray. "If I cleared all this away, I'd spend a lot more time searching for things. Uh-huh, I like this mess just fine."

"Better you than me." Octavia frowned at her excuse for an utterly appalling workstation. "With all the mess a woman has to deal with on an hourly basis, I try to maintain order whenever I can."

Cee-Cee settled back in her comfortable office chair, therapist-style, and interlocked her thin fingers. "Alright now, Ms. Longbow. I know that your young woman's woes are not what's kicking your butt this evening, so what gives? The clock is ticking." She smiled politely, posturing all serious-like, as if they were in a real session to be billed for later.

"Oh you're really trippin' but I'll play along. I'd never be foolish enough to pay somebody for telling them all *my* business," Octavia teased.

"Yeah-yeah-yeah, what-ever! Just get back to it."

"Don't get so pushy, Cee-Cee, sheeez."

"You know about me and Phillip and how we couldn't seem to make up our minds on how much we loved each other, so I have to live vicariously through you and Truest. Don't be acting all surprised." Cee-Cee Lovely was a top-rated deejay and a local celebrity in her own right. Oddly enough, she was often more interested in the eventful goings-on of her two closest friends than her own. "You never know when a girl might learn something she can use for her own sake further on down the line. So out with it."

"Yeah, I must admit that some of the things you've shared with me over the years have proven to be good seeds for me to grow from." Octavia reached across the desk to squeeze Cee-Cee's hand. "I don't know. I just get lost in the shuffle of regular living. I feel like there's another life inside me just begging to get out. If I knew how to open up and let it breathe, I would. I'm just concerned that it's dying a slow death being locked away. When I let it get to me, it leaves me feeling as empty as a drum." She slid off her shoe and began to massage the heel on her left foot. "Hey . . . have you ever wanted to be something other than what you are?"

"Well, I wouldn't mind being Halle Berry, but the position is already filled and she's working that joint overtime. Fine men wishing they had a shot, Oscar-winning performances, all those parties that she never has to stand in line for, and all the money a girl can spend. That's the dream life I want."

"Who're you telling? Get in line behind me. Ol' girl has found her niche in life and is managing the three-ring circus that I'm sure it can be, but that's not exactly what I mean. She's the best at what she does and she seems to be loving it all the way to the bone. Now, that's the part that eludes me. I want to know what I'm here on earth to do, what my purpose is. And feel good about it being my destiny, not someone else's . . . mine, no matter what it pays."

Cee-Cee nodded, flashing her perfectly aligned teeth. "My hat's off to you 'Tav because not everyone is serious enough to chase after what they feel belongs to them. Most people have dreams but rarely get past the just dreaming stage. I used to spend hours in front of the mirror pretending that I was a news anchor-woman but I never moved past pretending. Scared, I guess."

"Scared of what? You definitely have the looks for it and a person couldn't buy the type of presence you were born with. It's not too late to look into it."

"Aren't you sweet to go filling my head with lofty expectations. I suppose that I still do have a few good years left before gravity pulls all of my real talent south." She cupped her full perky breasts with her hands to accentuate her talent.

"Use 'em before you lose 'em," Octavia advised. "Although you could always get 'em fixed if they happened to need a boost. Promise me you'll give it some thought. About chasing your dreams, I mean. Anyway, you can't cheat destiny."

"Tell you one thing, I damn sure hope that destiny can pay the bills better that what-ever it is you call what I'm doing now." Cee-Cee glared at the thought of last month's overdue bills. "'Cause this is not my idea of making it. Not even close."

4

Thirteen Minutes and Change

Lazarus Whiles, the nighttime deejay, was fast at work cueing up the playlist for the ten o'clock hour when he noticed Cee-Cee and Octavia exit through the front door of the radio station. "Good. They're gone," Lazarus whispered to Benny, the only white intern ever employed by the minority-owned network. He was their affirmative action project. "Come to think of it, what are you still doing here? I've got this hottie swinging by later and I don't need anything or anybody getting in my way." His plans for the evening didn't include office associates who could disrupt his meeting with the woman he'd been running up his cell phone bill with firm hopes of getting to know her better.

Although Benny was as cool as a fan can get and handled himself well in mixed company, he was only twenty-one and had a lot to learn regarding all the fringe benefits that came with being in the spotlight. But he was eager to take notes. "Laz'rus," he said in his best manufactured homeboy voice, "Uhh-huh, I know how you roll. I'll bet you're gonna get with that and handle up. She's probably a dime piece from the deck up past the neck up."

Halting his nightly duties just long enough to respond, Lazarus shook his head violently. "Uh-uh, I said that I would show you the ropes and how to run the programming board but you don't want to know what I know about pleasing women. It'll mess you up for life. But I will say this. The sistah that's coming by here tonight is . . . ooh-wee. I don't even have the words to tell you how stacked she is. I'm talking about front-back and side-to-side buckle up and enjoy the ride."

"I feel you, Laz, but how did you get at her in the first place?"

"I shouldn't be corrupting you, Benny, but check it out. On Tuesdays, I hang out at the Goofy Gator."

"Isn't that an entertainment place for kiddies?"

"Yeah, and for their single mamas, too. Tuesdays are half price so that makes the hunt twice as nice. Last month she was there with some shorties from her class, a birthday party or something, but that didn't matter. I stepped to her, pitched my game, and the rest is history. When I found out that she was a grade-school teacher and goes to church every Sunday, I just about lost my mind 'cause that combo means she's a freak to go."

"Riiight-riiight, sounds like a winner to me. Goes to church and a schoolteacher too. Oh man, you hit the jackpot." Benny stood up from resting his skinny behind on the work desk. "Nahhh, dawg, you gotta let me hang around here to peep this one."

"Nope, I've got grown-folks business and you're too young to be seeing what I got planned. Besides, this is the kind of woman who'll eat you whole."

"She'll eat your what?" Benny was wearing a stupefied expression. In addition to being young and white, the bewildered intern was green to boot.

"Never mind, Junior." Lazarus's tone was peppered with disappointment. The younger protégé was not ready to dive into the depth of erotica that Lazarus had adopted as a way of life. "Just as I thought, You are not ready, but I am ready, for you to find somewhere else to be. Class is over for today. Better be glad that I'm not giving you homework. Now beat it."

Benny gave his baseball cap a reluctant tug and exited stage right, wanting to grow up faster than time allowed. He loved being around the on-air talent and Lazarus was his hero. He followed the popular deejay around like a lost puppy and emulated his sly way of talking when putting his moves on the microphone. After Benny slinked out of the pit, referring to the booth, he promised himself that he'd sponge all the knowledge from the disc jockey he could acquire, imagining the lure of women and fame blowing his way. Lazarus was not only his hero, he was also the standard to be measured by.

"Late Nights with Lazarus" aired Monday through Friday night from ten to four A.M. Lazarus was average in height, brown-skinned, good looking, and scandalous. He'd been a fixture at the top station since he was eighteen. His duties began with running errands and fetching whatever the radio talent needed but couldn't do because of their many commitments. He also delivered flowers to lovers who for many reasons had to remain nameless and faceless due to their secret relationships with other radio personalities. A full decade of watching and waiting patiently for his turn at the microphone proved very beneficial. Lazarus knew every inch of the station, where the surveillance cameras were, and how to sneak women past them when he wanted to order in some late-night physical activity to help him pass the time.

"*Late Nights with Lazarus,* what's up?" While Jill Scott crooned in the background, he poised his hand on the record button. Most of the calls on the station's listener line were taped and edited while songs occupied the airwaves, then played minutes later. He kept a sharp eye out on the wall clock, anticipating a delivery.

"Laz'rus, you punk!" an enraged woman's voice blurted out.

With clenched teeth, he recognized the voice as soon as he heard it. "Hey! Hey! I done told you once, Stamina, to stop calling up here on my job harassing me." Cringing, he barked back. "You know my restraining order says that you can't come within fifty feet of me and that includes contacting me on this here line, so later for you and everybody who looks like you." He slammed down the phone receiver, then nervously looked around the small booth as if someone might have overheard him admitting to being caught up in so much drama that it necessitated serving an ex-lover with cease-and-desist papers. Immediately he erased the call and went about his normal duties.

Suddenly the private phone line rang loudly. He smiled devilishly as he eagerly snatched the receiver from its base. "Yeah, this is Laz'rus."

"And you still a punk!" the same voice fired back. "You think you can just hump me and hang up on me whenever you get ready? You ought to know me better than to think a restraining order is gonna stop me from getting what's owed me."

Until then Lazarus had held his tongue, hoping the storm would pass quickly. He had gotten to know Stamina well enough to be certain of one thing, she would be ringing that line all night if he didn't give her an opportunity to vent and feel as though she was making her point.

"Okay Stamina, is that all?" he sighed. "I don't have time to be on the phone with you all night. I have a job to do."

"You weren't saying that when you were blowing up my phone and two-waying me all times of the night, were you? Hell naw, you had plenty of time for me then. Now that we've gone half on a baby, you can't find a minute to talk to me or visit your own daughter. I don't care how many other kids you got. This little girl of ours will be well taken care of. Oh yeah, I got me a little piece of paper, too, and it says you better pay up every month for the next eighteen years, playa!"

After listening to her tirade, Lazarus tried to hurry the call to a conclusion. "Stamina, I did what you wanted. I listened to you. Now, are you finished? I have to get back to work and if you don't cease and desist bringing drama up in my place of biz'ness, I'll place a call of my own to your probation officer and tell him that somebody is ready for her third strike."

"Mmm-hmm. I bet that your bizness ain't all you're tryna to get back to. I know all of your ghetto tricks. You probably got some hoodrat up in there with you right now but I'm not stressed. You just better be a man or I'ma put the attorney general, Tiny Trooper Day Care, welfare and a whole lot of other white people on you. Yeah, I heard about your new Cadillac truck, too. Better watch your back and where you park that high-dollar whip. 'Cause until you do right by me, ain't nothing you do gonna turn out right. As a matter of fact, I spent my last thirty dollars paying to put a root on that little thang you're so damned proud of, to shrivel up and fall off. Now run and tell that!"

"Alright Ms. Celie," he huffed with disdain, "but you'd better look out for Mistah." Lazarus slammed the receiver down with the angst of a man who was tied to an eighteen-year prison sentence. Then a slight chuckle emerged from the depths of his soul. "Ooh, I'm crazy about that girl," he admitted to himself.

Although the paternity test had yet to be concluded, Lazarus was 99.9 percent positive that he could very well be the father. He had frequently sneaked her into the station like she said. And even though he couldn't stand her constant prodding and downright homegirl street demeanor, their sexcapades were window-shattering events every time they hooked up. Eleven months later Lazarus was shaking in his boots, although he pretended not to be concerned with her numerous threats of appraisal to come from a lot of different entities, all of which could cause him more headaches than he was willing to deal with. He should have been more worried about Stamina's *Color Purple* innuendo regarding his other new baby, a cream-colored special-edition Cadillac fresh off the showroom floor. Stamina was hurting, embarrassed and embittered after telling everyone that she was slated to be the first and only Mrs. Lazarus Whiles, only to be dumped on her head when she told her husband-to-be that she was expecting her fourth child at age twenty-three.

"She must be crazy, talking about putting a hex on Mr. Happy."

Lazarus, alone in the booth, ran his mouth nonstop in response to Stamina's spiteful rants. "Can't nothing stop me from handling mine. Better ask somebody. They can't measure my kind of pleasure." He turned toward the telephone as he thought back on something the woman had dropped on him. "And it ain't little, neither!" he yelled. "Maybe a lil' short at times but it ain't little . . . and she wasn't complaining about it all those times she was all up and down on it. Believe the myth, baby. I'm a black man. Believe the myth. That's right, I'ma playa from a long line of playas," he bellowed, self-aggrandizing, while preparing additional music tracks for the night. "Long line of playas. Daddy was a playa . . . grand-daddy was a playa. You can't stop no third-generation Don Juan. I's a playa by design and ain't nobody got neggah tricks like mine."

The private phone rang again in the midst of his pointless rebuttal. "Hello!" he shouted, answering the call, his jaws tightening. "Yeah, this is Laz'rus! Who's this? Who?" Like a tropical sunset, his rough-cut attitude dissolved into pure ecstasy "Oh, it's you. Sorry, baby, but you know these radio groupies be calling up here bothering a brotha. What? You're down stairs. I'll be right there. Don't move. I'll be right there."

He ripped the headset off, then remembered he hadn't made a station identification announcement within the hour, which was an FCC edict. "This is *Late Night with Lazarus* here on the Monster Beats Hot 100," he said hurriedly. "If I don't have it, you don't want it. 'Cause I'm nice like that. Yep." It didn't matter that his voiceover interrupted the flow that listeners were bobbing their heads to. He had been vying for weeks to get biblical with the woman he met while cruising for some lonely single-mother action. She told him that she loved his show and couldn't wait to get to know him in the biblical sense. She had come up with every excuse in the book to put him off, until now. This was it. Finally she was perched outside, wearing the bedroom ensemble that Lazarus had ordered and paid for from a *Victoria's Secret* catalog.

After bounding down the back staircase with the agility of an Olympic athlete, Lazarus ran top speed until he reached the side door exclusively used by the after-hours employees. He caught a glimpse of an attractive woman the shade of cocoa through the small window in the metal door. His heart was pounding, and his testosterone raged. He took a deep breath and pushed the unlock switch to the right of the door. The buzzer sounded and he welcomed the woman in.

"Hey, Aliza." Lazarus was all pumped up, Mr. Happy included. "Let me get a look at you, girl." The woman parted a long silver taffeta trench coat to seductively display a chartreuse lacey two-piece getup barely covering what he'd been waiting to get at. "Oh yeah, that's what I'm talking about. You bring your precious self on in here. I have to get back up to the booth and take care of a few things, then I can take care of you."

When she leaned over to collect a brown leather satchel from its resting place near the door, her ample breast nearly toppled out of the bra that worked hard at containing more than it was suited to hold. Lazarus checked his watch. He had just enough time to hike two flights of stairs with a scarcely dressed woman in white stiletto heels in tow.

As soon as they returned to the small booth, Lazarus dashed to the programming board and pulled the headset over his ears. He composed himself, then pressed the "live" button. "Because I love y'all so much, get set for I. Rome's new one, titled *One Last Chance*." A broad grin the size of Texas gleamed on his face when he contemplated all the things he was anxious to do in the easy chair that his date lounged in. While he cued up the track, his guest's lacey panties landed on the microphone. Lazarus eyes bucked with surprise and his breathing became labored all over again. He tossed the half-naked woman his best I've-got-to-have-you-baby leer, then back to the airwaves he went. "Hey, check it out. I'ma do something that I don't usually do. I'ma hit y'all with the first three tracks of the album. You can thank me later."

With all that said and done, Lazarus moved toward his prey with calculated steps. "Come on, girl, we got thirteen minutes and forty-two seconds. I hope you're ready for this 'cause I've been dreaming about doing things to you that's got to be illegal in a whole bunch of states and a couple of small countries. I'ma give you something that'll make your ears pop." With all the excitement coursing in his veins, getting him all worked up, he forgot to deactivate the on-air button.

Lazarus had also forgotten the phone conversation with Stamina, her temper tantrums, and her ridiculous threats of paying to have a root put on him. He was in paradise now, for another thirteen minutes and forty-two seconds' worth. A moment in time that he'd never forget, regardless of how hard he tried.

5

In My Own Words

Most of Saturday had come and gone. Octavia's seventh-day ritual normally consisted of cleaning her apartment from top to bottom while listening to top-selling vocals of female singers who possessed overwhelming skills on the guitar as well. Her father had taught her a few simple cords when she was a young girl and those fond memories often came to mind whenever she did happen to sit down long enough to stroke her fingers through a bevy of tunes she loved.

After the housework was finished, followed by a long steamy bubble bath, it was customary to work on her master's dissertation, *The Wages of Fame*. Octavia was nearing completion for graduate studies in entertainment journalism. She based her entire study on the traumatic ups and downs of celebrity lifestyles and the pitfalls of success.

When it was apparent that she was failing miserably at concentrating on the task at hand, she closed her research folder before tossing it aside on the rectangular beveled smoked-glass coffee table. She opened a weathered army green tote bag and felt around inside until she found what she had been searching for in the soft leather oversized carryall—her private journal. She couldn't shake a nagging desire to revisit some of her personal thoughts of days and nights gone by.

Although she had no earthly idea why she felt so compelled to delve into the tablet, it continued to beckon her until she submitted to its bothersome and relentless summons. The tablet she had vowed never to share with a living soul stored several entries concerning the men she had shared laughter with, among other things of a more intimate nature, throughout the past year of her life. Much like the details penned on those lined pages, each of her suitors were merely mental exercises to help keep her mind off I. Rome; or at least that's what she kept telling herself each time it was made even more apparent that she was on the receiving end of another disaster.

For instance, there was Secret Service Steven. Love 'em and Leave Steve is the name she gave him after their last good-bye. He was a handsome man who possessed the intellect of a Latin scholar and a distinguished majestic stature. He'd earned a Ph.D. in criminal science and often disappeared for weeks at a time on "official business" as he put it. The ample dose of mystery had intrigued Octavia in the beginning but subsequently evolved into a bad case of mistrust and anxious intentions. The one thing she enjoyed most about him turned on her like the IRS.

When she was with Steven she felt safe, comforted, and secure. His strong silence at times was a challenge but she knew how to loosen him up when the mood hit her. He rewarded her with gratitude at every turn, praising her generous nature and kind spirit, but there was something about Steven's secrets, other than his occupation, that prohibited their relationship from fully developing. Octavia was sure that he was hiding behind something but her frequent inquiries about what was holding him back always resulted in unnerving bouts of animosity followed by Steven shaking his head slowly and offering a one-word reply—"Nothing."

One Thursday evening, she felt his absence moving her in a menacing way that she couldn't understand. She was missing him like the desert longs for rain and couldn't help it, although she and Steven had not once spoken about commitment or exclusivity. Without plan or presence of mind, she found herself cruising by spots where they shared some of their best times together. She stumbled upon him sitting in the huge window of the ice cream parlor where he liked to go because he craved their exotic flavors. Initially she was overwrought with joy, but the surprise that quickly followed that nearly caused a horrific automobile pileup when she realized that he wasn't alone. An eighteen-wheel gasoline truck slammed on its breaks as it backed out of the adjoining 7-Eleven parking lot. The driver's harsh words and obscene gestures were wasted on the woman caught up in a sea of jealous circumstance.

Octavia was still idled in the middle of the busy avenue when Steven's eyes eventually met hers. His mouth opened as if to apologize behind the thick sheet of glass and trepidation. His eyes pleaded for understanding while begging forgiveness as uncertainty engulfed him. The beautiful white woman who sat closely by his side possessed eyes that said something different altogether. She watched Steven and Octavia's interlocking gaze with contempt before asking who that woman was. Steven exhaled a dense stream of frustration as he often did, then he gently took a folded handkerchief to wipe away a renegade stream of Huckleberry ice cream from the chin of a little girl; there were three of them.

Octavia faded into utter disbelief when Steven calmly answered his wife with one of his patented one-word responses. She didn't have to be a world-class lip reader to know beyond a shadow of a doubt that his one-word answer concerning who the woman parked in the middle of the street and staring back at them was "Nobody." Although she and Steven had no long-term plans for commitment, that didn't ease the blow of seeing him with another woman.

That was the last time she had laid eyes on him. He didn't call once to seek redemption. Oftentimes she wished he had but she was thankful that he hadn't. And after a few months passed she finally decided to toss his spare belongings into a charity box at the nearest homeless shelter. She kept the handcuffs for herself.

Before the bruise of an almost love affair had adequately healed, Octavia met someone else to smooth out the kinks. His name was Elgin Castile, The Food Pimp. Actually, his title at *Big D* magazine was Food Critic but he was nothing more than a cheap freeloader with nice facial features and bad everything else. After four consecutive dates with Elgin, Octavia began to notice his M.O.: fine dining on the magazine's ticket. Each time they stepped out, dinner was the only thing on the menu. Not once had he offered a date to the theater or any other place where he would have to dig into his pocket. Instead, he'd phone a restaurant beforehand to inform the owner that a noted critic and his guest would be arriving for dinner. That meant a free meal in exchange for a favorable review.

While wrapping up their last date, Elgin overplayed his hand. The restaurant chosen offered impressive service. All of the attendants were gracious and pleasant. The ambiance was warm and inviting. The selections were numerous and the entrées scrumptious. It was by far the best dinner Octavia could remember enjoying and she wasn't quite ready to be driven straight back to her place in order for Elgin to receive his gratuity. Consequently, as the waiter cleared the table of silver and flatware, Octavia asked the server for an after-dinner liqueur list. Suddenly the entire night came crashing down around her. Before the waiter could oblige her request, Elgin was quick to inform her that she would have to fork over some money for cocktails because alcohol wasn't included in a complimentary dinner. It took a couple of seconds before she realized her previous hunch was correct. He had pimped the magazine food-critic angle, reducing her impression of him to an all-time low. It wasn't so much that she objected to paying for the drinks or the meal itself, but she was troubled with the rash way he halted the waiter until it was made clear that he would not be anteing a single dime. That's when it came to her that he hadn't up to that point, not even as much as a tip, after having been catered to like a king. He'd simply sign a comp card for another freebee, promise a smashing article that was sure to drum up additional business for the eatery, then hit the door picking his teeth.

The waiter looked on, uncertain of how to react. Octavia calmly cleared her throat. The awkward smile masking her face was one of total embarrassment. That a grown man would place her in a compromising position didn't sit right with her in the least. Taking the high road, she pulled a twenty-dollar bill from her small handbag and presented it to the order taker. "Please take this for your troubles. The food was excellent but I won't be having *anything* else this evening." She made sure that Elgin understood exactly what she meant by the comment. He understood perfectly, then promptly excused himself from the table, exited through the front door, and kept right on going. When the realization occurred to Octavia that he'd left her stranded without a ride home, she was greeted by the familiar twinge that always stirred deep within her bones when vengeful thoughts surged beneath her skin.

On the very next afternoon, a gourmet-style tray of ribs was delivered to Elgin's office at the magazine, from a supposed new restaurant owner who desired the critic's approval before adding the item to his menu. Octavia heard later how Elgin got his just dessert after he delighted in selfishly refusing to share the three pounds beef platter with any of his contemporaries. Despite not having a single drop of bar-b-q sauce to bathe the dish with, he was still true to form, just as the sender had anticipated he would be. Once the platter had nearly been devoured in the company's lunchroom, a long cylinder-shaped parcel arrived right on schedule. Elgin was gloating and picking his teeth as he uncapped the cylinder to get at the item inside. All the gloating ceased when he laid eyes on a poster-sized photo of a pudgy bulldog with thick layers of bar-b-q sauce dripping from his wrinkled chin. Tearful snickering from his coworkers, who had been snubbed, quickly boiled into riotous laughter when it became clear that the sauce had not been forgotten as Elgin assumed but rather lapped away by a squat pooch with overactive salivary glands. To make matters worse, a doggie biscuit fell out of the card accompanying the photo. It read, "Thanks for dinner last night. It was so dog-gone nice of you to treat. By the way, my neighbor's dog loved the sauce. Feel free to quote him on that."

It was the least Octavia could have done considering his behavior. The Food Pimp was no mental giant and didn't have much going on downstairs, either. As the saying goes, it's so easy to forget the little things.

The next entry of note regarded Strip Show Savon, a horse of a different color. Octavia loved reading entry number 117 aloud, especially when she got to the good parts.

Entry 117: After Sienna Felton's bachelorette party, she got married and I got Strip Show Savon Turner. If you ask me, she got the short end of the stick so to speak. Savon was the headliner and at night's end, who took off all of his clothes for two hundred screaming fans at Big Daddy's all-male revue, but he kept his eyes on me. Sienna didn't seem to mind at all when he kept working his way back to my roaming hands because she thoroughly enjoyed his front. Despite his rock-hard presence and show-stopping moves, I didn't think he meant it when he leaned over me and whispered softly "I wanna get to know you" in my ear. I just chalked it up as showbiz gamesmanship to make me dig deeper into my purse until the waitress offered an "I know what y'all are gonna be doing later" grin as she passed me a matchbook with his digits written inside. Hell yeah I took it. Couldn't say no if I wanted to.

He lived in a small place off the interstate in a two-room flat painted blue. I thought it was the oddest hue for a house, not too dark but somewhere between royal and indigo. After breaking my neck to get there for five nights in a row, he told me that the shade of blue was six A.M., which was about the time I got my worn-out tail up to head home in the morning. Each time, he'd leave the door unlocked for me when he knew I was on my way and my dress would be around my ankles before I'd get the door closed. He'd pull me to him and hold me tightly, like I was his last dying breath. We didn't waste words and I doubt he gave less than a damn how my day went. And after his tongue glided along my breast I didn't, either. His loving was so good that it left me feeling intoxicated, medicated, and sedated, all at the same time. I felt supernatural while he did a collage of freaky things to make my body quake. Some of them I never imagined possible. He said he liked it best with a pillow shoved under my ass so he could hit my spot better. I loved being overwhelmingly subdued and falling-asleep satisfied as he watched *Sanford and Son* reruns, eating Cheerios in the nude. The fun we made was delicious.

Once I got to know Savon better, I didn't mind knowing that he'd sent countless married women home feeling guilty, like they were returning to their husbands to cheat instead of it being the other way around. His ebullient childlike attitude and carefree way of looking at life made women stumble off-balance, then fall in love. He didn't mean for it to happen but it seemed to always end up that way. Savon had a knack for bringing out the woman in a lady and they thanked him for that, some with sexual gratitude and others with expensive gifts of appreciation. He could have cared less about all that. What he wanted most was for them to forget about their troubles while they were with him. Their laughter turned to tears when time came to leave that oddly shaded house of blue. I should know because mine did, too.

As with all good things, it came to a very abrupt ending when I thought I'd made it crystal clear that I needed some special attention after a long day at the office. We must have gotten our signals crossed, but I considered it fate when I showed up at his home unannounced to discover a man's face in the exact same place and time where I had hoped to put mine. Of course I went slap off and screamed my resentment concerning his free-spirited and shameless disregard for my life as I broke one of my shoes off in his behind. Getting it repaired did occur to me but there was no telling what else he's had stuck in there so I decided to leave it right where it was, then told him to keep it as a small memento from me to you. Although relieved after my trip to the doctor proved negative, I was still steaming over that one. I really loved those shoes.

The crooked smile Octavia wore by the time she'd finished reading number 117 was due to an otherwise self-incriminating tidbit, which she had purposely omitted from the entry. By the time Savon arrived home from the emergency room later that same night, his entire house, including the windows, had been painted a peculiar shade of hot pink. Octavia laughed uncontrollably at the thought of him driving up to her twisted idea of revenge, in her favorite color.

6

Don't Look Now

Evening cast a hazy shadow over the fabulous downtown landscape. Octavia cruised her Jeep along the scattered streets with hunger biting at her soul like a small dog nipping at its master's heels. She was charmed by the burnt orange hue that blanketed the dense clouds. Rain was in the forecast but she couldn't visualize it ruining such a beautiful scene. Unfortunately, the outcome was not up to her.

Café Brew was an out-of-the way breakfast house in Deep Ellum, the artsy district just seconds from the high-rise mountains of downtown. Octavia sat in the crowded parking lot, watching the sun settling in for the night until it was swallowed up by the darkness. She worked hard at forgetting about Secret Service Steve, Strip Show Savon, and that total waste of time, Elgin "The Food Pimp" Castile. Pushing men out of her mind completely is what she promised herself as an early birthday present. Like most delicacies we treat ourselves to, it was harder to give up than she expected.

The café was barely shy of standing room only. Octavia was lucky. A small table was vacant near the rear window. She hailed a petite freckle-faced hostess dressed in a daisy-yellow getup. The hostess smiled amiably, then escorted her customer to the far corner of the restaurant. "Hey, ma'am," the hostess announced politely, like a barmaid straight out of an old western movie. "I'm Nan. I can go ahead and take your drink order. Your waitress is swamped but she'll be along directly to tend to ya." *Directly.*

It took everything Octavia had not to burst out in a rude chuckle at the woman's absurd homespun Texas twang. The woman was merely offering a heaping portion of Southern hospitality. "Thank you very much, Nan," Octavia answered behind a suppressed snicker. "I'll just have a hot cup of your Columbian house blend with Amoretto cream." The woman nodded, smiled again, then darted off in the direction of the coffee bar.

Before the Columbian blend had cooled, a taller woman older than Nan appeared at the table. She whipped out a small order booklet with her left hand as she searched vigorously through her stained red apron with her right. "Whut you havin'?" was her rushed salutation. There went Southern hospitality, but her twang was as authentic as could be. Her weathered name tag read Dorothy. She was a dishwater blonde, but there's no way she could have ever been tall and fine like the striking character whom The Artist Formally Known as Prince once rapped about in a hit song. This woman was just plain tired.

Octavia considered matching her no no-nonsense speech pattern with some good ol'-fashioned Oklahoma barroom banter but thought better of it, mostly because she hadn't received her food yet and didn't want to think of her entrée with special sauce that all waitresses keep handy for smart-mouthed patrons. "I would love a Spanish omelet with diced ham and green onions, if you don't mind." That was a gold star for diplomacy and it came across a lot better than "witch you bet' not spit in my food."

Dorothy stomped away without as much as a kiss-my-butt, much less a thank-you, but Octavia's food was on its way minus the special sauce. The rationale to choose her battles proved sound. Within a few minutes, a piping-hot masterpiece arrived just as she'd ordered.

"Compliments from the kitchen. Javier thinks you're some kind of star or something so he skipped your plate to the front," Dorothy said, as if the enchanted cook must have been out of his mind. He was still peeking at Octavia, tiptoeing from behind the order window, grinning like a Cheshire cat who thought he might have a shot a eating the canary.

With a slight wave of her hand, Octavia conveyed her appreciation while two couples in her section complained about the cook's affections getting in the way of receiving their meal, despite having been seated before her. She giggled to herself at the thought of both couples getting a little extra something mixed in their dinner when it finally arrived, courtesy of dishwater-blonde Dorothy.

After having inhaled the largest omelet meant for one person, Octavia felt her eyes getting heavy almost immediately. No amount of coffee would have staved off the overwhelming desire to close them a minute, granting them rest. In what seemed like seconds she awoke to a much noisier diner and a booth full of young white women loudly slurring their words. With a sweeping once-over, she surmised that they had just left a bachelorette party like the one starring Savon. The woman wearing a long brown stuffed penis-shaped hat and a white veil streaming with rows of flavored condom packets was her first clue. They were all cackling as if it was going out of style and looking in her direction like they expected some sort of interaction. Instinctively she faintly brushed the back of her hand across her chin, hoping that she wouldn't find a trail of saliva there.

Before Octavia could make heads or tails of the odd situation, one of the girls at the table turned her head slightly toward the wait station. The others played follow-the-leader and did likewise. The scene grew more bizarre with each passing moment. Octavia continued thinking, what is the deal with these inebriated white chicks and what are they all gawking at? Suddenly the urge to join what had to be some kind of demented game drew her in as well.

When Octavia discovered what all the fuss was about, her mouth watered. She saw him standing there, casually collecting his things and tossing them into a gray nylon backpack. They were supplies of some kind, but the details were lost on her because she could not and did not want to stop checking out every inch of the fine man now standing at the register near the front of the room. Octavia did not mind at all that she was sharing the same eyeful as many of the other women present. In a word, the view was spectacular. From a fancy pair of rust-colored street boots, past the perfectly worn faded Levis and all the way up his cappuccino-colored face with a tailored low-fade haircut topped with thick waves. The man's appearance was *spectacular*. Octavia was afraid to blink because she didn't want to miss anything and had to consciously remind herself to keep her tongue in her mouth. Since curiosity has no shame, she allowed her curiosity to take over.

When it appeared that the stranger felt her eyes burning a hole through him, he pivoted slowly. She expected him to part his lips and salute her with a warm "Hello there, beautiful, where you been all my life" or something just as wonderfully clichéd, but his gaze drifted past her and landed on Dorothy the waitress, who acted as if she had free run of the place.

"See you next time, Mom," he said, much to Octavia's dismay. His voice was strong over the clattering of dishes being collected by a conscientious busboy at the next table. Dorothy gently touched her lips with her fingertips and blew him a kiss with a warm and sentimental flare. That must have be been the waitress' other side, the one that came out only when she was not waiting on tables.

"I know that rude mop-headed table-setter did not spawn such an exquisite hunk of a man," Octavia heard herself whisper to no one in particular.

Disregarding the notion, which Octavia had held firmly, of being looked over two or three times, the stranger threw several folded bills on the counter. He didn't seem to be aware that all the hungry women staring him down had more than just reasonably priced appetizers on their minds. Instead, he slung the backpack over his right shoulder and headed for the door in even manly strides. Octavia watched the scene frame by frame so she could play it back in her mind as often as she cared to once he was gone.

As suddenly as he had appeared, the door closed behind him. He walked out of her life like a leading man in the kind of dreamy love story where the handsome stranger always gets the girl in the end. That's when it occurred to Octavia that she could not let him pull a Houdini and vanish before her very eyes. She shoved her better judgment aside and immediately began begging Dorothy for her bill.

"So now you're in a hurry," Dorothy teased sarcastically. "Too bad you decided to take a happy nap at his favorite table or you could have met him. Yep, he watched you snoring, snorting, and huffing for over half an hour or so until he got tired of waiting for you to stop calling the hogs."

"Me snoring? I couldn't have been that out of it." Octavia eyed her modest timepiece. Just as Dorothy had informed her, she'd been asleep for close to an hour. "Oh my goodness, you're right. How embarrassing. I'm sure I looked ridiculous."

"I thought so," Dorothy answered on cue. "But someone else seemed pleased as punch, although the reason why alludes me."

Octavia hesitated while opening her purse. "Hmm, someone like who?"

"I'm not sure. My memory fades every now and again." She stuck out her hand, rubbing her fingertips against her thumb. When Octavia handed over a crisp ten-dollar bill, the waitress turned actress. "Oh, I remember faintly but it's getting clearer." After another ten-spot, Dorothy dispensed with the memory-loss bit. "Oh, now I remember."

"That's pitiful. You should be ashamed of yourself. Don't you feel the least bit guilty for extorting money for information on your son?"

"No. I've never been stupid enough to do the marriage thing and the last time I looked, I didn't have any children."

"But I distinctly heard him call you 'Mom,'" Octavia argued, beginning to feel that she had been duped out of twenty bucks.

Dorothy folded the bills and tucked them in her bra for safekeeping as she looked past Octavia and out the window. "I'll be, look at that. It's startin' to rain."

"What's rain got to do with that guy who just left here?" Octavia's annoyance had begun to spill over.

"Well, for one, everybody calls me 'Mom' 'cause I've been here since the place opened and I don't take anybody's crap, just like dear old Mom. Two, he left this for you. Said to give it to you if you ever woke up."

The waitress handed her an eight-by-ten-inch charcoal sketch that Octavia couldn't pretend wasn't amazing. The drawing captured her sleeping at the table with her chin resting on her chest and arms folded. The detail was so remarkable that Octavia had difficulty believing someone could instill her essence on paper in such a short amount of time. "That guy did this, for me? Why?"

"I'ont rightly know, miss, but if you weren't so busy yappin' your flap, you could ask him yourself." The tail end of that comment went right by Octavia, much like Dorothy's unexpected but thoughtful expression. "There he goes Darlin'." When Octavia finally glanced up from the beautiful artwork the stranger rolled his bicycle past the window as stately as you please. Who rides a bicycle anymore, at night and in the rain? She couldn't help wondering. Was he some sort of eccentric kook? Too confused for words, Octavia searched Dorothy's face for a hint as what she should do. "I've never seen him draw anything for anyone else, and he's been having dinner here for years. If I's you, I'da stopped yappin' a long time ago and done gone after him."

The biggest smile possible tipped across Octavia's face as she hugged Dorothy, then she headed for the door. "Thanks, Mom," she added on her way out.

She felt a bit foolish when she realized how it might look, going out of her way to catch up to a fine handsome stranger who was on a bike and in the rain. As absurd as that seemed to her, Octavia figured it would have been even more absurd if she never saw him again or didn't at least give herself a chance to thank the man properly.

As the wind pulled the clouds across the sky Octavia ducked her head, dodging the rain, as she jogged toward the parking lot. Once in the dry confines of her vehicle, she twisted the windshield-wiper knob on her steering wheel and began surveying the various movements around the restaurant. There was a family of four sprinting from a Volvo station wagon. Two pickup trucks idled while vying for Octavia's parking spot and other drivers traveled through, but there was no gorgeous hunk on a bike. As she waited in the rain, she decided it was a stupid idea to be searching for a perfect stranger. She was actually relieved that she didn't see him.

The rain continued to fall steadily as she backed out slowly. Both trucks inched toward her, too close for comfort in fact. She leaned on her horn in an effort to keep them at a safe distance until she could get clear. Just as she pulled away, one of the truck drivers roared his motor and bolted for the now-vacant parking space. Simultaneously the other driver raced ahead. With horns blaring, neither driver was willing to give an inch. Octavia watched the game of nerves from her rearview mirror. Unfortunately, she was still moving forward while doing it.

Suddenly there was a loud thump. Octavia screamed, mashing on her breaks. She didn't know what she'd hit but was certain she'd hit something. Terrified that it might have been a stray dog, she cautiously opened her door and stepped out. Expecting to find a scared injured animal, she screamed louder than before when she saw rust-colored street boots moving on the ground in front of her car. Instinctively she hopped back in her car and threw the gearshift into reverse, then winced when there was another thump. Whoever she ran over the first time had just been trampled again.

"Stop! You're gonna kill 'im!" Dorothy hollered. She was standing under the awning on the sidewalk adjoining to the restaurant, waving her arms frantically.

The man was now down on his knees, trying to make it to his feet. He was soaking wet and grimacing in pain. Octavia stood bewildered and distraught, especially when he began yanking at a wrecked bicycle frame lodged beneath her SUV. She realized immediately that he was the same guy who had only moments before cast an angelic expression Dorothy's way, but his face was now contorted.

He shook his head in frustration, then stumbled against Octavia's car door. When she rushed over to aid him, he turned toward her erratically as if she had appeared out of nowhere. When his eyes locked on the woman who had run him down, he backed away. "Oh, it's you!"

"I'm so sorry," she apologized, extending her hands to help him stand.

"Oh no, I don't think I want you near me. You're a lunatic."

"Please let me help you get out of this rain." Her words were sorrowful and heartfelt.

"No, I . . . have to get my bike. It's my ride home." As he took a step away from the commotion his knees buckled. He splashed butt first on the hard concrete and sat there in a sullen stupor. Dorothy looked on, as did others from inside the busy diner.

"Keep him there. I'll get an ambulance," Dorothy advised, heading for the restaurant's entrance.

"Mom, don't!" The man halted her with his adamant plea.

Octavia hustled over to his side. She was terrified for his sake as well as for her own. Fearing the worst, she rubbed her hand across her face to wipe the streams of water away. "Oh God, this did not just happen. Sir, please let her get a doctor. You may be hurt. Please."

While Dorothy awaited his response, he looked at his mangled bike, then up at his attacker. "I just need to get home. I'll be fine. Just need to get home." He climbed to his feet slowly. "Mom, please call me a ride. I'll be fine."

More confused than before, Octavia kneeled down for a last attempt to make a bad situation salvageable. "If you won't see a doctor, let me make sure you get home alright and—"

"You are a lunatic if you think I'm gonna let you drive me anywhere," he interrupted, wearing a scared expression. "I've seen you drive and, honestly, I'll take my chances in a taxi."

Octavia understood his reactions but wouldn't take no for an answer. She grabbed him with both hands and hoisted him with all her might. "I don't care what you say, you're coming with me and I'm going to see that you live. So come on and shut up!" The man fought back a grin when she forcibly apprehended him. "Now get in the car and buckle up," she added. "Most accidents occur in inclement weather, and my insurance is high enough as it is."

Dorothy watched perplexed as Octavia led the injured man to the passenger side, then tucked him in before returning to the driver's side. "I got this!" she yelled angrily in Dorothy's general direction.

Once the car began moving, the weary passenger adjusted his seat belt, then tugged at it firmly to assure that he was tightly secured. "I liked you better when you were asleep," he remarked sarcastically.

"Well, we'll just have to deal with that later. For now, you just tell me where you live."

Octavia dragged the remnants of the bicycle under her SUV for half a block before it was dislodged and abandoned in the middle of the flooded avenue. During the short drive, the man barked directions while his chauffeur remained steady on her course. They sat fuming like two well-acquainted lovers after a heated quarrel. When she made the last left turn into a ritzy subdivision with mansions on either side of the street, she thought for certain that she was going to be sued by her victim's wealthy family.

"Turn right here and slow down," he instructed nervously. "I'll just jump out. I'm still not too confident about your ability to stop."

She glared at him. "Just tell me which one of these is yours and I promise, no more accidents."

He glared back before acquiescing to her demand. "It's that one on the right. Two houses down." He pointed to a large stucco house the shade of a white sandy beach. It was huge, Octavia thought. Her eyes widened when she imagined the excessive doctors' bills, a highly probable call from the police, and a high-priced attorney.

She pulled into the long driveway and leaned forward to get a good look at the palatial estate, then breathed deeply and let out a labored sigh. "Well, it looks like we've made it, and without further incident might I add, so make sure you tell your lawyer that before he tries to haul me into court."

The man gazed at her peculiarly, then realized she was staring at the beautiful six-bedroom home. "Oh. Now I get it, Speedy." He raised his arm again and pointed to a small one-bedroom guest house in the rear. "That's where I live. You won't have to worry about a lawsuit. I don't know any lawyers on a first-name basis and even if I did, that wouldn't be necessary. But you will have to replace my wheels."

Somewhat relieved, Octavia tapped the dome light in the roof of her Jeep before reaching in the backseat for her purse. She couldn't get her checkbook out fast enough. "That's good to hear. Let me take care of this before you change your mind." She signed her name, then glanced up at him, suggesting he tell her how much this little mishap would actually cost her.

For the first time he caught a clear glimpse of her face at close range. He blinked his eyes rapidly to shake off a strong desire to gaze deeply into hers. He was captivated by her radiant deep-dark complexion and striking features. "Uhh, you can make it out for four hundred dollars and the check had better clear your account," he added in his best businesslike tone. "That was a perfectly good Schwinn Flyer you totaled."

By the expression she shot back, you'd have thought he requested four thousand dollars. "Four hundred? Are you telling me that you paid four hundred for that raggedy bike?"

"First of all, that bike wasn't raggedy before you stormed into it, and no, I didn't pay four hundred, but I do know that they're all out of two-hundred-dollar Flyers because you destroyed the last one they had!"

She huffed with grave disbelief as she penned in the requested amount. "Why couldn't you have bought a Huffy? I happen to know that Huffy makes a darn good Flyer. 'Had one myself when I was nine."

"Well I don't like Huffys. I like the Schwinn Flyer," he argued. "And why am I even discussing this with you? You hit me, ruining my transportation, and now I'm haggling with you over the price of it. This is crazy. You're crazy and I must be losing my mind, too."

"Yeah, whatever." She peered down at the check again and it came to her that she didn't know the name of the man she had assaulted. "Who should I make this payable to?"

"Thoughtful of you to finally ask after you *ran me down!* It's Legacy, Legacy Childs." He began to spell it out. "That's L-e-g-a—"

"I know how to spell, and I have a degree to prove it."

"Oh yeah? I bet you flunked driving school."

"Ha-ha, very funny. Looks like you're feeling better already. That bump on your head didn't seem to help your manners any, Legacy Childs."

"Maybe not, but it did help my bank account." He gave the check a onceover and nodded assuredly while unfastening the seat belt. Her phone number was printed just below her name and address. "I'll call you later, Octavia . . . Longbow."

Pleasantly surprised, Octavia fought off the smile wrestling inside her lips. "Uh-uh, you seem to be healing just fine and you've told me that you're not going to sue, so what makes you think I want you calling me?"

He opened the door and stuck one leg out. "Because you wrote a four-hundred-dollar check for a two-hundred-dollar bike. You're not that crazy." Behind those parting words, he strolled down a watery pathway without so much as the slightest limp or any signs of trauma. Octavia sat motionless as he unlocked the door to the small building he called home. She blushed from the feel-good emotions percolating down to her toes. She knew he was right, too. She wouldn't have minded it in the least if he rang her phone or sent smoke signals for that matter. There was something oddly endearing about this spectacularly handsome Legacy Childs, and Octavia was hoping she'd have a chance to find out what it was.

She backed out of the driveway slowly with thoughts of Mr. Childs heavily on her mind. At the same time, Legacy peeked at her between thin slits in the venetian blinds with Octavia weighing likewise on his.

7

A Perfectly Good Lie

Steady beads of rain tapdanced down the front windshield as Cee-Cee pulled over against the curb next the Vicious Cuts beauty salon to get her thoughts together. Although the building had been a family-owned bakery in a previous life, renovations had transformed it into a posh perm-and-weave palace. The high-priced cut-and-curl den was fashionably decorated in broad strokes of gold and trimmed in money-green accents. It also served as a veritable gossip fest for Truest, generally from Tuesday through Friday and by appointment only on Saturday. She liked to keep her weekend options open in the event that something tempting jumped off. When she had agreed to stay late to help one of the nail techs from the shop get her head together, she had not planned on getting caught in the rain or confronted by a storm.

The seasoned nail tech lounged in the comfortable salon chair, covered by a black nylon smock. Her head stuck through the top of it like a small child's doll after an unsuccessful first attempt at styling. Most of her hair was sticking straight up, as only a few micro braids had been woven in. Truest used one hand to comb a long part down the back of her customer's hair while pulling at thick strands of it and spreading oil to the roots of the woman's dense new growth with the other. "Hold your head down, Deja, I need to get up in this kitchen before I'm too tired to do justice to the pots and pans," Trust teased. She enjoyed the off-beat banter and discussing current events, who's doing who and catching up on the latest juicy hearsay to be consumed, which was as common to a beauty salon as oil and heat. "That reminds me. Lisa called from the church today and said her cousin Shay's wedding was called off when the groom got caught butt-naked with the best man and her maid of honor in the pastor's study. I don't wish any bad luck on nobody but I could've told Shay that Piper More wasn't trying to let getting married stand in the way of him getting his freak on. You feel me?"

"I feel you like a Siamese twin," Deja answered. "I did tell Shay, in a roundabout way, that her man was still out there and didn't seem like he had no plans of turning over no new leafs."

"Deja, I don't know why you wasted your breath. You know you can't tell a black woman nothin' about her man 'cause she can see the best in him when no one else can."

"Mmm, say that twice girl. Two times." Deja reached up to scratch her scalp but Truest instinctively deterred her with a subtle forearm block. "Anyway, she got what she deserved if you ask me."

"You' wrong for that. Shay's a nice girl, naïve but nice. And what makes you think she deserved to have her wedding plans ruined?"

"For the simple fact that the damned fool still didn't believe me about Piper even after I showed her *The Humping Homeboy* booty flick that he sold me out the trunk of his car just a week ago."

"That's nothing to leave a man over. Seems to me he was just trying to come up on some extra cheese."

"That ain't all he was trying to come up on, so let me finish. Truest, he was *in the movie*. You don't hear me, though. Starring, directing, and producing . . . all that. Piper *is* The Humping Homeboy."

"Nuh-uhhhh, tell me he ain't. Hell, now I gotta check it out for myself. He sold me one of 'em, too."

"Me and Shay rolled a blunt and watched the whole thang

together," Deja told her. "She still didn't want to believe it was her man, even though he kept walking over to adjust the camera in the middle of handling his business."

"That sounds like some talk-show shit. See, that's why I don't get caught up. Drama to the left of me and drama to the right. I do wish I was there at the church, though, when all hell broke loose."

Deja agreed wholeheartedly. "Sho' you right. I kinda wished I was the one who busted them. I'da showed Piper what real camera work is. Zoooom in . . . zoooom out." She threw up both hands and connected her thumbs at the tips, acting out what she'd said. While Truest laughed and heartily encouraged the woman's antics, Deja's eyes discovered a disturbed pair staring back at her. "Hey, ain't that your girl Cee-Cee Whatchumacallhuh from the radio station out there scopin' us from that Benz?"

Truest stopped laughing like her life depending on it. "Cee-Cee, where?" She started off in the direction of the front window. Slowly she slapped lotion on both of her hands, although she hadn't finished with Deja's hair. "It sure is. Hmm, I wonder how Cee-Cee knew I'd be here. No one knew except you."

As Cee-Cee stepped out of the car, Deja confessed, "Well, don't trip, Truest 'cause I know you got a temper, but I did get a call while you were in the restroom. I know y'all cool so I told her you'd be here late hooking me up."

Truest caught a glimpse of Deja's pensive expression in the wall mirror. "That's cool this time, but never offer my whereabouts to anybody," Truest reprimanded sternly. "Big mouth." The short stroll to the head of the shop was laced with uncertainty. Although Cee-Cee had been a good friend in the past, something was bothering her. Since the Hat Chat event, Cee-Cee had made constant attempts at getting to the bottom of her concerns, but Truest had been uncharacteristically unavailable for comment. And now she was finally cornered as well.

After unlocking the dead bolt, Truest pulled the door open to invite the late caller inside. Cee-Cee extended her arms for an embrace. "Hey Tru, glad to see you're still alive. We need to talk." Deja studied their interaction then half spoke, taking her cue when Truest didn't say anything at all, but not out of spite. Truest couldn't find words to disguise the emotions traipsing through her. "Sistah, can you excuse us a minute? Tru won't be long." Deja was as nosey as nail techs come. She watched them carefully as they trekked back to the far end of the building, then disappeared into the manager's office.

Cee-Cee imagined herself kicking the door off the hinges and marching in, snatching up Truest by her collar, and dragging her off by her neck. Fortunately for her, she'd witnessed her girlfriend's fisticuff prowess. A levelheaded approach served better at getting her point across, because getting that level head knocked clean off was the ugly alternative.

"Cee-Cee, you telling me that whatever is killing you to talk to me about can't wait until I'm finished with Deja's head?" Truest asked vehemently, once they were behind closed doors.

"Uh-uh. I wouldn't even be here if you'd just returned one of my calls, but you like doing things the hard way. Look, I couldn't sleep another night until I got this off my chest." Before Cee-Cee could address the matter head-on, Truest plopped down angrily on the edge of the office desk. "Tru, you know I'm not one to jump in another woman's affairs concerning a man but I can't believe you."

"What you mean, you can't believe me?" She was apprehensive but wanted to hurry up and face the music Cee-Cee felt it necessary to dance to. "What's all this about, anyway?" Truest had done so much dirt to so many people that she wasn't at all sure of what Cee-Cee had learned about her misdeeds.

"I can't believe that you've been seeing Isaiah Rome."

"Isaiah . . . Rome?" Truest repeated. The tremor in her voice bordered somewhere between alarm and surprise. "Where did that come from? I don't even . . . even know him?" Her eyes couldn't conceal the lie, so she looked away to hide the shame.

With her arms crossed defiantly, Cee-Cee stepped closer toward the accused and took a deep breath to compose herself. "You're just gonna sit there and lie to my face. Truest, I was at Octavia's place last week when the man called and asked for you. I'm guessing he got the numbers crossed by mistake somehow, but I'm sure it was him because 'Tavia's caller ID flashed his name."

Truest knew she had been busted, but that didn't stop her from trying to fake it. "So, he's been trying to get with me, but that's all. We both know how Octavia feels about him. She'd do just about anything for that fool."

"And what about you? What would you do for that fool? And don't think about pitching some more of those tired lies. That three-timing jerk told me all I needed to hear to be too through with you."

Biting at her nails, Truest could barely speak. "What . . . what did he say, when he called?" She couldn't stand being at the mercy of someone else, no matter how wrong she was.

Although Cee-Cee was put out with what one girlfriend had done behind the other's back, she eased up when she noticed the obvious embarrassment on Truest's face. "Well, before I could tell him that he had the wrong number, he'd already run his mouth. 'Hey Tru,' he says all low and secretive-like as if he had ducked in a closet or something. 'Baby, this is Rome. Your ticket should be hand-delivered tomorrow.'" It was difficult to read Truest's expression as she peered down at the floor. "If Octavia had answered her own phone that afternoon and heard what I did, it would have torn her heart to pieces." Cee-Cee was not prepared for the reaction that her words had evoked when Truest scraped the bottom of the barrel to make a valiant effort at spin control.

She sucked her teeth with a renewed calculating swagger. "It's a good thing that she'll never find out about any of that, huh? I know you, Cee. You haven't told her 'cause you think I'll see the error of my ways and tell her myself. Well, I ain't in a repenting mood. Ahh, don't twist your face up like you want to do something to me. You got your nerve coming up in here like your shit don't stink." Cee-Cee was confused, wondering what Truest was driving at. "Uh-huh, I'm not the only one doing dirt. Let me tell you what I know about the first woman Devin ran to when he couldn't take no more of Sylvia's so-called Prissy Priss routine? That's right, you can't miss me when it comes to Devin. We've been tight since junior high and I know a lot more about him than his wife does, but I'm guessing not more than you." Truest paced circles around her accuser until a sly remark came to mind. "Now, does that make you the kettle and me the pot, or is it the other way around? I forget."

Sylvia's husband Devin had been out the house for over two months for, as she put it, abandoning her. In actuality, Sylvia had spent more time building her well-established interior design company than her marriage. Also, her sexual hang-ups, prudish non-compliance, and ultraconservative views regarding what was acceptable behavior evolved into a flat reluctance to indulge him beyond the missionary position. His frustrations had manifested. She felt that her willingness to give him some every now and then should have been sufficient. Understandably, it wasn't. Their affection dwindled, and subsequently all intimacy was extinguished. She was complacent. He bounced. Imagine that.

With Truest spinning a nasty web, it was Cee-Cee's turn to sit in the hot seat. She was visibly uneasy with the accusation thrown in her face. "Truest, Devin is a good friend of mine as well but no, I don't know anything about what his wife should or shouldn't know about him. True enough, he did call me when he packed his bags. I let him come over to talk. *Just talk!*" Her last words come out louder than she expected them to. "I'm just saying that I respect their marriage despite the struggles they've had trying to hold it together. We just . . . talked."

A loud chuckle rolled from Truest's wide-open mouth. "Seeing as to how Devin's car was still parked outside 2009 Bateman Drive the next morning, y'all must've had one long-ass marathon of a conversation." When no reply came forth to refute her claim, Truest reveled in her suspicions. "Don't that make us a splendid pair?" Cee-Cee didn't have to guess what she thought they were a pair of.

One night of loneliness and vulnerability did give Cee-Cee pause to check her own suspect morality. But it was only one night, not two years of sneaking around, meeting in out-of-the-way hotels and other more unspeakable arrangements like the one Truest had subjected herself to while smiling in Octavia's face at the same time. In comparison, Cee-Cee had stepped away from her mistake and felt remorseful about it immediately. Sylvia was not a part of the threesome's inner circle, but Octavia was the nucleus of it. Without Octavia in their lives, the ladies from opposite sides of the tracks would have never become close. Chances are they never would have met. Now they found themselves standing at the crossroad of friend and foe.

"Listen, I'm not going to dignify what you think I did with Devin," Cee-Cee offered, eventually. "Besides, that's neither here nor there. What's important is Octavia. She represents the best of us and you know it. With I. Rome due in town on Thursday, I need to know where you stand. It's going to be rough on her as it is. Each time that man blows through here, she drops everything to make herself accessible. She's addicted and can't seem to kick the habit but you don't have that excuse, do you? With you, I'm sure it's just a thrill thing . . . pay-your-bills thing. You should consider squashing that for Octavia's sake."

Truest walked near the office door, where Deja's ear had been firmly pressed the entire time. "Not that it's really any of yours nor nobody else's biz'ness who I let pay my bills, but you do have a point. I love Octavia just as much as you do and yes she does represent the best of us. That's why I told Rome that I wasn't available to meet him in Chicago last week. He's been blowing up my phone and sending flowers every day since. My place looks like a damned mortuary or something. Ooh, if I see another rose, daisy, or daffodil I might hurt somebody. I should have said no to him a long time ago."

"Better yet, you never should have said yes."

For the first time since Cee-Cee had arrived, both women felt at ease with the difficult situation at hand. They agreed, then embraced like real friends, whether they're going into a storm or coming out of one.

Cee-Cee glanced at her watch. "I didn't mean to take so much time but like I said, I was tired of losing sleep over it. I'm sure you'll handle things in a womanly fashion."

"Yeah, you can bet on that. Oh and Cee-Cee, Devin told me that nothing really happened that night . . . you know. I just don't deal with it too well when someone has the upper hand on me, including you. It's the street in me coming out, but I'll work on it."

"Tru, we all have issues we can work on. Some more than others."

"Wheww, maybe now I can get some sleep, too. Right after I figure out how I'm paying for that new Corvette sittin' out front. It's in me and Rome's name and I'm sure he'll have it repo'd when it finally hits him that I was serious about it being over." Cee-Cee motioned for the doorknob but Truest beckoned her. "Cee, one more thing. We cool again? I mean, like before this? I know I act tough and all but I ain't never had no sistahs. You and 'Tavia are the closest thing for me. I'd hate to lose that." When the nosey nail tech heard the steps drawing closer, she tiptoed quietly back to her chair.

Cee-Cee read between the lines, long before Truest could ask what she didn't have the words to convey. All had been forgiven. "Don't sweat it. If Octavia gets wind of it, won't be from me. Everyone makes mistakes. It comes with being human. You never know when I might need you to knock some sense into my head if I let a perfectly good man like Devin walk out on *me*."

"You know I'm good for it," Truest said in jest, thumbing her nose like a prizefighter ready to do battle.

Once she was safely locked in her new car, Cee-Cee felt relieved for doing the right thing, hoping that Truest would do the same. It's not every day that a friend has to put a coveted friendship, as well as expensive dental work, on the line.

As Cee-Cee pulled away from the curb, Deja wasted no time tying to get to the scoop on what went down in the backroom. She'd heard I. Rome's name but couldn't clearly make out what the entire beef was about. "Hmm, that Cee-Cee what's-her-name seemed pretty pissed. I know I wouldn't have let nobody come up in here and lead me around by the nose. I thought y'all was tight. So . . . what got into her?"

Truest grabbed the full bag of synthetic hair lying on her workstation. "Uhh-uhh, Deja. If you don't want to be punched in *that nose you wouldn't be lead around by*, then mind your biz'ness." When Deja made a last feeble strike at pay dirt by starting in again, Truest gave a hand full of real hair a vicious yank.

"Ahhhhhhh!" Deja screamed.

"Mind . . . your . . . biz'ness," Truest reiterated venomously through gnashing teeth.

8

Liquor in the Front, Poker in the Back

Alphonzo brushed the soles of his Timberlands against the gold-trimmed welcome mat more times than necessary while taking in the view from outside Tony Tune's mansion. "I gots to get me one of these when I grow up," he heard himself say. When he rang the bell, a symphonic hip-hop rendition of "We're in the Money" played over the intercom throughout the station's number-one deejay's new home. After signing his second consecutive million-dollar contract, Tony Tune had treated himself to the former mayor's house in an upscale, exclusive gated community.

Alphonzo was bobbing his head to the bass beat when a tiny Asian woman answered the door, adorned in a traditional maid's uniform. "Please to come in. Mistah Tony is in back." She smiled agreeably as she invited him in. "Please to take your coat, sir?" Alphonzo removed his thick jacket, then felt awestruck by the inviting but Las Vegas–style ostentation. Fine crystal thingamajigs and gold-plated knickknacks stared back at him as he took in the expensive trappings of a thirty-year career in the biz.

The tiny woman guided Alphonzo to the back of the first floor where laughter came pouring out. As she ushered him in the enormous game room, the distinctive aroma of marijuana and liquor greeting him. "Hey, thanks for the tour," he said. "What does a man have to do to get his hands on a drink?"

The maid cackled, holding her miniature hands over her mouth. "Deejay so funny, so funny." She dismissed his request. "It no work like that, homeboy. Mistah Tony too cheap to pay for bartender. How 'bout you please to get *me* a drink? Second-hand chronic smoke give big headache." She placed both hands on her hips, waiting for a reply.

"Hang around for a hot sec, I got you covered. What you drinking?" "Hennessey's straight, no chaser. I like it neat." He left her idling outside the game room entrance and quickly forgot his promise when the enticement of joyous entertainment lured him in.

Alphonzo fell in the doorway, grinning from ear to ear. "Now we can get the party started," he shouted above the music emanating from the '50s-style jukebox. "Dayum, Mr. Tune. I heard your new digs was hype but man, this is wrong."

"Hey 'Zo, glad you could make it," Tony Tune hailed from the other side of a tall water glass filled with Crown Royal on the rocks. "We're just getting the show on the road and young brotha, it can't get much righter than this. Make yourself at home. The bar is open but hey, don't get yourself in trouble with the law. Racial profiling ain't no joke. The police spend the better part of each shift waiting on a black man to mess up." He shuffled a fresh deck of cards, then took a long drag from a fat rolled blunt. "You got to be responsible when you take it to the head." Alphonzo laughed at the ironic comment, a millionaire with one too many vices preaching about responsibility. But he took it all in stride as he poured himself a stiff four-fingered glass of orange juice over a jigger of gin.

Sitting to either side of Tony were Ebony Jones and Floreese Taylor, the tag team duo known as Eb and Flo to their audience between the hours of 2 and 6 P.M. "'Zo, I caught the show last night. You was in rare form, boy," Ebony said between mammoth puffs. "But what was up with that stuff about taking the fortieth caller for the new I. Rome joint?"

"Ah, that was a little something to get Octavia going. You know she's been kicking it with him on the low-low."

Floreese passed on the herbal enticement making its way around the green felt-covered card table. "I thought ol' dude was married to that *Jet* centerfold from Cleveland. You know, the one who works for the phone company and likes moonlit walks and sex on the beach."

Ebony choked on his drink, then wiped the spillage from his chin. "Man, I keep that issue next to my bed. That's the one they tried to recall. "Had her nipples hanging out and everything. I know one copy they won't be getting back."

"I've got mine in a wall safe upstairs with my other valuables," Tony added. "They should've shipped it in a brown paper bag." Actually her bio listed Sex on the Beach as her favorite drink. "Boy, if I ever get to Cleveland . . . I know one call I got to make." The boys in the back room had a good laugh over that one.

When the telephone rang, Tony asked Ebony to get it while he dropped a bit of advice on his young protégés. "Fellas, I almost forgot. Ms. Patricia is on a rampage so you'd better watch your step. Saul the security guard hipped me that she was up to something because she wanted to know what really goes on when she's not looking. I think she might have hired a mole working on the inside." Each of the men shared the expression of death warmed over, knowing their own mischief while on the clock.

"You' kidding, Mr. Tune," Alphonzo questioned nervously. "Please tell me she didn't."

"I believe she did. Something's been going on for a couple of weeks now and I also heard from Mooney in the mailroom that she's going to drop some news on us at the Monday meeting." That revelation cast a thick shadow of panic over the well-lit table. "I meant to tell y'all yesterday but I had to get home to meet the man putting in my Jacuzzi and sauna." Unfortunately, Lazarus hadn't benefited from that little jewel of information in time to be on his *p*s and *q*s. He wished his lucky stars he had come in Monday morning.

Once Ebony returned from the phone call, he rejoined a much more subdued group than he'd left. "Why are y'all looking like somebody died? Somebody get fired from the station or something?"

"Not yet, anyway," Alphonzo answered with his head in his hands. He proceeded to fill Ebony in on the latest 411, lamenting over his own business done on company time, including the photocopies he'd made of his penis one night during his shift. It had seemed like a fairly safe thing to do at the time, considering he merely faxed them to the attention of an ex-girlfriend who refused to see him again after she stumbled across his vast collection of listener fan mail; most of which had risqué pictures of females enclosed in them. He thought it was a good idea to remind her of what she was missing.

"By the way, who was that on the phone?" Tony asked as an afterthought.

Ebony spread his poker hand carefully. "Oh, that was Laz'rus. Said he couldn't make it. Sounded tore up about something. I couldn't make out what he was saying, though. Too much crying on the other end."

Alphonzo thought that seemed odd. "What, is he mixed up with another upset hoochie?"

"Nah, he was by himself but crying enough for three people. I bet it had something to do with that crazy chick Stamina. He ain't had nothing but troubles since she stepped to him that night at Pimpsters."

"Yeah, I remember." That was Floreese, laughing and stomping his foot against the floor. "She'd just won the five-hundred dollar best-dressed contest. You know how it always ends up with some sistah getting freaky? Uh-huh, that night Stamina won, clinched it in the last round. Did the whole dance-off in a short skirt but forgot to bring her panties."

"Ah, man, the whole dance-off?" Ebony yelled in disbelief from across the table.

"Yep, and she got down to 'Back That Ass Up,' the extended version."

Tony studied his cards, then his visitors. "Don't fool yourselves. She didn't forget to pack the panties. That's the oldest trick in the book. Back in seventy-six or maybe it was seventy-seven, I remember like it was yesterday. Studio Fifty-seven was the hottest thing smoking and people would drive or fly in from all over Texas to party at the wildest nightclub in the state. Well, one Saturday night the police had to shut the place down when this voluptuous thang with a fine brown frame stripped down to her unmentionables during a Brick House contest."

"Say it ain't so?" Floreese argued for the sake of arguing.

"The Hell if it ain't. I was there when her stiffest competition did her one better and got as naked as the day she was born, then did a split on stage. The club owner had to call the law to stop the riot."

Alphonzo was captivated by the absurdity of the story. "What were you doing when all that madness was going on?"

"Man . . . after I'd seen enough, me and the winner tipped out the back door and spent all night getting acquainted." He took a deep breath as he laid his cards on the table. "I ain't never been the same since. Come to think of it, that's how me and my second wife Gladys met." Everyone around the table listened in until they were fighting back tears. When Ebony lost his breath, he reached into his pocket and came out with an asthma inhaler. That story was a three-puffer if ever he heard one.

"Tony, Tony you've got to stop, man. You' gonna hurt 'im," Floreese begged jokingly. "Don't do it. I need him for the show."

Tony sipped from his tall glass, thinking back on younger days and much wilder times. Suddenly his attractive smile fell flat. Not all of those wild times had proved expedient. "Yeah, that was two life times ago and it's good that some things stay in the past where they belong." The others adapted a similar demeanor when they realized he was sincere. "Wild nights and wild women. Boy, I'll tell ya, it didn't take long for me to find out that Gladys couldn't keep her drawse on, period, whether I was around or not. Some women are dogs, too. But I did my share to bust up our marriage. I can't deny that. I was a young man making too much money and spent too much time away from the house at night. I thought that keeping a woman's pocketbook full was the answer to keeping 'em happy. Don't fool yourselves. Women need their men home and taking care of business or else someone'll step in and take care of business for you." The younger men looked on solemnly at a man who'd seen the errors of his youth and thought it necessary to pass on what he'd learned the hard way. "It took me a long time to figure out what every sistah wants is reciprocity."

"Reci-what?" Ebony spoke up, but all the others were wondering the same thing.

"I said reciprocity. That means they want the same thing they give to their men, nothing more and nothing less. It's what they all want and they deserve it. If a woman shares her body only with him, she expects the same in return. When she tells him how much she loves him in spite of his shortcomings, she ought to get to hear those same kind words whispered in her ears, too. That is the real secret to a good relationship lastin' and it'll keep you from running the streets. Give a sistah that and she'll love you better than your momma. Most people think it's communication, but bad communication can ruin a good thing faster than a man who won't say much at all. Reciprocity, gentleman," he reiterated before taking another sip of bourbon. "That is the sum of the whole matter. Every sistah wants it." When no one had a word to add to a flawless dissertation on making a good thing better, he picked up his cards again. "Now that we got that out of the way, I'ma school y'all in some poker."

Somehow every syllable uttered from the depths of Tony Tune's wisdom rang home with those who couldn't escape the honesty shared in his thoughts. He spoke from years of heartache, trial, and excess.

Alphonzo looked over his shoulder and out the door of the elaborately redecorated room. It was plain to see that all the money and fame mustered by the legendary voice of Hot 100, minus a good woman to share it with, was barely worth having at all, although Alphonzo wouldn't have minded trying it on just to see what it felt like for himself. Sometimes, a man can teach his brothers as much about women as the fairer sex can. It really doesn't matter who's doing the teaching, as long as a man is willing to listen. Reciprocity.

As the night dwindled down to nothing, Tony bid good-bye to his guests but offered no apologies for fleecing them on the poker table. It was a small price to pay for the knowledge he had dropped on them, a very small price.

Alphonzo was halted at the massive front door as the other visitors casually passed through it. The feisty trial-size maid grabbed his shirt tightly, then spun him around. "Not so fast, homey," she hissed. "Spread 'em." Similar to an arresting police officer, she kicked his feet apart, instructed him to extend his arms to the side, then proceeded to wave a metal detecting wand up one side of his body and down the other like a bouncer at a nightclub entrance.

"Hey, hey. Watch that. You're getting a little too friendly with your hands." Alphonzo wiggled when her fingers danced freely between his pant legs. "Why'r you frisking me? I told you I wasn't gonna take nothing."

"Gotta shake you down, homey."

"Hey! What happened to that other lady? That very nice pleased-to-get-you-this-and-that lady? You done changed on me." The maid's gentle demeanor had transformed. Now she was the house Gestapo on a mission. What mission, Alphonzo wasn't sure.

"That's right. Nice lady Ms. Kim-Kim turn into maniacal bitch when man promise drink but no deliver," she answered, continuing to run her hands through his pockets.

Alphonzo watched the other guys rolling around on the front lawn, laughing at his expense while he was all but cavity searched. "Ms. Kim-Kim, what about them? Why you didn't jack them up, too?"

"Oh, them nice boys, they deliver. Bring drinks like promise. But you get girl all worked up, then no produce. That not right. Homeboy must pro-duce." She flipped the off switch on her wand finally. "Next time you bring gift. Ms. Kim-Kim be nice again. Hooka you up maybe."

"Alright, Ms. Kim-Kim. I feel you." He'd internalized Tony's lesson about what women want. "You just want a little reciprocity. Is that it?"

"No, no want reciproci-tee. That for kinda lady who wanna get jiggy. Ms. Kim-Kim too old for that. Want drink onnnly. Hennessey straight, no chaser."

"You're right. I'm sorry. I won't forget next time. I'll be honored to hook *you* up."

She began to shoo him away, shaking her head while muttering in broken English. "You keep honor. Bring beer may-bee, we kick it."

"Yes, ma'am," he offered with a bright smile. "Have a good night."

"Peace out, homey," she saluted back.

Ebony was still rolling when Alphonzo received his clearance to leave. "My bad. I should've warned you, 'Zo. Ms. Kim-Kim ain't nothin' nice when she don't get what's coming to her. Tony told me that he pays her first. Then if there's anything left, he pays the mortgage."

"Obviously, good help is hard to find."

9

Steady Pimpin'

When Legacy had no other place in particular to be or something too heavy to contemplate alone, he'd often end up at his home away from home, Marshall and Jasmine's house in Atlanta. Though he'd bought a ticket and headed for the airport, Octavia gave him second thoughts about leaving town. He saw something special in her. Even while she had slept, Legacy felt as though their paths were destined to cross. He resigned himself to the premise of sometimes you just know as he boarded the plane, hoping that his intuition wouldn't betray him, looking back over his shoulder and hoping he'd have more to return home to than he left.

After he arrived, watching little Deuce toddling around the enormous living area, Legacy couldn't stop brimming with pride, as if the healthy mocha skinned two-year old was his son instead of his godchild. The baby's father was Marshall Coates, a superstar football player with the Atlanta Falcons. He and Legacy had become good friends a few years ago on the campus of the University of Texas Consolidated, when Marshall's teammate committed suicide after struggling with AIDS. Afterwards, Legacy had immortalized the fallen athlete in a lifesize mural in the team's locker room, and a bond was forged between him and Marshall from that point on. They also shared their affinity for Jasmine, Marshall's wife and college sweetheart. She understood her man's need to have friends he could trust, more so now than ever. Jasmine was often overprotective of Legacy, too after the only woman he had ever loved died suddenly. His relationship worked well, with Jasmine as a mainstay in the overbearing but loving sister role.

"Marshall, what are y'all feeding that boy?" Legacy asked, marveling at the small child and gushing with even more pride than before. "He'll be too big to break all of your collegiate records if he doesn't put that bottle down."

Marshall took his eyes away from the ESPN sports update long enough to dote on his firstborn. His son was every bit a looker as his father, whose dominant features screamed *all man*. Marshall's six-foot-two-inch frame idled comfortably against a magnanimous sand-colored pigskin sofa. "Let my boy alone. That's about as big as I was at that age," he said eventually. "We make 'em thick like that in Texas. Ain't that right, Deuce?" When the child heard his nickname, he turned on a dime and smiled back at his daddy.

"How many times do I have to tell y'all that Deuce is not my child's name?" Jasmine sashayed over to the boy, scooped him up, then nuzzled her nose against his tummy until he cooed with excitement. "I chose the name "Marshall" because that's the sweetest name I know. Isn't that right, baby?" She bent over to plant a loving kiss on her husband's lips.

"Ain't what right?" Isaiah Rome asked, entering the large room. He wiped perspiration from his forehead, awaiting an answer.

Jasmine's lips smacked as she walked away in disgust. I. Rome and Marshall had grown up in the same South Dallas community. Although they were not close friends back then, wealth and power drew them together after the entertainer's music career took off. He loved the idea that Marshall's notoriety benefited him when their humble beginnings were made known in a two-page spread in *VIBE* magazine. Jasmine didn't think much of I. Rome when he was an over-the-hill student at UTC and thought less of him after learning of his constant overt philandering. The fact that he and wife number two were estranged made her no difference. She'd nearly had a cow when he showed up unannounced three days previously with his luggage and the mistress of the month in perfect step right behind him. He introduced the slender woman with a supermodel's stature as his publicist. Jasmine smacked her lips, then muttered under her breath, "So that's what they're calling them these days." As far as Jasmine was concerned, a ho' by any other name was still a ho, although she considered herself too much of a lady to use profanity and say it out loud. She couldn't wait until they were both out of her house so she could disinfect the mattresses and torch the sheets. The thought of a married man parading his other woman around like they were on a business trip made her sick to her stomach, even though she'd only once met the Mrs. and didn't think too highly of her, either.

"Oh, nothing, Rome," Marshall said, eyes locked on the big screen. "I thought y'all would never come up for air. You need to give yo' *publicist* a raise." He winked at his homeboy knowingly. "I heard her puttin' in some overtime late into the night."

The attractive tan-skinned publicist sauntered up behind her employer to give him a sensual kiss on the back of his neck. When I. Rome felt her there, he rudely shrugged off her affection. "Gone now. I done told you that the lady of the house ain't too cool with our arrangement." The woman's feelings were obviously bruised. She pouted, expecting an apology. "Oh, I'm sorry, Naturale," he said softly. "I didn't mean to hurt those sensitive feelings. Be a good girl and get a brotha a beer. You got a niggah thirsty." She perked up immediately and moved to do as she was ordered, wearing a brand-new smile to match the sparkling tennis bracelet she'd flaunted since they arrived. I. Rome grinned devilishly as he playfully slapped her on the rear.

"Yeah, Jazz, get a brotha a beer." Marshall was playing king of the castle.

"I know you didn't!" Jasmine objected. "Don't be tripping, Marshall. Long after Isaiah is gone, you still got to live here. Don't you forget that!"

"Uh-oh, she's misconjugating verbs," Marshall joked, sitting up. "She must be salty. I'd better go handle up."

He lumbered off in her direction, knowing what had to be done in order to make amends. "Come here, baby." Marshall trapped Jasmine in the corner between the massive stainless steel refrigerator unit and the pantry door. He whispered sweet nothings while holding her head against his thick chest. "You know I have to play the role like I run things around here. I can't have everybody knowing who the real boss is. Let a brotha front for the fellas."

Jasmine tried to push her way by his assuming guard. "Move, Marshall . . . move, honey." Her words came out as mere whispers. Her attitude weakened as much as she had, instantaneously and utterly. "Why are you always doing this to me when I'm trying to be difficult? You know I never could resist all this attention." She slid her hands down the front of his lounging pants. "I'll try to play nice while your friends are here, but I can't stand it too much longer. Isaiah and that tramp cavorting—"

"Cavortin'," he interrupted. "What's that mean? Now, if you're gonna be fussing at me, I should at least know what you're saying."

"Marshall, don't play with me. You know what that means as well as I do. You didn't graduate with honors not knowing what "cavorting" means, but that's beside the point. What I want to know is when you're getting that adulterer out of our house. He's a bad influence on lil' Marshall, and Legacy, too, for that matter."

"I'll speak to Rome about doing things around Deuce, but Legacy is a grown man. He can handle his own peer pressure."

They exchanged subtle glances. "All better?" Marshall asked, between light pecks on her forehead and cheeks. He had his answer when she playfully pushed him aside. In record time Jasmine met him at the sofa with a party tray topped with finger snacks and beer, served like a true hostess who didn't have to be told that she was the one running things.

"Dayyum, Marshall. What did you say to her in the kitchen?" I. Rome asked, visibly impressed. "I could use some of that butter for my new song. The melody is sweet but I just can't feel the lyrics yet."

Before Jasmine could offer her two cents about him perhaps returning home to *feel* his wife for a change, Marshall hurriedly shoved the toddler in her face. "Here-Jazz-the-baby-needs-changing." She took her cue in stride, accepted the child, and gladly strutted away, where the air would be undoubtedly more agreeable, dirty diaper considered.

Although Legacy was not married with children, he wasn't oblivious to Jasmine's rage. He'd been there to help pick up the pieces when Marshall was sowing his wild oats on campus. Since then, his respect for her hadn't waned one iota. "So Rome, where's the next stop on tour?" Legacy had taken up playing the piano in his spare time and was interested in seeing a good concert.

"I'm going home, man. Dallas. It's been a good while since I've seen my mama and I have a couple of homies to look in on." He gave Legacy the sly eye, the one that signaled he was alluding to homegirls. "Speaking of homes, I've been meaning to talk to you about the work you did for my man Marshall. That game room you hooked up wall to wall is the mega-bomb-diggity. I want something like that done for the house in Chicago. That's where I'm building a studio in the basement."

"I could put something together for you," Legacy said, gazing up at the ceiling. "I'm seeing a full stadium, a screaming-fans scene with you behind the keys and setting it off."

"That's what I'm talking about right there. Palm me yo' digits and I'll holla at you when I hit town."

Marshall chuckled. "I don't know, Romey Rome. That boy ain't cheap. You don't even want to know what he got me for. And, that's when he was just starting out. I was his first and got that starving artist discount. After Freelance hooked up Emmit Smith's joint, *MTV Cribs* shot the footage and the price doubled overnight. Ain't that right, dawg?"

Legacy nodded. He was grinning because Marshall was the only one on the planet still calling him Freelance—a name he'd earned in college by working several jobs to keep his skills sharp and his hustle on point. "We'll talk about prices when you get there. I'm sure Double Platinum money is the kind of money I can make friends with. Maybe we can work out a barter and I'll cut you a break."

"Oh, now you're talking my language. A deal?"

"Yeah something like that. I've been fooling around with this tune in my head but it's like a cry that won't come out."

"A cry that won't come out? That's deep. Deep. I might have to lift that one from you myself."

The publicist must've felt left out of the conversation. She'd huffed for attention more than once while the men were discussing business. "Hey man, I'll get with y'all in a minute. This lady needs something to do with her hands," I. Rome gloated. "Know what I mean? Peace. Come on, baby." He stuck his chest out, slapped the woman on the fanny again, then followed her back to from whence she came.

"They've been here for three damned days and I ain't heard her say a single word outside that bedroom," Marshall informed Legacy. "Gotta give to Rome, though. That publicist of his might be high-maintenance but she's all that and a Cadillac. Loud too. You should've heard her last night. Sony Surround Sound." The two of them laughed but Marshall knew Jasmine would have been in his face had she heard him going on about the late-night acrobatics happening under her own roof between a married man and his *publicist*.

Legacy had his own issues to deal with, including a very beautiful lady Jeep driver. Once they were alone, Marshall had a chance to see about his friend's well-being. He had been there for Legacy when the bottom fell out of a hopeful love affair that fizzled too soon when his last love interest died a few years ago. Legacy had disappeared for a year, then reemerged as one of the most touted young artists in the country. His showings were flooded with reporters and art connoisseurs alike. Paintings sold for thousands more than he could have imagined. Soon he began receiving calls from the obscenely rich who wanted to boast of having a one-and-only Legacy original. He'd done well for himself, but there was no one to help him enjoy it. Fortunately, there was hope on the horizon.

"Hey man, you alright?" Marshall asked, giving him that have-you-found-a-woman-yet wide eye.

"Yeah, you know me. I get by."

"Get by? Who's talking about getting by?"

"It's been cool enough for me. I mean . . . I met this one sistah. It's promising."

"Promising, huh?"

"You gonna keep repeating everything I say?" Legacy was more embarrassed than annoyed.

"Am I gonna keep repeating everything you say? Are you gonna keep speaking in code? What the hell you mean, promising?" Suddenly Jasmine appeared. She took a seat next to her man.

"Yeah, what do you mean promising, especially if you're talking about a woman?"

"Jazz, this is menfolk talk. Baby, I thought you were seeing to Deuce."

"I put lil' *Marshall* down for a nap and now I'm seeing to my friend, if you please. So, Legacy, is she nice?"

"Forget nice," Marshall argued. "Is she fine?"

"What do you care whether his woman is fine or not?" Jasmine questioned Marshall. "Your woman is and that's all you need to know. Marshall, you've been around Isaiah too long already. By the way, where is the rolling porn show?" Neither of the men made a move. They just sat there, avoiding eye contact with her as well as one another. "I know I asked a question because I was here when I asked it," she stated insistently. "Where is Isaiah and the loudmouth freak of his?" Reluctantly Marshall motioned toward the bedroom with a slight head tilt. "Oh heck, no. They're at it again? She should be charging him by the hour and maybe then she could afford some real food to put a little meat on that Popsicle stick body of hers. And Marshall, you better not say a word. Don't think I haven't caught you sneaking a peek at her tail hanging out of those booty shorts she had pulled up in her behind yesterday." Marshall was smart to take his wife's advice to remain silent.

"So, Freelance," Marshall said abruptly. He couldn't change the subject quick enough. "What's the scoop on this woman you've got designs on?"

Legacy thought to himself over Jasmine's tirade. She was the same hot wire as she was in college and a suitable match for Marshall. With two sets of eyes locked on his, wanting to hear the usual answers regarding a man-woman what's-she-really-like, he gave in. "Well, her name is Octavia Longbow."

"Octavia Longbow?" Marshall repeated the name as if it were Greek. "What kind of name is that? Is she a sistah or an Indian?"

"The politically correct term is Native American," Jasmine said. "You wouldn't want people calling you a spear-chucker now, would you?"

"Jazz, please, I didn't mean no disrespect. Freelance knows that, don't you, Free? This man can date whoever he wants and I'll treat her like my own sistah." Marshall looked Legacy over suspiciously. "She ain't no . . . Native American, is she?"

"Actually, I'm not sure. We just met kind of suddenly. You could say that our worlds collided, so to speak."

Both husband and wife were perplexed. "Why do I feel that there's a story in this somewhere?" Jasmine was with Legacy on the day he met Kennedy, when she nearly dropped a full can of soda on them from an upper level in an art gallery. "How'd you meet this Octavia?" Her question came out soft and slow.

Feeling interrogated, Legacy moistened his lips with the tip of his tongue. "I, uh . . . let her hit me with her SUV."

"What?!" Marshall jumped up off the sofa, rolling in the midst of a thick cloud of disbelief.

"See, I knew it," Jasmine squealed, only not as loudly as her two-hundred-pound spouse. "I love being right."

"It was nothing. I saw her. She was sleeping at my favorite table at Café Brew. I sketched her and . . ."

"Ah, naw," Marshall said, more quiet than before. "It's over now. She don't stand a chance. When's the wedding?"

"Chill out, man, we haven't even had a date yet. I'm going to take it slow and easy until I get to know her."

"I got a bad feeling about this, Freelance. If memory serves me correctly, the last time you took it slow and easy, they were pulling a Ford out the front of your new girl's ex-boyfriend's house. Most women just call up and tell ol' boy that it's over, but not after you start putting your magic pencil to 'em." Marshall realized that what he had said sounded like a sexual metaphor, knowing that Legacy's last flame discovered she was infected with AIDS before any serious intimacy had taken place. "Not that magic pencil but . . . y'all know what I mean."

"Forget him, Legacy," Jasmine apologized. "Are you hurt? Okay, good. Then would you please explain how you let her hit you with an SUV?"

"It's not like it sounds. I wanted to make an impression but I was out of practice. There hasn't been anyone else since Kennedy and there was something about this woman."

"Uh-huh, it's just like it sounds," Jasmine surmised, and she was right again. "What's wrong with just plain old introducing yourself? The standard still works."

"I wanted to but . . . I didn't want to appear desperate."

"There was no chance in that." The sarcastic tone in Jasmine's words hit its mark.

"Wait a minute. Let's not be too quick to dis," Marshall reasoned. "Letting this lady run over you isn't the route I would've taken, but it gives you a back door if she turns out to be psycho. Actually, your strategy wasn't that bad."

Jasmine disagreed vehemently. "Not that bad? Honey, that's terrible. Two crazy people don't have any business getting together, because if they do their kids would be just as loony."

Suddenly silence attacked the room. No one knew exactly what to say, not one of them. I. Rome reentered the room to a wordless conversation that only moments before bubbled with merriment. "What were y'all making all that noise for? You're gonna wake my publicist."

Marshall scratched his head. He opened his mouth but nothing came forth initially. "I'm speechless and that ain't never happened before. I'ma call Ripley's, right after I fix myself another sandwich." He popped up, patted Legacy on the shoulder, then disappeared into the kitchen.

"Yeah, I'm still hungry, too." I. Rome rubbed his stomach to emphasize his point, which insinuated he expected Jasmine to hop to it on his behalf. When she caught the gist of what he was implying, she rolled her neck, then did likewise with her eyes.

"I know you don't think I'm going to house and serve you. If you wanted the Hilton you should have stayed at the Hilton," Jasmine threw in for good measure. "See this, all this up in here? This is not the Hilton, Howard Johnson, or the Holiday Inn. This is *Casa De Jasmine*, so you'd better make yourself useful while I'm still feeling benevolent."

Realizing that he'd have to fend for himself, I. Rome sought to join

Marshall, who was rummaging through the icebox. "And wash your hands!" she yelled to her unwanted houseguest in particular. "Twice!"

Legacy sat with his head in his hands, like a child just moments from hearing the sentence for his mischievousness, while Jasmine stared him down. "So meeting Octavia meant that much to you? It's been a few years since Kennedy passed away. You think you're finally ready to try it again?"

He pondered for a minute before putting his words together. "I need to be. The problem is, I just don't know how to go about." Jasmine walked over and hugged him. It was the warmest embrace he remembered having since Kennedy.

"Don't be concerned about the how. That'll take care of itself. Call me if you need me. Just like before." She had in fact assisted him in working his charm on the lady he lost. Why should this time around be any different? Marshall's family was the closest thing Legacy knew to feeling a part of one. Growing up orphaned caused him to be leery of people he didn't know and guard his feelings, some times to a fault. He wasn't sure if hiding his wealth and fame from Octavia was the appropriate thing to do, but for now it was much better than his plan B, which didn't exist.

10

The Beat Goes On

Monday morning came right on schedule. The Hot 100 Morning Dream team featuring Tony Tune and his longtime sidekick were wrapping up their fourth hour on the air. Over the past twelve years, he and Gwendolyn Tyme had set numerous records for holding the top rank in their time slot hostage. Twelve years together at the top had cemented Tony's legacy as Dallas's super deejay and turned Gwendolyn into somewhat of an arrogant witch that no one but Tony could stomach. Her manufactured British accent was a big hit with the listeners, but her contemporaries at the station wanted to smack her every time she opened veneered teeth and pushed out nasal, chopped words. It was one thing to think she was better than everyone else, but to insinuate it with each passing breath was unconscionable.

"That just about does it for this beautiful Monday morning," Tony said, making notes on possible topics for the Tuesday show. "Keep it right here and listen up for your chance to win the I. Rome platinum concert package sponsored by none other than the station that hits you like you wanna be hit, your Hot 100. We'll be right back at you tomorrow at the five A.M. hour and you can tell us all about the night before." Tony hit the off-air switch, then motioned to his cohost to wrap the show.

Gwendolyn smirked as if it were asking too much for her to close the program as she did each morning. "It's Gwendolyn Tyme. Make it a good one and remembah, if you can't be good, at least be careful. Take your time and do it right." As soon as she went off the air, she began her usual whining routine that typically lasted until she had lunch. "Tonee, if I get one more request from these stupid listeners for that insidiously no-talent I. Rome, I will just pull my hair out in clumps."

Tony looked over at her, eyeing the thick synthetic mane cascading down her back. He didn't say what he wanted to but it was written all over his face. The fact that she had a standing weekly appointment with Truest to have her weave tightened did not lend credibility to her statement. It would have been much easier to have a track or two removed if she wanted to lighten her load. "Relax, Gwendolyn, the concert will be over and done with this week, so try to hang in there. Actually, the album is pretty good. I've heard a lot worse."

"Yah but, I just don't get-tit. A pretty boy takes off his shirt and the crowd goes wild. It's all so overrated. The idol worship is nothing short of spectacle, I tell you. Three records and he's already viewed as an institution, as if he has devoted his whole life to his craft instead of merely sending fans into a frenzy by gyrating his words out on stage." She carefully dismantled her headset, huffing discontentment. "Where's the real appreciation for good musik?"

"Just because you think Michael Bolton is the second coming doesn't mean other people can't move to what they groove to. To each his own. . . . And don't be so quick to dismiss those idol-worshipers you don't seem to understand. They do pay your rent and your bills down at that day spa you can't seem to do without."

"Now you're speaking my language, Tonee. Magnolia's is the end, the living end. That's a real institution, a beautiful place for beautiful people. Lovely, simply marvelous."

Tony looked over at her again with the same bothered expression. Magnolia's was a hospitable wellness emporium owned by a successful businesswoman turned best-selling novelist, who went to great lengths to create a star-studded atmosphere that regular folks could afford. "Uh-huh. If I was paying to have somebody, who I didn't know, to rub me up and down once a week, you'd be ready to call the morality police on me. But it's like I said, to each his *or her* own." He winked at her, then glanced at the circular wall clock. "You can sit there looking defeated if you want to, but I am not going to be late for Patricia's monthly meeting. You're really going to have something to be upset about if you're late again." Gwendolyn had been late for the last meeting and was immediately and thoroughly embarrassed by the station's producer, Patricia Maria Stapleton, a former radio personality legend in her own right.

"I could have done without that little remindah of a woman with too much power for her own good."

"Well, she's the boss and we're running late . . . so buck up ol' gurl and snap to it." He smiled politely after rendering worthy advice in his own manufactured homage to the Brits.

Gwendolyn was inspecting her hair in a pocket mirror kept in her overpriced Prada handbag when his words hit her like the bad joke they were meant to be. "Nice try but nought funnee. I'm off to a bad day and it's nought going to get any bettah, I'm afraid."

"You'd *bettah* be afraid to show up late for the meetin'."

Octavia sat at her desk, staring back at a blank solid-blue computer screen. Thoughts of the stranger she'd run over on Saturday night had plagued her from the time she dropped him off. Finding his backpack on her floorboard had added to her dubious mood. She wanted to forget ever meeting him, but was instead looking forward to seeing him again when she returned his belongings. He was poor, living in the guesthouse of some extremely wealthy landowner, Octavia assumed, and she was not prepared to take on a charity case, no matter how handsome he happened to be. Not that money was high on her list of must-haves for a possible suitor, but Octavia thought it was best to get a man who already knew where he was going and on his way to getting there. As far as she could see, he was the proverbial talented artist one step from being homeless. She'd had more meaningless flings than she was prepared to claim, and after reading her journal entries that chronicled the time wasted in the process, she was determined to save herself like an aging virgin until the right man came along. Although Legacy was ahead on points in the looks department, his lack of must-haves quickly evolved into ain't-gots. Her brief encounter with him had left her thinking, *He ain't got no home, he ain't got no real mode of transportation, he ain't got no potential chance at changing his ain't-gots, which means he ain't got no chance with me.* After she drew a thick line through his name written on her daily planner, she tried to shake him out of her head.

"Come on, 'Tavia," Cee-Cee announced, her notebook and pen handy for mandatory note-taking. "Patricia's monthly meeting is about to start, and you know what happened last month when Gwen paraded in like she was the Queen of England."

"How could I forget? I can still envision that thick vein popping down the center of her forehead when Patricia let her have it but good."

"Riiiight. I almost peed my pants tryna keep from laughing when she told Gwendolyn the Bad Witch that she was expendable and would gladly purchase a one-way ticket herself for that fake-tooth heffa to head back to wherever she came from. That British accent of hers is as counterfeit as a three-dollar bill. Who she think she's fooling? Everybody knows she's from Jersey."

"Ooh, you're wrong for that." Octavia thought the slams were a bit harsh, but she laughed nonetheless until she noticed Gwendolyn rounding the corner from her lavishly decorated offices, reserved for the big-timers. "Speak of the devil and in she walks."

Cee-Cee cut her jovial mood down to size when Gwendolyn made her way past them. "Mornnning Gwendolyn," she bade pleasantly. "I loved the show, girl. Do your thing, girl." The stuffy prima donna offered a quarter smile in return for the compliments, but neglected to offer one syllable of gratitude. When Gwendolyn disappeared into the conference room, Octavia folded her arms while looking up at Cee-Cee, disappointed with her friend's two-faced accolades. "What? Octavia, why are you mean-mugging me like that? You never know when I might need something from that plastic Barbi Doll," Cee-Cee said, in an attempt to save face. "She might be hard to like but she's been in the business a long time and has a lot of powerful friends. I'm just looking out for me. Don't hate the playa. Hate the game. Hate. The. Game."

"Uh-huh," Octavia huffed, disappointed. "Be careful you don't play yourself."

"I got this. Now let's get in there before we both get played."

"Come on, playa. That's one thing we agree on."

They nodded simultaneously as they made a beeline in Gwendolyn's path. When they arrived, Patricia was annoyed and guarding the door. "Does anyone know why I cannot begin my meeting on time?" she asked, pacing the floor. "Tony, can you please find out where *the boys* are."

"Yes, ma'am," he offered, getting out of his chair. "I'll see what's going on and round 'em up." Tony walked the floor, searching all the normal hangouts where the younger talent congregated between shifts. There was no one in any of the break rooms and nobody loitered behind the station in the back parking lot. When he was tired of making laps around the second floor, he stopped by the reception desk where the station's sixty-something jewel of a gatekeeper sat, applying another coat of makeup. "Mornin', Ms. Pitman. Have you seen any of the fellas?"

She licked and sucked the excess Bright Red Number Nine lipstick off her gold-capped teeth. "I ain't seen hide nor hair of them since they all went downstairs 'bout ten minutes ago. They was carryin' Laz'rus off like he was ailin' somethin' fierce."

"Downstairs, huh? Thanks, Ms. Pitman. I see that Number Nine is still the lady's choice."

She winked at him suggestively. "Mr. Tony, Number Nine always does the trick. But I can show you better than I can tell you. You know my peoples is from Missouri. That's the show me state."

"No, I'll have to take your word for it, but thanks for the warning."

Ms. Pitman's eyes paced up and down the backside of his trousers as he marched away with hurried strides. Tony couldn't get away from the woman's powers of suggestion fast enough. "Ooh, if I just had five minutes with that man," she whispered seductively while he made his getaway.

"Remind me to stay out of Missouri," slid out of his mouth when he reached the staircase.

"What's that about Missouri, Mr. Tony?" Saul the ancient security guard asked, eyes half closed, awakened from his second nap of the day by Tony's words. Saul was a retired postal carrier working a second job to make ends meet. He had been delivering the mail since a first-class stamp cost a nickel.

"Nothing, Saul, just thinking aloud. Actually, I'm looking for some of the guys. Meeting's about to start."

"They ducked into the men's room all nervous like there was a fire that had to be put out."

"Thanks, Saul. If Ms. Patricia comes this way, try to stall her for me. I have a feeling there's gonna be trouble."

He wrestled a long black flashlight from his belt holster as if it were a deadly six-shooter. "I'm your man, Mr. Tony. Nothing's gonna get past me. You have my word on it. Uh-huh, you can take that to the bank and cash it." No sooner had Saul given his word than he quickly nodded off to sleep again.

Inside the men's room, Lazarus stood at a urinal groaning intensely through agonizing pain. His extensive and labored nature break was taking a toll on the other men, pensively watching him. Floreese tipped up from behind with exaggerated anticipation as Lazarus finally completed his business. "Alright y'all. I think he's finished."

"That's got to be a world's record," Ebony surmised, hoisting up his wristwatch. "It shouldn't take no grown man that long to take a piss. Hurr'up and shake that thang, Laz'rus, so we can see what the deal is."

Alphonzo stood the furthest away with his hand over his nose. "Me-myself-personally, I am in no hurry to be eye level with another man's Johnson. As far as I'm concerned, you can take all the time you need time, dawg."

"No way," Benny argued. "We gotta help him. He's been trembling all morning behind this. If we don't do something, he might not make it."

"Man, don't say that," Lazarus protested. He was genuinely terrified. "I need my Johnson. We go back too far for me to lose him now. Benny's right. Y'all gotta help a brotha out."

Despite his adamant displeasure with the ludicrously sordid situation, Alphonzo pinched his nose and exhaled deeply through his mouth. He stepped cautiously in line behind Ebony. "Aw-ight then. You may as well drop 'em."

Lazarus lowered his eyes while lowering his pants. Slowly Ebony inched closer to see what had a grown man trembling. When Lazarus's baggy jeans fell past his rusty knees, Ebony recoiled in astonishment. He nearly stumbled over while trying to get out of his own way. "Dayyyyyyum!"

"I told y'all it was bad," Lazarus whined. "That's why it took me so long to pee. It don't wanna work no more. I gets no cooperation."

"Man, you're gonna need another one of those," Ebony advised him. "It looks dead to me."

Benny bent over to get a better look. He was dangerously closer to it than anyone else felt comfortable with, including Lazarus. "Hey man, don't touch it," Lazarus begged, fearing Benny might actually try. "It's too sensitive."

Floreese peaked over Benny's shoulder to give a second opinion, but he was not prepared to offer any in his ignorance. "What's that black thing hanging down right there?" Wearing a disgusted expression, he pointed his finger jab-fashion at Lazarus's manly region.

Benny wondered about it too. "Yeah, what is that?"

Looking the troubled area over more intently than before, Alphonzo's eyes squinted into thin slits. "And where's the rest of it?"

"Y'all shouldn't get that close." Floreese frowned, then turned away when he couldn't handle the sight of it any longer. "Looks infected."

Tears gathered in Lazarus's eyes. "See man, I knew y'all were gonna be trippin'. Just let me limp off and die in peace like a bear with its leg caught in a trap."

"Nah, he don't have enough there to get caught in anything," Alphonzo joked.

"Maybe that's what happened to the rest of it," Ebony added.

"There goes the myth," Benny teased. "After everything I've heard about the brothas, I must admit I'm thoroughly disappointed. I expected *a lot* more out of you, Lazarus."

"Hey-hey, cut that out Benny. I feel bad enough as it is. It's not small, just a lil' short. You should have seen it before it got sick."

"Whatever, dawg," Alphonzo debated. "You just keep right on sticking to your story, but there is something definitely not right about that . . . your . . . little soldier." Alphonzo was serious about doing something to aid a fallen comrade but didn't have a clear diagnosis. "What is that other thing hanging off to the side of it? That saggy pouch . . . thing-thing."

After Lazarus had gotten down and dirty in the radio booth with the late-night visitor he'd sneaked in, paranoia of having contracted a sexually transmitted disease got the best of him. He had begun imagining symptoms and pains associated with gonorrhea, an unwanted gift he had previously been given on more than one occasion. His adamant fear of needles inspired him to seek another and less conventional method of curing the phantom ailment. He'd received a ridiculous barbershop recommendation that lead him to Ms. Cloveen's *House of Cures and Conjures*. The old Creole woman, who made a good living as the neighborhood witch doctor, sold roots, rare herbs, incense, and everything else from love potions to pickled pig's feet. Lazarus should have made a U-turn when he entered her home and stumbled upon a glass gallon jar of pork-covered huffs. Instead, he'd let her hook him up with a spell to chase away any evil spirits lurking about, including ones that carried diseases. She guaranteed her work or the pig's feet were free—and then she attached it to him.

Two days later, there was Lazarus, looking down sad-eyed and sorrowful. When Tony Tune swaggered into the men's room, he was concerned about what appeared to be going on with all the other male deejays huddled up around an exposed set of hook-and-tackle. "What in the hell is going on up in here? I've been looking all over for y'all and it looks like we all need to have a long talk about Adam and Eve not Adam and Steve." Eventually, his eyes wandered to a place where he hadn't intended on looking. "Laz'rus, how long have you had that sack of garlic cloves and monkey knuckles tied around your privates like that? You're gonna stop the circulation and lose your pride and joy if you're not too careful. You might need to have 'em lopped right off. I've seen it done back in Vietnam."

"Ooooh, there's got to be another way," Benny countered, crossing his legs.

"I think he already lost half of it, if you ask me." Alphonzo couldn't resist taking another jibe at a man on his last leg, however short it may have been.

Without warning, Tony took a few steps toward Lazarus. He pulled a pair of reading glasses from his shirt pocket and leaned over to give it a thorough look-see. Inspecting the problem up close, Tony nodded assuredly. "Uh-huh, just as I suspected. Laz'rus, take a deep breath and close your eyes."

Fearing the worst, Lazarus backed against the wall in retreat. "What you gon' do to it?"

"Something you should've done when Ms. Cloveen first strapped this "stank sack" on your family jewels." With the precision of a skilled surgeon, Tony reached out and grabbed hold of the sack tightly. He pulled and tugged and tugged and pulled. Lazarus screamed out, both from the tormenting pain and the uncertainty of what might have happened if Tony was too aggressive at detaching the long black sackcloth.

While Tony operated, Lazarus screamed continuously. The others turned their faces away, wincing. The men's room door swung open. Tony heard it go smack against the adjoining lockers but he refused to relinquish his steady grasp on the task in hand. Patricia marched inside the men's room ranting about the meeting when her eyes took in the awkward display in progress. Frantic, Lazarus tried to cover his private parts, but it was out of his hands. "Hey, this is the men's room," he protested. Hey!"

Tony was not about to give up after he'd committed himself. "One . . . more . . . tuuuuuug." There was a loud snap. The straps broke free. Tony wiped sweat from his brow with the backside of his hand. He held the bag up like a trophy, then tossed it in the trashcan. Lazarus fell to his knees, grimacing and moaning. The tears streaming down his face said it all. Patricia placed the tips of her fingers over her nose in the same way Alphonzo had done earlier.

"I don't even want to know," Patricia said, backing out of the crowded room. "The meeting is postponed for fifteen . . . no, make that thirty . . . minutes." She fought back the urge to gag. "I need time to call my shrink."

As Tony celebrated his defining achievement, Lazarus squirmed around on the ground trying to catch his breath. Alphonzo sidled up next to them. "Hey, Mr. Tune, how'd you know what was in that sack and who in the hell is Ms. Cloveen?"

"You think Laz'rus is the first deejay to pass up a penicillin shot for a hoodoo home remedy stank sack instead? Believe me, he's not the first to call on a hoodoo priestess and he won't be the last. The saddest part of it is, after all this, he's still got to go see the doctor. He might not think so now, but I did him a favor. The doc would have used a needle to numb his goodies. It always works better when you just take hold and snatch it right off." Again the men turned their soured faces away, expressing sympathy from Tony's description.

Tony hummed a happy tune while washing his hands vigorously, like a surgeon after performing a delicate operation. "Hope I didn't pull nothin' out of socket, Laz'rus. And consider yourself lucky. Ms. Cloveen could have fitted you with a collard green-molasses wrap. Sometimes you gotta burn those off. Just make sure you see a real doctor to inspect my work."

"Oh-kay," Lazarus answered from a fetal position on the floor. Oddly enough, a smile traced his dry lips. "Thank you, Mr. Tuuune."

"Don't mention it. Glad to help."

Tony strolled out of the men's room whistling the same happy tune he'd scrubbed up to. The elderly security guard woke up, startled and stammering, when the carefree melody tickled his ears. "Ssssee-see-there Mr. Tony, told you nobody gets by me. I got the situation on lock."

"Like nothing I've ever seen, Mr. Saul, that's for sure." Tony was still playing the role of diplomat. He'd learned a long time ago that the old adage about not saying anything at all if you can't say anything nice was as important as bread to a starving man. A kind word just might put food on the table when nothing else could. He remembered how it used to be when times weren't so good. Tony Tune was one of the first black deejays in the South when all music was played on the AM side of the dial, before FM ruled the airwaves. Times were much tougher then. Most black-owned stations were limited to eight hours of airtime and spent the remainder of the day hustling the streets for sponsorship dollars to keep afloat the little piece of radio programming they did have. He'd put in a lot of work in order to get where he was, both lawful and otherwise. Despite his shortcomings, he was an old-school "lend a hand to help your brothers when you can" kind of man. He remembered how it used to be.

11

You Wrong for That

When Octavia caught word that the meeting had been put off due Lazarus's unforeseen incident—which quickly made its way around the station—she returned to her desk to catch up on a bit of business that should have been taken care of on Friday. She logged on to the Internet and waited for AOL to boot up. In the meanwhile, she opened her purse and pulled out a black checkbook to make an entry in the register. She wrote the number four hundred and actually smiled to herself when she couldn't think of anything to put on the comment line next to the amount, so she penciled in a question mark and kept right on smiling. Thoughts of running into Legacy the way she had conjured up laughter when she remembered him sitting in a rising puddle of water in the Café Brew parking lot. Although he was unmistakably a full-grown man, he had resembled a distraught little boy who looked as if he didn't know what hit him or how he would explain returning home without his prized bicycle. Unfortunately, the good vibrations didn't last.

Her laughter dissipated immediately when her e-mail account revealed sixteen messages from I. Rome, all marked urgent. Since he hadn't been calling as much as he usually did, she assumed he had begun working things out with his wife, which she encouraged him to do although she wasn't sure if that's what she really wanted. Their in-again, out-again we-love-again romance now spanned five years. The last three had been the most hectic and so full of ups and downs that she didn't know which way to turn. Octavia wanted to be in love with him even though she needed to get on with her life, but all she managed to do successfully was float back and forth, caught between what she wanted and what she needed.

Cee-Cee appeared behind her. She read all the e-mails entitled "I Need You" to the side of I. Rome's name. She checked her expression before offering a comment on the obvious. "Hey. You all right? I see he's still at it."

"It would seem so."

"That sure is a lot of messages. He ain't too proud to beg, either."

Octavia stared at the screen. She was frozen by the thought of allowing her languishing desire for I. Rome to get her caught up again, which is how it always went down when he felt like reaching out to her. "See, there you go again from the outside looking in. I've been doing this a while and I should have seen this one coming. It's his patented four-touch program. It's smooth but I'm hipped to it by now."

"Four-touch program?" Cee-Cee repeated, awaiting clarification.

"Umm-hmm. The first touch or contact is e-mail. Next come the phone calls, two of them. I received those yesterday. Then there's dinner. There's always dinner. Four steps to draw me in. That's his program and it works like a charm. Took a while to figure it out but in the end, his pattern is as predictable as you trying to help me through this."

After pulling up a chair, Cee-Cee sat down and locked her fingers to prop up her chin. She was not going to share the conversation she'd had with Truest but she felt the need to say something helpful. "What my untrained eyes also tell me is you're still not past this thing you have with him. I realize that relationships are difficult. That's the nature of the beast, but try to keep one thing in mind. You deserve better than him blowing in and out of your life like this. You deserve better."

Still facing the monitor, Octavia's eyes dimmed. She knew that her girlfriend was right, and she also knew better than anyone how much trouble and heartache a woman should expect when she lets a love affair linger, especially if it should've died a long time ago. The fact that I. Rome was a commitment-phobe and married didn't help the situation any. As Octavia exhaled the anxiety away, she chuckled peculiarly. "I'm still a pushover and too tired to front, but you wanna know something? Every time I think that he's forgotten what we've had between us, he starts this up again. I get e-mails when he's in trouble, lonely, or has spent too much time reminiscing on what could have and should have been. He goes on about how his children should have been mine and how I should have been a bigger part of his life." Suddenly she appeared to be at peace with it all. "He named his first child Madison, 'cause that's the name I'd chosen . . . for my first. I spent two days in the hospital with chest pains when I heard. I knew then I'd never share his last name."

Octavia turned toward Cee-Cee, still wearing an expression of resolve. "I'll just delete these messages unopened and try not to wonder what it took him sixteen e-mails to say." She glanced at the screen again, then back at Cee-Cee. "He may want me. He might even still love me. But I will not fool myself into believing he ever needed me." Octavia clicked "delete all," then pressed "enter." Every one of the messages disappeared simultaneously. "That's why I've made up my mind to steer clear of him when he arrives. No phone calls, no booty calls, no heartaches at all. Simple as that." She and Cee-Cee both knew that it would not be that simple, despite what Octavia had in mind. I. Rome would see to that.

On the other side of the building, Floreese sat on the lunch table in the upstairs break room. Benny, Ebony, and Alphonzo stood around counting out money and placing bets before the Fan Mail Monday festivities got under way. Each Monday, Mike Mooney made his way up to the break room with stacks of fan mail from listeners. There were short notes of thanks for encouragement offered from on-air talent during their broadcasts. Others consisted of everything from birthday cards to triple-X-rated photographs and much worse. Mooney was a chubby, dark-skinned, thick-lipped brother in his early forties who idolized the deejays. For him, life couldn't get any smoother than if he got his shot at the limelight. Unfortunately, his tongue was fastened on the thick side. That prevented him from persuing a career having anything to do with talking for a living. For one thing, the microphone would have been drenched with saliva after each radio show.

"Hur-yee, hur-yee. E'rbody gathur 'round," Mooney announced. He took a pencil from behind his right ear and jotted down the names of the contestants. The others grew more anxious to get to it. "Aw-right, hold yo' hoyces. Today, we have somethin' for Alfonso, Eb'ny, and Flo'reese. Sorry, Benny, nothin' fuh you today. 'Sides, you still in trainin' pants. Don't wet ya'self now." Benny expected the jealous older man to crack on him. That was par for the course.

"Ahhhh-ahhhhh . . . hater!" Benny shrieked, disguised in the midst of a fake sneeze.

Mooney looked at him suspiciously from the corner of his eye. "I know you better have some snot hangin' out yo' nose, 'cause if you tryna clown me, I'll cut you. I ain't scurd of white peeples." He went back to conducting the anticipated ritual, then paused when he hadn't quite said his piece. "I'm a grown-ass man. I'ont play wit' udder folks' kids. I'ont even play wit' ma own kids." He shot another stinging stare Benny's way. "I ain't scurd of white peeples. Hell, I got's good credick too, good credick." Mooney scratched the cusp of his forehead with his stubby fingers. "Well, there is that one thang but they gon' take that off when I get my income tack check. But that's a nudder storee."

"Come on, Mooney. We heard you the first time," Floreese insisted, tapping his foot and waiting. "Benny is cool people. He ain't white people, he's an intern. They don't even pay him, so come on and stop trippin'."

"Awe-right, hur we go." He laid three envelopes of different sizes face down on the table so that no one could read the names of the addressees. "If'n you wants to bet, put yo' cheese down right hur." Everyone threw in twenty dollars, including Benny.

Mooney gave him a thorough once-over, up and down like he didn't think much of what he saw. "Jess foe the sake o' intress, who you puttin' yo' money on, white boy?"

Benny wisely overlooked the racial tone in his question. "I'm putting my money on Alphonzo. He's won the last two weeks and I like rolling with a winner." Benny was searching for a new hero since Lazarus had been, um, exposed.

"Gone then and do your thing, Mooney," Ebony demanded. "I'm feeling kind of lucky."

Floreese swallowed hard. "I'm feelin' kind of freaky."

Two stacks of crisp bills lay on the table, just waiting to go home with someone. Mooney flipped the first envelope, which happened to be the smallest. It was addressed to Ebony, who after reading his name cussed up a storm. The smallest package typically didn't contain much smut, so his chances were slim of taking home the pot. As the second envelope turned over, Floreese gritted his teeth. His name was written on it longhand. "Man, dayyum," he whined. "That can't be big enough to have nothin' real juicy in it." Of course that meant the largest one had been sent to Alphonzo, whose grin was effortless and glowing.

"That's right, who's the man? Who's the man?" Alphonzo howled. He hopped off the table, then proceeded to strut around proudly.

Floresse, like a broken man, slowly pulled back the flap on his envelope. "Just what I thought, a birthday card . . . from my insurance agent. I ain't never liked that dude."

"'Told you Alphonzo was on a roll," said Benny, slapping Alphonzo some dap before reaching for the bills laid down on the side bet.

Ebony let out a sigh, then halted Benny with a stiff open palm to the chest as he picked up a letter-sized white envelope. "Not so fast. I want to see what I spent forty bucks on. He tore at the edges as the others gazed steadily, not expecting much. "Let's see here. Ooh, I'm feeling a lot better about my chances. Peep this." He began to read from the small rose-colored stationery. "Hey Ebony, I've been listening to you for about two years now and I just had to write. Last month when you were rappin' about what a woman can look forward to when she spends time with you, I had to sink deep down in my warm bubble bath and pretend it was your fingers dancing between my legs instead of my new roommate's. She told me that she met you at the club before and thinks you're as sexy as you sound. I'd like to find out for myself. Take a look at the picture we took just for you and let me know if you're interested in joining us. If you're wondering, I'm the one on top." Ebony's smile continued to grow as he held the Polaroid out for all to see.

"They're buck naked!" Floreese yelled as he grabbed the front of his jeans. He leaned in closer for a more intimate analysis. "They're fine as cat hair! Both of 'em."

"And . . . they're buck naked, too!" Alphonzo reiterated, much too loud to be at the job.

"Uh-oh, I've gotta bad feeling about this one." Benny was the first to take his eyes away from two honey-tan-skinned Latinas posing bad-girl style in a tub frothing with white satin bubbles. "Alphonzo, I hope you can top that. I got my gas money riding on you."

"Well, Gilligan, look like you and the Skippa gon' be wwwalkin' foe a wwwhile." Mooney pulled out a handkerchief from his back pocket and ran it across his package full of lips and broad forehead, but he didn't move his bugged eyes from that photograph, not once.

Alphonzo calculated his chances of winning to be between slim and none, but there was still hope. He wasted no time ripping into the manila package. His eyes grew wide, then squinted like he didn't understand what he saw. "What the—"

Benny snatched the contents from Alphonzo's tight clutches. After he scanned the eight-by-ten glossy, he threw it down on the table and romped out in disgust. The small room erupted with gut-busting clamor when Ebony and Floreese discovered what Alphonzo and Benny were repulsed by. Tears came pouring from Alphonzo's laughing eyes as he joined in merriment with the others. "I think I went to school with that cat."

"That ain't no cat," Floreese argued. "That's a dude with a fresh set of Ds. The only thing missing is the price tag hanging off those bad boys. Look at 'em. They're pumped up and still got that showroom shine."

Ebony read over the note enclosed. " 'Zo, ol' boy says he's got a Web site if you get down like that. Check it." He started laughing all over again. "It's www.chixwitdix!" Afterwards, Ebony counted the stack of bills, held it up to his nose to take a whiff, then shoved it in his front pocket. "Smells like a buck-naked good time to me. This ought to pay for some new bathtub accessories. Sorry, 'Zo, unless you do get down like that?" Alphonzo bounced a dismissive glance off Ebony's head before turning away to leave behind Benny. Ebony was bent over holding his stomach and pointing at the sender's anatomically incorrect figure. "He could give Laz'rus a run for his money though, in a lil' wee-wee contest."

Mooney was the only one still amazed by what he saw lying on the table. He wiped his forehead again, then cleared his throat. "Uh, that's something you don't see every day, a fella wit' two great big ol' breast-'es. Look here, Eb'ny. You don't mind if I do away wit' this, do you?" It was obvious that he had plans for more than just doing away with it. When Ebony waved Mooney the go-ahead, he unbuttoned his dress shirt and slid the contents inside for safekeeping before walking out as if no one knew what he was up to.

"Remind me not to shake his hand for at least a month," Floreese hissed, placing his hands in his pockets. "I don't even want to imagine what he's planning on doing with that."

"I got a good idea, but I think that package was sent to the wrong dude. I wouldn't have guessed that Mooney was the type to take the bull by the horn."

Suddenly Patricia appeared in the doorway like a stiff breeze preceding a hurricane. With her arms folded and dander up, she couldn't believe they were casually hanging out as if they had no better place to be. "I was sure that I made myself clear when I said the meeting would be starting in exactly half an hour," she informed them harshly. "Don't make me suspend another deejay this morning. And you know I will." Both men jumped to attention and ducked out before she made good on her threat.

On the way to the meeting, Ebony bumped into Brad Mayberry as he read the *Wall Street Journal* business section. Brad was the top advertising salesman, who openly detested the on-air talent. He was a man of short stature with the complexion of maple syrup. His clothes were impeccable, although that didn't halt the numerous bouts of insults that were commonly exchanged between him and the deejays.

"Watch where you're walking, boy," Brad popped off. He was angered that drops of spilled coffee ran down his hand, staining his monogrammed cuff.

"Boy?" Floreese snapped back. "Don't get it twisted. I don't see yo' mama up in here."

"And you'll never be half the man she is, anyhow," Ebony added.

Brad digested their insults and considered joining in a war of words, but money was on his mind. "It's not enough that Lazarus ruined a big account for me last week when he forgot to run a very important spot for Willamena's Weave World. He should've gotten more than a slap on the wrist and a two-week suspension for getting his kicks while on the company's clock."

"Laz'rus was suspended?" Ebony asked, shaking his head. "Man, that's what Patricia was talking about."

Brad brushed at his solid-gold cuff link vigorously. "I would have fired his black ass. His little party in the pit cost me ten thousand dollars in contract revenue and I'm going to see to it that I'm compensated. I don't care if he has to pick up club gigs for a year to do it."

"Why you always so hard on the fellas anyway? We put a lot of grip in your tight little leprechaun pockets. You and everyone in that sales department ought to be *kissing* our black asses every chance you get."

"Believe that!" Floreese chimed in, signifying. "Rumple Stillskin."

"You can call me what you want. But as long as I take home three times as much as you'll ever make, standing on my wallet makes me taller than the two of you together. Don't fool yourselves into thinking you're running anything around here but your mouths. It's the sales group that keeps this station riding high. You scrubs are merely along for the ride. How you like me now?" The expression he brandished adequately displayed his satisfaction when he left them standing there with their mouths hanging open.

"I know Tiny Tim didn't just try to clown us like that?" By the way Ebony was peering down at the floor, Floreese figured he was up to something and hoped it had everything to do with getting even. He had grown weary of Brad and his *compadres* in the sales department treating them like a bunch of welfare recipients. The fact that Brad's sentiment was shared by his entire group, whose average income was at times considerable compared to what the deejays counted on for paying the bills, didn't help the situation any.

"He did come at us pretty hard that time, Eb. I've gotta give him that round. But I see you working on something."

"You know it. We still have a few minutes before PMS gets started. Floreese, you still have some of that eye wash?"

"For my contact lenses? Yeah, I just bought a new bottle. Why?"

"Follow me."

They took off down the hallway, mischief in mind, and darted for Floreese's locker. After he handed a twelve-ounce bottle of saline solution to his partner in crime, they double-timed it up to the sales area. When the coast was clear, Ebony pulled his cohort into the break room next to the sales floor. He grinned sheepishly at a pot of coffee in the middle of a brew cycle. "Man, I got you on another bottle. Brad and his whole stuck-up clique needs a little loosening up, and I'm just the man for the job." He explained that the contents in the bottle held nearly the same ingredients as laxatives as he squeezed a healthy dose into the coffee pot. "I'm going down in history for this. I saw it on an old *Quincy, M.D.* rerun. It worked then, it'll work now." After their mischievous deed had been dealt, they were well lathered in suspense while fleeing the scene.

12

You Shouldn't Have

Standing by the door with her fist balled and resting on her curvy hips, Patricia scolded Ebony and Floreese with her eyes as they rushed past her to take their seats at the large mahogany conference table. They sat next to one another with their heads bowed, praying that she would go lightly on them. Lucky for them she did, much to Gwendolyn's displeasure.

"That's naught bloody fair." She voiced her objection in Patricia's direction, wanting to gain support from her associates sitting at the table. No one stepped in on her behalf, so she stood up to escalate her protest. "When I was running behind for the last session, I was ridiculed unbearably for my troubles. And now, Amos and Andy come shuffling about . . . detestably tardy even for my taste, and naught a word is uttered in opposition. What do you have to say to that?" She stuck her neck out, literally as well as figuratively.

Patricia was writing notes on a pie graph when she realized the comments were meant for her. Calmly she turned to face the group and the renegade Jersey girl with the gloss-on British finish. "Gwen, sit your skinny butt down before I make last month's episode seem like a friendly girlfriend chat by comparison. And, don't make me say it twice. I hate repeating myself." With all eyes on Gwendolyn, she contemplated the situation quickly, then did as she was advised, fearing her manager's wrath. "Good," Patricia stated soundly. "Now we can get started."

Floreese imagined what else was getting started down in the sales department's break room. He laughed inside, thinking about the sales team swigging his concoction and the rumbling that was sure to ensue. It was sheer genius, setting up seven stuffy sales heads with their stomachs in knots, just before receiving what he considered a necessary cleansing. Patricia disrupted his thoughts of revenge served piping hot and called the meeting to order.

"Guys, it's no secret that another station is going live next Monday and receiving a lot of press as a formidable foe. They're bringing a top morning team from Atlanta and the word is, they're pretty good at what they do." Tony Tune's expression conveyed unswerving confidence to the eyes watching him, expecting a reaction. He wasn't shaken in the least, but Gwendolyn was visibly disturbed. She'd been ousted once before when a rival morning show stole her listeners, hijacking the ratings and the advertising contracts along with them. She'd forgotten about her brief standoff with Patricia after hearing the latest. "Don't be concerned, I have faith in all of you," Patricia continued. "You have proven worthy of all my praise and I'm certain that you'll continue to do what has made all of you the best at what you do. I'll get back to you with more on that topic when the time is right, but for now, let's concentrate on getting our own house in order. I've already begun by adding six additional security cameras around the office to maximize productivity, because we have to be up for the challenge ahead." *Six additional cameras?* When the horror of getting caught tapped Floreese on the shoulder, he wanted to jump up out of his chair and bolt for the door. He contemplated how much trouble he'd be in if one of Patricia's maximum productivity devices had recorded what he'd done to the java. Floreese looked over at Ebony, noting that his ability to breath appeared troublesome and intense. Patricia noticed before the others did. "Ebony, you don't look so good."

"I need some water . . . and air," he wheezed nervously. He needed more than air. He needed to stop anyone from drinking that coffee.

"Excuse yourself before you get sick and get us further behind."

Without hesitation Ebony popped up from his chair and sprinted out of the conference room. When he hit the hallway, he beat it all the way to the break room where the scheme had been committed, thinking if he could dispense away with the laced coffee pot, he just might save his job. Coincidentally, Brad was pouring the last drop of coffee and eye wash in his favorite mug while reliving the words he'd used to demoralize Ebony and Floreese. Brad's cronies bellowed harder when Ebony stumbled in their midst.

"Here's one of them now," Brad heckled. "You may as well take a bow."

Ebony was terrified. He went from person to person, snatching cups and mugs from their grasps, like a madman. Puddles of coffee rested on the floor when he approached Brad, guarding his. No one understood what to make of Ebony's wildly erratic behavior. Some of the women were actually a tinge frightened.

"Come on, man. Give it up," Ebony warned.

"You must be on crack if you think you're getting this from me. You'll have to get your own, podna." Brad chuckled to himself after ending his statement with the street-corner colloquialism.

Ebony scanned all the perplexed faces around the room, uncertain what should happen next. "Aw-ight then. Be like that." He surveyed their faces again as he backed out the same way he came in, bewildered. "Don't say I didn't try." He sauntered back to the conference room having no idea what his sentence would be when it all hit the fan. Floreese searched Ebony's face for a sign when he returned. Ebony's gloomy demeanor mirrored that of a man condemned, suggesting that trouble was brewing for the both of them. From that point on, all he could think of was how long it would take him to find another job after Patricia got wind of what was going down and his part in it. Floreese grimaced when he suddenly remembered that the culprits on the '70s *Quincy* television show had been busted for the same prank in the end.

Patricia watched Ebony and Floreese while they did their best to communicate telepathically as she explained the next item on the agenda. "Ebony, I'm glad you're back in time to hear this. I hated having to make a tough decision, but Lazarus painted me into a corner with his last stunt. You may as well hear it from me before the office grapevine lets the cat out of the bag. It seems that Lazarus refused to adhere to my policy prohibiting anyone not associated with the station in the pit during your respective shows. On Friday night, he thought he was sneaking a woman up the side staircase, but I have it on tape. I also have undeniable proof of what went on during his decision to play two restricted cuts from I. Rome's album. Because the songs were aired before the official release date, we're in hot water with his record label. That I can fix, but if the woman who was unauthorized to be in the booth has the notion to cause trouble for us, a good team of lawyers could have bodies scattered everywhere when they're done. Believe you me, that kind of stupidity will not be allowed. I could make an example of Lazarus, but I won't. The numbers for his show have catapulted since the . . . incident. Some people are born lucky, I guess." She broke into a smile when she explained what elevated the ratings. "Lazarus must have forgotten to flip the "live" switch on his microphone when he was seeing to his guest. Some of their pillow talk was over-heard on air and the phone lines blew up when they thought it was a remix. That's right. They loved it and have been requesting it nonstop. I guess that sex really does sell." Snickers rang out when Patricia found it difficult to hide her amusement. "Alright, that's enough of that. Calm down. It could have been a lot worse when Lazarus put the station at risk. He is suspended for two weeks, without pay, and Ebony will take his spot until he returns."

"I get my own show?" asked Ebony, somewhat astounded. "I'm sorry it had to jump off like this but I'm diggin' it just the same."

"Well don't dig it too much," Patricia advised cautiously. "Like I said, it'll only be for two weeks, so don't get caught up. I like the chemistry between you Floreese."

Cee-Cee cackled and teased when the opportunity presented itself. "Ooh, chemistry. Ebony and Flo'reese sittin' in a tree, k-i-s-s-i-n-g."

"Whatever's clever, Cee-Cee Lovely, 'cause if Ebony gets Laz'rus's time slot I gets to run the boards alone, too. That's a win-win like getting down with some twins." Congratulations were being passed around the table like bottles of cheap wine at a high school skip-and-ditch party. Everyone shared in the good news, even Gwendolyn, almost.

She checked her fingernails thinking they could use some patchwork and perhaps another coat of polish was in order, so she folded them under and out of sight. "That's just great," she said, annoyed. "Hip-hip hoorah. That's smashingly good news but can't we move this thing along? I've got loads of things to do."

"For once I agree with Gwendolyn," Patricia remarked, still committed to sticking closely to her agenda items so as not to veer too far off-track. She read from a list of songs to be played on each show, discussed a couple of housekeeping issues, then confirmed the recording artist slated to slide by the station within the next month. When she didn't read an obvious name among the guest list, Octavia had mixed feelings. Just as she was getting comfortable with the thought of not having to deal with the superstar breathing down her neck, Patricia dropped the bomb. "By the way, if you're wondering why I didn't mention I. Rome among the other notables, it's because he hasn't consented to an interview. Well, not yet, anyway." Octavia felt a heavy weight bearing down on her shoulders. She was certain that it had to be serious when Patricia poured herself a tall glass of water and took a long sip before continuing. "He says he will not grant an exclusive interview unless he can get the station to answer his demands in writing."

Gwendolyn seemed perturbed, as usual. She had all but taken a mental trip out of the room until she became interested in what those demands were. "Patricia, what could a pretty-boy millionaire with a mountain of things want from this station?"

When a thunderous scream pierced the walls from out in the hall-way, Patricia was glad that something had come between her and the answer to follow. In fact, the bloodcurdling howl was welcomed.

She marched over to the door, then whipped it opened. Brad from the sales department went flying past with both hands cupped over the seat of his pants. At full stride he howled again, like the devil's wife was after him. As if they were playing a game of tag, Ebony and his for-mer showmate Floreese, along with Alphonzo and Benny, barreled out of the room to get closer to the action. They scurried off in the fashion of little boys chasing a fire engine up the block, balls of excited testos-terone expecting a free thrill.

With her lips pursed, Ms. Pitman rolled on another fresh layer of Bright Red Number Nine with one hand and pointed toward the stair-case with the other as they scurried past her workstation. Saul was sit-ting in his favorite chair at the downstairs reception area, fast asleep as usual, and of no assistance. Another unnerving yelp drew the guys to the same men's room where they had played snatch-the-sack earlier. Floreese was the first to inch nearer to the door. "Oh, man. If I'm gonna get fired for this, I gotta see."

Neither Benny nor Alphonzo could say for sure that they under-stood what was transpiring on the other side of that large oak door, but they couldn't stand the sales team, either, and Brad especially. Flo-reese pressed against the door with Ebony on his heels.

"Oh, the funk," Benny complained. "Something must've crawled up him and died."

Alphonzo's eyes watered. "Whatever it was must be tryna claw its way out."

"Shhhh," Floreese begged. "Be quiet. Y'all stay here and keep watch. Me and Eb will be right back."

Ebony and Floreese heard whimpering noises emanating from one of the stalls, then another chorus of loud screams mixed with the unmistakable sound of Brad's bowels flushing out everything that wasn't attached and a few things that used to be. They tiptoed closer and braved the funk as Benny so aptly put it. Floreese stepped up on a toilet seat so that he could peep over the top of the metal partition separating the stalls. He peered over and looked down. Brad sat there rocking back and forth, doubled over with his head hanging low. He was stark naked except for his shoes and socks, cradling his stomach and shivering between powerful contractions.

Floreese held his breath for obvious reasons as he lifted an expensive pair of tailored dress slacks from the door hook. After he'd successfully pulled Brad's pants over the partition, he climbed down and made off with the spoils of war.

Meanwhile, Patricia had been biding her time. She was floundering akin to a fish out of water, busying herself by shuffling papers from this side to that until someone spoke up. "I know what I. Rome is up to. He wants me." Those three words came out of Octavia's mouth like slow drips from a leaky faucet. She had been staring into space, but her next sentence needed to be accompanied by eye contact. "Isn't that it, Patricia? He wants me."

Lost under a sea of confusion, all eyes were trained on Patricia's now. Having to admit that Octavia was correct in her assumption concerning I. Rome's demands was a difficult task. But it was twice as hard for Patricia to suggest that Octavia comply and give one for the team. The entertainer's devious ploy had nothing to do with business. It was personal. I. Rome sought to get under Octavia's skin because she refused to answer his phone calls or return the gang of e-mails he'd sent. The millionaire playboy had no plans of being dismissed that easily. Octavia's relationship with the radio station served as his ace in the hole, and he played the trump card when it appeared his luck had changed for the worse.

Patricia nodded. Her reluctance to ask the unthinkable thwarted a verbal answer from coming forth. Octavia thumbed through her daily planner casually. "So, what *does* he want . . . exactly?"

Tony Tune was severely put out. He clenched his teeth in opposition to the proposed innuendo while looking away in utter exasperation. Patricia had reservations, but stated I. Rome's wishes nonetheless. "It's like this, in no uncertain terms. He expects dinner and dancing, Octavia, a lavish date with you." Cee-Cee nearly voiced what had entered her mind when it became obvious that The Four Touch Program had been activated to perfection. She was certain of Octavia's feelings toward her long-term, part-time lover, her loyalty to the station, and a predilection for coming through in the clutch. I. Rome counted on that one most of all.

"He and I are old friends," Octavia responded evenly. "And, I sure could use a good dinner. I'll start the interview during the appetizer and have it wrapped up by dessert. Consider it done. Just let me know what evening he wants to hook up and I'll give it a go." Although her voice was steady and sure, no one was fooled into believing that she was comfortable with accepting his inappropriate requests.

Patricia concluded the meeting abruptly, despite several remaining agenda items. For the first time in her tenuous career, she'd asked something of an employee that she wouldn't think of complying with, had the shoe been on the other foot. Carrying the company's torch left her feeling less than the upstanding manager she was known to be. Due to new competition in the marketplace, the station's owner had laid down the law to ensure the upcoming concert prove to be a huge success—including every event leading up to it. Patricia didn't approve of I. Rome's demands or her role in seeing them to fruition, but she did have a job to do as station manager. Had the offer been declined, Patricia was prepared to handle the rejection accordingly, up to and including her own resignation in order to protect Octavia, but she was glad it wouldn't come to that.

13

What Else Is New?

Around lunchtime, Alphonzo began his usual plea for Octavia's attention. He had heard about I. Rome's proposal but couldn't understand what all the salty sentiment was about. Patricia had been locked away in her plush office since she delivered the news and Tony Tune was making phone calls to see if there was anything he could do about it, short of delivering Mr. Double Platinum a fat lip on arrival. Gwendolyn Tyme displayed a somewhat surly disposition but that wasn't much of a stretch. As far as he was concerned, it was much ado about nothing.

When Alphonzo caught up to Octavia, she had purse in hand and was heading for the back parking lot with Cee-Cee. "Hey, wait up a tick," he yelled. "Are we taking the Jeep or the Benz?"

"What's this 'we' stuff?" Cee-Cee asked, not expecting an answer.

"For real," Octavia snarled. "You'd better catch up to the fellas." She wasn't in the mood to be chased around the lunch table all afternoon. "They took off to Cuzzin Cora's. We need some girls-only time and the only time we can hang in the middle of the day is after the monthly meeting, so run along."

"Run along?" Alphonzo repeated, taken aback. He was thrown for a loop and embarrassed to the point of saving face by matching ego-bruising blows. "Oh, I get it now. Unless you're a megastar with two wives and some babies at home, a man can't get no time with you."

"Cee-Cee, will you get this fool away from me before I have to go in my purse?" Neither of them had seen Octavia so upset before. Her lips were taut and twisted. She took a step back, ready to swing on him over the thoughtless comment. Instinctively Cee-Cee jumped in between them.

"Gone on, 'Zo!" she warned him earnestly. "This is not the time to be losing cool points, and what you just said was straight foul. You don't know the deal and I'm not the one to tell you, so step."

Alphonzo stood his ground, looking them over. He licked his lips and eased up when he realized that there was nothing he could say to fix the mess he'd only seconds before put his foot in. It was very dangerous to irritate a woman hurting over a man that wasn't hers. The level of uncertainty alone was sufficient to cause irreparable damage. Throw in the other fifty thousand emotions flowing within her and the police might have been taping off a crime scene.

"Look, Octavia, I didn't mean to take it there but—"

"Enough already, 'Zo!" spat Cee-Cee, trying to stop the runaway train from derailing, but it was too late.

"No, girl. Let him keep on pushing me." Octavia rammed her hand in the bottom of her spacious handbag. "I know how to calm all this."

Alphonzo got the idea when Cee-Cee backed out of the way hurriedly. "Alright, alright. I get it!" Alphonzo mimicked Cee-Cee's gesture and recoiled, fearing Octavia just might have come out of that fancy bag of hers with something that he couldn't talk his way out of or apologize fast enough to stop. "I'm sorry! Sorry!"

"Damn straight you're sorry!" Octavia shouted hysterically, still frantically rummaging through her purse. "But I've got something that'll lean you."

Cee-Cee was more frightened that Octavia would make a costly decision in a fit of rage. " 'Zo, I think she's serious. You'd better move around." In the time it took her to blink, Alphonzo was gone. Good thing, too, because the most harmful weapon she could find was a shiny tube of lipstick, which wouldn't bode well for her being taken seriously. Cee-Cee looked at Octavia as if she were an escaped mental patient. "All that drama over a tube of lipstick? You've got to be kidding me. Where'd you get that street talk from?" She pretended to pull a gun from her own purse. "I got sumthin' to lean ya!"

"Well, I had to say something to shoo him away. I saw Truest pull that deranged sistah routine one night when we were leaving this after-hours spot in the hood that she likes to slide by. The kinda joint that mostly pimps and wanna-be playas hang. Anyway, some mean-looking chicks ran up on us when we were getting in the car after Truest called one of them a *kitchen-tician* and clowned her in front of some clients."

"What on earth is a kitchen-tician?" Cee-Cee questioned.

"I guess it's the worse crack you can make on a hair stylist. It insinuates their work looks like it was hooked up over a kitchen sink. And oh, she was a big girl, too, about three-fifty, and so mad she was blowing snot bubbles. Truest went in her purse and that backed 'em up. But forget about all that. I need to talk to my big sistah and medium-size friend over lunch and I can't do that with Alphonzo the Radio Ho tagging along. Now can I?"

"What were you going to do, smear him to death? And I'd better be the medium-size friend 'cause I'm not trying to be a big anything to anybody."

Octavia laughed it off on the way to her jeep. "Just come on and get in. Got something I want to ask you, big sistah."

"Alright now, I've already told you about that once."

They pulled out of the parking lot still laughing and wondering why Brad Mayberry's pants were hoisted up the flagpole and blowing in the wind next to Old Glory. The short drive over to MaGuire's allowed Octavia the time to get her thoughts together concerning what refused to stay in its place, a ton of mixed emotions playing games in her head. When they arrived at the busy restaurant, Cee-Cee dropped her comb between the seat and the console. "Hold up 'Tavia, I can't seem to find my comb." She climbed out of the automobile and opened the rear door, then lifted a silver nylon backpack to continue her search. "Ah, here it is. Octavia, what do you have in this bag, an Uzi or a few hundred lipstick grenades?"

Octavia peaked inside the rear compartment through the back window. "What bag? Oh, I almost forgot about that. It belongs to this guy I ran over the other night," she answered mater-of-factly. She headed for the restaurant entrance, leaving Cee-Cee to decide if she were for real this time or overexaggerating for effect like she had to scare the wits out of Alphonzo.

Luckily, the ladies were shown to their table right away, but in an undesirable section near the bar area. Cee-Cee was chomping at the bit to inquire about the bag and the alleged man who'd met with an unfortunate accident. "Don't think you're getting away with leaving me with my mouth opened about hitting someone, then dashing off. I saw the scratches on your front bumper, but I want to know what really happened?"

Octavia laid it all for her to consume, explaining it as best she could. But the explanation left more to questions to be asked. "I don't see what the big deal is," she said innocently, "I crashed into his bicycle then I took him home and that was it." With that, she bit into her shrimp po'boy sandwich nonchalantly.

"That's not it," Cee-Cee argued, staring at her strangely.

"Hey y'all," Truest announced, when she approached them. "Is this the best table two attractive divas could come up with? Y'all should have worked that magic a little better. Where's the manager?" She began waving the hostess over. "Just 'cause we're black doesn't mean we have to put up with this."

"Truest, sit your behind down in that seat," Cee-Cee insisted. "If you can sit in those tight hip-huggers. You just got here and you're already making trouble." Looking on, Octavia took another bite and nodded her agreement.

"We don't have to deal with this kind of treatment. Black folk been here four hundred years and it's about time we got some respect," Truest continued.

Octavia swallowed hard behind a healthy gulp of ice tea. "Tell her, Cee-Cee."

"Tru', we asked for first available seating because we don't have the leisure lifestyle to come and go as we please. Our schedule allows us to have lunch not *do lunch*. That's what we have to look forward to when we grow up and have it going on like you do."

"Excuse me! I pay dearly for the privilege to *do lunch* among other things that require busting my behind when you two have called it a day and gone on about your biz'ness. Sometimes I feel like I live at that shop." When the hostess made her way over to see what Truest seemed so adamant about, Octavia apologized and sent her away.

Truest was relentless. "I bet I could have gotten us a better table." She was still pouting when the waiter returned to discover that another hungry mouth had joined his party of two. He didn't seem to mind, though, nor could he take his eyes off all the skin in plain view as Truest leaned forward to run her painted nails up and down the lunch menu. "I'll have the shrimp po'boy, too. She's making it look too good to pass up." The waiter smiled at Octavia, who was destroying the sandwich like it was her last meal. He took the order and hung around longer than he should have, seeking another cheap thrill. "Uh, did you lose something?" Truest asked, rolling her eyes back at the ones popping out of his head. He quickly composed himself, then vanished.

"If you didn't want men ogling over your body, you should have bought some pants that fit your behind," said Octavia as she pointed at the low-rise jeans. "*All* of it. Freak."

"Ooh, don't be jelly 'cause I got some extra jam. Hating is habit-forming. Don't get hooked on it. It's not cute."

Cee-Cee had to cover her mouth with a napkin before some if her lunch came flying out over Truest's comeback. Although Truest was underdressed in her tight pants, Octavia did have a bad case of booty-envy when it came to the way men fell over themselves to get a good look at that package, underdressed or not.

Picking over her sandwich once it arrived from the kitchen, Truest hummed. "Pass me the salt, Cee-Cee."

"Uh-uh, salt isn't good for you. Eat it like it is."

"I left my mama at the house," she protested. "'Tavia, hand me that salt, please. Cee-Cee is out of line. Thanks, honey." She poked her tongue out jokingly at Cee-Cee. "That's what I'm talking about. By the way, what's so important that I had to cancel my pretty feet-and-hands appointment?"

After she shoved the last bit of bread in her mouth, Octavia began to speak with her jaws bunched. "See, I wuff meanin' to geff . . ."

"Uh-uh, stop, Octavia." Cee-Cee assumed the mothering roll again. "I know you know better than to talk with your mouth full. Hand over your diva card. I'm revoking your passport. Privileges denied."

"I'm sorry but I haven't been able to eat since the accident."

Truest displayed genuine concern. "What accident?"

"I'm not going to relive that story a second time today. I'm okay but I'm not so sure the man I ran into is."

Truest had to put her po'boy down. Octavia acted as if it were an everyday occurrence to hit someone with a one-ton vehicle. "Somebody had better tell me what the hell she's talking about. Who'd you hit, Octavia? And did you mean to?"

"Truest, please," Cee-Cee objected, shocked at the accusation.

"I'm just sayin'. You know that rich white chick in Houston ran over her husband not once but three times when she caught him sneaking out of a hotel with his employee, and she was straight-faced when she told the judge that she didn't mean to do it."

"No, I really didn't mean to," Octavia contested quickly. "I didn't even see him until it was too late and the rain was coming down. It was too much."

"This is where the story takes a turn," Cee-Cee added, with alarming enthusiasm. " 'Tavia was about to tell me how his backpack ended up in the backseat of her Jeep."

Truest smirked at Octavia knowingly before she spoke her mind. "Backseat, huh? He must be fine." Cee-Cee hadn't considered that and was immediately reminded that Truest bestowed extra-sensory instincts the FBI could benefit from.

"Was he, Octavia, fine?" Cee-Cee prodded.

Octavia's eyes drifted away from theirs. Guilty Eyes is what her mother used to call them when she couldn't maintain contact after having been confronted with the truth. As much as she hated to admit, Truest was on to her but good.

"I knew it," Truest answered for her. "She ran over a fine-ass man, took him home, stole his backpack so she can see him again, and she calls me a freak. Uh-huh, too trifling."

"You ho," Cee-Cee exclaimed. "Octavia Longbow, you didn't tell me anything about him being fine. It took Truest to show up and drag the truth out of you."

"It wasn't about that. He is fine, but I would have taken him home if he wasn't."

Once again Cee-Cee fell short on street skills compared to Truest. It seemed to be second nature for her to conclude things having nothing to do with her. It was an uncanny ability and Cee-Cee openly envied that blessing. When Octavia didn't contest the accusation, Cee-Cee was outdone. She squinted her eyes at Truest in a suspicious manner. "And how do you know she kept his bag purposely? You weren't even there."

"Simple. 'Cause that's what I'd have done if he is as fine as I'm willing to bet he is." She went back to her meal and left Cee-Cee to sort out the rest.

"You may as well give it up, Octavia. Just how fine is he?" Cee-Cee's arms were folded, her expression stern. "And don't leave out one detail."

"Y'all gonna make me go there?"

"We're already there, waiting on you to catch up," Truest cracked before digging into some extremely salty French fries.

Octavia regretted getting involved in this discussion. She had nothing to gain by drudging up thoughts of the mystery man and everything to lose. But she had one persistent investigator staring her down and a know-it-all waiting to hear all about it. "Okay, okay. To make a long story short, for the sake of time, this is it in a nutshell. I was sitting at a quiet table in Café Brew."

"I love that place," Truest threw in, much to Cee-Cee's displeasure. "Javier makes these huge omelets to die for. You can't eat the whole thing by yourself."

"Shhhhush!" Cee-Cee wanted to strangle her for interrupting. "Truest, please, you are . . . wrecking the flow."

"I know she didn't just shush me," Trusted objected. "I ain't to be shushed. My mama don't even shush me."

"I apologize. Please forgive me but I'm in desperate need of a juicy story and this sounds like a doozey. Didn't mean to shush."

"Well, since you apologized I'll hold my comments to the end." Truest went back to nibbling fries and listening attentively.

"Are y'all through 'cause I don't want to tell this story no way?" Octavia advised them.

Cee-Cee snatched the butter knife from the table and playfully waved it across the table. "Don't make me cut you over this, girl. Get back to tellin'."

"As I was saying before I was so rudely interrupted, several times might I add, I was at the spot. After I devoured the whole omelet, prepared by the fabulous Javier—" When Truest's eyes grew wide, Cee-Cee grabbed the knife again to stifle any extemporaneous comments.

"Despite whether Truest believes me or not, I did eat the entire thing. In fact, it put me under. I'm talking asleep at the table in the middle of the dinner rush. When I came to, it was almost an hour later and there was this gorgeous specimen of manly handsomeness sitting at the counter. Every woman in the place was checking him out, and a few had their men with them. He was nice on the eyes and stirring to the spirits, if you know what I mean. He had a smooth cocoa-butter complexion, looked kinda Creole, nearly six feet or so, a gorgeous smile, his hair was faded, nice and curly on top, and the sexiest thickest eyebrows imaginable. There was a charming Denzel way about him and a Wesley Snipes build to go with it." After that description, Cee-Cee needed a drink of water. She was hanging on every word and Truest nodded as if she were there when it had taken place. "He'd been watching me sleep. I knew it because he drew this beautiful pencil sketch of me catching some zees while the entire non-smoking section watched him. Knew I shouldn't have tried to eat the whole omelet, but it was so good." She hurried back to the story when Cee-Cee flinched the knife her way again, urging her to continue. "So, I wanted to thank him but he left before I got the chance to pay the bill. This annoying waitress had the scoop on him, but she was not tryna help a sistah out. Can't say that I blame her, though. Anyway. When I got in my car, these two trucks were waiting on me to give up my parking space. The lot was full. It was raining . . . a recipe for disaster. And that's exactly what happened. Disaster struck. Out of nowhere, the man appeared in front of me and I ran him over. Don't worry, he's not going to sue. I wrote him a check for the bike and persuaded him to let me take him home." Truest winked at her. "Don't you be winking at me. If you won't be shushed, I won't stand for being winked at like I had ulterior motives for getting him home safely." Now, Cee-Cee was catching on too. She returned the wink that Truest offered with a reasonable facsimile of her own. "What-ever, y'all. That's my story and I'm sticking to it."

Cee-Cee had learned a thing or two from Truest, who was not so overly suspicious as it turned out. "Heffa, you did keep that man's backpack so you could see him again, didn't you?"

"Told you," said Truest, nodding I-told-you-so fashion while wading through the truth, or as much of it as Octavia was willing to admit. "So what's Mr. Super Fine's name? And, I'm sure you got the man's digits so you can call and check on him from time to time."

"His name is Legacy Childs and he didn't seemed all that impressed with me at the time, so I didn't think to get his number. In all honesty, I kinda hoped he'd have used the information on my check and called me by now but he hasn't, so I guess I read him right."

"He'll call," Truest said, with conviction. "Unless he's gay. Hell, he still might call. You almost converted Strip Show Savon. I heard he's as happy as a queen living in that little pink house you painted. Uh-huh, turned all the way out."

"Don't even try it. I'm not trying to think about Savon's crowded behind right now. I've got bigger issues."

Cee-Cee finally rested the butter knife on the table. She'd had her fill and seemed satisfied. "One thing's for sure. If Tru says he'll call, he'll call." She slipped the woman with too much intuition and a wealth of street sense some dap. "Truest, use your powers for good, girl. For good."

"Uh-uh!" Truest objected harshly. "They work better for evil."

Octavia broke out in a rash of loud animated snorts. She had been with Truest when those extra-sensory powers proved formidable in dire situations. Regardless of when she used them, they were awesome powers to behold. And she was grateful they'd kept the conversation away from her enforced date with I. Rome.

14

Compensating Factors

The bill for lunch arrived, attached to the leering waiter. Octavia handed him a credit card before either of her friends had a chance to offer covering the tab. "It's the least I could do, plus I haven't told y'all why I called a meet-and-eat today."

"There's more to this story?" Cee-Cee asked, hoping there was. She went for the knife again, just in case.

"No Cee-Cee, there isn't so there's no cause to get excited. Running into Legacy was interesting and he is extremely easy on the eyes, but . . . you know I have this thing about compensating factors."

"Compensating factors?" Truest echoed, confused by Octavia's choice of words.

"You know, the compensating factors a woman's got to consider when a man is missing some of the standard essentials."

"Oh, you mean something that gives a brotha extended time on the court when he would have otherwise fouled out."

"Yeah, compensating factors." Octavia went on to explain that Legacy had been riding a bicycle when she met him. She assumed that was his sole mode of transportation, which was understandable. Then there was the fact that he did live in someone's guest house, for God's sake. She didn't know if he was a kind-hearted soul, thoughtful, and charming beyond compare, or if he had the kind of bedroom skills that relegated compensating factors to a nonissue status. "Think about it for a minute. When you've met a man who hasn't acquired the standard package of stability, what have you done? Did you throw him back, or try to work with him until he ascended to where he needed to be?"

"That depends on if you're talking about working with the brotha until he's where *I* think he needs to be or where *he* thinks he needs to be," Cee-Cee said, in retrospect. "I've learned the hard way that the two can be worlds apart and damned near diametrically opposed. As far as I'm concerned, there isn't a compensating factor for a brotha who does not have his stuff together." She'd dated a med student for six years, watched him work eighteen-hour shifts and helped him study for one exam after the next. He'd waited until he was a resident, nine months from completion to decide that being a doctor was his father's dream, not his. Suddenly he up and quit. It had become her dream, too, somewhere down the line but that was of no consequence when the man needed to find himself. Two years post-catastrophe, he had yet to find himself or a job to replace the promising career he didn't want. Cee-Cee was willing to put up with a lot of ain't-gots and lacks-thereof, too, but a man trying to find his place didn't have any business putting his face in hers. She was not having it.

Octavia turned toward Ms. Know-It-All for her opinion. "What about you, Truest? I've seen you with all types of men. What criteria do you set for keeping a man around?"

"Criteria? Don't matter to me where a brotha's going or where he's been," Truest answered plainly before making her point. "I live in the now, accept things as they are, and I expect a man to do wrong. That way, I don't get disappointed when they break their promises about what they're gonna do for me. I don't get my hopes up every spring for a wedding in June and I'm not surprised when I catch them with other women. I had my heart broken in the tenth grade by a young thug named Ronald Sims, from the projects. He asked me to the senior prom but took another girl instead and had me waiting all night for him to pick me up from my grandmother's. Since then, I don't put myself out there like that. What I do know is what I need. Most women don't have the slightest idea. Too many of us go after what we want, and as soon as we're shackled with a marriage, we spend the rest of our lives wishing we had the real thing. Uh-uh, not me."

This was intriguing to Octavia. She thought they were one in the same. Wants and needs were at least interchangeable at times, a difference in semantics. People often said how they needed a new car when the latest models rolled off the assembly line and others whined about needing another pair of black shoes to compliment the five pairs they currently owned. "I don't know if I follow you, Tru. What you consider to be a want, I might view as a need and vice versa."

"Exactly, but you asked about wants. I don't get caught up in wants when men are concerned. You see, I like a man who says sweet things and holds me tight, but what I *need* is a man who can handle the kind of woman I am and keep me up late at night."

"Preach on, sistah, preach on," Cee-Cee signified like a sinner on the front pew.

Octavia raised her right hand in the customary testifying position. "Say amen if you can. We may as well have church up in here. Cee-Cee and I are already late for work. So you may as well preach on."

By the time Truest climbed down off her soapbox, both the other ladies were the better for it. "Uhh-huh, see . . . some sistahs want a man who is fifty percent sweet and fifty percent freak. Y'all don't hear me, but I know I need a dyed-in-the-wool sho'nuff make-you-break-a-sweat strong-backed rough-neck. Don't matter to me if he's committed a crime or on probation from doing time. I needs at least a seventy percent thug, thirty percent lover kinda brotha. I ain't tryna have a watered-down thug 'cause I'm a hundred percent thug-tress. I need him to be true to his thugness, then he'll know what a real thug is supposed to do. Don't cheat yourself. Treat yourself. Get what you need."

"Wellll . . . make it plain, sistah pastor. Make it plain."

"Monday through Sunday, I needs a gang o' drama," Truest continued. "'Cause I'm bringing some of it with me, through the winter, fall, spring, and summer. And if by chance I do discover he's not a thug lover, I won't concede. I'll drag him down to thug headquarters. And trade his perpetratin' ass in for another, who's bonafide and pedigreed. Let the church say amen."

"Amen and back again," Cee-Cee hailed wholeheartedly.

"Check his papers, girl," Octavia suggested. "Check 'em."

"Y'all know I'm joking, but I do know that more than half of the marriages are failing these days, and most relationship fall apart before folks can even make it down the aisle. I can't count all the times some sad-faced sistah has come in the shop, crying about her own man not giving her what she needs and how she's confronted with the dilemma of what's a woman to do when she finally bumps into the kind of man who can represent, but she can't get out of her marriage so she can move on it."

"I can't imagine how difficult that must be," said Octavia as shook her head, trying to envision countless women who had chosen the wrong man and for all the wrong reasons. "Do you think it's all about sex?"

"No, that's usually such a small part of it. I'm talking simple stuff, like spending quality time together even if the football game is on, him taking the steps to share what happened at the job when she gets home, picking up after himself to help lighten her load at the house, or running her bath water every now and then. Don't get it twisted, though. Let's keep things in perspective. Good sex don't hurt none, but I'm from the streets so that's my comfort zone. That's what I need and that's who I am. I can live with that. Like I said, no man will get the chance to break my heart again. However, I will give 'em a shot at breaking my back, every day of the week and twice on Saturday."

"Heyyy now." Cee-Cee giggled while fanning her self with an open palm. "That'll make a sistah look forward to the Sabbath."

"It'll make a sistah long for the right man to come along and spend those Saturdays with her," Octavia agreed. She stared past the eyes looking at hers. "Sometimes, I think of having a special man in my life who can do that for me. One who'll stop in the middle of what he's doing just to look at me right. I mean the kind of look that whispers *I'm so glad you crossed my path* and the same look that conveys *what-ever where-ever when-ever, just ask.*"

Sighing together in simultaneous harmony, the three of them reserved a moment of silence to appreciate the thought of experiencing a subtle glance hot enough to melt butter. Octavia brushed on a smidgen of light powder, then closed her Clinque compact case. "We've had such a good time catching up, but I still haven't told you why I needed my girls in my corner today. It won't take but a second, and I don't expect your two cents right away." Cee-Cee and Truest were both tuned in. "Because of the time and effort I've spent with Isaiah Rome, I'm going to tell him that I've made up my mind and there is no chance of us continuing whatever it is we've been doing." She sighed again, this time alone. "I just hope that I'm not cashing in my chips too soon. I've known since the beginning that his father ran out on him when he was young. Isaiah hasn't gotten over having been abandoned, and I just don't want to be added to the list of people he hates for doing the same."

The peeping waiter was back, standing there grinning and staring suggestively at Truest. When he asked if she needed anything else, she went off. "Hell, no!" she barked. "Security!" Suddenly she was no longer interested in being the object of any man's affection or a part of the threesome. There was something in what Octavia said that caused her emotion to run amuck. I. Rome made several stops each time he came home and Truest had to deal with being only one of them, knowing that he was lying to Octavia in order to keep her on a string as long as possible. He took no issue with sharing intimate details of his relationships with other women during the pillow talking sessions with Truest. But at no time had he discussed the way he felt about Octavia. Now she knew why—his feelings for her ran deep. "Hey girls, I'm sorry to break up the hen party, but I need to run."

Truest hopped up from the table. Octavia wanted to ask what caused the quick mood swing that took her and Cee-Cee by surprise while Truest traded hugs, grabbed her purse, then hurriedly walked out the front door. Grief is the emotion Truest did recognize, but guilt was one she'd never met. Now it was clear that Isaiah Rome truly loved Octavia, why he refused to discuss anything having to do with her. Because he hadn't reserved that honor for either of the women who benefited from carrying his last name, it was finally so clear, and Truest had missed it. When it revealed itself, she was sick to her stomach. She could justify her poor decision to sleep with him as long as she thought he was incapable of love. As far as she was concerned, their affair was a financial and physical arrangement. Realizing that there was another side of I. Rome, another side that he reserved for Octavia, rocked her. Suddenly she felt like a woman who was losing her man instead of one who, against her better judgment, had shared some woman's husband with her best friend. Cee-Cee had it right when she stopped by the shop to set Truest straight about complicating her life. Truest never should have said yes to his advances in the beginning, regardless of how much he had given her in return.

15

Twinkle, Twinkle

The afternoon glided by much smoother than the morning had. Octavia skipped out of the office early in order to make her last class on time. Twenty-four months of night school had come to an end, and that meant she was finishing what she started, a master of arts in journalism. Now that another chapter was closing, she wondered what new chapter would open, because that was how it generally worked out. Maybe now was the right time to replace some of those obsolete ideas of what she thought life was supposed to hold for her. Since success was relative, keeping up with her undergraduate schoolmate's accomplishments was pointless. But whenever she had a run-in with any of them, she caught herself inquiring about their career moves since college and whether they had heard rumblings about others doing well. Then she would immediately begin kicking herself after each unnerving occurrence, hating the thought of comparing her current employment status to that of former classmates. She also despised the thought of overanalyzing the decision she had made four years earlier to pass on an assignment to write for Johnson Publishing in Chicago. Instead, she'd followed I. Rome to Dallas and waited. She continued to wait when his first hit single took off like a rocket and so did he. The irony was, he up and moved to Chicago to further his singing career, only without her. The forty-two mile hike back from the university gave her time to think. Time was just what she needed. Time to mentally replay the latter stages of her life, time to sort out what was standing in front of her, and time to decide what should be left behind.

While parking in front of Legacy's guest house, Octavia felt like a trespasser. She stepped out of her SUV with only the shimmering November night to witness her creeping along the driveway, timid and apprehensive. Having been there only once before, she had overlooked how the house appeared to stretch out. This time around, it seemingly took up half a block and lounged on twice the amount of land of the other lavish homes. Just when her mind began to question what kind of business someone had to be involved in to afford such an estate, a sudden gust of wind brushed against her. Texans have a saying about the indecisive weather patterns they can count on changing at a moment's notice from desert heat to freezing cold, sometimes within the same afternoon: "If you don't like the weather in Texas, just wait five minutes because it's destined to change."

Eight years in the Lone Star state had made Octavia a believer. She drew her arms into her body instinctively to stave off the stiff breeze. Her pace quickened as her mind drifted back to her mission: Leave the backpack and don't complicate things any more than they already are. Carry out that simple plan.

Immediately her simple plan suffered an unforeseen hiccup. A few steps from the guest house, she felt her fingers tingle with excitement as the light came on inside. The moment she saw someone walk past the front window her plan was put on hold. Perhaps she should take a minute to do more than drop off the man's personal belongings and forget they'd met, she thought. That renegade idea occurred on the heels of Octavia catching an innocent glimpse through a vertical space between the ivory-colored drapes. There stood Legacy, bare-chested in blue jeans and gazing out the side window. Somewhere in the midst of taking in his broad shoulders, strong back, and muscular arms, innocence was lost. When she continued peeking inside, all apprehension of trespassing disappeared temporarily and her simple plan evaporated. Now she was conflicted over whether to knock at the door and perhaps ruin the view she cherished, or letting the moment play itself out. While the conflict raged on inside her, Legacy leaned over a large telescope, then adjusted several knobs on it. Whatever it was that he saw brought a pleasantness to his face. It must have been contagious because Octavia was smiling, too.

When it seemed that he was going to turn her way, she lunged backward to move out of view. Tripping over a small potted plant by the door caused her to stumble. That misstep created a loud clanging sound, obliterating her anonymity. It also brought Legacy to his front door. He yanked it open, wearing a tight workout shirt and a disturbed expression.

"Who's—oh, it's you again," he said, his eyes landing on her just after she'd landed on her pride. "Come on, let me help you up," he offered with an extended hand.

Octavia's eyes drifted up to rest on him. She blushed hard while she dusted herself off and noticed how strong his hands were. Too strong to be that soft, she almost said aloud. "Hey uh, Legacy. Seems I can't stop crashing into things when you're around." She was embarrassed, and since there was no sense in denying the obvious she ran with it. "You know it was funny, so go ahead and laugh."

The demeanor Legacy had adopted when he found Octavia distressed was quickly transformed after he looked back over his shoulder at the gap in the drapes she'd used to look in on him. "I don't know if I should laugh or call the police. Be'n a Peepin' Tom-ika is frowned on in these parts, ma'am." His exaggerated Texas twang removed any room for doubt that she was in fact welcomed.

Busted, Octavia threw her hands up willingly. "Then you'll just have to arrest me. Huh, sheriff?" For some reason, the handcuffs left over from her fling with Secret Service Steven came to mind.

Continuing with the icebreaking exercise he'd initiated, Legacy enacted a Southern brand of justice. "Hmmm, let's see here now. That's uh . . . peepin' with the intent to peep some more, general disorderliness, disturbin' the peace, and some other transgressions against the law that I could fabricate, have I need to."

"Have you need to?" Now she was flirting back, shamelessly at that. "Sheriff, you might not want to sentence me until you've gotten to know me better."

Legacy sensed that she enjoyed their running joke. "Uh-oh, that sounds like bribery. Gonna have to add that to the charges." He almost laughed at how ridiculous he sounded, but he was working an angle. "Tell you what. I'll offer time served standin' here listenin' to my sherf-f'n routine if you help me out with sumthin'. I want to give you a gander at something remarkable and you tell me what you think about it."

"Okay, but it'd better be good."

He nodded slightly and stepped aside to invite her in. By the time she crossed the threshold, her simple plan had dwindled to little more than a memory. Legacy stuck both of his thumbs through the front belt loops of his blue jeans and tugged at them, wrapping up the lawman act. "Alright ma'am, it's a deal. Raise your right hand." When she raised her left, he grinned. "Ma'am, your other right hand. Good. Okay then, by the pow'rs invested in me by the great citizen of this'n here guest house, I reckon you've suffered enough, and 'cides I'm tired of hearin' myself sound lyke this. Time served, now pay up."

Following him in the quaint studio-fashioned living quarters, Octavia took in the sights. There was a long bookshelf on the far wall, too long and filled with far too many books to be in such a small space. A Murphy pull-down was hanging along the other wall, next to a weight bench and a tall workout tower used for chin-ups and upper body dips. That explained how well developed his shoulders and chest were. A miniature kitchenette separated the restroom from the makeshift office area where an electric keyboard sat on an elaborate black metal stand adjacent to a computer desk. By the looks of things, he had everything he owned in that small room, or at least everything he needed.

Feelings zigzagged through Octavia when she remembered what Cee-Cee said about not wanting to get involved with a man who didn't have his stuff together. Then Legacy shot her a Pepsodent smile, his perfect teeth aligned like a battalion of ivory cubes. *Forget about Cee-Cee and all that she stands for, 'cause I'm feeling this*, Octavia reasoned. She wanted to see that man smile at her like that as often as possible.

"It's kind of crowded in here, I know, but it's home," Legacy said eventually, after watching her assess his digs. "Step over here. This is what I wanted you to see." He motioned for Octavia to have a seat behind a three-foot telescope, covered in chrome metallic paint, which was angled up toward the sky.

Once she settled in, Legacy instructed her to look into the lens, then he stood over her like a tutor with his prized pupil. His expression was dripping with exuberance. Octavia had no idea what to expect. She had gazed up at the sky her whole life, as it was common to Native Americans, whose culture is heavily inundated with astronomy. Even though it was a viable part of her up bringing, she was not prepared for what brilliance lay in store.

When her eye focused, she rattled back away from the telescope, frightened. "Is that a meteor? It looks like it's heading straight for us."

"No, it's just a blazing star," he answered behind a slight chuckle. "I call her Twinkle. You know, twinkle-twinkle, wish upon a star, and all that. She's the star I wish upon."

Octavia eased back up to the lens again, marveling at the collage of colors flickering glimmers of beautiful purples, hues of violet mixed with shades of orange and fiery reds. She was captivated by the sheer magnitude of what she saw. "My God, I've never seen anything like this," she whispered, not taking her eye away.

"It's the only one in the sky. Until yesterday, it was just another bright diamond, beckoning me to visit her each time the clouds allowed me to. Twinkle is shy sometimes. She likes to hide, but she shows up when I need to say hello." He moved beside Octavia and peered up with his naked eye. "Twenty-three degrees from the tip of the Big Dipper has been her home since 1562, at least that's when she was discovered. But, she and I became acquainted a few years ago." He glanced down at Octavia, still engaged in her amazement. "On a clear night like this, I swear I can see heaven from here."

Finally, Octavia leaned back and looked Legacy square in the face. That Heaven comment sounded like one heck of a compliment, if he were talking about her, but she didn't want to take it for granted and end up with an egg on her face. Instead, she decided to play it safe. "Wow, Legacy. Thank you for sharing Twinkle with me, but why do you sound so intimately attached and why the name Twinkle? Did you come up with that one all by yourself?"

Legacy leaned his back against the wall, kind of smooth like. "I guess I could have named her Flaming Ball of Gaseous Matter, but Twinkle has a nicer ring to it." He didn't dare tell her that Twinkle in some way stood in place of a woman who'd died before he could give her all the love he'd been saving up. He'd read in the Bible somewhere that a man who finds a good woman findeth a good thing. He wondered if that scripture applied to Octavia.

"Yeah, Twinkle does sound a lot better at that," she said, amused. "Growing up on the reservation, I've heard it called Canopus or the Alpha star, the closest cousin to Sirius, but I think I like Twinkle the best."

"Whaaaat? You a stargazer too? And a reservation? An Indian reservation?" He was obviously enchanted but didn't know what to make of her now. Regardless, his face lit up like a Christmas tree.

"I was introduced to the diamonds in the sky as a child. And is there any other kind of reservation a person would live on?" She didn't know what to make of him, either, a man with charm, wit, a sense of humor, and interested in more than what happens here on the third rock from the sun. "You got a problem with my heritage?" Octavia snapped at him jokingly.

"No, not hardly. I'm just surprised to meet a black woman who really does have Indian ancestry in her family." They laughed, both having encountered black people with naturally straight hair, high cheekbones, and soft features claiming to be descents of ancient tribes that walked open the plains of America.

"Yeah, I've heard that a lot since I moved to Texas. It's hard not to laugh out loud every time I run across one of my distant cousins."

"So where do you hail from?" asked Legacy.

Octavia took note of the way he seemed genuinely interested. "Where do I hail from? What, are you trying to sound educated or something?"

"I have all the education I need at the moment." When he didn't own up to having a college degree, she assumed he didn't. He let it go because graduating at the top of his class in the Art Department hadn't made him the man he was, nor had the internship he'd earned to study in France. He wasn't about papers hanging on the wall to boast his achievements, which was why his diploma was stored in a box some-where in that gigantic palace of his.

"All the education you need, huh? I see." She was sizing him up and he recognized it, but he wanted to see what she was made of while she remained unaware of the fortune he had amassed in a very short time. "Where am I from, you asked? Near Tulsa. Have you ever been to Oklahoma?"

"No, I can't say that I have but I'd have to take a guess that you're Crow or Pawnee. No, on second thought, Cherokee? Despite your dark complexion."

143

This time around it was Octavia's turn to savor interest in this unusual man who continued to blow her mind with how much he seemed know about things most men were clueless to. She assumed he had taken a shot in the dark and decided to call him on it. "Now you're trying to hard. What do you *think* you know about the Cherokee nations?"

Legacy stepped away from the wall. He proceeded to pace slowly in a small circle, stroking his chin like a professor about to drop some nuggets of higher learning. "More than you think I do, that's for sure. I know there are three nations of Cherokee in the state of Oklahoma alone and the third is the largest." He paused when her mouth flew open. Now she was impressed. "Shall I continue, or have you been sufficiently intrigued for one evening?" He winked at her as he continued pacing the floor.

"By all means, Dr. Childs, do continue." Her eyes reflected his intelligence like dark sapphires underneath a jeweler's magnifying glass, dazzling and radiant.

"I've studied more cultures and civilizations than some people get paid to. I wanted to know more about people in general, I suppose. The three nations of Cherokee have some of the most interesting subcultures and traditions, and they've somehow managed to maintain their heritage in spite of being subjected to live the white man way." He had studied cultures so extensively because he was undoubtedly of mixed ethnicities but had difficulty guessing which ones, considering that he had been orphaned at birth. After searching for information about his parents led nowhere, he'd hoped to draw some conclusions by studying various ethnic groups. He chalked it up as a long shot that proved futile, other than becoming a walking encyclopedia for how various groups of people happened to end up where they are now.

"Brotha, you are really scaring me. My father would trip if he heard you talking about our people with so much intuitiveness." She assumed he was black because his skin was dabbled with melanin, and the way he carried himself with utmost assurance said *brotha* all over. "He's full-blood Keetoowah and holds on to the old ways with a death grip."

"The Keetoowah Band," Legacy repeated with the same authentic pronunciation. "That's the third nation and the largest of the three if I remember correctly."

"Okay, see, now I'm concerned." She stood up from the comfortable chair and started for the door. Legacy headed after her.

"Oh, I see. You meet a man with a decent amount of intelligence and you head for the hills? I thought you would appreciate that, not run from it."

Octavia stopped in her tracks. As her eyes began to mist, she turned away to hide her face. "You don't understand. I've been caught between the pride of my people and their shame. Growing up on a reservation, where everyone was dirt-poor and couldn't conceive of anything else, still follows me like a shadow. No one outside the Keetoowah gave a damn about us, or what it was like getting third-rate hand-me-downs, from our schoolbooks and clothes to our citizenship. And being half black didn't get me any breaks either way. Now you speak of my people like my father wished I did." She spun on her heels to face him. New tears fell on her cheeks after the others had been wiped away. "I don't even know you, nothing about you, and you walk in my life seemingly knowing way too much about me." After Octavia caught her breath, she noticed that his smile was gone. Legacy's expression displayed a painful resonance, one bearing a striking resemblance to hers. "Honestly, I'm not sure what's happening to me right now. I am delighted that you're different from any man I've known, regardless of race. Also, I'm as infatuated with the way you've got my mind going a hundred miles an hour as I am enchanted by the way astronomy moves you. And at the same time I'm bothered because you've neglected to call me by my name in all the time I've been here."

She overlooked Legacy's warm smile as it made another guest appearance. "You couldn't understand," she huffed. "It's a woman thing."

"No, I understand."

"What?"

"It's not that serious . . . Octavia Longbow. That's right. I haven't forgotten your name, if that's what you're thinking. There was no forgetting anything about you."

Crossing her arms, she exhaled frustration, which had been bottled up inside her. "You must think I'm a kook? I wouldn't blame you if you didn't want to see me again."

"You can't shake me that easily. No, I don't think you're a kook. Maybe a little high-strung, but it depends on who you're asking. And anyway, who's talking about seeing you again? I'm not through seeing you now. Tell you what. Let me treat you to dinner and I'll pretend that you didn't cry, that I haven't disturbed you with what I've learned about Native Americans, and I'll also overlook all the preconceived notions you probably have about me and how penniless I must be to live all cramped up like this. I think I can scrounge up enough change to spring for dinner."

Having begun to wonder how a man could have come to know so much and have so little to show for it materialistically, Octavia was confounded when Legacy had read both her and her mind correctly. Coincidently, she wasn't too confused to pass up an impromptu date with him.

"Octavia, what's your curfew? I would hate to cause you trouble with your man."

"I wasn't aware that I had a curfew and you're not that slick. If you wanted to know if I was seeing someone exclusively, you could have asked me outright." She purposely left his question unanswered. With things moving so fast, she wouldn't be too quick to broadcast her availability.

"Hold that thought. I need to get a couple of things before we go," Legacy said before walking away.

She watched the rhythmic sway in his stride, exuding confidence step by step, and disappeared into a smaller closed-off area. Octavia slowly approached the massive bookcase to get a better idea of what was really happening. She ran her fingers up and down the spines of textbooks in various subjects, both contemporary and dated novels, dictionaries for Spanish and French, and how-to manuals from building model airplanes to constructing life-sized model homes.

Looking away to survey the rest of the room, her initial suspicion was confirmed. There was no television or radio to be seen. Did he like being shut in from the rest of the world, or was he shutting it out? She couldn't understand why a man with apparent upside potential didn't capitalize on his energy and knowledge to provide for himself a better living. Then an old quote that she remembered came to mind about unrewarded genius and how nothing was more common than unsuccessful men with great talent. Legacy had proved to be extremely talented considering the sketch he drew freehand at the coffee shop, and any man who adopted a thorough interest of so many topics had to be more cerebral than most of the people she'd met. The more Octavia surmised about this strange man, the more uncertain she was that any of her assumptions were accurate. Regardless of what she'd find after stripping away at his outer layers, she looked forward to the process, and more of those effervescent smiles of his. *Ooh-wee.*

16

Whutcha' Call Me?

From the street outside, the laundromat looked more like a day care than a washateria. The large storefront window framed the brightly lit, privately owned business, stacked deep with long rows of pastel-green washing machines and banana-yellow dryers. The ceiling was painted like a midday summer sky, soft blues sponged over with patches of white made to look like clouds. The custom paint job created a comfortable setting, as laundromats go. A large hand-stenciled sign hung above the door: SUDS, written in red and trimmed in navy blue.

Octavia was at a loss when she followed Legacy into the building that adjoined a Chinese fast-food joint. The aroma of Musiu pork tickled her nose just before a good whiff of laundry detergent made her sneeze. She should have asked what was really going on when Legacy climbed in her Jeep earlier with a faded green army-issue duffle bag. It must have weighed thirty pounds or more, but he carried it effortlessly like a schoolboy with a lunch box.

Octavia heard her stomach growl disagreeably as she looked around the exceptionally clean room. Two Hispanic children nibbled on egg rolls while playing checkers on a plastic tiny-tot-sized table. There was a section devoted as a play area where kids could enthrall themselves in arts and crafts or try their hands at watercolors. Octavia figured the owner either must have been a parent or a have good head for business, because the layout provided grown-ups a chance to handle their chores without continually chasing the little ones around. That meant fewer bumps and boo-boos and more in-and-out traffic. After another broad look of the place, the good head for business won out.

"Sorry, Octavia, I'll be finished in a minute," Legacy yelled above a chorus of machines on spin cycle. He sorted his colored clothes from the whites and tossed them into washers, sprinkled powered deter- gent, and loaded the coin slots with quarters. "Ready?" he asked, voice raised. She didn't answer, too busy eyeing two small children just fin- ishing their predinner snacks. Octavia joined them at the small table to look on as they had a field day with a color-by-numbers Crayola set. Moments later, she felt someone standing behind her. "Legacy, did you say something?"

"Oh, pardon me, señorita. Hay no necesita," a woman's voice answered instead. The meek, accented voice belonged to Maria, the evening manager. She was as round as she was short and spoke in a slow deliberate pattern, attempting to translate two languages in her head simultaneously. "Eh, if de eh . . . ," she muttered, searching for the English words, but failed to convey what she wanted to get across. Octavia wanted to put her at ease, so she stood up and placed her hand on Maria's shoulder, with a mind to calm her.

"Qué tienes, Maria?" Legacy said, approaching them. "Hay proble- mas esta noche?"

"No, estoy bien. No hay problemas, Señor Legacy. Miro la señorita con las ninas. La elle ayudame. Como se dice', eh . . . muchas gracias en inglés?"

"Un momento, por favor. Un momento." Legacy felt that he had better explain what was going on to Octavia, who watched them con- versing like old friends. "Octavia, this is Maria. She's the evening man- ager here and a very sweet lady. I asked her what the problem was. She just wanted to say thank you for helping her children with the books while she worked. Believe it or not, her English is better when she's not concentrating so hard." Maria nodded and grinned through his entire explanation. She saw the way he looked at Octavia and didn't have to speak the language well to see sparks flying in front of her. As for Octavia, another treat had seemed to fall out of the sky regarding Legacy. He was actually fluent in Spanish, not merely displaying the books to perpetrate a facade.

"That was nice of her Legacy. Tell her it was nothing. I love kids."

He turned back to Maria. "No hay de que." Then Maria's nose started to grow. She had also seen the way Octavia was throwing enamored glances at Legacy.

"Está la esposa futura?" Maria asked if Octavia was the wife-to-be. Her tone was low and sneaky, slightly ashamed for talking about the woman like she wasn't standing there. Octavia's disposition changed as her head teetered back and forth between them.

"Ya no sé," he offered, laughing. "Pero podré decirlo mañana." Legacy replied that he didn't know about Octavia yet, but he would have a clearer idea by tomorrow.

Legacy's date grabbed him by the arm and pulled him out the door. Maria giggled with her hands over her mouth as the pretty lady dragged Legacy onto the sidewalk.

"Qué lástima!" *What a pity,* Octavia spat. Legacy was surprised, hoping that she had not understood his entire conversation with Maria. "Hablo español muy bueno y yo sé ahora," she continued. "Ahora!" Legacy was at a loss for words but Octavia had plenty of them, in both languages. "It is such a pity that you'd talk over me like I wasn't there. Maybe the next time someone puts you on the spot, you handle it better than you just did. And what exactly did you mean, telling Maria you'll know by tomorrow? What do you think you'll have accomplished between now and then? Huh?" Legacy didn't flinch. His expression remained blank. "Well, it can't be too much, because you still haven't fed me dinner and I'm so hungry I could eat a horse." Not sure what his next move would be, Legacy remained planted on the concrete in silence until Octavia snapped her finger to direct him. "Meet me at the Jeep. I need to get my purse." He was on his way to doing as ordered when she snapped at him a second time. "By the way, *señor*, you could use a little work on your verb conjugations. Sounded a bit like second-year Spanish to me."

Taking a minute to formally introduce herself to Maria, Octavia let her know that she wasn't upset by their disregard when they spoke about her jokingly, thinking she couldn't comprehend what was said. Octavia also felt the need to clarify something with the woman on the outside nosing her way in. She was diplomatic when she affirmed who would be the one deciding how, when, and where the relationship moved forward, or if it would be going anywhere at all. Maria giggled again, then waved goodbye to Legacy, who was languishing next to the car, in exile.

"What time will Maria lock up?" Octavia asked, backing out of the parking lot. "I am so hungry." When Legacy didn't answer, she was forced to hold in a whopping grin. He wasn't the only one with a lot on the ball. In their battle of wits, round three went to the pretty lady.

"She'll close up in about five minutes but the service will package and deliver my things," he answered eventually. Octavia headed north on Greenville Avenue. Legacy enjoyed her profile as she kept her eyes on the road, making it harder for him to step up to the plate and give her what was due, an apology and her props. "Uh . . . I'm sorry for discussing you like you were a child and the worst part is, I can't stand it when other people do that to me. It was thoughtless and not too bright to talk about you like you weren't an adult."

"A grown woman!" she insisted, with her lips pursed.

"A grown woman who hablas español, very well. Muy, muy bueno."

"That's right, you don't know what I might come out with next." She was really feeling herself now.

"I'd like to be around for it . . . when you do. What-ever, whenever, where-ever. I just need to know if you can forgive me for being thoughtless and underestimating you."

Octavia replayed his soft heartfelt words, then abruptly pulled the vehicle to the shoulder of the road, then pushed the gearshift in park and pressed the hazard button to kick on the flashing taillights. "What did you say to me?"

"I was trying to apologize. If you want me to do it a thousands more times, I will."

"No, no. You said something about wanting to be around for . . ." She couldn't be sure of his exact words.

"Oh, that. I was just sayin' that I'd like to be doing whatever you're doing, whenever you're doing it and wherever you're doing it."

Remembering the conversation she had with Cee-Cee and Truest over lunch, Octavia took a deep breath. She'd practically said those same words then, although it now seemed like days ago instead of hours. If this was a dream, she wasn't ready to awaken from it.

"Octavia, this probably isn't the best place to have this discussion." The avenue was busy, too busy to be idled on the side of the road as cars whizzed by. She agreed, maneuvered the vehicle back into traffic, then pulled into a convenience-store parking lot. She stopped and climbed out without saying as much as a word before walking around to his side of the automobile.

"Legacy, maybe I've waited too long to eat. My head is swimming. Would you mind driving . . . to the restaurant?"

"Sure, seeing how it's my fault for keeping you away from your dinner. I know of a nice place near here. What are you in the mood for?"

"When I said I was hungry enough to eat a horse, I was not playing with you. Dip Mr. Ed in some hot sauce and it's on."

Legacy pulled a small flip phone from his jacket pocket. He dialed a number then pressed the send button. "Hey, Rudy. This is Legacy. How's it going? Good, glad to hear it. And the kids? Hey listen, I have a beautiful woman with me and she's starving. Yeah, it's my fault, so

I'm trying to make it up to her. Is the kitchen still open? What is it? No, it's just the two of us. That's excellent, the best seat in the house. Okay, we'll be right over." As soon as he flipped off the phone, Legacy made a U-turn and took off in the other direction toward downtown. The look on his face suggested that he had something up his sleeve. "I hope you like Italian," Legacy said with a promising wink.

Within a few minutes the fabulously constructed American Airlines Center loomed over them. It was the entertainment showcase of the Southwest and home to the Dallas Mavericks basketball organization. Octavia had been there for a concert or two before, but no events were scheduled that evening. "Legacy, I thought we were going to a restaurant. I didn't know this place served anything but fried appetizers and popcorn."

"They have one of the best chefs in the country cooking for the team. The Maverick's owner, Mark Cuban, takes care of his players. Only the best." Although uncomfortable with having a late dinner inside a basketball arena, a wealth of anxiety gnawed at Octavia when a security guard unlocked the closed facility to welcome them in. "Thanks, Thomas, this is Octavia. She's a new friend of mine."

"Hey there, Legacy. Ma'am," saluted the guard.

After they exchanged a firm grip, Legacy stood back to get a good look at him. "You're still on that diet, I see." The squatly built white man in his midforties seemed generally happy to see Legacy. "Yep, lost fifty pounds so far, thanks to you. Rudy sees to it that I keep it up. He won't let me near the heavy stuff. Go 'head on, he's ready for you on the circle."

"Great, I bet there'll be way too much food. He thinks everybody eats like those seven-footers he feeds twice a week. Be good to yourself, Thomas. Afterwards, we'll let ourselves out." He and Octavia started off toward the tunnel door on the lower level.

"Oh, Legacy, I almost forgot." The security officer hustled over to them before they entered the tunnel. "The wife would kill me if she knew I talked to you and didn't thank you again for what you did. Corey's doing better now and Cindy says we're never selling that house. There's no way we can repay you so . . ." He stopped talking when the need to sniffle attacked him. Octavia could have sworn she saw that grown man choke back on his tears.

"Come on, Thomas, you're making me look like a nice guy in front of my date and I've got her thinking I'm a heathen," Legacy joked. Don't ruin it for me."

The oversentimental guard shook Legacy's hand again, this time for an extended period. Now Octavia was itching to hear all about what had spawned the wealth of emotion. "Ma'am, you've got a great guy here," he told Octavia. "They don't make 'em like this anymore."

She hesitated briefly, not yet ready to claim the great guy for her own. "Uh, thank you Thomas. I'll . . . keep that in mind."

"You'd be smart to. You two kids enjoy your dinner." He pulled out a stack of tissue and tooted his nose loudly into it. Octavia turned around when she heard it.

"Well I'll be, he is crying. Legacy, what did you do for his family that brought tears to his eyes?"

"No big deal. His boy was sick a while back and had to stay at the hospital for two months. I heard he was going to be sent home, so I wanted to do something nice for him."

"So you're going to make me ask you again?" She didn't like the runaround he was laying on thick.

"It was nothing. I just threw some paint up on the wall in his son's room. Superheros and stuff like that. You know, boy stuff." What Legacy omitted was that he'd designed a masterpiece, covering every inch of the child's room from ceiling to floor. After he'd finished, neighbors came in droves to see the room designed in a 3-D comic-book motif, including villains and battle scenes. The *Dallas Morning News* had put together a full-page spread with photographs to highlight the wonderful welcome-home gift. He declined to grant an interview for the piece because he didn't do it for the hype of accolades. Anonymously, he submitted a one-line quote. "He's a good kid who would have done the same for someone in need."

Octavia suspected there was more to the story Legacy downplayed as a random act of kindness. She didn't push but it was pulling at her from the inside, tugging at her like an important to-do that couldn't be crossed off the list until it had been completed. They entered the stadium through two enormously tall metal doors. Legacy expected her to inquire about the questions that had to be running through her mind, but she reserved them. She was content at the moment to go along for the ride. They entered a long hollow tunnel painted pure white with silver and dark blue brushstrokes along the walls in the form of a swoosh, like the Nike symbol. As they emerged from the carpeted walkway, a gray cement floor was beneath their feet, which lead to a large polished rectangular hardwood surface. When it occurred to Octavia that they were actually about to step onto the Dallas Mavericks' basketball court, she pulled off her leather hard-sole shoes, so as not to scratch the surface, and let them dangle from her fingers. Legacy looked down at the rubber bottoms of his boots and then at Octavia's toes wiggling inside a pair of brown nylon stockings. "Here. Get on," Legacy offered as he bent over so that she could climb onto his back. Without hesitation she hopped on and threw her arms around his neck as if she'd done it a million times. Like a little girl being packed around by her older brother, she enjoyed the sensation while taking in the awesome view of the state-of-the-art facility from ground level, the fresh scent of his cologne casting a fine veil over her other senses.

She noticed a spotlight shining a beam down from the rafters that landed on a small cloth-covered dinner table planted in the middle of the court, right over the team's wild-stallion logo. The table was set for two, with an intimate candlelit centerpiece. Legacy's astonishment was mirrored by Octavia. She slid down his back as a heavy brown-haired man appeared from the darkness pushing a stainless steel cart on wheels toward them. He wore a fluffy white chef's hat, apron, and pants designed in a houndstooth check. Octavia peered up at her date, with light dancing off her eyes. She couldn't have imagined anything of this magnitude if she'd tried. Nothing like this had happened to her or anyone else she knew. The grandeur wasn't an illusion. It was real and meant for her consumption.

"Good evening," the man saluted. "Legacy Childs, a party of two?"

Octavia squirmed with excitement. "That's us," she squealed, as if they weren't the only ones there. "Childs, party of two."

"Hi-ya doing, Rudy?" Legacy announced, grinning uncomfortably. "This is Octavia, the lady I told you about. Octavia, this is Rudy Slantiano, the team's personal chef. I hear he can really cook," he added in jest. The chef took his bow, then quickly added dinner plates and bread saucers.

Watching the handsome man organize the flatware, Octavia looked up at Legacy again and squeezed his hand tightly. "Hey, how'd you pull this off? You do a favor for Rudy, too?"

"I didn't expect an extravagant candlelit dinner when I mentioned that I'd met a special someone who I wanted to impress. I'm not sure what Rudy has in store for me to compensate him for this one, but it is really going to cost me."

"I'm not sure what that means, but consider that special someone impressed."

After a lovely prepared dish consisting of manicotti, cheese potatoes and asparagus spears had been served, Rudy poured two glasses of blush wine and filled the water glasses as well. "Will there be anything else this evening?" he asked, standing at attention. "Then enjoy your dinner, compliments of the house and might I add, Mr. Childs, that the lady is as beautiful as you promised she would be."

Legacy turned blood-red despite trying to hide his embarrassment.

Octavia thought it was cute the way he refused to make eye contact with her sitting across from him at the quaint table. "Thanks, Rudy, but you're over doing it."

"That is the only way to do it, sir," Rudy replied, still piling it on thick. "Bon appétit."

As soon as Rudy made himself scarce by disappearing into the same dark surroundings he had appeared from, Legacy gave the entire moment a second to sink in. "Yep, this is really going to cost me."

Octavia chuckled hard. She was genuinely happy that it was she who was sitting there with the most adorable man she'd ever laid eyes on instead of hearing about an evening like this second-hand at the beauty shop from some other woman who'd benefited from sharing Legacy's company. She was filled to the top, like a blushing bride in a white gown and the whole bit, who'd waited eons for her wedding day and it finally arrived. No one had ever thought enough of her to go to such great measures for the sake of making a good impression. And like most brides, she hoped that the illusion of Shangri-la would still be intact long after the rice had been swept away. Likewise, she hoped the man she was falling head-over-heels for remained all he seemed cracked up to be, a simple man who didn't need compensating factors to make her happy. She also hoped that he would continue to seek her company once the wrapper was removed from their new association. There was always the outside chance that he wouldn't. But at the same moment, concerns like that had to wait. Nothing was going to steal her enjoyment while she basked in it, so she wiggled her toes and relished a scrumptious dinner with a vastly different kind of man than she was accustomed to, the kind of man that books are written about and Hollywood has committed billions to personify on the silver screen, the same kind of man that she always wanted for herself.

17

Something to Hide

Over dinner, Legacy stared across the table, remembering Octavia sleeping in the café. That night, he'd wanted to wait until she awoke so he could claim his favorite table and have his usual masterpiece signature dinner of steak, well done, and hard scrambled eggs. Instead she'd continued her marathon nap until something else happened. He'd begun to study her in the midst of a peaceful sleep, the curves in her face, the texture and color of her skin. Then another thing happened. When he decided to chalk it up as a bad idea to stick around, he tried to leave several times. The harder he tried, the harder it became to deny just how much he wanted to stay. Octavia wasn't the first woman who stood in his way of having dinner in his usual venue, but she was the first and only one who had him wanting to hear her speak, the resonance in her voice, and her laughter's pitch, but most of all he was netted in the wonderment of what she might be like.

Legacy was still wondering as he made small talk, continually tossing the conversation back on Octavia's plate. "I notice you don't talk about yourself. Got something to hide?" she asked before sipping from her wine glass.

"No, nothing worth mentioning. I like talking about you and watching your cute lips flatten out when you really get excited. You're very good at setting up a story. I like that, makes me feel like I was there."

She'd told him a story that stuck to him like gum to his sole on a hot summer day. "I must have been seven or eight at the time and my class went on this field trip to the movies. I wanted to go so bad but my parents didn't have two dollars to spare, so I was the only one left behind. I ended up spending the entire afternoon sitting in the nurse's office crying my eyes out, imagining all the fun the other kids were having without me. Oh man, I'd forgotten about that. Wow, the feature was *Snow White and the Seven Dwarfs*. That's probably why I can't stand little men now. Happy, Doppy, Doc, Mini-Me . . . none of 'em." Legacy nearly dribbled water down his chin when she added the character Mini-Me along with the famous dwarfs she despised for no fault of their own.

She told other stories just as endearing, but not any of them floored him like the tale of a little girl having to miss out due to a lack of money. It reminded him of all the things he went without while growing up, having to count on an occasional Christmas gift from some bleeding heart who wanted to feel good about helping out underprivileged children during the holidays. That was a part of his life he often made efforts to forget but couldn't. Instead, those experiences helped to make him the kind and generous man he came to be, incrementally shaping his character along the way. Each time he was forced to go without, he became more determined to help others one day, when he had the money.

Legacy traded smiles with Octavia and laughed each time Rudy appeared from the shadows to refill their water glasses and later to insist they make a selection from a gourmet platter of decadent deserts. After his persistence prevailed, Octavia spoon-fed her potential leading man with the only spoon Rudy provided.

Because there wasn't much of an opportunity to delve deeper into the type of grown-folk conversation that first dates generally consist of, due to Rudy listening in the wings, Octavia waited until they had returned to Legacy's home. She followed him to the front door, not wanting the evening to end but not quite settled with the idea of getting into something that might lead to finding her clothes spread across his bedroom floor and regretting it by morning. This man was different, so different that Octavia felt good about holding back, and hopefully onto this man she'd already grown to admire.

Legacy unlocked the deadbolt and stepped inside. "I want to thank you for your time and company tonight. You've probably had a long day and didn't plan on giving what was left of it to me so, good night."

Good night? Oh, hell, no. "What, you're not inviting a sistah in?" Her expression displayed ample measures of disbelief and disenfranchisement.

"It is late and I realized that I neglected to get a confirmation on whether you were spoken for or not. I got involved with another man's woman before and it wasn't pretty." Octavia couldn't have guessed what Legacy meant about his last girlfriend's love interest, Simpson Stone, who had been a trifling rich blueblood with a predilection for sleeping with men, too. Legacy was so stricken with grief when the woman died from AIDS complications that he made a phone call to a mobster associate and informed him how Simpson was skimming money in their illegal drug partnership. Although Legacy didn't pull the trigger himself, he knew what outcome would transpire after the damaging phone call was made. He later regretted causing the man's death, but he wasn't sorry that he did what he thought was right. Simpson had known he had the disease but continued to have unprotected sex with the woman Legacy loved. He'd rationalized it as a necessary evil and hadn't lost one night's sleep over it.

"It couldn't have been all that serious," Octavia surmised incorrectly.

"Alright, don't say I didn't warn you," he told her. "And, it seems yet again you have avoided the question. Since I don't have time for boy-girl-boy dramatics, it's like I said. Thanks for your time." He motioned to close the door.

Octavia threw her hands up to stop him. "Hold on a minute! I'll be honest with you. I am kinda seeing someone right now but it's not . . . it's not working out."

Legacy was visibly disappointed by the sugarcoated update. "Oh, you're *kinda* seeing someone? Holla back when you're not." In a strictly businesslike manner, he shut the door and walked away. Octavia wasn't sure how to feel, but in a split second she found herself knocking on both of the doors, the door that shut her out of his house and the other one that potentially shut her out of his life. Octavia's chest heaved when Legacy returned to open the door, wondering why she felt the need to stick around after she had been dismissed.

"Yes, did you forget something?" Legacy asked. His voice was void of malice, but the same shroud of disappointment remained evident while he waited for her to say whatever it was she needed to get off her chest.

"I'm not," Octavia stated sullenly.

"Excuse me?"

She rocked on the balls of her feet, agitated and apologetic. "I said . . . I'm not. You told me to holla back when I wasn't seeing anyone. Well, now I'm not."

"Just like that?" Legacy asked, studying her face for signs of uncertainty.

In essence, he was asking her if she knew what she was doing and if she meant it. Octavia had to decide if what she stood to gain was more promising than what she was giving up. She remembered a conversation she had with her mother regarding the right time to let a bad thing go on about its business. She had told her, when you have more reasons to go than to stay, it's a good indication that the time in question has arrived. Octavia considered the years she'd spent waiting for I. Rome. And here it was staring her in the face. If it wasn't the most exciting thing to come her way, she was willing to try it out until something better happened by.

When all of her hardheaded indecisions had evaporated, she nodded, assured. Standing on the line she thought she'd never have to cross, she bet it all on what she stood to gain. "Yes, Legacy, just like that."

"Well, I guess you'd better come on in out of the cold then." Octavia graciously accepted his invitation. She stepped inside and closed the door behind her. "You'll find a spare key on the desk, if you want it. Excuse me, I have to check on a few things."

It seems that her mother's wisdom paid dividends once again. It was the right time to let I. Rome go and move on with her life. Octavia had a key to Legacy's humble abode to show for making a sound assessment of her future. By granting her the right to come and go as she pleased, Legacy surrendered plans for seeing anyone else. The fact that she didn't have to ask or wait years for him to break down and give in made her giddy. So far, everything about him was covered in charm and sprinkled with generosity. Getting to know him was simply delectable and Octavia was confident for the first time in her life that she would not have to share. Seeing as how she looked forward to spending extended periods of time there, she sought to ease the tension caused by the, albeit brief, moment of fear outside by running her fingertips over a variety of things belonging to the man of the house. She touched a leather binocular case and a multicolored globe that appeared to have been painted while it was still spinning. Then she closed her eyes and held her thin fingers out, searching for the bare wall. Legacy watched her as she began walking parallel to it with her eager fingers leading the way. He had seen a blind woman duplicate the act while at an art museum several years ago. Later he learned that people who had either lost their sight or needed more tactile stimuli to serve as an information source, often preferred a light touch to using their eyes as the sole reference. What she planned on gleaning from the experience was a mystery, but that didn't stop Legacy from enjoying the exercise just the same.

Slowly Octavia traveled along the wall until she came to the window where the telescope was anchored. She peeked in the lens. "Hey, Twinkle. You'd better get yourself another man. 'Cause girlfriend, this one belongs to me now."

Legacy overheard the declaration although he didn't let on after he eased up behind her. "What's on your mind, sweetheart?"

Octavia took her eye from the contraption and stood up, then allowed her body to lean against his. Instinctively he wrapped his strong arms around her shoulders and locked them, hand to wrist. Her eyes closed before she could beg them not to. His embrace felt better than good. It felt like an old but treasured pair of jeans, broken in to conform to her curves after years of wear. His warm embrace felt like it belonged to her and would not fit anyone else as perfectly.

"Ooh. Sweetheart?" she teased. "Is that sweetheart like you call all women sweetheart 'cause you're a nice guy or the kinda sweetheart that's only meant for me?" Legacy chuckled softly while planting a tender kiss on the crown of her head. "It was the "you're the only woman I've ever considered giving a key" kinda sweetheart."

"Wow. That's even better," Octavia cooed, still with her back to him, intimately sharing the same space. "Legacy, when does a person know if they've met their soul mate?"

"Soul mates? That's deep. Dinner wasn't that good."

"Don't joke. I'm serious."

"Well, if I was one to believe in the legitimacy of soul mates, I'd have to say . . . if a person has to ask, chances are she probably hasn't met him yet."

Octavia pondered a moment to digest his answer. "I guess you're right. That would be kinda hard to miss, huh?" She nuzzled closer against him, if it were possible to get any closer. She envisioned waking up with her face against his developed chest and falling asleep to something a little lower and a lot harder.

"If it's the real thing," he added in a whispered tone. "Something like that has got to be destined."

"Like a woman meeting a man by running over him with her Jeep?"

"Mmm-hm, something like that, or maybe a man creating his own destiny, like I did to meet you."

When his words pierced the cozy confines of their warm embrace, Octavia turned to face him. She playfully parked her hands on her narrow hips and rolled her eyes. "Are you saying that you meant for me to run over your bike that night in the parking lot?"

"And what if I am?"

"Then you owe me four hundred dollars."

"Is that all?"

She softened even more. "Let me think about it. I'll get back to you."

Legacy looked around the guest house, taking inventory. "Just let me know. As you can see, I've got it like that."

"Uhn-uhn, you do not have it like that and besides, I don't need a mountain of things. I need this." She pressed her breast against him, allowed her warm tongue to ramble around his welcoming lips then swooned, wondering if she felt his heart beating against hers or if it was just the echoes of hers racing. In either case, it seemed as though their hearts were beating together.

Just as the heat between them boiled to the point of exploding, Legacy backed off, bracing himself. "Let's uh, give it a break. We'll have plenty of time to do . . . more . . . of that. I'm not going anywhere." He slipped both hands into the front pockets of his jeans, making an unsuccessful attempt to conceal a tremendous erection.

"Nice try, but you couldn't hide that thing if you had three hands," she told him, thrilled that she did excite him when the opportunity presented itself. "However, you might be right about this being a good time for me to call it a night. I almost forgot that I have to go to work in the morning."

"Sweetheart, please be careful going home and give me a ring to let me know you've made it." He pecked her on the lips a second time while on her way out.

"But I don't have your number."

"I left you a message today. Check it when you get there. I was hoping you'd stop by this evening and return my backpack."

Octavia rolled her eyes again. "Let me guess. You purposely left your bag so I would have to see you again, working that whole destiny angle?"

"Now you're catching on. It's like I said, every now and then you have to create some of it for yourself."

"I'm happy that you did. And, I'm even happier that you chose me to share it with. I'll call you when I get home."

Octavia was falling and falling fast. She hadn't given I. Rome a passing thought since Legacy had invited her inside his world and handed over the key. The moon was shining, the sky was clear, and anticipation was oozing out when Octavia's cell phone rang until the word "private" flashed on her readout screen. That all but diminished her after-the-first-kiss buzz when she assumed it was I. Rome. She thought about letting the call go unattended but what if it were Legacy instead. Yes, that was enough to convince her to take the call.

"Hello," she meowed into the receiver, batting her eyelashes.

"Baby girl," a man said, in a semi inquiring tone.

Octavia pressed her lips together, then smacked them. "Yyyeah," was her sullen one-word salutation.

"Baby, it's Isaiah. I've been trying to catch up with you but it seems you've been too busy to return my calls."

"Hey, Isaiah." *Why did I answer this phone*, she asked herself throughout the entire conversation. "Yeah, I've been busy."

"Don't sweat it, I've got you now. Look here, I'll be coming to town soon. I don't know if you've talked to your station manager but I asked that you interview me over dinner, if that's alright with you."

"Oh . . . I got the memo. It came as a shock since months have passed and I haven't heard from you."

" 'Tavia, you sound different. Don't tell me you're changing on me. This is not a good time, baby. If I ever needed you in my corner, it's now. Check it, I have a surprise for you. I think you'll like it. I'm really looking forward to making things up to you. I've grown up and I've made some changes in my personal life. I'm getting a divorce and I'm coming back to do what I should have done years ago. Baby girl, the best memories in my life have been with you. My words might not be coming out right, but I need you to know that I want some more of those memories."

"All right, Isaiah," she said, without signaling a response in one way or another to all that he'd dropped at her feet. "But right now isn't the time for this discussion, either. I need to go."

"Well, we'll talk about it when I get there. And baby, I miss you. There will never be nobody else for me."

Despite his kind words, Octavia was positive that he was still up to no good. She disconnected the call thinking, *nobody else*. His problems had always stemmed from getting involved with *anybody* and *everybody else*.

No sooner had I. Rome heard the dial tone than he punched in another phone number while sipping champagne until Truest's answering machine began suggesting that the caller leave her a message. He gulped the remaining two ounces of Moët, then placed the receiver on its base before crossing through the common area of a high-priced hotel suite. As he strolled into the bedroom, he shrugged a fluffy white bathrobe off his shoulders and grinned devilishly as it fell to the floor. "What time you get off?" he asked the woman getting comfortable beneath the sheets. A front desk clerk's uniform was folded neatly and resting on the chaise lounge next to the bed. The young lady with an alabaster complexion, who had checked him into his room stroked her long blonde hair while staring endlessly at the business end of his question.

"It's been slow tonight, so after I got your call in the lobby I opted out of my shift and took the rest of the evening off."

"Good girl. I like the way you think on your feet. You know, I could always use another publicist."

"Publicist?" she repeated naïvely. "What's that?"

"Oh yeah, you' gonna work out just fine."

Morning came too fast for Octavia's taste. Had it not been for the splendid night she'd spent brushing against the fringes of Legacy's world, Tuesday would have been met with the usual ho-hum obscurity that accompanies perhaps the most useless day of the week. But this was the Tuesday after Legacy, "Tremendous Tuesday" she coined it when Cee-Cee popped by her desk before starting her show.

Starry-eyed and lost in la-la land, Octavia didn't know where to begin with the evening that had left her in a tailspin. Because Cee-Cee's time slot was ten to two, the jog down memory lane had to wait. Unfortunately, what Patricia had to say wouldn't. "Octavia, do you mind stepping into my office when you get a chance?" Her request came across as more of a plea than a demand, which is how her in-office coaching sessions were typically initiated. There was something fishy about the pleasantness in her voice, and Octavia was interested in what this impromptu get-together was about.

"I can do it now, Patricia," she replied suspiciously. "Let me get my notebook and I'll be right there."

"No, there won't be any need for that. We'll just chat, like sistahs." *Like sistahs?* Now Octavia was more than interested; she was troubled.

After a few years in the workforce she had learned by watching others spiral downward in a fiery crash to be troubled when a by-the-book senior manager started acting out of character, whether by limiting extemporaneous conversation at the water cooler or by becoming too friendly. In either case, she knew to steer clear of the flames.

"Yes, ma'am?" she said as she set foot in the boss's office, not positive if she should sit, roll over, fetch the morning paper, or play dead.

"Please come in and close the door." Patricia sat behind her desk, poised as usual, fingers locked and resting on her broad mahogany desk. Octavia wondered if she should have had a lawyer present and a tape recorder rolling by the tone in her manager's voice. What happened to the sistah-talk they were supposed to have? She hadn't been there two seconds and already had orders to close the door.

While Octavia made her way across the plush carpet, Patricia motioned with an open hand for her to have a seat. The expensive desk was absent of important-looking documents that normally decorated it when such a closed-door affair was called to order, so Octavia waited on Patricia to make the first move. "You're probably at a loss as to why I asked you to meet with me. Yesterday I was out of line, and so was the company, for suggesting that you put yourself in a compromising position and accept a date with I. Rome. We discussed it, the owner and myself, and I was against it from the start." Octavia sat there hoping she'd hurry up and make a point. "I'll say it again. I'm against it and will understand fully if you change your mind and decline." Octavia didn't have a clue where this was going but continued to listen attentively. "I just needed you to know that I stand behind you. The only reason I brought the proposition to you in the first place was . . ." She hesitated awkwardly, allowing her eyes to fall on the blank space where the important-looking documents would have been. "Well, it's been rumored for some time here at the station that you and I. Rome have or had a *relationship* of some kind."

Patricia paused, her eyes rose in order to read her subordinate's reaction, but Octavia remained aloof intentionally, still waiting on that seemingly elusive point to be made. Rumors were common at the office, Octavia was well aware of that, but she refused to cop to it at first pass. It was bad enough when the deejays hinted around to hearing *the rumor,* but having the boss-lady call her in and spring it on her like that caught her in a net of mixed emotions. She had one guess how *the rumor* worked its way to the top. The woman she most respected was all but asking her to lay it on the line for her company, since it was common knowledge that she'd been laying on her back for personal gratification.

When more time had passed than was typically allotted between two people engaged in a dialog, Octavia assumed it was her turn to foster the conversation. "I'm somewhat confused. Are you asking me if the gossip about me seeing Isiah Rome is true, or are you asking me if I've changed my mind about interviewing him over dinner?" Patricia's eyes laid down on her for a second time when she realized how out of line the entire conversation had been and should not have occurred on office time. That was not her style. The workplace was reserved for making things happen, not digging into someone's personal life, and inquiring about what actually had or had not been the case, then subsequently attempt to skew the details to benefit herself.

Having seconds thoughts about calling the meeting, Patricia cleared her throat, followed by a deep exhale. "I uh . . . I'm simply saying that I respect your decision, but in all honesty, I would feel better about the situation if you two were currently involved."

Octavia's eyes widened when the figurative lightbulb finally flashed on over her head. "So, you want to be let off the hook?"

"Precisely," admitted Patricia in a rushed manner.

"I understand."

Octavia looked away momentarily. She felt the need to let Patricia fry in her own grease while turning up the heat and to enjoy perhaps the only time she would be the one mixing the batter instead of the one being dipped in it. "Not that it is any of your business or any of the gossip's here at the station, but I will say this. I make no apologies for my relationship with a married man who changes his women like he changes his clothes but we are friends now—nothing else. I have not been with him in months and, quite frankly, I had not planned to. Actually, I've decided not to see him again on any level, but this will give me the opportunity to let things go amicably, after the interview, of course. I guess what I'm *simply saying* is, you can consider yourself, for all intents and purposes, off the hook."

After receiving her pardon, Patricia managed a quarter-smile, then pushed away from her desk. "Then why do I still feel like a fish out of water?"

"Because you've never let anything get in the way of protocol, as it should be. That's the way you're put together." Satisfied, Octavia turned her back to exit the office. She'd held her own and came away smelling like a rose, with her dignity still intact.

"Octavia!" Patricia called out from behind her desk. "One other thing. I also wanted to tell you that your raise has been approved, but I'll expect you to diligently seek the next level of advancement to properly enhance your journalistic talents. You and I both know that you've topped out here. Oh yeah, and thank you."

"Don't mention it."

"I didn't plan to." The quarter-smile made another brief appearance before running scared.

Octavia left the office laughing on the inside while restraining the glee that nearly escaped from the corners of her mouth. Business as usual had been restored and Patricia Maria Stapleton actually said thank you. Tremendous Tuesday forged ahead with great optimism, but Octavia couldn't stop contemplating whether she'd just been complimented or condemned. "Diligently seek the next level of advancement," she heard herself say, repeating Patricia's exact words. "Does that mean I'm fired?" It had better not, because she was going to be working overtime trying to figure out a way to go on a date with a not-so-distant lover when her new romantic interest had almost put his brand on her the night before. Now who was in the grease?

A dozen brilliantly yellow tulips and a matching greeting card rested on Octavia's desk when she returned. The card read: "Thanks for a wonderful night. Use the key. L." She looked around, thinking just maybe he had delivered them personally. Her other thought was how less expensive tulips were than roses and how he'd made the most of his meager finances.

Little work was attempted throughout the rest of the morning. Octavia sat huddled at her desk, rearranging the flowers in the crimson vase. She thought, how nice it was to receive flowers without the pressure of Valentine's Day or her birthday goading a man from the other end. "Just because" flowers were the best kind, because she didn't have to do anything in order to receive them and she didn't have to wait on a special occasion or the next he'd-better-send-me-flowers day to roll around.

18

They're Outta That!

Floreese walked the second floor, bobbing his head to the silent funky beat no doubt going on inside it. Benny was in perfect step behind him, imitating his cool homeboy strut as best he could, having once been told that being a good deejay came by feeling the music even when there wasn't any. He took that advice literally.

"Hey, Octavia. Nice flowers. Ole boy couldn't afford roses?" Floreese assumed, while reaching over her to touch them. Octavia frowned at the thoughtless comment before she blocked his attempt with a brash slap on his rusty knuckles. "Ouch!" he wailed. "I wish I would send my girl anything but roses. That's why I hate Valentine's Day. They always tryna get in a brotha's pocket."

"Yeah!" Benny chimed loudly.

"Not that you'd believe me, but you ought to try it sometime and see what it gets you in return," suggested Octavia.

"Uh-uh. I did a promo for Flowers-R-Us one time and had 'em send my lady a bunch of carnations to her office." He put up his dukes and started swinging. "She went off on me, talking about I must have done something wrong to be guilty for or else I wouldn't have sent 'em." Octavia flashed him an I-bet-she-was-right expression as if she were sticking up for all women in general. "Okay, so she was right but she didn't know with who. She was just guessin'. Ain't that right, Benny?"

"Yeah!"

"Benny, do yourself a favor and find someone else to hang with because some of Flo's trife' might rub off on you," Octavia advised with a slight head tilt. "Anyway, I thought you were assigned to pal around to Alphonzo this week."

Floreese was offended. True enough, he didn't have the charisma that Alphonzo was blessed with or the above-average physical appearance, but he could hold his own in the pit. "Benny's my white shadow and I'm gonna teach him everything, even the bad stuff about black folk that we don't want white people to know. Ain't that right, Benny?"

"Yeah!" Benny grinned graciously, then he became suspicious. "Really?"

"Nah, I'm just trippin'. Unless you're gonna trade secrets, cause I need to fix my credit."

Octavia had had her fill of double trouble. They belonged together. One was short on common sense and the other shy on insight. When Floreese made another stab at feeling up her tulips, she objected. "Why are y'all still here?"

"Forget you then," Floreese retorted, like a disenchanted five-year-old. "We came by to take you to lunch. The word is out about you doing that I. Rome thing. Much respect for that."

As Benny opened his mouth, Octavia spun around in her chair. "Benny, if you start with that *yeah* mess again, I'm going to scream and ain't no telling what's going to jump off after the screaming is done." On cue, he slammed his mouth shut. "Alright then. Thank you, Floreese. Much appreciated."

"Cool. Let us treat you to some grub, then."

"Where are y'all headed?" Not that Octavia was going anywhere with those two, even if they were having the last supper with Jesus himself, but humoring them seemed harmless.

"We're gonnna run on over to Cuzzin Cora's for some soul food," replied Floreese, massaging his empty belly.

"Nuh-uh, not again," Benny argued. "We went there yesterday and it took thirty minutes to get our eat on. Nah, Flo. I'm not going through that again. It was aggravating as hell. Every time they brought a plate out from the kitchen, I got all worked up and I know it was 'cause I'm white they took their time serving us. And, when my food finally came, it was cold!"

"That's 'cause you ordered a South Side Sub chilled to order." Floreese tried to represent in the restaurant in the owner's stead but Benny's evil stare stopped him dead. "Okay, you' right. It was cold, but next time you need to order a hot plate. Fish and grits or chicken and waffles, sumthin' like that."

For the sake of avoiding a fight, Octavia let their disagreement slide. "Cuzzin Cora's is tempting, guys, but I think I'll pass. Thanks for offering, though."

"Suit yourself. This time, we'll get there before they run out of waffles," Floreese added, noting the time on his watch.

"Please, Flo, don't make me go back there. That mean lady at the register looks just like Mike Mooney from the mailroom and he can't stand white people. Dawg, they've got to be related. They have the same mustache and everything." They both marched off, huffing up a storm, Octavia laughed when she overheard Benny's complaints regarding the neighborhood haven for patrons who didn't mind a good meal served up with much attitude. Truth be told, Cuzzin Cora's was known for excellent home-cooked cuisine, but it also had been accused of taking their own sweet time serving customers of European descent. They were just doing their part to even things out.

Patiently waiting on Cee-Cee to come out of the pit, Octavia's project of finding things to busy herself with became a job all in itself so she looked over the notes she'd taken from the previous months on at the Hamilton Park Writer's Forum. Struggling novelists and several other aspiring writers who sought to pen what plagued their minds met once a month to talk about writing and share what actually had made it to paper since the last session. She enjoyed the forum because it allowed writers to grow from open discussions and hone their crafts while having a published author help them make the bridge from wanting a book deal to getting one. Generally, she walked away from it with more insight than information, because the facilitating author seemed to thoroughly enjoy the sound of his own voice. But the forum was free and, more importantly, inspiring, so Octavia continued to wade through his lengthy dissertations on the publishing biz to gather nuggets to include in her master's thesis.

"How'd you like that new one from P. Diddy?" Cee-Cee hummed rhetorically into the microphone. "I know you did because I'm still dancing and the song stopped five seconds ago. You are jamming to the Hot 100, the Monster Beats, and I'm Cee-Cee Lovely. It's one o'clock in the P.M. and I'm hungry. Somebody send me a plate," she jested. "Wait a minute, I have a call." She looped the tape to record as the caller held. "This is Cee-Cee, what's for lunch?"

"Hey, Cee-Cee, this Floreese from the Hot 100 and formally of the Eb and Flo dynamic duo. If y'all haven't heard, Laz'rus had to take an unscheduled vacation. Had something to do with coming up short. You can catch me in his slot from ten to four in the mornin' and we can do the damn thing. Please believe me."

"Ooh, sounds like a party, Flo," Cee-Cee howled, as she danced to the instrumental hook from Heather Hadley's latest chart-climber. "Now that you got that shameless plug out of the way, our peeps in the streets want to know . . . *what's for lunch?*" She tried to keep him on task for her section of the show where listeners called in to brag about what they'd eaten before returning to the job and fight all afternoon to stay awake.

"Check this out, Cee-Cee. Since you're always looking out for our listeners I'ma hook you up."

"It's not my birthday but we can act like it, anyway. What's on the menu?"

"Cee-Cee, it ain't even like that. I'm at Cuzzin Cora's and the menu for today is Chicken pot pie, fried chicken, chicken and dumplings, baked chicken and chicken surprise . . . that's yesterday's chicken. Surprise!"

"I guess I'll have the chicken," she said underneath the comical rapture. "Put Ms. Cora on so I can phone in my order."

"Hold on." Floreese pulled his ear away from the receiver while standing at the cash register. "Cuzzin Co-ra!" he yelled above the dining room noise. "Cuzzin Cora!"

The older black woman put both meaty balled-up fists on her thick hips and glared at Floreese before she took a step toward the phone. "Who's that holl'in up in hur? This ain't Pappadeaux's. Ain't yo' mama ever told you to use yo' indo's voice when you indo's? And who said I was yo' cuzzin, anyway? Just 'cause the sign say Cuzzin Cora's don't mean nuthin'. You don't look like none of my peeples." Benny stood back, trying not to bust a gut, thinking the whole time that he was glad it wasn't him getting played like that over the airwaves. Besides, Cuzzin Cora did look just like Mike Mooney from the mailroom. Just like him, especially around the mustache.

"Uh . . . *Ms.* Cora," Floreese said, backpedaling. "Could you please take the phone, ma'am? We got you live on the air at the Hot 100. Cee-Cee Lovely wants to holler at'cha."

"Speakin' of holl'n. If'n you come up in hur agin holl'n like you ain't got no home train'n," she pointed downward at her feet, wrapped inside a pair of lime green runover fuzzy house slippers, "you'll leave with these tens stuck where the sun don't shine. I don't cur if you leave hur hungrier than a hostage neither. Give me that phone and let me talk to Cee-Cee." Now, the entire restaurant listened in as someone from the hostess stand turned up the radio, then shoved a microphone in front of it.

"Hello, is this Cuzzin Cora?" Cee-Cee inquired with a grave attempt at holding it together.

"Yeah, it's me. Hi-ya doin'?"

"Good, and you, ma'am?"

"These kids today, I just don't know." Cuzzin Cora threw her right hand on her ample hip again and shot another stinging leer at Floreese. "I've been better, that's for sho', but the Lawd is good so I won't complain. Uh-huh, what can I do you for today? Got lots of hungry mouths to feed."

"Cuzzin Cora, this is Cee-Cee Lovely from the Hot 100 radio show. You're live on the air."

Suddenly, the woman perked up and straightened her apron. She struck a pose as if someone had rolled up on her with a television camera crew. "Cee-Cee Lovely? Is that really you? Don't play with me now. I loves me some Cee-Cee Lovely. The way you say "What's for lunch" gets me er'ry time."

"Cuzzin, that's why I had them call me from your restaurant. I want to phone my order in and have Floreese and Benny bring me back a plate."

The older woman looked from side to side. "Who? I hope you ain't talkin' about this potato-head fella and the scurd white boy he got wit' him."

As soon as Cee-Cee caught her breath from laughing, she tried to save the boys. "Yes, ma'am, I'm afraid that sounds just like the two I sent over. Please take it easy on them."

"Well, tater-head is standing on my last good nerve and the white boy, he don't say nuthin'. Heck. I thought he was a mute. Sho' honey, I'll do any thang fuh you, Cee-Cee. Tell Cuzzin what you hungry fuh and I'll wrap it up in some wax paper real tight so these two don't botha it none."

"Alright, let's get cracking." Cee-Cee licked her lips, anticipating. "Cuzzin Cora?"

"Yes, honey, I's ready."

"Are candy yams on the menu today?"

"Uhm-hm, but we outta that. 'Used all the yams for the sweet potato pies."

"How about a side of collard greens? I just love your collard greens."

"Yeah, they's on the today's menu."

"Good, I'll have some."

"Naw, you won't."

"Why not, ma'am?"

"'Cause we outta that, too."

They went back and forth. No matter what Cee-Cee ordered, they were out of it. She didn't know whether to be frustrated or keep right on laughing at the whole thing. While she was trying to decide which, the radio station's phone lines lit up like a switchboard at the phone company. Cuzzin Cora was an instant hit. Patricia opened the door to the pit, silently applauding. She twirled her finger to instruct Cee-Cee to keep it going.

"Cuzzin Cora, maybe you ought to tell me what you do have."

"You could've saved yo'self some trouble if'n you'd said that in the first place, baby. Let's see hur." She put on her reading glasses, which hung around her neck and were attached by an old tan spiraling rotary telephone cord. "The chitt'lins ain't ready yet 'cause they still be'n cleaned back yonder. And the stove's too hot to cook the potpies. Don't nobody wanna get over that hot stove. Now, we do have corn-bread-black-eyed-peas-and-your-English-green-peas-snap-peas-pinto-beans-green-beans-fried-okra and some okra not-so-fried-maccoroni-with-cheese-fried-mashed-taters-taters-not-mashed . . . them-they's uh some of what you might call Julianne, and then pret'near just about er'ry kind of chicken you'd wanna wrap your lips around, baby." After she rattled off her list of menu items, she took a breath and sucked her teeth. There was a resounding ovation inside the down-home eatery.

Cuzzin Cora dipped her bifocals with her index finger, then peered over the top of them and took a bow. "Thank you kindly."

"Whew, it all sounds so delicious," Cee-Cee saluted. "You said a mouthful."

"I usually do, baby. By the way, we also have red kool-aid."

"What flavor?"

"I said red! Red!"

"Tell you what Cuzzin Cora, please fix me up with whatever you think is best and I'll be forever in your debt."

"Like the kids say, it's all good, but you don't have to owe me nuthin'. I'll trade you fuh a shout-out, though. I want to say hey to sistah Cloretta'nem over at the nursin' home and to my play niece down at the welfare office. Don't you let them triflin' heffas get yo' blood pressure up, Daisy. And one last shout to my baby boy Mikey. He's workin' down in the mailroom with y'all over at the station."

Benny was hopping up and down now, frantically tugging on Floreese's shirttail. "I told you. I told you she looked like Mike Mooney. I told you."

"Cee-Cee, I gots to go, child. That white boy you sent is havin' a seizure or sumthin'. Somebody need to call the number fuh 911 or sit him down and shove a stick in his mouth 'for he swallow his tongue." She handed the phone back to Floreese and shuffled her house shoes back to the kitchen, popping gum and singing Negro spirituals. "Mmm-hmmm . . . Jesus on ma' mind."

Floreese scanned the handwritten menu chalkboard. He was elated to find waffles listed as one of the side items of the day. "Cuzzin Cora!" he yelled as the woman passed through the swinging doors. "Cuzzin Cora, can a brotha get some waffles to go with that fried chicken I ordered?"

She ducked out of the kitchen with her thick fists saddled on her hips like before. "I ain't got time for this. Will somebody please tell him?"

"They're outta that!" shouted all the other customers, simultaneously.

"Yeah!" Benny chimed, rubbing it in. "I told you. You wouldn't listen but I told you."

From that day on, Cuzzin Cora's was the talk of the town. Interested diners rushed over to stand in line, hoping to get a shot at that infamous menu board and meet the owner personally. Cora was an instant celebrity. Cee-Cee called her up once a week and had the toughest of times ordering by phone. One guess, they were always outta that!

19

Too Fast, Too Serious

Listening while programming her playlist for the following day, Cee-Cee was amazed by Octavia's date with Legacy, including the stars, the moon, the kiss, and just about every other detail. Cee-Cee was brimming with excitement for her girlfriend, although she caught herself wishing she could have been there to witness things firsthand. "I can't believe all that happened just because you hit him with your car. Hell, if I had known it was that easy, I'd have been hanging outside the fitness center to nail myself a hunk years ago."

Octavia fingered the house key Legacy had given her, that lay flat on her desk. "I'm sayin', but he came clean last night and told me how he engineered the entire thing."

"No, he didn't?"

"I'm afraid so. He said sometimes you have to create your own destiny and he went for his."

Cee-Cee's eyes danced, thinking how clever this Legacy was that she'd heard so much about. She was excited that a real man existed, who went after what he wanted with reckless abandon. "He sure does show initiative. You have to give him that. I like this brotha already." She watched Octavia's expression change like the Texas weather, fast and without notice. "Uh-oh, I don't like that look. What did I say?"

"It's not you. I'm so ahead of myself that I just realized I don't know much about him. You know, no background four-one-one to speak of. On the other hand, the stuff that matters I do know. He's sweet, smart, caring, and thoughtful. Take last night, he was speaking Spanish and didn't think I understood him. He told this woman that he wasn't positive that I was his cup of tea. I had to read his behind."

"Was he surprised when you put that la vida loca on him?"

"Yeah, he was diminished when I let him know that I was not to be played to the left, 'cause you know I'm right." Octavia slapped her a fresh high-five, girl-power style. "He landed on his feet though, Cee-Cee. The man apologized."

"Whuuut?"

"If I'm lyin', I'm flyin' and I ain't never had wings. He said he was sorry and if he had to, he would say it a thousand times to make it right."

"Girl, you'd better conjure up some old Indian spirits to tell you how to hold on to that brotha. A man like that is worth the risk of waking up the dead. I don't see how he's still on the market."

Remembering what Legacy told her about having gotten involved with a woman who was then seeing someone else, Octavia's expression grew dim. "You know, I think he was scarred by a relationship with some lady he busted with another man. He probably needed time to get over it."

"Do you think he is, over it I mean?"

"Over it enough to give me this key to his place." She shot Cee-Cee a sly glance from corner of her eye, then began tickling the edges of the key like she had been for the better part of the day. She hadn't questioned Legacy's motives for giving her the green light so easily, to show up when she felt the need to. Inviting her to come around often and unannounced would give him plenty of opportunities to feel her out, too. Besides, he wanted to keep her close without having to say it.

" 'Tavia, you've got him open like an all-night store. Girl, just be glad you found him first. A man who hands over unlimited visitation privileges is ready to share everything else he has, too."

"That's just it. He doesn't have much of anything. No car, no home. But he must have me open, too. It hasn't crossed my mind to ask him what he does for a living or if he even has a job." She suddenly felt at odds, getting all worked up over everything and nothing. "Do you think I should return the key and back out until . . ."

"Until what? 'Tavia, you're sitting here blushing and you haven't *did the fool* yet? Have you?" Octavia shook her head slowly, as if she resented the fact that Legacy hadn't approached her for sex. "Well then. That's a conversation y'all need to have, but under no circumstances do you think about giving him back that freedom pass to come and go as you please. Women all over the world have their fingers crossed, hoping for something like that every day. You can't surrender it that easily. Believe me, that key is worth its weight in gold. Don't leave it on the ground for someone like me to come along and swoop it up. It might be too early to call, but I have a good feeling about him. Hang in there, you'll see. But if by chance it doesn't work out . . ." Cee-Cee playfully reached for the key between Octavia's fingers.

"Don't make me cut you, heffa."

"See, 'Tavia, he's already something worth fighting for, homeless, jobless, walking, or not. Don't judge him by my standards. I've been known to be a little full of myself every now and then. The last time I climbed on my high horse, a few hours later I found myself naked when I climbed off . . . well, just be careful about saying what you won't do."

Alphonzo puttered by the ladies' intense conversation. He'd learned his lesson the last time not to interrupt two black women with serious issues on their minds, so he kept right on walking.

"Hey, 'Zo, can you come here for a quick minute?" Octavia yelled pleasantly. This time, she was all smiles.

"Is it safe?" he asked, assuming the duck-and-cover position. "My life insurance ain't paid up."

"Come here, boy," she assured him. Her expression conveyed genuine warmth. "I owe you a big fat please-forgive-me. Yesterday, I was igging and you let me have my space. Big ups for that."

"With his cute self," Cee-Cee threw in, on her own account.

"See there. That's why I'm giving up women," Alphonzo threatened. "I can't read y'all and you don't come with a manual."

"Men don't read directions anyway. Wouldn't do no good if the instructions were written on our foreheads," Cee-Cee joked. "Ma' girl is right, though. We needed to talk and after you feared for your health, you didn't even press one little bit."

"Whatever, I'm still done with y'all. I'm thinking about buying a dog. A dog is a man's best friend."

"Uhn-uhn 'Zo, a dog is a man *without* a drivers license," Cee-Cee deliberated in fun.

While they basked in the amusement from the comparison that sounded too much like the truth, Alphonzo waited until the laughter cooled to go tit-for-tat. "So funny I forgot to laugh, but you know what they call female dogs?" he replied crassly, holding up two fingers and looking down his nose at them.

"'Zo!" Octavia's eyes almost popped out of her head. "You bet' not."

"I'll handle this before he gets himself into some real trouble," Cee-Cee offered, grabbing Alphonzo by the arm to haul him away. "'Zo, why do you keep putting your foot in your mouth? That's the worse thing you can call a sistah."

"I didn't say it. I just implied it. Anyway, Octavia is wound up too tight behind I. Rome to care what I think about her."

"Actually, she's moving on to someone else. But that's beside the point. Let's talk about where you keep going wrong. You are a very attractive man, Alphonzo the radio gigolo, although it's hard to see sometimes when you say immature things that turn women off. You need to handle up and utilize your charm a little more instead of resorting to wisecracks when you don't get your way. The bottom line is that you should grow up and move up to a better class of woman than what you've been spending your time with." Cee-Cee winked at him after she did her part to lend help. Alphonzo stroked his chin, playing back her words and wondering if what he heard her say was the same as what she meant.

"So you find me very attractive, huh?" He'd missed the finer points in her analysis.

"Yes I do, and if you didn't have Octavia on the brain, your big head might been telling the little one what to do for a change."

He was rocking his head now, catching on finally, like a joke that was way over his head. "I'm feelin' you, Ms. Cee-Cee Lovely."

"Play your cards right and you could be doing *that* on the regular."

Cee-Cee had been interested for quite some time in seeing what all the fuss was about. Alphonzo had the female audience drooling since he got the late-evening spot two years ago. Discretion was something he didn't have. Cee-Cee was willing to help him with that, too. Sweat equity was as good a way as any to achieve a fair return on her investment, she concluded. And if the word on the street about Alphonzo held any legitimacy whatsoever, she could count on a big dividend yielding a widespread margin. That's the long-term gain she was hoping for.

Legacy didn't catch any of the thank-you messages Octavia left on his answering service. He was busy sketching out ideas for a new account he'd landed with the French designing house, Cachet. They were visiting with a Dallas advertising giant when someone from that firm mistakenly passed his work off as one of their own artist's. The following day, Legacy had their business and a thirty-thousand-dollar advance check for a new logo to inspire their upcoming fall line. A month later he was still staring at a drawing book full of images that weren't close to the concept they envisioned. Cachet wanted something original and breathtaking. He didn't want to let them down, nor could he see giving back the easiest money he thought he'd ever make. Legacy might have been wrong about the time it would have taken him to bring the client to their feet, but he was right about Octavia, and she would inspire a winning creation.

20

The Others

Approaching Tommy Tune's house, Alphonzo felt good about having the chance to atone for his blind promise gone awry. He told Benny to stay in the passenger seat and keep his hands off the stereo knobs. The younger protégé raised his hands to ask why not. "Benny, I don't know what Floreese has been teaching you, but pleeease believe me, you don't want to know what'll happen to you if you put your hands on a black man's radio." Alphonzo picked up a wooden box from the floor of the backseat, then squinted his eyes at Benny in a gloomy sinister manner while biting into his bottom lip. "They won't even hear your body drop." After the declaration had been made, Benny returned a weary expression. He wasn't totally convinced that Alphonzo meant what he said but he wasn't willing to risk it. Having been around black men for an extended period of time provided an experience he wanted to live to talk about, so he watched his hands fall on his lap, where they remained until Alphonzo returned.

"We're in the money" played just like it had the first time Alphonzo visited Tony Tune's estate. He was more impressed at the extravagantly constructed home in the setting of the evening sun. While he wiped his leather sneakers against the welcome mat, the door opened. "Mr. Tune, what's up?"

Tony lounged in a matching set of black silk eveningwear. He peeked outside, as if he expected other people to accompany his uninvited houseguest. "Hey, Alphonzo, what brings you around these parts?"

"I thought Ms. Kim-Kim would have answered the door." Alphonzo attempted to look inside the large oak double doors. Tony eased in front of him to limit his view, so Alphonzo held out the box to show why he wanted the maid. "I brought her something. Lil' makeup gift from the other night."

Tony ran the back of his hand across the side of his chin, kind of suspicious-like. "I thought I knew you better than that. You trying to get with the help now?"

"Whut?" Alphonzo asked, somewhat puzzled.

"Shouldn't you be picking on women your own age?"

"Ohhhhhh. No. That's not, I mean she's not . . . naw, Mr. Tune. Ms. Kim-Kim was probably a hottie about five or six . . . decades ago and I'm sho' she can still hold her own, but I can't get with that. I'm just trying to be a man of my word. You know, trying to slow up and grow up."

"What's this all about? What'r you up to?" Tony ducked his head out again, as if a swat team was all set to swoop down on him for whatever he had going on behind all that oak.

"This is a peace offering for not coming through. I told Ms. Kim-Kim that I was going to do her a solid then I crawfished on the deal. That wasn't cool of me, so I wanna make it right."

After stroking his face like he did before, Tony stepped aside to allow Alphonzo to enter his towering abode. "Come on in, then," welcomed Tony finally. He was proud of Alphonzo for doing the honorable thing. "I'll get her for you, but don't you tell nobody what you might see here today."

Now Alphonzo was looking forward to seeing something, anything that might challenge his ability to keep his mouth shut. He had to look no further than the end of his nose when a sensual and leggy Asian woman built like a swimsuit model sauntered down the winding staircase. She was attired up to her chest in sheer lingerie. With each step she took, her flowing gown brushed back, showcasing why breast implants had become so popular.

Alphonzo wanted to turn away, but why bother. The scantily clad temptress didn't stop strutting toward him and he was happier about it with each step she took his way. "Hey, handsome," she whispered as she approached him. Initially no reply came to mind, so he continued to gawk instead of trading words. "New titties. Oh, how I love new titties," he wanted to say. The woman smiled anxiously when he stared at her with a painful expression that complimented her flawless body in the worst way.

"Are you one of those cute deejays?" she asked, hoping he was. "I go wild for deejays."

"Yyyyeah, I'm one of them." He swallowed hard. "Uh, one of those."

"And he was just leaving," Tony remarked, from behind her. "He's a good boy, Tyler. Don't be trying to corrupt him with none of your sexy tricks, neither. He ain't that far gone yet and I want to keep him that way. Besides, I thought I told you to get started without me if I wasn't back in three minutes."

"I got lonely, Tony," she whined seductively, giving Alphonzo another long inviting eyeful. "And the oils were getting cold, too."

Tony reached around the woman's waist to usher her back in the direction she came from. "I got that covered, like you should be. Now get your sexy self back up there with the others and close the door," he demanded, with a soft squeeze on her behind.

Watching the leggy woman slowly making her way back to the staircase, Alphonzo took a step to follow. "Mr. Tune, you gotta put me down with that. Come on, man." His eyes were pleading. His manhood was begging. His mouth was salivating and he was raring to go.

"Alphonzo!" Tony announced, voice raised and stern like a dog's handler usurping authority. "Son, you're not ready for that. Ain't no going back once you've had the likes of women like Tyler, and that's just her stage name. I can't even say her real name. That's an ancient Chinese secret."

"But Mr. Tune, I heard you. You've got *others* . . . *others*, man. Come on, now. How about some of them *others*."

If Tony owned a choke collar, he would have been jerking on it for dear life. "The *others* are for me, too. They cost too damned much to share 'em with you and I'm too old for anything that kinky, anyway."

"Hell, I'm not. We can take turns, man, with the *others*." Alphonzo was chomping at the bit to break free from Tony's tightfisted grasp.

"Alphonzo, I warned you. Now don't make me have to go to upstairs and get Mr. Speaker to say a few words to you. My forty-fo' ain't had to talk to nobody in a long while and I want to keep it that way." Alphonzo didn't want to push Tony and find out if his threats were legitimate about getting a gun. "'Zo, you don't want to end up like me. Take my word for it. You don't want this. It'll take you down slow." Tony Tune had been offered the same advice by his mentor many years before, but he didn't take heed and now he was addicted to the lifestyle and erotic perks. Money, fame, and women were a dangerous combination when enjoyed in excess, and Alphonzo was heading down the same path. "Despite what's going on through your troubled mind right now, Alphonzo, you do not want this. You deserve better for yourself than all that sensual butt-nakedness goings-on upstairs."

"Ahh man, but the *others*," Alphonzo continued to plead.

"I told you to forget about all you might see here. You need to find yourself a good girl and settle down. Raise some kids, ruin your credit buying things you can't afford, and live happily ever after. That's the American way." Alphonzo kept peering over Tony's shoulder, wishing someone else decided to come and hurry his mentor along. "See. I told you, 'Zo. It's a sickness, son, a sickness."

"Sickness? I can get with that for a minute. We can go right on up there with your friends and play doctor, then. I always dreamed of being a gynecologist." Alphonzo pulled Tony close to him so the maid couldn't overhear his devilish thoughts. "Mr. Tune, how about you just let me watch? I ain't gonna tell no-body."

"I know you're not because there's nothing to tell, remember?"

As Alphonzo's chest heaved with exasperation someone yelled from the top of the stairs, but he couldn't see who it was. "Tony, hurry. We're bored," the soft voice pouted.

"Ohh!" Alphonzo panted, getting excited all over again. "Who was that?"

Reluctantly, Tony felt compelled to answer. "That was one of the *others*. But don't lose sight of what's in store for you. A good clean life with good clean women." Although Alphonzo was willing to take his chances with the women waiting upstairs, he knew it was a lost cause as the maid trekked down the stairs, wiping oil from her hands with a white wash-cloth.

When Alphonzo saw her, he was appalled, assuming she was part of the traveling freak fest. "Awwwe Mr. Tune, now you're trippin'. Ms. Kim-Kim, too? This *is* a sickness."

"Boy, you lost your mind? On the down low, she keeps them separated. I pay her extra for that," he added in a hushed tone. "Do what you came to do and remember . . . forget everything and say nothing to nobody about this. You hear me?"

Begrudgingly, Alphonzo acquiesced. "Yes sir, I'll remember not to say a word." He stood there like a broken-down racehorse on his way to the glue factory.

"Now that we understand each other, I must say that it warms my heart for you to keep your promise to my ace here." The maid looked on, clueless as to what had transpired between them. "Is there anything *else* I can do for you before you go?"

Thinking that Tony hadn't done anything for him up to that point, he shook his head. "Nah, man. Just get on up there and represent."

After they shook hands firmly, Alphonzo did have one request. "Could you at least tap each of 'em one time apiece for me? Make 'em say *my* name or something?"

Smiling heartily, Tony agreed. "Now that I can do. See you at the office, kid."

Alphonzo noted how many paces it took for Tony to get to the first stair. Fifteen was the number. Fifteen steps to immortality he counted while the maid grinned eagerly at him. "Oh, Ms. Kim-Kim, this is for you."

She accepted the gift graciously, then grabbed his hand to shake it. "Mistah Toony was right, Alphonzo. He good man with many troubles. He think much of you. 'Say pretty boy deejay have much potencha. You go. Have many baby and get pretty wife to do many freaky-deaky thing with. Save money that way. Be good boy and forget what see here. Very bad thing, much pain in the morning. Mr. Toony, can some-time no get out of bed. You go. Made Ms. Kim-Kim very happy. Man of word important."

Somehow her speech made Alphonzo feel better about being where he was rather than involved in the sexploits popping off upstairs—well, almost better. "Thanks, Ms. Kim-Kim. You're alright in my book."

She looked in his empty hands but found nothing there. "What book?"

"Never mind. I'm just saying thank you." They exchanged salutations as he headed out the door, with more thoughts of Cee-Cee than when he entered Tony Tune's pleasure palace.

When Alphonzo returned to his shiny green BMW, Benny was per-turbed. "Dude, you could've told me that you were going to be in there a long time. I could've been out here kicking it. Anyway, why couldn't I come with?" Benny asked as Alphonzo settled into the Beamer.

"Because you say goofy stuff like . . . *come with.*"

Alphonzo was two times as emotionally twisted as Tony probably was physically, upstairs with Ms. Kim-Kim refereeing, although Alphonzo wasn't enjoying it half as much.

"Hey, 'Zo, where'd you get that oily stuff on your hand?" Benny was getting his own ideas.

"From the *others*," he answered sullenly, backing out of the cobble-stone drive way. "Something you wouldn't believe if I told you." Although it was difficult for Alphonzo to decipher what to make of the advice Tony Tune offered, he left with a new resolve. One that chal-lenged him to look past all the glitz and glamour the spotlight pro-vided to seek another avenue of fulfillment that involved one woman instead of allowing his testosterone to run amuck and have him inevitably sharing the same fate that had Lazarus in tears with a stank sack tied to his most prized possession. That scene should have suffi-ciently served as a wake-up call if for no other reason than guilt by association. The rank-smelling treatment of soiled garlic cloves and roasted monkey knuckles could have as easily been an old home rem-edy prescribed for him, harnessed just as tight.

21

Promises to Keep

Legacy strapped on the blindfold as Octavia giggled over the excitement. She didn't have the slightest clue where he was taking her. Actually, she couldn't have cared less. She was with him and that was sufficient for her. "Now don't you try to peek or you'll ruin the surprise," he said, waving one hand in front of her eyes while steering her Jeep with the other. "It's not anything major and I've been in the mood for something classic, too, so it's as much for me as it is for you. We're almost there."

"Legggacy," she called out in a voice just this side of sensual. "Don't tease me like this. It's not fair." What also wasn't fair was her pretending that she didn't like to be blindfolded.

After making a sharp right turn that made Octavia squeal, Legacy stopped the vehicle. She turned her head in his direction as if to ask, what now? Slowly he untied the blindfold, then pointed past her to a large nostalgic-style movie marquee at the landmark Wynnwood Theater. The letters spelled out in big block letters: SNOW WHITE. TONIGHT ONLY.

"Oh, thank you, honey!" she screamed, jumping up and down like the second-grader who'd missed it the first time around. "How'd you know this was showing here? It was so sweet of you to bring me." She leaned over to show him how thankful she was. Legacy couldn't help thinking how much more thankful she was going to be once they were greeted inside.

Her eyes were so wide that it didn't occur to her there were no box office attendants selling tickets, nor were there people milling about waiting for the movie to begin. She pulled him across the street like a child rushing to the bright lights of a carnival stopping through a small town on its way home. Suddenly the sold-out sign on the door stifled her joy. "Oh, it's sold out," she pouted miserably.

"Don't sweat it, they're saving seats for us," he assured her. Joy was restored but immediately metamorphosed into panic when Octavia finally realized they were the only ones standing at the concession stand.

She looked around the barren theater lobby, then stared suspiciously at Legacy. "Where is everyone? If this movie was sold out, there would be other people. And come to think of it, we parked right up front."

"Hey, Legacy," a young pimply-faced kid hollered, running down the side stairs leading from the film projector room. "Glad you could make it."

"Christopher, good to see you again and thanks for hooking this up." Legacy's greeting was warm and cheerful. "How's your mom doing?"

"Rehab is for quitters so she's still tryna kick, thanks to you," he replied, with a happy smile in the midst of pubescent woes. "She was glad when I told her you were coming by. Said to say hey and that she's not going to let you or me down. I really think she's gonna go all the way this time."

"Let's hope so, Chris. By the way, this is Octavia. Isn't she something?"

The young man's eyes glassed over like Octavia's did when she saw the sign outside. "Pleased to metcha, ma'am. Mama said you'd be pretty and boy was she right."

"Well, thank you and please tell your mother thank you, too." She peered up at her date for answers.

"Chris and his mother inherited this theater days before the city was about to condemn it. We raised money and wrote to the newspapers to cause a fuss, and the community jumped on the bandwagon and pitched in to save it. This is the oldest theater in the city."

"Okay," she uttered, still lacking the answer she had hoped for, but the one he rendered would have to do.

"Come on, y'all. The movie's about to start and I have homework." Christopher stuck his hand out like a doorman expecting a sizable tip.

Legacy, remembering the setup, began patting at his pockets. "Uh, I seem to have left my wallet at home. Did you . . . Octavia, happen to bring cash?"

She squinted at them both as she pulled a twenty from her purse. "How much are the tickets?"

Christopher smiled larger than had initially, enjoying the opportunity to give back some of what he'd received from his association with Legacy. "That'll be two dollars each, ma'am."

When she heard the ticket price, she remembered sharing her story with Legacy the night before. It was the exact sum that stood in her way all those years before. She fell into his capable arms to avoid boohooing runny mascara on his white T-shirt.

"Still getting used to a man who cares about your happiness, huh?" he asked, holding her against his chest.

She rocked her head, insinuating that this surprise had her trapped in an extremely sensitive state of mind. "Thank you, Legacy. This is too much. I could never repay you for this but you probably don't even want anything from me."

"That's where you're mistaken. I want everything from you. Actually, if we're not raising grandchildren together in about thirty years, I'll be very disappointed."

"And I'll be very disappointed if I don't get to finish my homework assignment." That was Christopher, tapping his wristwatch. "Don't make me call security," he threatened with a crooked smile. "Grown-ups," were his parting words before he dashed back up the side staircase.

Legacy escorted the woman he wanted everything from into the auditorium and followed her to the seats she chose, the middle row in her very own private viewing of her most favorite movie she'd never seen.

After Octavia caught up on years past and the story about a white girl hanging in the forest with seven little guys, she stayed close to Legacy as they exited the theater. Arm in arm, they stood on the sidewalk. "Legacy, I'm not ready to head for home yet. Do you mind if we walk a bit?"

"Are you kidding me? You think I'd pass up the chance to show you off?"

Octavia held Legacy's hand with a secure grasp, as if he might get away if she loosened it. They strolled the sidewalk, delighting in the brisk air and in each other's company. Her heart was opened to him and she smiled to herself over the idea of unlocking his front door with her key. Not having to call ahead or hold her breath while turning the lock, for fear of finding him with another woman or worse (like the time she stumbled in on Savon with another man), made her feel that much more special. Just then, the mere thought of coming and going as she pleased caused goose bumps to tickle her all over like the heart-quickening dizziness of receiving unsolicited flowers. She had a distinct feeling that this dizziness would still be with her long after the tulips wilted and bit the dust.

"Legacy, I'm really getting used to all this attention. Please tell me that this is the way you are. You've got me thinking things I shouldn't be thinking this soon. It's all very new to me. And quite frankly, it's kind of scary."

"Scary? Well, what you see is what you get. Monday through Sunday, I'm going to be me. That's what I do best."

"See, that's what I mean. I have so many questions about you. We've only just met and there's so much mystery to who you are. You know that I was raised on a reservation and I'm from Oklahoma. I work at radio station and I'm finishing up grad school. That's me in a nutshell. Who is Legacy Childs in a nutshell?"

He knew that line of questioning would be forthcoming so he'd rehearsed canned answers, but he didn't want to begin their relationship with lies. Not telling the whole truth was something he could live with, for now. "Let's see. I'm from the Carolinas. I grew up in an orphanage."

"An orphanage for children?"

"Is there any other kind?" He wasn't comfortable divulging that part of his life so he lightened the mood by tossing her question back at her.

"Ha, ha." She pinched him on the arm.

"Ouch, what was that for?"

"For being such a smart butt. A man with a quick wit, that's dangerous."

Legacy smiled when he remembered how Jasmine had said those exact same words years ago, when they were completing their senior year at UTC.

"What else?" she asked, soaking up their conversation like a sponge.

"There's not much else to it. I'm just an average Joe who likes talking about you."

"But we're not talking about me, your name isn't Joe, and there is nothing average about you. I want to know about this fine orphan who is unlike anyone I know. What kind of man names a star, speaks foreign languages for no apparent reason, feels that he has everything he needs, happens to be living in a guest house, rides bicycles in the rain, does things for people like encourage them to diet, paints their kid's room, and gets a famous chef to serve him gourmet meals on the center of a professional team's basketball court? If that's average then I am crazy."

Legacy slowed to a stop and gazed deeply into her curious eyes. How many not-the-whole-truths would he tell? "What is this, an interview?" he asked, dodging her inquiries.

"Don't avoid the questions. And no, this is not an interview. It's more like an audition."

"I thought I already had the job."

"When I give you a key to my place, that's when you've got the job. Right now you happen to be the only applicant, a very attractive applicant, but I want to feel better about who you are. I want to know, who's got my nose so wide open when we've not even *done the fool* yet?"

"Is that what they're calling it now?" He was actually blushing. "I think that's the best one I've heard yet. Doin' the fool. Yeah, that sounds good to me."

"Don't go thinking that doin' the fool is in your immediate future just because I let you hold my hand and escort me around the block."

"I wasn't thinking about doin' the fool," he insisted, looking guilty as sin. "Well, not right at this moment," he added, inspiring another playful pinch from Octavia. "Hey, is loving you going to hurt? 'Cause if it is, I don't know if I'm up for it."

"Plan on me doing that every time you try to change the subject. Anyway, who said anything about love?"

Immediately Legacy reverted back to the questions she'd asked. Talking about love was out of bounds and too soon to be considered. He should have known better. "Okay, would you like me to respond to the questions in the order you asked them, or can I answer in any order I chose?"

"As if you could remember the order. I'll give you a nice one on the lips if you can remember any three of them, in any order."

"Piece of cake. You'd better get ready to slob me down and I'm not talking about some dry sisterly kiss, either. I want a long drawn out, fog up the windows, steamy, wet as the bottom of the ocean tongue dance that'll make a man want to change his religion." The way Legacy put it, Octavia locked her eyes on his, anticipating his best shot. Legacy rolled his head from the left to the right, stretching it out as if he was about to begin a physical exercise rather than a mental one. With his eyes focused on Octavia's, he started in. "Here goes. First things first, I'm not an orphan. I was, but as you can see, I'm now a full-grown man. Second and thirdly, I ran across and named Twinkle after teaching myself Spanish, French, and German because I had too much time on my hands and decided to make the most of it by doing something constructive. Forth, and keep up 'cause this is getting good, I don't feel that I have everything I need because I'm at this very minute auditioning to get you. Fifth, yet while it is true that I currently reside in the guest quarters, I do have full run of the main house while the rich guy who lives there is not home, which is quite frequently might I add." Legacy continued to rattle off his answers with a smooth poetic staccato flow as Octavia followed every syllable, utterly astonished. "I do believe that makes five, for five, and how about number six, which puts me on my Schwinn Flyer, while unbeknownst to me that rain was in the forecast. Seven, Thomas's family needed him to be around year after year, not get bigger and more round, year after year. Painting his son Cory's room did me as much good as it did for the small boy, who much like me could've used a change of everyday scenery." When Octavia opened her mouth to verbally display her awe, Legacy sped up his pace to discourage her from interrupting his flow. "That makes eight and I see that you're thoroughly impressed, but please don't interrupt. Nine . . . while Rudy is a famous chef, he wants to be in the good graces of the even more famous guy whose house I reside behind, who shall remain nameless due to his desire to maintain his anonymity, although I must admit the whole spotlight candlelit dinner table on the basketball court thing was overkill on Rudy's part. And for the coup de grâce, the term average is relative. You are not as crazy as you think and not as crazy as I am about you. Now, that's a perfect ten."

"Can . . . I . . . speak now?" she pleaded, about to burst. Her expression was cloaked in an overwhelming need to shower him with her fascination.

"You sure you don't want to go for the bonus?" he asked, knowing good and well that he had the floor as long as he needed it. With stars in her eyes, she pretended to contemplate for a split second before pitching Legacy a what-ever-you-want-is-fine-with-me expression. "Good. Let me make you aware that I want to spend a long time getting to know you lock, stock, and barrel. That's your mind, body, and soul. Both the perfect and not so perfect. The dreams you run to and the nightmares that chase you. All in all, as is."

Now Octavia was visibly shaken. When she tried to speak, nothing came out. Oddly enough, she didn't honestly think that she deserved to have a man say those kinds of things to her, much less try and live up to them. She had to say something, but nothing could come close to the perfect ten or the bonus that sent her reeling. Was this what every little girl dreamed about while making mud pies and watching them burn through the windows of her Easy-Bake Oven? Octavia's idea of Prince Charming had never been nearly as fine or as blessed with Legacy's mastery of the King's English in poetic verse.

Running away entered her mind, but that meant some other woman might be honored with his words the way she had, so running was not an option she was prepared to live with. She'd have to steady her feet and face a real live, gentle-hearted and sensitive man where she found him. That was a better plan compared to her fears associated with too much man, too fast, so she went with it.

"Hmmm, what does a woman say when a man does what all women want a man to do? And why do I feel like a sixteen-year-old girl with the first boy who saw something in her that she didn't know she had?"

"Maybe she's with the first one who mattered," he answered after a solemn sigh passed between his lips.

"Legacy, I'd be lying if I said I wasn't terrified right now. What if I'm not who you think I am? I have done some things I regret, made some decisions that still haunt me to this day, and I am so flustered with all this emotion that kicks up another notch when I'm near you. Look, I need you to promise me that in the event I do something you might despise me for, you'll try to find it in your heart to forgive me."

"I promise."

"I need to know another thing." She glanced up toward the sky to insinuate that God was listening, so he'd better be truthful. "I need to know what you believe in." Since Octavia hadn't met a man who was so forthcoming and willing to shoulder the burden for a potentially serious relationship, she found herself feeling her way around the walls of Legacy's soul just as she had with the walls of his apartment.

Contemplating the question with grave discernment, Legacy realized that Octavia was not accustomed to a man who made decisions on the fly, when all signs suggested that venturing ahead presented an extremely favorable outcome. At the risk of complicating the issue further, Legacy explained it in the most subtle and honest manner he could.

"I believe that people pass through each others' lives for a reason, some for a season and some for a lifetime. I also believe that our roads crossed when and where they did because they were supposed to, and that's good enough for me." He assumed what her next question would be and tackled that one too. "Maybe we've been given a special chance to journey through this specific moment in time. Maybe I'm supposed to see you through a rough spot in your life, who knows? But that's not what's important. I'm in your life now, and I believe that's where I belong."

"Maybe I came along that way . . . for you," she said, easing into the idea that perhaps it was him who needed her in order to move past a difficult spot in his life. "One last question. Of all the women you could have, why me?"

"I could ask why not you, but I won't because I knew the moment I saw you that our paths were intertwined. I've spent a lot of time alone, Octavia, a lot of time wondering, waiting, wishing for someone to come along that I couldn't pass up or look past without feeling that I'd regret it for a lifetime if I did. Somehow, the angels put you to sleep in my booth just long enough for me to make sure. At the risk of scaring you any further, I need to ask you something." She wanted to let her eyes fall from his but couldn't. "What would you do if a man said . . . he knew you existed long before he met you and that some day he'd find you?"

The wind blew strands of hair in her face. She shooed them away with her nervous fingertips before attempting to put her apprehensions aside. "Whewww. If a man was that certain I was the one he'd been waiting for . . . I would be honored, but I would hold on tightly to my heart until I was certain that his feelings for me were the kind that lasts. And I would ask him to bear with me while enjoying every day together, sharing moments like this, until I could let go completely."

"In the meantime, that man would be more than happy to accept those terms and seal that semicommitment with a—." Octavia lunged into his arms and pressed her lips against his before he could utter another word. She hadn't planned on a man offering unlimited access to all he had to give and everything she wanted. It was the first time she'd ever been in control of a relationship. The chill of uncertainty that traipsed down her spine was warranted. Fortunately, Legacy's persistence adequately subdued it, at least for the time being. I. Rome was coming to town with promises of his own and with history on his side and the wherewithal to make history repeat itself. In no time at all, Octavia would find herself in a predicament that most women would kill for: the man she always wanted and what she always wanted in a man. Even though the two would be diametrically opposed, she could find herself standing smack-dab in the middle of her future and her past, staring both of them down. Face-to-face.

22

Jail Bait

Listeners were still raving about having been officially introduced to Cuzzin Cora on Cee-Cee's show the day before, when Cee-Cee tried to order out on the air. A sea of calls poured in about that eccentric restaurant owner more than any other topic, and Cee-Cee ran her show on autopilot. Patricia was loving it that Hot 100 had cemented the weekly segment before the new station, which was days away from powering up down the block, could add it to their programming cycle. Then Patricia ceased to bask in her good fortune as station manager long enough to make time to handle a few housekeeping issues left over from Monday.

Ebony and Floreese sat on pins and needles outside the boss's office like schoolboys who had been caught letting the air out of the principle's tires. The longer she made them squirm, the more panicked they became. Since both of them had masterminded more than their fair share of pranks, neither knew which of their sophomoric acts was behind the meeting they waited pensively to begin.

"Remember, no matter what she has on us, we're denying everything. Deal?" Ebony's lips were dry and crusty after visions of impending doom flashed before his eyes.

"Sho' you right?" Floreese asked nervously. He raised his hands shoulder-high, turned his palms toward the ceiling, then began speaking in tongues. He ended his strange ritual with a rushed Hail-Mary, crisscrossing his chest. Ebony was confused about the pseudo-Muslim-Holy-Ghost-sanctified prayer with a splash of Catholicism thrown in at the end for flavor.

"Man, quit playin'. What was all that for?" Ebony seemed more annoyed than confused.

"Just covering all my bases. One of 'em's gotta work. They always work. Sometimes they work." His face scrunched up when he felt helpless. "Damn. Oh, I just said "damn" right after praying. Now, ain't none of 'em gonna work. I knew I should've went to church last Easter but my suit wasn't back from the cleansers and . . . ahh man. It's a long story." Floreese was trying to keep his emotions in check, but it didn't look good.

When they heard voices getting louder from inside the closed office, Ebony turned to Floreese. Looking him in the eye, he grit his teeth. "Flo, we're sticking together. If she can't divide us, we can't be conquered."

"Uh-huh, I'm with that, and I'm all prayed up now," Floreese testified after completing another Hail Mary for good measure. "She can't touch us. Can't touch us. I might look scared but I ain't no punk . . . on the inside where it counts." He took two sustaining deep breaths to help fortify himself after pounding on his bony chest.

The office door opened. Floreese jumped back against Ebony. Both of them popped up from their seats, looking like pitiful POWs anticipating a lengthy and brutal interrogation. A short, well-dressed man came puttering out of the open door, pushing a metal walker. Ebony almost bit a hole in his bottom lip when he realized it was Brad, the arrogant sales jerk, whose intestines they'd served up a good flushing.

Ebony nudged Floreese with his elbow. "Check it. I bet his whole ass fell out. Or at least his asshole."

"Yeah an I'll bet we get ours *snatched* out once we get in there. You know PMS don't play."

"Just don't forget we made a deal to stick together," Ebony reminded him. His eyes narrowed to display the seriousness of their pact.

Brad slowly exited the office and puttered their way. He paused to rest, it seemed, when he was parallel to where they stood. "You two niggah's are in for it. And I'm not finished with you." He took another deliberate step in the other direction, surveyed his surroundings before he stood erect and broke out his best cabbage-patch move, then bent over again to pretend he needed the walker. The whole act was a hoax.

"Ain't that a blip?" marveled Ebony. "He ain't even hurt, Floreese. And he called you a niggah to yo' face."

"He couldn't have been talking to me 'cause I ain't no niggah. I'm black."

"Good!" Patricia shouted from inside her office. "Now that you've cleared that up, get your black behinds in here." From the echoes resounding off the walls, the deejays knew she was on the warpath.

They trotted in single file. Floreese was determined to hold up his end of the bargain. He put on a more convincing game face, jaws locked tight. Ebony was too busy avoiding eye contact with Patricia to notice. "Sit down," she demanded, standing near her leather high-backed chair. They sat, like two obedient little doggies. "Who's going to tell me exactly what happened to Brad? I've spent half the day talking him out of a civil suit for being poisoned and charges for attempted murder."

"*Murder!*" Ebony screamed in a shrill voice. "No way this is falling on me. I ain't going back to jail. It's a gang of brothas in there who I still owe cigarettes, from being sent up on the last thing I didn't do. I can't go back to braiding hair, Ms. Stapleton."

Sitting with his head in his hands, Floreese began to moan something terrible while rocking back and forth like a mental patient behind on his meds. "Ma'am, I know what you think because we're always up to our old tricks, but this time it wasn't us."

"It wasn't *me!*" Ebony yelled in his own defense. "It was him!" He hopped up, pointed his finger straight at Floreese, and commenced to sell him cheap like a nickel-per yard carpet warehouse during a going-out-of-business sale. "It was Flo's eyewash. It was Flo's idea. And, and it was him. Right there's your man. You can cuff him, too. He ain't no stranger to handcuffs, neither." Ebony pitched a wide-eyed you-know-damn-well-what-I'm-talking-about expression to his partner in crime while dropping dime on him. "Flo', go on and tell her about that time, you know that time . . . with them strippers. The ones that got us drunk and naked, then robbed us. Don't act like you don't remember."

Floreese was blindsided by his total disbelief. Ebony was paying off like a Vegas slot machine, clattering and giving up the goods. Floreese was obviously disappointed in the friend he thought he could trust.

"Man, how'r you gonna play me like that? And, what happened to all that stuff about let's make a deal, man? Let's stick together, man? Eb, you' a trip. Had me doing all that Muslim, Hebrew and Holly Ghost praying, and you come up in here and start screaming "Murder! Murder! I can't go back to braiding hair" like a sissy. I bet you was good at it, too. You probably still hold the prison record for crisscrossing and weave extensions and designs . . . and a whole bunch of other stuff a grown man ain't got no business doing when he's locked up."

"We'll never know 'cause I ain't going back. I keeps a suitcase packed at the house. I'll jet. I will. I've been practicing some Spanish from watching the Latin TV channel and I ain't scared to drink the water, neither. I'll run."

Floreese was ready to fight. He pushed his chair back, preparing to scrap. "You won't get far with a broke neck. Snitch!"

"Enough!" Patricia shouted when she could no longer stand their antics. "Floreese, pick up my chair and Ebony, you're not going any-where. Floreese was right. You were wrong to betray his confidence like that. Both of you all calm down." She picked up a remote control off her desk and cued up the VCR, which rested on her credenza. When the tape rolled, it revealed Ebony squeezing contents from a large white bottle into the coffee pot with Floreese bent over laughing and rooting him on.

Laughing again, Floreese nearly lost his breath as he viewed the incriminating evidence that caused tears to stream down Ebony's face. "That's right, podna'," he cheered the turncoat's misfortune. Floreese worked his fingers to simulate the art of hair-sculpting. "Yeah, Ebony, you'd better get to practicing yo' braiding techniques. Right over left, or is it left over right? Don't really matter as long as they tight. But I know something else that won't be tight after the boys in cell block D get wind that you're baaack. I hear they like to get real physical and we don't have to guess what the D stands for." He was laughing so hard that he almost fell out of his chair. "Which . . . which dress are you gonna wear to the prison social?"

Patricia turned her head away momentarily when Floreese's outright silliness forced a chuckle from her as well. "I thought I said enough," she stated, regaining power. She cut off the television and took her seat across the desk, then burned a hole in the two of them with the evil eye. "You two act as if you don't get paid to work here. If I didn't need both of you, I'd call the police myself for pulling such a ridiculous gag. There's no telling how many people could have gotten hurt behind it."

Ebony's tears stopped flowing when he heard her say what he thought she said. "Ms. Stapleton, did I hear you say you're not calling the po-po?"

"That's precisely what I meant. Whewww, sometimes I don't know why I bother."

"Oh, please don't bother," begged Floreese. "Uh-uh. Jails are full of lonely sex offenders who just love snitches. Eb'll probably win homecoming queen . . . again."

Patricia dismissed his banter as she opened her desk drawer, pulled out two identical documents, then placed each in front of the radio rascals. "In case you read as badly as you stick together, I'll tell you what these promissory notes declare. I've taken the privilege to have them drawn up on your behalf, of course. They state that you will never pull another prank, regardless of how small or insignificant you think it to be, as long as you are employed here." She peered at them as if to ask what they were waiting on. Within a heartbeat they willingly signed the documents. Ebony held his hand out for some congratulatory dap, but all he got from Floreese was a snide smirk.

"Don't think you've gotten off so easily," Patricia informed them.

"What else we gotta do, boss-lady?" Ebony asked. "We'll do anything you want us to do. We'll even play the wack tracks we're supposed to."

"First thing. Never, as long as you're black, call me boss-lady again because you do know my name and I won't stand for it. Secondly. You will clean the men's locker room thoroughly, from top to bottom, and find some way to rid it of that garlic stench."

Floreese turned up his nose. "Is that all?"

"No, that's not all. And, you will do everything in your powers to hold your ratings over the next year, both time slots."

"But what about when Laz'rus gets back?" Floreese reminded her that he was covering the late-night shift temporarily.

"That's why you're not going to jail," she answered plainly. "Lazarus isn't coming back. He's taken a position with the new station. Starting Monday."

Although both pranksters felt a slight void for losing a team member, who was an all-around cutup as well, they were bubbling over now and excited about navigating their own shows individually. All things considered, they got off like OJ, except they wouldn't be pledging the remainder of their lives to clear their good names.

"Thank you, Ms. Stapleton. Thank you."

"We'll make you proud, you watch."

She glanced at the television screen briefly, then at them. "Oh, I'm counting on that. Now, unless I'm mistaken, and that never happens, there should be two scrub brushes and a water pail in the locker room just pleading for some company."

They practically skipped out of her office, delighted with the news. But Patricia had promised Brad retribution over the coffee incident. Since it wouldn't have served well to fire Ebony and Floreese, she gave the disgruntled sales star a free pass to get even, short of someone ending up in the hospital. Patricia was reminded yet again that the most challenging mission of management was keeping the employees from killing each other. Whatever she was getting paid, it wasn't nearly enough.

23

Imagine That

A trail of tears had all but dissipated when the other two remaining stylists cleared their stations and hit the door. Deja had been crying a river since she'd received a call from the school nurse earlier in the day concerning her fifteen-year old daughter's pregnancy. More unnerving than having a child who was expecting a baby, was Deja's total denial that the girl was sexually active. Truest had less to say compared to the other stylists over the past six hours due to her being consumed with her own out-of-control issues. I. Rome's relentless calls had taken a toll, especially the ones at 3:00 in the morning, followed by the 7:00 A.M. wake-up calls pledging his admiration and plans to take their relationship to another level, once they had a better understanding, that is.

"Keep your chin up, Deja," Truest encouraged her. "I know you must be coming unglued, but that won't help fix what you and Dena have to deal with."

"It'll help me feel better after I kill her lil' hot ass," moaned Deja. "And when I find the mannish punk that did this to my baby . . ." She didn't say the words she really wanted to. Words that she might have to deny if served with arrest papers for taking the young man's life, who'd robbed her daughter of her innocence.

"Despite what happened, she's a good kid and she deserves to have you be there for her during this." Truest genuinely empathized with the nail tech's woes but lacked the stamina to argue the point. "It's your place as a mother, irregardless. Don't let nothing come between you and your child, not even this. And, I'm through." Truest turned her back on any further discussion on the topic. She remembered leaving home at sixteen after falling out with her mother over the same phone call, only it came from the boy's mother claiming that Truest was trying to trap the promising prep-school basketball player. Pressured into having an abortion and subsequently running away from home, Truest had regretted giving up her baby, at least once a day over the past twelve years.

"You can turn your back on me, and it is my problem and my child to deal with, but I am not ready to be a thirty-five-year-old grandmother. My grandmama was younger than I am now when I came along, and I said I wasn't going out like that." Deja slinked off, moaning sorrowfully and wringing her hands. "I'm too young for this." She seemed more bothered about becoming a reluctant grandparent than her only daughter becoming a young mother. Somewhere in her blurry vision the line of demarcation had been washed away. Deja was going to have to work things out at home, so Truest decided to save the drama for her last visitors. She would need the energy to carry her own load.

Cee-Cee hadn't told Sylvia where they were going when she'd arrived suddenly at the woman's home. She merely mentioned that Sylvia needed to have a long talk with someone. After spending too much time alone, Sylvia was willing to go just about anywhere—just about.

Her marriage wasn't that bad, considering, it just wasn't that good. It was a typical story of noncongruent sexual appetites, but it did deserve a shot at salvaging before either one of them got the idea that they were better off going it alone. That was Cee-Cee's aim when she swooped up Sylvia to join her for a short car ride over to the Vicious Cuts.

As soon as Cee-Cee whipped around the last turn, Sylvia began to shift uncomfortably in the passenger seat. "Why are we stopping here?" she asked, somewhat miffed.

"This is one of the best places to be when you have man problems. You can get pampered here, supported here, and maybe learn a few . . . useful tricks."

"I don't need the kinds of tricks that Truest and women like her ought to be ashamed of, I don't need pampering, and I don't need anyone's half-baked support." Sylvia was on a roll, rolling her eyes and rolling her neck. "And, I do not have *man problems*."

"Your man left home. That's a problem," Cee-Cee informed her. "Now get out of this car and if nothing else, let Truest apologize to you for what went down at the Chat."

"Cee-Cee, you don't know what you're asking of me. I have no plans nor desires to be in the same building with her."

"Look, Sylvia, you're always running your mouth about what's scriptural. If you don't allow Truest the chance to say how sorry she is, you'll be blocking her blessings and that doesn't sound to scriptural to me. I might be wrong but I doubt it." Cee-Cee had figured out a couple of things. She'd used Octavia's insecurities to push her closer to Legacy. Alphonzo was already acting his way to becoming a better man. And, Truest was softening around the edges in every way since they went nose to nose over I. Rome splitting his downtime. Now it was Sylvia's turn to go up against what she held dear, the *Word*.

Not surprised at how quickly Sylvia was standing on the sidewalk once she'd leaned on a worthy crutch, Cee-Cee had one thing to say before entering the shop: "Amen." With Sylvia dragging her cross behind, the spiritual angle Cee-Cee had taken was probably the only avenue to pry the woman, who was sheltering self-righteous indignation, from the car.

In the rear of the shop, Truest soaked combs and trimming shears in the oversized sink. She was too possessed with a multitude of decisions to hear the women approaching until Cee-Cee startled her from behind.

When Truest felt someone drawing into her personal space, she grabbed a set of trimming shears from the sink and brandished them in a panicked defensive manner. Cee-Cee lunged backward. Sylvia nearly ran out of her shoes, fleeing apparent danger with her heart pounding. She trembled in fear over what almost happened.

"Truest, what's gotten into you?" Cee-Cee reprimanded. Sylvia kept a safe distance, halfway across the room.

"I'm . . . I'm sorry, y'all. I didn't hear nobody come in and . . . and—" Truest gasped, trying to catch her breath as she wiped water from the sink off her hands. "I must need more rest than I thought."

"Are you okay?" A worried expression covered Cee-Cee's face like cheap cosmetics. "You probably need to come over here and sit down."

Truest held firmly to Cee-Cee's arm. "Wheww, I'm kinda dizzy."

"Did you eat today?" Sylvia asked from the other side of her human buffer. She appeared to be as concerned.

Truest looked up oddly, as if she'd forgotten that Cee-Cee hadn't come in alone. "I've been too busy to run out and pick up something, I guess. Whew. I haven't ever felt this light-headed without being deep in a bottle. Or just as deep into something else," she added suggestively.

"Drinking should be the last thing on your mind right now," Cee-Cee debated. She didn't care to ponder over Truest's sudden lapse of energy, but Sylvia had her own ideas. "No one should stand on their feet all day without eating. You of all people should know that."

Sylvia pulled up a chair for Truest to have a seat after she refused to sit in the chair reserved for her clients. "I never sit there," Truest stated in a peculiarly leery tone. "If y'all knew the stuff that a stylist's chair can make a woman say, you'd think twice about it, too."

"It's just a chair, Truest. You act as if it has special powers," Sylvia contended, obviously feeling more at ease due to Truest's slight debilitation.

Truest waved at it while she sipped from a water bottle. "That's why I call it the Truth Chamber. It'll make you tell all of your business and some other people's, too, if you're not careful. I'd write a book, if I had the time. Humph, a best-seller."

Cee-Cee laughed for the first time since she'd arrived. "Girl, you're crazy. I've heard you call it that before but I always thought it was a play on words. You know, Truest . . . *Truth* Chamber?"

"Uh-uh. If my name was Gertrude, it'd still be the Truth Chamber. Ain't no play on words needed. That's the truth." Both visitors scoffed at the chair, then shared the same that's-preposterous frown. "Alright, I can show you better than I can tell you. Cee-Cee, have a seat." She didn't budge an inch, afraid that the first question Truest might have been bold enough to ask would have had something to do with another woman's husband staying the night.

"No, ma'am, you just converted me. I now stand on the side of believers." Cee-Cee also knew better than to have placed herself in the middle of Truest trying to make a point. "Anyway, you know too much about my dark side already. I am not trying to read about it in some best-selling novel. I've got more issues than I need right now to be adding some tell-all book to my troubles."

Truest eyed Sylvia, who was seriously considering it. "Mrs. Everheart, you want to give her a whirl?" Truest challenged. Her voice was laced with respect. Sylvia hadn't heard Truest call her by her married name before. It sounded surprisingly refreshing, coming from the woman she suspected of having a lot to do with her and Devin separating. Against her better judgment, she sat her Prada bag down, accepting the challenge. Cee-Cee watched attentively, steadying herself to break up another brawl if things took a wrong turn. So far, no one had addressed the fight that had occurred the last time they were in swinging distance of one another.

"How are you today?" Truest asked in a pleasant professional manner. She popped a black nylon smock, then carefully laid it over Sylvia and fastened it around the neck, like she'd have done for an ordinary paying customer.

"Ok Truest, I'll play along. I've not had a good day in a while. Want to take a guess why?"

"Sure, but it wouldn't be guessin'." Truest winked at Cee-Cee, who was now more intrigued than on guard. "Before we get started, I owe you an apology, Sylvia, for showing out in your house. That was wrong of me and I hope you can forgive my behavior." Cee-Cee was concerned again. It was so unlike Truest to make amends for anything she'd done, once riled up.

Sylvia watched her expensive shoes clicking nervously at the tips and nodded her head briskly. "Well, if you can find it in your heart to say that, I should be big enough to find it in mine to accept. I know this is suppose to be me testing the truth out, but I have another question for you, if you don't mind."

"You're wondering if I've been with your man and the answer is no. You also want to know why I seem to hold so much hostility for you and the answer is . . ." From the corner of her eye she caught a glimpse of Cee-Cee leaning in as she began to comb through Sylvia's thick overgrown hair. "Honestly, I'm a little jealous," Truest confessed.

Sylvia whipped her head around in disbelief. "Jealous of me? Why? You've gotten every man you've ever wanted, and you make the kind of money it takes some people two college degrees and two nine-to-fives to rake in."

"I'm jealous because you have Devin. Well, not Devin particularly, but the kind of man you need. He's sweet and caring, not to mention thoughtful. But, most of all he loves yo' dirty drawze." Cee-Cee and

Sylvia had to laugh. It was funny to hear Truest giving some props to another woman about her husband. Usually, she would have commissioned some of his time, leaving the wife in tears and despising her over the affair.

"I guess he does at that," Sylvia snickered. She covered her mouth as if she'd said a bad word. "However, that wasn't nearly enough to keep him there."

"No, it wasn't, but it's not too late." Truest tossed another wink at Cee-Cee standing in the shadow of amazement. "Why'ont you tell me why you think he left?"

Studying the question, Sylvia wanted to stretch a one-sided lie but had a distinct sinking feeling that Truest already knew a lot of what lead to their breakup. She had no idea that Cee-Cee knew even more. "I, uh . . . we've had some disagreements over how money should be saved and appropriated."

"And?" Truest said, knowing that wasn't all they'd had disagreements about.

"And, we've not come to terms on how ambitious I've been regarding my career."

"And?"

Sylvia shifted in that chair, just as she had when she was in Cee-Cee's car, uncomfortable as could be about taking on Truest again. "And, I'm only sharing this because I want to, not because of some silly *Truth Chamber*." She lowered her head before rendering an answer. "And, because I think that a woman diminishes her self-worth when she throws her legs open any time and any way a man thinks she should." Her explanation spit out rapid-fire like it had been waiting centuries to do so.

Shaking her head slowly, Cee-Cee said the first thing that popped into it. "Oooh, that chair is a motherfuh—"

"Cee-Cee!" Truest yelled. "You're in the presence of Christian folk."

Thoroughly astonished, Cee-Cee had forgotten herself amidst Sylvia's spicy and uncensored testimony. "Y'all, please look over me. I'm . . . stupefied."

"Y'all," Truest objected. "I was talking about Sylvia. Bible-beaters meet too much for me. Ursher board meetin', Deaconess meetin', young disciples meetin', choir rehearsal meetin' and meetings to schedule the next meetin'. Uh-uh, that's more time than I want to spend with Jesus or any other man." By the time she was finished, Sylvia and Cee-Cee were nodding agreeably at how some church members get overextended while trying to devote themselves. "But back to you and your ideas on sex and the married man." Cee-Cee was certain that Truest had further expertise to provide, although she'd never been close to jumping the broom. She had barrowed a few married men from time to time, but that was beside the point. "I do remember one thing, and that's the bed is undefiled. I learned that from a preacher man. Won't tell you which one 'cause you might attend his church."

"See, now you've gone too far," said Cee-Cee. "I don't want to think about giving my money to have some smooth-talking, backsliding pastor who sponsors his women on the side with it."

"Cee-Cee, your act of tithing is the blessing despite what an evil-doing minister spends it on. That's something he'll have to answer for, not you." Sylvia had spoken the truth and couldn't stop there. "That scripture you're referring to, Truest, is found in the New Testament. It's overly used by men in the congregation if you ask me, but the Word is the Word."

"Ah-huh, since you know what the Bible says about that, I'm guessin' you also know what it says about the wife's body not being her own but her husband's and how she should submit herself to her husband?" Truest was flowing and coming correct, further catching the ladies off-guard.

Cee-Cee moved closer to the chair Sylvia was confined in. "Tru, just how much time did you spend with this minister?"

"I'll say this, the kind of time that would get him ousted by his congregation if they knew that I was just one of the women he sponsored. But don't get all bent out of shape," she instructed, trying to sound dignified, ". . . we repented right after, every time we hooked up." She neglected to explain that she and Brother Pastor repented while butt-naked by the bedside, which frequently lead to the same sin they'd previously asked to be forgiven.

"Y'all repented right after each time you hooked up," Cee-Cee repeated, mimicking Truest's tone of voice. She couldn't understand the logic. "What y'all did wasn't repenting, that was *reporting!*"

Sylvia couldn't control herself. The thought of Truest and some pot-bellied middle-aged preacher asking forgiveness for the very act they surely resumed as soon as the last amen had been offered up was preposterous. Oddly, she was doubled over laughing as Cee-Cee and Truest stood at odds.

"What, Sylvia? Cee-Cee's lil' joke was funny but it wasn't all that funny."

"No-no, I can't stop because it just occurred to me, the real reason why I never let myself relax when Devin wanted me to loosen up and be his private freak. It's the way my mother raised me. She'd drag me to all those church meetings and preached how she didn't want no ho' for a daughter, but she couldn't keep a man, either. Oh my goodness, this is too funny. I didn't want my mother to think that my husband could run me or control me, not even in the bedroom. How foolish could I have been?" She wiped her eye after having the epiphany of the century. "Truest, Devin wants me to be more like you. He cherishes you, your free-spiritedness, your zest for life, and your friendship. He always said there was nothing between you two and that he chose me because of what we could build together. I'm ashamed to admit that I wouldn't believe him. All I could see was him wanting to do all those kinky things he'd been asking of me, with you. To think I might have lost my man, a good man, trying to be what my mother envisioned for me . . . *a wealthy entrepreneur who don't need no man!*" she roared, as if the sentiment had belonged to someone else but saddled on her. She started to cry when her house of cards came crashing down around her. "My mother died . . . frigid, bitter, and alone."

Cee-Cee stepped forward to comfort Sylvia after her awakening. Truest was leaning against her workstation, snacking on a candy bar and virtually unmoved by Sylvia's true confession. She knew all too well what powers resided in the Truth Chamber.

Sylvia settled into the chair like she planned on being there awhile. "Truest," she called out, "I need my man to come back home."

"You sho' do."

"I think I can manage to get him there, but . . . a *sistah* might need some helpful hints on keeping him there. Are you down with that?" She snickered again when those words sounded far less cool coming out of her mouth than she imagined before she'd said them.

"I am, now that Devin's wife is a friend of mine," Truest answered. "We'll make sure he gets what he needs and a whole lot of what he wants. We can go over technique while I hook you up with a wash-and-trim, on the house."

"Well, well. If I hadn't been here and seen it for myself," Cee-Cee heard herself say under her breath, not wanting to spoil the moment that ushered in budding new friendship. "Y'all, let me know how it goes. I have a show to catch. Truest, can you drive Sylvia home when y'all get through? Thanks. If I hadn't seen it for myself."

Cee-Cee tipped out figuring it was a good idea to leave well enough alone. Truest had always been a good friend to Sylvia's husband despite her tumultuous relationship with his better half. Cee-Cee didn't feel quite comfortable discussing methods to please the man who she had given serious consideration to making magic with herself, when he reached out to her in his time of weakness. Cee-Cee had hoped that Devin would concede to taking another stab at making his marriage work. Otherwise she would be kicking herself, wishing she'd given him what he came for instead of sending him away unsatisfied and with hopes of him finding the way back home, where he belonged.

24

What She Really Wants

Alphonzo was transfixed when Cee-Cee tapped on the door to the pit, then invited herself in. "I've been listening to the show and you're flowing tonight," she said when Alphonzo went to a commercial. "What's all this serious talk about romance coming from? Last time I checked you were still Alphonzo the Radio Gigolo."

Smiling at her, he went back on the air as if she should have known the answer to that question. He laced the extended-play version of "Moments of Love" by Art of Noise to carry the background. The mellow beat chaperoned as he began the next segment. "I'm back and I know you missed me 'cause I'm feeling y'all, too." Alphonzo's voice was relaxed and velvety smooth. Cee-Cee enjoyed the strong vibe and listened in as he continued a man's maturation before her eyes. "The first part of the show was dedicated to the sistahs, and by the way my phone lines are lit up like a casino, I can tell I wasn't wasting my time. Now I feel it's necessary and long overdue to rap to the fellas, my brothas. And men, don't go all ballistic at what I'm putting down tonight,'cause you know I'm right. Tonight, we're gonna talk about what every sistah wants." He smacked his lips when he caught Cee-Cee blushing from the comforts of the new loveseat. The other one had been removed expeditiously after Patricia viewed the videotape of

Lazarus getting buck wild on it with his last late-night in-studio guest. "That's right, I said every sistah. They all want it. That includes your woman, her best girlfriend, your sistah, your mama, and your mama's mama, too. All of 'em, each and every one . . . that's if they haven't lost their mind yet over some of the trifling stuff we've been serving up. Don't get mad at me because the truth hurts, and I'll hip you to something else. A wise man once told me that women want to be held, that's right, and talked to. You heard me. I said talked to. Not yelled at, not punched, not dogged out, not pimped, not played and played with. And don't think I'm hatin' because I want you to do right by the woman you're claiming. She deserves at least that much. If you want to keep her and keep her happy, do what she wants you to do. Yeah, I know you might think that's selling out and you're thinking I should keep it real. Well, I'll do you brothas one better. I'm telling you how to really keep it."

He was feeling himself and had a fair idea that the women who listened to the first part of the show were still tuned in and praying their men hadn't flipped the dial and turned their backs on some brotherly advice to rekindle the mojo they had somehow misplaced.

"Remember back fellas, to the first time you saw that sistah you got now and how you lost yo' mind when she gave you the digits. Remember when you would have done anything to get at her? That's the same way you should feel about her still. Let me tell you something I had to learn the hard way. A woman's love runs deeper than any man's. You cannot began to quantify how much a woman can love you when you love her back, the way she wants to be loved. Money and gifts ain't to be sneered at, women appreciate a lil' sumthin'-sumthin' and you should treasure her enough to open the wallet to make that happen. Trinkets and whatnots go a long way and they should, but I'm talking about the everyday, toss a smile her way, anything but ordinary love. You don't believe me, just ease up behind your girl when she comes home from a long day at the job and tell her that you love her. Tell her that you care, then show her. Try running her bathwater every now and then, light the candles for her. Don't go tryna get your rusty butt in the tub, too. Make that her special time. Put on some mood music to help her calm down from battling the man at the office who's holding a promotion from her because she won't let it go past having lunch with him.

As a matter of fact, why don't you show up at her office and take her to lunch. I'm talking unannounced. Just pop up and tell her that you were thinking about her. Send her an e-mail with a smiley face or even better, send her flowers just because. Just because she's yours and you're proud to have her." Cee-Cee was on the edge of her seat, digesting every syllable. "Every sistah wants one simple thing from us brothas. They want exactly what they're giving. If her love is strong, give her some strong love in return. When she goes out of her way to make your house a happy home, or if she goes to the grocery store or to pick up something the family needs to improve the quality of life in yo' house, you need to be right there with her pushing the basket down aisle after aisle. That's what I'm talking about. Move her the way she's moving you. And for the kinda of brotha who likes to put his hands on your woman, next time you want to make your point, try messaging her neck instead of wrapping your hands around it. Hell, rub her feet while you're watching the ballgame. You might find yourself smacking on more than chips and dips during the halftime show if you come correct and handle yours. Uh-huh, and if you happen to be one of those type of brothas who wanna be hard and you ain't tryna have all that, then you may as well wait on the other shoe to fall 'cause I guaran-damn-tee you that for everything you're not willing to do there's at least two brothas waiting around the corner just hoping you slip up and give them the chance to step up to the plate. Pleeease believe me, there's plenty of fellas out there swinging for the fences. You heard? They call it reciprocity."

Alphonzo smiled when Tony Tune's words came to him like a song he couldn't shake loose from his head. "It's not a city in a faraway place but it could be paradise on earth if you're willing to take your relationship to the next level. It simply means, gentlemen, give her the best of what she's willing to give to you, nothing more, nothing less. Confess how you feel with your words, thoughts, and deeds. And, don't be surprised how she's all of a sudden as beautiful as she was the first time you laid eyes on her and the freak you thought faded out on you. Don't forget, she put something on you to get you sprung in the first place. Hmm, if all else fails, just send the kids off to mom's for the weekend, pull down the shades, unplug the phones, and walk around the house naked for two straight days. If that don't help restore some of what's been lost, looks like you didn't have much to begin with in the first place. Maybe she ain't the one for you and chances are you're the wrong man for her, too. That's right, it goes both ways. Let her go so she can find the right brotha who can put a smile on her face that goes all the way down to her toes instead of you complaining about being too tired to represent. Y'all better be glad I got my eye on sum-thin' new 'cause I'm just the type brotha to step up and smack a home run when you don't think it's not worth taking a swing. Uh-huh, I bet you used to look forward to batting practice. Better ask somebody." Cee-Cee snickered like Sylvia had when she was embarrassed by the ladies' back-alley discussion. "I think by now I might've made a few dents in the walls of that macho box we try to hide our feeling in. Brothas, I'll say this, then let you and your girl rap about it. Fellas, hear me well, ask your woman what she wants, how she wants it and how often you should give it to her. After all that's out the way, y'all can talk about sex. I's just seeing if y'all were paying attention 'cause if you didn't know, it ain't all about sex. Never was and never will be. If I did have to sum it all up in one word, it would have to be reciprocity. You can't say you don't know, now that you've heard it from a former gigolo. I'm handing over my player card. Shoot, I'm over the limit anyhow." Alphonzo smacked his lips again, slow and sensual-like, for Cee-Cee's benefit. "I have to cut to a commercial and pay some bills but check it. If half of y'all ain't there when I get back from this next break, I won't be mad atcha for handling up on some good advice. For the rest of you who are alone or wishing you was, keep it right here on the Hot 100."

The phone lines lit up, the back lines rang continually, and Cee-Cee was glad to assist with the endless pursuit of listeners, both men and women, wanting to discuss Alphonzo's recipe for good love with all the trimmings. Although they fielded a smattering of calls from opponents who accused the deejay of going soft, the slew of listeners who did get an opportunity to go live on the air with him thought his topic and the way he brought it to them was a welcomed change of pace. And so was Alphonzo's decision to grow into what Cee-Cee saw in him all along, a better man than he knew he could be.

Down in the men's restroom, Floreese and Ebony sat on the dressing bench, tired and drained. It had taken them over six hours to get that place spick-and-span per Patricia's demands. To meet her specifications, they bleached the floor, twice, scrubbed it, washed the walls, and fumigated to eliminate the putrid smell. Ebony didn't have the strength to carry his own time slot that night and didn't know what to do about it. A nice hot shower had to be mixed in his plans because he had worked up a powerful fury of funk while trying to live up to the agreement they signed.

Floreese shuffled over to the sink to wash what filth he could off his hands. "Yo, Eb?" He shook his head when the exhausted face looking back at him appeared to be a lot older than it did earlier in the day. "I don't know how you're gonna pull off making it through your show tonight. I know good and well that you've got to be as broke down as I am. If I had to clean one more spot, man, I'd damn near try to kill myself."

Approaching his locker to see what decent gear he'd have to wrestle on after a quick run through the water, Ebony gazed over the work they had put into making the room spotless and stank-free. "Yeah, I think I can make it. But you were right. I'd rather be back in the gray-bar hotel than to have to clean up this joint again. And we both know I'm too thin to be locked up." He pushed out a deep sigh as he turned the dial on his combination lock. When he opened the small locker door, a fully extended balloon waited inside. Someone had to have inflated it after the balloon was already inside because it would have been too large to fit otherwise. "Floreese, c'mere and see what some-body left in my spot." The two of them leaned in simultaneously when they noticed something had been written, in extremely small print, on the nose of the balloon. "What does that say? I'm too tired to make it out but I need to get my. . . ." Ebony reached out to dislodge it from the tight space. No sooner had the very tip of his finger met with the tightly stretched rubber than the enormous orb exploded, flinging a thick brown sticky substance all over what used to be their neatly cleaned stay-out-of-jail project. Before either knew what had hit them exactly, they were splattered with five pounds of gorilla dung. While they stood there, in a room sprayed with something far more funk--a-fied than garlic cloves, the restroom door opened slowly.

Brad peeked his head in, looked over the mother of all messes, and cackled loudly while pinching his nostrils closed. "I've been hanging around for hours waiting on you to open that locker and get what you deserved. I thought since you wanted to prove how big of an ass you two are, then it's only right you smell appropriate for what comes out of the biggest ass I could find, a pregnant gorilla's. If either one of you fools could read, this wouldn't have happened. The balloon said, 'Don't touch.' Gorilla poop wasn't cheap but it was worth every penny. It was in high demand for gags such as the one that had Ebony and Floreese thinking of murder. Too distraught to care about jail, Patricia, or keeping his job, Floreese took off like a rocket toward the doorway and the short man standing in it.

"Get him!" Floreese yelled as he dashed over to squeeze the life from Brad's stumpy neck. Unfortunately, the gorilla droppings were a lot more slippery than he imagined. "Ahhhhhh!" he screamed out slamming to the cold hard floor. Ebony was cracking his side at the way his former cohost was stretched out in remnants of an apparently extremely regular primate. As he bent over to help Floreese off the floor, he learned firsthand just how slippery it really was after landing just as hard right next to him.

Alphonzo wandered into the restroom. "Who done messed—?" he said, then fell silent while his eyes did laps around the room and didn't stop until they came to rest on the fellas calmly stretched out on their backs. "I'm not even gonna ask what y'all have gotten your-selves into, but Ms. Patricia ain't having this. By the way, Brad from the sales group asked me to give y'all these." Alphonzo tossed two tickets their way.

Floreese caught one as it fluttered over him. "Very funny. A season pass to the zoo."

"Hey, I gotta run. This is too strange and I was never here." That having been said, Alphonzo backed out with a suspiciously watchful eye. "Uh-uh, too strange."

Octavia sat at a lonely table in the library of UTC, making final notes for her master's thesis and coming up with interview questions for I. Rome. She took a study break when Legacy rang her cell phone. "Hey, you," he replied when she answered. His voice was unseasonably tired but she would have recognized it in the midst of a hundred-mile-an-hour hurricane.

"You sound so subdued. Is everything all right?" She crossed her legs as she leaned back in the wooden chair covered with a cheap fab-ric far from leather.

"I've been working on a project for a client, but it's not going anywhere," he answered eventually. "Too busy thinking about my baby, I guess."

"You've been on my mind as well. Too bad. I'll be tied up here for a while or I'd stop by to see about you." She tried to imagine him working but realized that they hadn't discussed what he did for a living, if anything. "Hey, that's the first time I've heard you speak of working. What is it that you do exactly?" Not that it mattered much. She just wanted to picture him doing his thing but lacked the necessary stimuli to make her vision complete.

"I was starting to wonder if you cared. Usually that's the first thing out of a woman's mouth. Not that it isn't important but I've appreciated talking about other things with you." He was stalling and sensed that Octavia knew it. "I'm a painter, but you might have guessed that by now."

"A painter? What do you paint—houses, cars? What?"

"Everything that needs painting and some things that are perfect just the way they are, only I want to see them in another color." How vague was that? Octavia didn't push for him to elaborate. Instead, she changed the subject.

"By the way, I had this sensual dream about you last night," she admitted boldly.

"Only one?"

"A sistah's gotta start somewhere," she said, twirling a stand of her hair around her index finger. "Oh, before I forget. Cee-Cee, the girlfriend I've been bragging to about you, wants to meet at the Zanzibar Room in Deep Ellum tomorrow night for karaoke. It's a sixties theme and should be fun."

"Are you inviting me out on a date? If I'm meeting your friend, it must be getting serious."

"Are you in or not? And yes, it is getting serious."

"Count me in as long as I don't have to sing. You wouldn't want me to clear out the joint and have Cee-Cee looking at you cross-eyed."

"That's a chance I'll have to take, baby, and I'd love to continue this conversation, but I'll regret it if I don't get back to what I drove down here for."

"You do that and be careful on your way back to the city. Oh, by the way. Before I forget, are you free for Friday night?"

"I'm open," Octavia answered without thinking. "What time?"

"I'll get my hands on some wheels, four of them this time. I want to pick you up for a change. How's seven-thirty?"

"Cool, I'll see you tomorrow night then."

"Yeah. I'll try not to shame you too badly in front of your girlfriend, Bee-Bee."

"Legacy, her name is Cee-Cee."

"Just kidding. I'm looking forward to meeting her." When neither of them hung up, Legacy gave her something to think about. "Hey . . . love is."

"I know," was her sultry acknowledgment, before disconnecting the call. She smiled, thinking about how much she'd been looking forward to seeing him. In a single heartbeat, the playful hair twirling ceased. It hit Octavia that she was set to meet I. Rome at the same time on Friday evening. She spent the next two days trying to get around the dilemma of being in two places at once. Either way, she had the distinct fear deep inside that she was going to find herself on the bad end of the wrong decision.

25

Heels Over Head

Thursday afternoon, I. Rome strutted through the airport like he owned the place, draped in a black tailored Armani three-button suit and velvet Gucci loafers. He had two skycaps tracing his every step with his Louis Vuitton travel bags under arm. His dark sunshades didn't fool anyone. He agreed to sign autographs along his route to the exit, where Ty the Limo Guy patiently awaited his arrival.

Tyrone Wallace was six feet seven inches of beefy thickness, a former ball player who couldn't keep his nose clean and inevitably snorted his way out of the NFL. He'd fallen to the ranks of chuffer and served as I. Rome's personal driver each time the entertainer came home to visit family or to stop in to rattle some local cages. However, this time I. Rome was on a mission.

"Make sure they don't scuff the bags, Ty," he whispered, "them Louie's is the real thing." Then the superstar handed the huge driver a stack of assorted dead presidents before climbing into the back of the stretch Mercedes Benz. Ty marched to the rear of the shiny black luxury car to do what he was told. The baggage handlers gladly accepted generous tips, then stood on the curve ogling over the fine automobile.

"Ty, you have everything I asked for?"

"Yes sir, Mr. Rome. The bar is stocked, the rubbers are in the ashtray, and the DVD is loaded."

"What about the camera?"

"It's hidden in the digital clock this time."

"That's good looking-out. I'll take care of your expenses on the back end." I. Rome enjoyed watching the latest porn flicks while journeying between stops. The last time he was making his own movie in the backseat, the miniature hidden camera had popped out of the over-head compartment when the woman he'd picked up from a bar was all too eager to kick her feet up. That little mishap had cost him fifty thousand dollars to make an impending lawsuit disappear. Although that was a high price to pay for a brief roll in the hay, it didn't deter him from getting his kicks on the open road. This time, he'd be more deceptive.

Leaving terminal C, Ty heard his passenger demanding him to stop the car. He coasted over to the curve and idled there.

"Sir?"

"You see what I see?"

Ty scanned the sidewalk, knowing what to look for. "Yes, sir, I do."

"Then what are you still doing sitting there? Get your big ass out and make it happen, homie."

Ty unfolded his legs out of the driver's side, put on his chuffer hat, and proceeded to do what he'd done too many times to count. There was a young woman sitting on a bench. Although she appeared to be stranded, it was her attractive features that warranted Rome's attention. He knew how to pick them. "Catch a woman who's down on her luck, pour a few drinks, and she'll be give'n it up," Rome had crooned on his first platinum album. *Love Potion* hit the charts at number one for a reason.

The woman's eyes narrowed suspiciously when the limousine driver offered her a ride to the destination of her choosing. Her initial apprehensions subsided after she was informed of who it was actually doing the offering. She squealed with glee, then quickly took off for the back door of the long black Benz before Ty could open it for her. "Allow me to get that for you, miss," he said, hustling to do his job. "I'll also secure your bags."

"The bags? Oh yeah, just throw 'em in the back. They aren't mine anyway. They belong to my roommate. She could use some new ones. That'll serve her right for having me sitting up here all afternoon."

Ty pushed a hand-held remote to pop the trunk while holding the rear passenger door for her to climb her hot tail into the lion's den. "It takes a ho' to know a ho'," he hissed under his breath. "I wouldn't want it if it's that easy."

The woman was as happy as a hooker on payday as the door closed behind her. Ty manhandled the cheap luggage, tossing them in the spacious storage compartment as if they were nothing more than garbage bags. He couldn't help thinking that it wasn't the only cheap baggage along for the ride.

"I'm guessing by the way you're sitting there with your legs open, you know who I am," said I. Rome, in the ultracavalier manner he was known for. He was certain that his hunch would prove correct yet again. She was so ready to do whatever he commanded so he didn't bother with his usual I'll-act-like-I'm-getting-to-know-you routine. He poured her a drink, then made a mad dash for her stash as soon as Ty's foot mashed the gas. She was literally heels over head with the camera rolling before they reached the airport exit.

She fastened her pants and ran her fingers through her micro braids after a scenic route to her condo. "Here's my number." She wrote it on the back of a napkin used earlier to wipe up some of the mess they made. "You're still gonna call me, right?" Hope anchored her ridiculous presumption.

I. Rome stretched out the soft paper so he could make out her name, scrawled above her home number. "Uh, Aliza, I'll get atcha before I leave town."

"You'd better. I already got front-row tickets from the radio station. One of the deejays is an associate of mine. I'll talk to you later. Don't forget to call me."

"I won't. See'ya." He waved, all nice and sweet like they had embarked on the beginning of something beautiful. "Ty, make sure she gets some change for her time."

The bags were delivered to her door with a crisp hundred-dollar bill hanging out of a zipped compartment. "Mr. Rome wants you to pick up something nice for the concert."

"What? No backstage pass?" she said, insulted. "Don't stress, I'll work that out when he calls me."

"Yes, Ma'am. What-ever you say," Ty huffed as he made his way down two flights of stairs. "Don't hold your breath."

Ty removed a canister of air freshener from the glove box and administered a thorough fragrance shower while Mr. Rome made a quick phone call. "Where to, sir?"

The passenger sipped cognac from a brandy snifter. "There's a list of stops on the front seat beside you. Let's do 'em all this time. One right after the other." Rome sat in the back, counting condoms and watching the movie he only moments before had starred in. The rear window lowered slowly and out went the napkin with Aliza's phone number. Why call when they'd already done it all?

The Thursday night hotspot was the Zanzibar Room, an old renovated fire station. It was packed to the gills with music enthusiasts and people who were eager to get their karaoke on. Cee-Cee arrived first, checked on the table she'd reserved near the stage, then took a seat at the bar to wait for the others to show up. The bartender slid a mixed drink in front of her. He explained that it was an icebreaker from the chubby fellow sitting on the end. Cee-Cee turned to see who he was talking about. The brother was already hovering behind her, wearing a gang of confidence and a suit that went out of style when Lionel Richie was still a member of The Commodores.

"Hey, Cee-Cee. Long time no Cee-Cee," he joked, licking the tiny straw in his cocktail glass. "You've been taking care of yourself, or is that somebody else's job?"

Sad for her, she did recognize him. He'd put on more than a few pounds, but the cheese-eating grin that caused her to cringe was the same, only cheesier. He was Nicholas Nickleby the name-dropper. In his slimmer days, Cee-Cee had made the mistake of going to a house party with him. She remembered how much she regretted not taking her own car after he mentioned for the hundredth time that he knew the Dallas Cowboys record-breaking running back, personally, and how he'd sold cars to many of his teammates. Cee-Cee was a fly's breath away from screaming "Loser!" when he'd followed those tired lines by bragging that he'd once been on the same elevator with Tito Jackson.

"So how've-ya been, Nick?" she said in his general direction, avoiding eye contact.

He continued to flash his gold tooth with a star in it, despite her cold hello. "I can't complain. Bid'ness been good. Last month I bought a house on the same block as Emmitt Smith'nem. You want to come by for a little soirée I'm throwing to celebrate all my success? I invited the mayor and all of the Dallas Mavericks. None of 'em have RSVP'd yet, but they will."

She arched her back to ease the tension marching up and down it, dreading the thought of another endless night of his mindless jaw-jabbering. "No, Nick, I'm not going to be available for that."

"But I haven't told you when it is yet."

"I'll be busy whenever it is." She flashed a quick I-wish-we'd-never-met sneer to blow him off, but he didn't budge.

"You can think it over while I buy you another drink." He waved over the bartender. "Yo, get the lady another one of them. She's Cee-

Cee Lovely, the Hot One Hundred lady deejay. Told you I roll with celebrities."

Cee-Cee wanted to crawl into the same hole that Nicholas crawled out of and hide there herself. "No, bartender, that won't be necessary," she said, louder than she intended. "I'm waiting on friends." She arched her back again as she handed Nick the first drink he'd purchased for her. "I'll say this the nicest way I can. Not only do I not give a damn who you know or who knows you, I will have you arrested for stalking if you tell anyone else that you know me. Get it? Now move around before I have to ring for security. I bet you know them very well."

"Oh, you trippin'. Give a sistah a little radio show and she's too good for a brotha."

The bartender had been keeping an eye on them, guessing that Nick would get shot down for the fifth consecutive time. "Look, man, you might want to try another club. This ain't your night. Step aside before the boyz have to remove you from the premises. You feel me?"

Nicholas calmly placed the empty glass on the bar top, then chugged the one Cee-Cee had refused. "May as well drink it. It's paid for. But I'ma tell all of my famous friends to boycott this joint and—"

"Tell your story walking, fella," the sturdy barkeep warned him.

"Some people just don't know when they're out of their league," a smooth operator said from Cee-Cee's other side. "Hi, I'm Carlton." He was neatly dressed and leaning against her chair, a bit too close for comfort.

"Carlton?" She waited on a last name that was not forthcoming. "Carlton what?"

"Just plain old Carlton," he said quietly, with a suave veneer wrapped around it.

"I see." She noticed how he had his left hand conveniently tucked in the front pocket of his dress slacks. "Just-Carlton No-Last-Name, you must be married." His guilty expression affirmed her suspicion.

"So what's your story? The wife a bitch, she changed after the wedding, she got fat, or—let me guess—is it that she doesn't understand you?" The bartender chuckled when the slick dresser was at a sudden loss for words. "Thought so. Beat it, Just Carlton."

"Hey, I'm not giving up that easily. I might be married but I'm flexible."

"Well, you should and I'm not," she replied rudely. "So, do be a stranger and say hello to the Mrs. for me."

The attempted adulterer slinked off with a bruised ego. "You probably wasn't my type no way," he remarked harshly when he was at a safe distance.

"And we shall never know, toodles."

Cee-Cee Lovely, two points: lame men at the bar, zero. When the bartender placed another drink down she feared another plague descending on her. "Who's this one from?"

"It from me. Those two have been hustling here for months and I've never seen a woman dismiss them the way you did. Good luck enjoying your drink in peace while the other sharks settle in to test the waters." He tossed a glance down the bar at several men who were sizing her up.

"Thanks. It's hard work, but somebody's got to do it."

26

The Zanzibar Room

Minutes later, Octavia came in with Legacy, arm and arm to ward off various unattached women in the club who might have inclinations about making her man's acquaintance. Cee-Cee was impressed by Legacy's striking features and athletic physique, although Octavia's lengthy description didn't do him justice.

"Hey, girl," Cee-Cee cheered.

"Cee-Cee, you're all geared up." They hugged like old friends who hadn't seen one another in years. Perhaps it was the festive setting along with the pomp and circumstance of their first double-date. "Who are you all G'd up for, in your good clothes?"

"Wouldn't you like to know?" Cee-Cee was peeping over Octavia's shoulder, prodding her for an introduction. "I see you brought the handsome stranger."

"Oh yeah, him." Octavia blushed at Legacy while he played the strong silent type. "Baby, this is Cee-Cee. My girl who can't do no wrong if she tried."

"Cee-Cee, I'm pleased to meet you after hearing so many great things. From what Octavia says about you, she's lucky to have such a good friend."

"Charmed, I'm sure, Legacy." She nudged Octavia, impressed from the outset. "Wow, 'Tavia, manners and two compliments in the first sentence. I like him already."

"He'll do until the real thing comes along," Octavia joked, scanning the room. She discovered that all but one table had been commandeered. "I'm so excited about the sixties theme they chose for tonight but I don't see any open tables. There's one over by the stage, but it has one of those reserved signs on it."

"And guess who it's reserved for?" Cee-Cee asked knowingly. She grabbed her purse off the barstool and strutted away with a confident swagger to claim the reservation. "That's right. What's my name?"

"Cee-Cee," Octavia announced with bubbling assurance as she strutted off in the same parading manner her girlfriend had. "Come on, Legacy. We shant' be late."

"I guess we shant'." This was the first time he'd gotten the opportunity to see Octavia in her element, with her best friend. He continued beaming, being pulled behind her, all the way to the foot of the stage.

The waitress stopped by the table to take their drink orders. Her towering blonde beehive wig looked especially ridiculous atop a deep brown complexion as dark as hers. A mellow yellow chiffon off-the-shoulder dress was very authentic, but a busy evening of schlepping drinks and hot wings would make her wish she'd passed on the sling-back pumps rented to accentuate the costume.

She struck a pose, allowing them to take in all her splendor. Her fitted dress had a slit up the side, cut farther up her thigh than the designer had intended. Octavia slid her chair closer to Legacy's when the waitress started paying way too much attention to the only man at the table. "What are y'all drinking?"

"The ladies will have cosmopolitans and I'll have an orange juice," Legacy said, as if it had been discussed beforehand. Octavia was surprised. She hadn't told him what the cocktail of the season was, but he seemed to pull a rabbit out of his hat.

"That's right, baby, she applauded. "But, how'd you know?"

"I read about it in this magazine. It was in this article about who's who and what they drink. Cosmopolitans were far above the others and I figured a couple of social-climbers like yourselves might find it appealing."

"That's why I'm keeping you. 'Cause you're so appealing, too."

Cee-Cee was too busy giving the room a thorough once-over to catch wind of what happened. She enjoyed people-watching more than just about anything else, and the collection of highbrows and regular folk packed in the small venue made for outstanding observation. "Hey, is that Devin over there?"

"Where, girl?" Octavia spun around in her chair. "Ooh, it sure is but that's not Sylvia with him."

"Who's Sylvia?" asked Legacy, not wanting to be left out.

"She's in our Hat Chat group. You know, girl stuff."

"Who's Devin?" His question was flanked by a subtle determination to understand the importance of his woman excited to see another man, for any reason.

"Sylvia's husband," she answered, as if he should have guessed.

"Then why is he with another woman?"

"That's exactly what I'm going to find out," Cee-Cee answered, getting up from the table.

While Cee-Cee was off to put her nose in affairs that had nothing to do with her, Octavia considered breaking her date with Legacy for the following night but couldn't bring herself to do it. He seemed so happy to be in her company and she couldn't see bringing that to a screeching halt. He had given her so much in the past week in the way of simple bliss that it made her feel sick to her stomach when she contemplated his disappointment. She received a temporary stay of self-persecution when the waitress reappeared with a cool remedy to help her gloss over the decision she made to remain reluctantly silent.

Legacy lifted the mug of juice from the table. "What should we toast to?"

"Not without me," Cee-Cee said, plopping down in the seat like a Raggedy Ann doll.

"So, what was Devin up to?" Octavia asked hurriedly, expecting some titillating gossip.

"Nothing. That's his sister. She's visiting in from Cali."

"That doesn't look like any sister to me," Octavia challenged, taking in another eyeful. When she got caught peeping, Devin waved and smiled. "Hey, Devin," she yelled in his direction, returning his energy. "I don't care what you say, Cee-Cee. I think he's testing the market."

"Believe me, they're related. Got the same cute little teeth and everything. Sylvia's safe for now." Cee-Cee hadn't had the chance to apprise Octavia of what had gone down at the beauty shop involving the Truth Chamber experiment. "Anyway, I thought we were toasting."

"Umm, that's right." Octavia had taken a sip while two-facing Sylvia's man. "Honey, why don't you say something sweet so Cee-Cee can see just how lucky I am."

"I'll try." Legacy squinted his eyes, thinking up something appropriate for the occasion. "I've got it. Let's raise our glasses to love and happiness. Shall they forever co-exist, hand in hand, kiss after kiss after kiss."

"Ahh, he is so special," Cee-Cee congratulated, leaning over toward Octavia. "Can we share him?"

"Don't make me hurt you," Octavia remarked, sneering playfully. "I love you but I will not hesitate to cut you over this man." Legacy laughed, then softly planted his lips on hers.

"I'll drink to that," Cee-Cee saluted, her glass lowered to her mouth.

"Cee, you'll drink to anything."

"I know that's right. Times like these, I'll drink to everything, too."

As they entered into the usual small talk that didn't make their office-time did-you-know, the first act was called to the stage. Four men trumped up there and dug in to The Temptations' hit song, "I Can't Get Next To You." Most of the talent emanated from the tall thin

baritone who carried the quartet for most of the number. Octavia sang
along in perfect harmony while Legacy tried to follow the lyrics scroll-
ing up on the gigantic projector screen. The crowd congratulated their
effort with louder whistling and clapping than they deserved.

"I didn't know you like the Temps, Legacy," Octavia yelled over the
crowd noise. "They're one of my favorites."

"Who'r the Temps? I was impressed by the way those guys put their
dance steps together."

Cee-Cee sipped her drink, routinely checking the door. "Is he for
real? Work with him, girl. Work with him."

"He needs me. I know it. He does." Octavia stroked Legacy's face
softly with her fingertips. "And he's too fine to throw back."

"I know that's right, 'Tavia. When you leave for work, chain him to
the bed, then unplug the phone and give him just enough food and
water to keep his strength up."

"One slice of bread and a Dixie cup," Octavia added.

"Ooh, you' wrong for that, but I wouldn't blame you." The cosmopolitans were running their course. Cee-Cee tried hard not to resent
the fact that she was alone, for the time being, as Octavia continued
showing her tail.

An hour glided by, more drinks were delivered, several acts went
up, and a few of them actually shined among those who couldn't carry
a tune between them. Nonetheless, their bravery was rewarded with
the audience paying tribute to each one, regardless of how many notes
fell flat. It was a team effort to keep the show moving and the good
times rolling. Octavia chased the inevitable away when it made multi-
ple attempts to trample her spirits. How she was going to renege on
her date ran circles around how much information she planned on
divulging when doing it.

The new announcer revved the crowd with a hilarious imperson-
ation of Little Richard. Cee-Cee laughed until her sides ached when
the man unfastened his shirt and dabbed his chest down with a hand-

kerchief made of lace. Also enthralled in hysterics, Octavia didn't hear him calling her up to do a number. Someone had passed him a note informing him how well she could blow. When he called her name a second time, Legacy nudged her.

"Octavia, he wants you to go up there. The guy is calling for you."

Initially, she clung to her chair. The man on stage bid everyone to encourage her aboard. Cee-Cee's urging screams were the loudest. The riotous applause grew until Octavia gave up all hopes of staving them off. Since she'd omitted her singing prowess from their previous conversations, Legacy floated back and forth between apprehension and anxiousness.

Octavia flashed a nervous but thankful grin to those who made it impossible for her to refuse. With the microphone held loosely, she whispered something to the host, then walked to center stage. "I'm in an Sistah Etta frame of mind. I hope you'll indulge me."

The audience settled in for some of what they've heard before—Octavia tearing the roof off the joint. As the music began, she bowed her head and started in low. She wowed them with the soul stirrings of Etta James's chart-topper "At Last." The screen had been turned off so the words to the song would not scroll. Not one person would have dared to utter a note if it had because she sang it so beautifully alone. Legacy was inadequately prepared for her sensational solo. If he hadn't already had it in mind that she was the woman for him, the way she piped out those lyrics would have removed any doubt. Her soulful essence poured out with each word she sang.

After a standing ovation, her fans pleaded for an encore. "More," they shouted, from the front to the rear. Inspired to give the people what they wanted, more is what she gave them. "This time I want you to bring up the screen so the sistahs can do this one with me. This is for my Boo. Isn't he fine, ladies?" Legacy was too flattered to hide his face, although he had to fight the urge. The women applauded with too much enthusiasm for their dates' liking, but they represented honestly. "I know he is," Octavia agreed. "He bet' not leave me neither. I'd sic the law on that man to drag him back home to me if he did." The next song had them dancing in the aisles. It would have done Etta James proud to hear her beloved favorite, "Something's Got A Hold On Me and It Must be Love," bringing people to their feet all these years later. Octavia convinced everyone to help her bring it home by drumming up audience participation as if she were getting paid to do it. Her energy was returned in spades. Several minutes after she had reclaimed her seat at the table, customers were still riding high on the tune that she had enjoyed as much as they did.

"Come on, now. It was not right of you to keep something that good from me," Legacy complimented, overwhelmed with her singing voice and stage presence. "I think you've missed your calling. They were screaming at the top of their lungs for you. It was stupendous."

"They know soul when they hear it," Cee-Cee asserted. "Strange' girl. Go, girl."

"Thank you very much. I do what I can," Octavia replied humbly.

Legacy was mesmerized. "Octavia, why didn't you tell me that you could sing like that?"

"I can't let you know everything about me all at once. I want you to take your time learning each and every one of my many talents. Men get bored too easily. A sistah has to make it last."

"Ooh, I heard that. String him along," Cee-Cee advised from the other side of her fourth glass of artificial stimulation.

"What's up, y'all? Sorry I'm late," Alphonzo apologized, then took the seat next to Cee-Cee. "I must've just missed something special, 'cause folks were walking to their cars going on about Etta James and somebody ripping it up."

"Heyyyy Honey. You missed 'Tavia bringing . . . down-the-house," Cee-Cee informed him slovenly, her eyes bloodshot red.

"Looks like I did miss out. 'Tavia's got the chops." He extended his hand for an introduction. "I'm Alphonzo Greenbriar."

"Legacy Childs. Nice to meetcha."

"I hate I missed something too," Octavia quipped, expecting an explanation for the "Hey, honey" Cee-Cee spread on Alphonzo. She expected to be clued in on the haps before her best friend started keeping time with a new love interest. "Uh, Cee-Cee . . . Alphonzo? I'm waiting on somebody to fill me in. Come now, there's no business like your girlfriend's business so, hit me with it."

"We gon' have'ta discuss this in the mornin'," Cee-Cee groaned. "I don't feel so good." The night was fleeting and so were Cee-Cee's chances of making it home without leaving her dignity and all the vodka she drank on the sidewalk.

Alphonzo's disapproval was written all over his face. "How many of those cute pink cocktails did she have?" he asked Octavia, watching Cee-Cee fall asleep at the table.

"My guess would be one too many, Zo. Could I trust you to get her home safely? She's wasted."

"Yep, I'll run her home." He read his watch before taking Cee-Cee by the hand. "Let's go, Stumble Bunny. I'd better get you to bed by midnight, or else you might turn into a pumpkin."

Both Legacy and Octavia eventually understood his misguided Cinderella reference. "Let me get her purse and we'll help y'all out to your car." Octavia searched the table to see if they were leaving anything behind. "Cee-Cee can swing by here tomorrow to pick up hers."

"Naw, 'Tavia, we can't leave a Benz down here overnight. They'll strip that car of everything, including the alarm system," Alphonzo explained. "Can you drop it off at Cee-Cee's place while I drive Ms. Daisy here?"

"You're probably right. Legacy, do you mind following me in the Jeep over to Northwest Highway?"

"No, not at all. Anything to help."

Alphonzo had been wondering just how close Legacy and Octavia were. Not that he was interested for himself—he was curious as to what type of man had the skills to finesse Octavia away from I. Rome. That had him checking Legacy's every move. When Octavia's date reached in his pocket for Octavia's keys, he had his answer. No woman allows a man behind her wheel unless he's allowed other places, too, Alphonzo reasoned.

"Thanks man, I really appreciate this." Alphonzo was genuinely grateful. He nodded his thanks in an ultrahip manner, then helped Cee-Cee away from the table. It seemed she'd had her fill of both entertainment and intoxicating elixirs.

Since Cee-Cee lived closer to Octavia than to Legacy, they decided, after the Benz was safe and sound, that it was more sensible for Legacy to stay the night at Octavia's apartment. Good news, bad news; Legacy had fallen asleep on the sofa by the time she emerged from her bedroom, having stripped down to almost nothing at all. She remembered to thank Cee-Cee later for buying her more time via an extremely timely drunken stupor.

Octavia was conflicted over wanting to make love with Legacy, to share his passion, be taken in and subdued by his power, and hoping that it all lasted passed beyond the rise of the following sun. He wasn't like the other men who provided little more than something to do until the time came to find something to keep. Legacy was much different. His inner qualities shook her to the core and touched her in places that no man had before. Octavia had begun a metamorphosis of change. The casual romances of her yesterdays were no longer enough to sustain her hunger for a love supreme. Legacy was alluring. Her first taste proved addictive. Now that she had her heart set on getting more of it, there was no settling for anything less. She understood that most people only got one shot at true love, if they were lucky. The time had come for Octavia to take her shot before her luck changed, and slam the door shut on what she had with I. Rome.

There was a silver lining in the storm clouds above, not the clouds outside, but the ones hovering above Octavia's head, as she covered Legacy with an authentic Aztec blanket, then climbed into her bed alone. Sleep couldn't have come fast enough if it had jumped in the sack before she did. There was a long night of tossing and turning in store for her, and lots of praying for it all to turn out right.

27

Not If I Can Help It

"Just tell me if I embarrassed myself as much as I think I did last night," Cee-Cee whispered, her head hanging down. She'd been wearing a cold towel wrapped around the back of her neck for most of the day.

"Cee-Cee, don't let falling asleep at the nightclub get you down," Octavia said, trying to comfort her past one heck of a hangover. "No one knew that you were sloppy drunk but us. Me, Legacy, and *Alphonzo*. She tossed Alphonzo's name real slow, like she was asking a question.

Cee-Cee caught it. "I was going to tell you but it happened kind of fast. We got to talking about you and the next thing I knew, we were talking about us, me and him I mean."

"Well, I'll forgive you this time, but I'll say one thing, he was great at taking care of you last night."

"You don't know the half of it." She finally looked up, eyes still tired and red. "I made a mess of my bathroom, praying to the porcelain god, Ooh-Rallllph." Each time she regurgitated the night before, that's who it sounded like she was calling.

"Ehhhh, yuck!" Octavia imagined her throwing up, hanging on to the toilet for dear life. "Did you make the same promise as always when you've had too much to drink?"

"You know I did. I promised for the umpteenth time that I would never drink another drop if I was allowed to make it through the night." A smile tickled at her lips. It was her first one of the day. "This time I was serious, kinda." Then she laughed at how ridiculous it was to beg for temporary redemption from something she was not trying to give up permanently. "Hey, that Legacy seemed wild about Octavia. He stayed all up in your grill. So, how does it feel to have a man's undivided attention with so many other women tryna catch his eye? I saw 'em showing their teeth, including that shameless waitress."

Octavia's eyes drifted down like she was thinking about something other than the question that Cee-Cee was wanting an answer to. "Yeah, I guess. Never noticed, really."

"Then why the long face? You look about as bad as I feel."

"Cee-Cee, I'm jammed up over having to see Isaiah tonight. Legacy's a good man, and I'm afraid to screw up and miss out on the real thing. He told me that he'd planned something special and considering our first two dates, I'm expecting dinner at the White House."

"I could be wrong but it sounds like a certain sistah wants her cake and eat it too? Greed is an ugly monster, Tavia."

"No, that's not it at all. I can't see past Legacy. My future is tied to him and that's the way I want it. I've even decided to put the booty on the shelf."

"The way I see it, there's two ways you could handle it. Tell the station to go jump in the lake and look out for Octavia, or tell Legacy that you have something to do for work and hope he'll understand. He sure seems like the reasonable type." When Octavia didn't respond, Cee-Cee knew there was more to it. "Unless there's some unknown secret that you haven't told mama."

"Can't get anything past you. I think that I need to see Isaiah again more than I realized. I want to let it go on my terms."

"Then that's what you'll have to do. Me, on the other hand, I've got to find a place to lay this pounding head of mine. Can you hear a five-piece horn section from there?"

"No, not from here." Octavia rubbed the back of Cee-Cee's hand in an effort to say thank you for making it plain what she *had* to do.

Legacy was openly taken aback when Octavia called and explained how she had to back out unavoidably due to something that came up, something work-related. But he said that he did understand and that her career was important. If it was so easy to stretch the truth, then why was she left feeling so deceitful? She agreed to call him later that night and discuss plans to make it up to him over the weekend. Octavia didn't think too highly of herself after she hung up the phone.

Later that evening, Legacy practiced chords on the baby grand piano in the foyer of the big house. His eyes remained closed for most of it because of how much the melody moved him. I. Rome watched him carefully from the royal blue loveseat shaped like a rising ocean wave. Legacy had agreed to discount the artwork I. Rome requisitioned for his Chicago home, and in return his tutelage was required for down payment.

When Legacy came to a change in the music that he couldn't nail down after several failed attempts, I. Rome went over to show him a few tricks he came across in his early years of tickling the ivories. "Peep this. Let your fingers follow the music that's in your head, not the other way around. Try it again but go a lil' faster when you get to the part you're struggling with." Legacy composed himself and started in again. This time, he played with the assurance of a concert pianist. When he approached the troubled spot, he internalized what his instructor said and let the music move his fingers right on through it, without a hitch. I. Rome leapt off the wave of blue when Legacy's fingers stopped moving. "See? That's it. Man, that was tight. How long have you been playing?"

"About six months," Legacy said, still in shock after playing his song from beginning to end. "I didn't think I could do it. Thanks, Rome. I'll have to knock off a few more bucks from my fee. You don't know how much you've helped me."

"That's all. In six months I was still playing chopsticks. You might be a whatchamacallit, one of them prodigies. And I want you to remember who helped you realize that when you're tryna decide how much to bill me for that Legacy original."

"No doubt. I'll put together something you won't believe." Legacy stood up from the piano bench with something on his mind. "Rome? I have some recording equipment in the guest house. You think I can play it again, perfect like that?"

"I don't see why not. You done it once, so ain't nothing to it but to do it again. I've got some time to help you set it up before my hot date with this lil' philly I've been seeing from time to time. She can wait, always has befo'."

Disconnecting the recording equipment, Legacy unplugged wires and gathered everything he needed to put his song on tape. I. Rome flipped through an art portfolio to get a better idea of what he could look forward to, once Legacy's masterpiece was completed. He eyed his diamond-beveled watch and realized he'd better call and inform his date that he would be running late.

While the number he dialed from his cell phone rang, something fell from the leather-bound collection of assorted sketches and multi-colored prints. He picked it up to put it back, then something about it caught his attention. It was a long strip of black-and-white pictures that had been taken at a cheap photo booth. In each frame, Legacy was cheek to cheek with Octavia. They were all hugged up and happy, too happy for I. Rome, in fact. He turned his back to Legacy to take a more serious look at it. The sinister grin that crept on his face was only a prelude to the drama he was set on bringing to the enchanted couple's lives. He walked out of earshot to put his devious plan into action when Octavia answered his call. "Oh, hello. Baby girl, I'm caught up right now but I thought it would save us some time if I had the limo roll by, swoop you up, and bring you to me. You ready?"

"I guess as ready as I'm going to be," Octavia replied with reluctance. "I thought we'd have a chance to talk before dinner but you haven't been taking my calls. Never mind, when is Ty coming?"

"Give him a few ticks, he ain't too far away."

After making another call to Ty in the car, I. Rome helped carry the heavy electronics inside the big house. He watched his expensive timepiece while Legacy played again, as flawlessly as he had before. One take and it was done. They cued the tape player and listened to the one song Legacy knew, the one that popped in his head one day and refused to leave. He couldn't wait to share it with a certain special someone. The title, "Octavia's Theme," seemed appropriate.

I. Rome had been uncharacteristically quiet. The anticipation was killing him. Now he understood why Octavia had not seemed herself lately. Other men had dropped in and out of her life—Rome wasn't so naïve to believe otherwise—but they hadn't affected her like this. For the first time during their tenuous relationship, he felt like a second-teamer wanting his starting position back and concluded that he'd found a way to engineer it.

Octavia rolled the same single bead on her pearl necklace between the tips of her forefinger and thumb while the limo glided through the city streets. Lying to Legacy had her swimming in a blue funk. No matter how many times she thought of backing out on the interview, knowing that it would be over and done within a few hours kept her steady on-course. Besides, it was something she *had* to do.

As the car turned into a familiar subdivision, Octavia snapped out of the guilty spell, then fell headlong into a deep well of worry. "Tyron, where are you taking me?" she asked. Her tone was strained, as if she had been kidnapped.

"To Mr. Rome. He's at this house just up the street. We're almost there."

Oh no, she thought, settling back against the seat. She was not trying to be introduced to one of Legacy's neighbors as a friend of I. Rome's and have Legacy find out about it later. Despite the dark tint over the windows, it couldn't have been dark enough to distort the shame running rampant in that backseat.

"Ms. Octavia, are you okay?" Ty asked, scoping her from his rearview mirror. Octavia cowered behind a labored expression, afraid to respond as they stopped directly in front of the mansion, which dwarfed the guest house she had unrestricted access to.

"Ty, is this the place where Isaiah asked you to bring me?"

"Yes, ma'am, that's him coming out now."

Octavia was about to implode with a cry that wouldn't come out. It was devastating to see her worlds heading on a collision course. She wished she could have disappeared. Even dying a sudden death was a more tolerable sentence than seeing Legacy step out of that front door behind her date. "God, what have I done?" Ty overheard her say, as the two men marched casually toward her.

"So Rome, who's the honey?" Legacy asked. "Another *publicist?*" There was the bright luminance in Legacy's smile that Octavia had come to cherish, although she was all but certain that it would be the last time she'd get to enjoy it. I. Rome didn't seem to think Legacy's brand of humor was all that witty, although that didn't dampen his sheepish grin one bit.

"Naw, I had to let the *publicist* go. She was too clingy. This one here is a real freak that I've been keeping around when I want to get triple-X-rated. She does this trick with her tongue and . . . never mind all that. I think you'll like her." There was that sinister expression, leading the way to a gruesome cataclysm.

Ty emerged from the front to attend the back door. Legacy was still smiling when the door opened; however, his joyous tenor faded when the introductions began. "Come on out, baby," I. Rome insisted when Octavia didn't move an inch. Her hesitation broadened I. Rome's grin twofold. "I want you to meet my boy, Legacy. Come on now, this is a very busy man." With the wind taken out of her sails, she inhaled to keep from crying as she climbed out to see what the face of doom looked like up close. "That's a good girl," he prodded, eager to watch the fireworks. "Hey, Legacy, this is the one I told you about. Octavia, holla at ma' boy."

Legacy swore his heart stopped when she slowly made her way outside the luxury sedan, all dolled up. I. Rome and Ty studied the interaction, for apparently different reasons. Rome's was obvious only to him but Ty knew his M.O. The stoic scene reeked of raw despicability.

I. Rome stepped up his game plan when silence wedged between Octavia and Legacy. Octavia couldn't bring herself to look at him, fearing the stinging glare of disappointment shining back at her. "What, don't tell me y'all know each other?" Rome said with a dash of make-believe innocence, pretending to be surprised over the despair he'd manufactured.

"No. I must've been mistaken," Legacy replied evenly. "She looks a lot like someone I thought I knew but I couldn't have been more wrong. I don't know this sistah at all." He turned away, visibly disturbed.

"Let's go then, I'm starvin'," I. Rome gushed. He was really feeling himself when he escorted a bewildered Octavia back inside the car. Legacy stood in the doorway of loneliness as the limo pulled away. The taillights blinked at him before disappearing out of sight.

The restaurant sat along the row of eateries on Beltline Road in Addison, a small adjoining suburb to Dallas. Octavia was understandably subdued on the way. I. Rome allowed her the time to mull over what he had happened, but he began working a new strategy as soon as they were seated at a quiet table.

"What's been up with you, baby? I thought you'd be happy to get some quality time." He appeared utterly frustrated when it was clear that she was consumed with a man other than him. "I came all this way to tell you how I've missed you and want a new future, with you at the center of it."

"You were supposed to call me when you got here. Why didn't you?" Octavia was working a strategy, too. Hers began with changing the subject to facilitate it.

"Why are we talking about me calling or not calling?"

"Why are you answering a question with a question?" she replied to get under his skin. "You tend to do that, you know, just before you lie."

"Okay, look. I'll be honest," Rome said, just before lying. "I've been looking into buying a home here, being closer to my moms and closer to you. I don't care about the concert tomorrow. I was saving it as a surprise, but I might as well ask you now."

"I hope you're not about to ask me to be wife number three," she wanted to say. Instead, she sat there listening and waiting on the lies to start flying out of his mouth.

" 'Tavia, you might not remember but I'll never forget how happy you made me back in the day, when we were full-timing it. You made me laugh and made me feel special, like I could do anything I set my mind to." Octavia worked diligently at not remembering while he continued to pour it on. "When I'm on the road, alone in those hotel rooms, I keep coming back to you when I think of the happiest times of my life. You made me feel special every day. And, that's why I've decided to ask you to . . . join me on the road, sing duets with me, and be a part of the platinum tour." He gloated like the offer was a can't-miss.

"Isaiah, this may come as a shock, but I'm not in the least bit interested in shutting down my life and traipsing around the country behind you."

"We're doing three shows in Europe, too," he added, as if it made a difference.

"I don't even like Europe. There're not enough of us over there for my taste, but that's neither here nor there. You are so full of yourself that I'm embarrassed for you 'cause I know you're not. If you took a minute to listen to yourself, you would be." She shook her head, annoyed with him. "Since we've been at this table, you've not once complimented my dress or how nice I look. It's been all about you. You-you-you. 'Octavia, I've missed you. Octavia, you make me so happy. Octavia, you make me feel special.' It's always been about you. I've been too afraid to lose something that I never had." I. Rome turned his head and looked away. That didn't stop Octavia from going for the jugular. "No, you don't have to look at me to know what I'm saying is true. You and I both know it." She took a much-needed deep breath to let out what had built up over time. "Let me tell you about me. What I've been going through while you're on tour *with who-ever* in those hotel rooms. I've grown tired of spending Valentine's Day, Christmas, and my birthday alone or with *who-ever* I choose to fill the void. I've grown tired of trying to hold on this fairy-tale princess fixation you had me believing in and that I was lucky to get the little piece of your love that you were willing to give me."

"You finished?" he huffed, temper flaring.

"No, I'm not finished. I've also grown tired of a man who doesn't deserve me while he was renting space in my heart and messing up my head. I'm not sure if the worse part is your being stressed that I'm finally standing up for myself or that it took me so long to realize just . . . how tired I am." She had to control her emotions, noticing that people from nearby tables were staring in her mouth. "I almost blew my chance at something real. A real man, mine. He isn't into games or jumping from woman to woman each time another video ho' comes on the set. No more fairy tales, Isaiah, no more. I'm meant to be a real live princess or at least be treated like one. I guess what it all boils down to is my need to make you fully aware that I've grown tired of everything having to do with you." She lifted her purse from the table as she stood to leave. I. Rome snatched her by the wrist to stop her until he had his say as well. Instinctively she tried to pull away, but he refused to release his grasp.

"That's some performance. I've done you one better, though. You sure you want to up and walk out on me when you already tore yo' drawze with Legacy!" Suddenly Octavia gave up on her earlier decision to retreat, so I. Rome loosened his grip. "Uh-huh, yeah. I know about you and that mutt. He ain't even a real brotha and look at you, 'bout to break outta here hoping he'll take your black-ass back. Too bad I had to hip him to our arrangement." Octavia didn't want to believe what she was hearing. How could he have known about her feelings for Legacy?

"I should've guessed it when you popped out of that front door. I should have known it wasn't a coincidence. How could you? Are you so screwed up that you'd ruin my good thing on purpose? Fool that I am. Humph, fool that I was. Just what kind of sick bastard are you?"

"One who's willing to buy you dinner and let bygones be bygones," he replied with his smooth demeanor restored.

"Then you're a bigger sucker than I thought. You need to call Tyron 'cause I'm ret' to go." She turned her nose up, expecting him to summon for the limousine.

"You'd you'd better kick dust then. Ty is *my* limo guy and I'm *not* ret' to go!" He spat her words back with a heavy dose of malice heaped on for good measure.

Insulted yet again, Octavia gathered herself before throwing caution to the wind and casting all intentions of landing her interview aside. Finally, salvaging her career took a backseat to holding on to the last bit of integrity she had. When she stormed past several tables with patrons gawking at the woman who'd been rudely advised to get home the best way she could, she felt renewed and refreshed. Despite having to pay for it later, Octavia knew she made right decision. Hopefully, it wasn't too late to salvage what had been torn and tattered. A chance at love with Legacy.

28

Color Me Naked

"Taxi!" Octavia screamed as she tore out of the swanky eating establishment. Although it was primetime Friday, there was not one cab it sight. Ty had been chatting with the valet attendant when he saw Octavia waving her arms wildly like the woman on the bad end of a date that never should have happened.

"Ms. Octavia!" he called out. His concern was evident. "Ms. Octavia, did something happen to you?"

"You bet it did, Tyrone. I finally woke up from that messed-up dream I. Rome had me believing was real."

"Good for you, ma'am. Good for you." Over the years, he had come to see her lied to, disrespected, and handled rougher than a woman should have had to deal with. He'd seen I. Rome step over the line with other women as well. It seemed that Ty had also grown tired of the oversexed musician manipulating his success to use people as pawns in his psychotic dysfunctional world. "If I didn't need this gig, I'd drive you home myself."

"Don't put your money on hold because of me. I'll be just fine." She flipped on her cell phone, then pressed speed dial while pacing in front of the restaurant.

Legacy sped down the tollway, en route to meet Marshall and Jasmine for dinner. He was thinking up ways to explain why he was showing up emptyhanded after bringing them down on a private chartered jet to meet Octavia. Marshall's next football game was two days away, in Atlanta, so it was arranged for them to fly in for a late meal, then hop back on that plane.

With the stereo blaring in his fire engine-red Lamborghini, Legacy nearly missed the phone ringing from its stand on the console. "Hold on," he yelled in the speaking end of it. He pressed the power window button then picked up the phone again. "Marshall, is that you?"

"No, this is Octavia. And . . . before you hang up, I was wondering if it was too late to apologize." She winced when asking his forgiveness.

"Where are you?"

"I'm at La Palacade on Beltline, standing out front."

"I'm exiting on Beltline now. Don't move. I'm on my way."

The distant sound of screeching tires caused Octavia to take notice. Her mind had drifted several times in the three-minute window since their call. What her knight in shiny armor would be riding up in to save the damsel in distress wasn't one of the questions it drifted past.

She was searching the busy avenue in both directions when the sports car skidded to an abrupt stop, inches from where she stood. Someone with too much money was in a big hurry, she thought, still looking out for Legacy to arrive.

The power windows of the sports car lowered. "Just get in!" Octavia heard the driver demand from inside the hundred-thousand-dollar high-performance machine. "Get in, Octavia, we're late." Although Legacy hadn't made an attempt to look her way, she graciously accepted his invitation. She assumed the extravagant automobile belonged to the rich man that Legacy was house-sitting for.

"Legacy, I know that I owe you an explanation. It was just going to be dinner and an interview," she said, speaking to his profile when he continued facing forward. "Trust me. Just dinner. Nothing more."

"Who are you trying to convince, me or you?"

"Please let me tell you what I should have in the beginning, about me and Isaiah."

"Save it. I don't want to know. I just need you to meet some very important people who've made special concessions to get here." Neither of them uttered another sound until they were in the presence of Legacy's closest friends.

Sambuca's Jazz Café was happening, as usual. A local band played the last number in a forty-five minute set. It must have been well received because the place erupted with cheers while Legacy asked the hostess to point out his guest's table. "There he is," Jasmine screeched, louder than Marshall felt necessary. "Heyyyy, Legacy." She threw her arms around his neck and squeezed hard.

"What's up, Freelance?" Marshall's hello was less amorous. "I've been smacking on bread for the past thirty minutes, man. We almost gave up on you and got to grubbin'." Octaiva was too disposed with her own woes to catch the nickname Marshall had used for Legacy.

"We did not," Jasmine argued, hushing her husband's complaints. "I knew you'd show up." Like a doting sister, Jasmine was looking over Legacy's date to see if she approved.

"I'm sorry. I had to make a stop and pick up a package," Legacy explained before he led in with a short and curt introduction. "This is Octavia Longbow. Octavia, that's Jasmine and Marshall Coates."

"Hey," said Marshall, still reading over the menu as if he hadn't been studying it from the moment he'd sat down.

"Pleased to meet you, Octavia. Legacy's told us a lot about you," Jasmine offered. "Hurry up and get comfortable so we can get in your business," she added with a quirky flip of her hair.

"I'm pleased to make your acquaintance also, Jasmine." Octavia's face was riddled with questions. Why was this Jasmine person all over Legacy and why didn't Marshall seem to mind? She turned toward Legacy, who was perusing the menu, too. "Legacy, it seems, has neglected to mention that he knew Marshall."

Now Jasmine had questions. "Octavia, I had no idea you knew my husband."

"Remember, all of us went to UTC together," Legacy responded in his woman's stead although he had yet to set his eyes on her face.

Marshall had something on his mind that he couldn't shake until it finally came to him. "Octavia Longbow! I knew that name sounded familiar," he said, ah-ha fashion. Jasmine was getting ready to slap him upside that big head of his if Octavia was one of the women who had tapped on her man's door when they were back in school. "Octavia Longbow, you're a legend. I heard this story about some skunks locked in this brotha's dorm room. They had to shut down a whole wing for a month."

"Actually, it was only three weeks, but who's counting." She was surprised that the superstar had knowledge of her get-even tactics when a conceited fraternity brat ran his big mouth after she shared his bed.

"Free, I like this one," Marshall yelled, slapping him on the shoulder. "You'd better check yourself 'cause from what I've heard, she don't play."

Legacy peered at him, not so sure he agreed. "Oh, I beg to differ Marshall. She's got much game."

Staring at Legacy in disbelief, Jasmine jumped in his behind with two feet. "Legacy Childs! I know you know better. What's gotten into you? I didn't fly way down here for dinner only for you to show out."

"What'd I say?" Legacy asked, looking confused.

"Don't make me take off my shoe at this table and shame all of us," she answered back. "I didn't know you had it in you to be actin' like . . . like a typical man."

"Ahh, there she goes," Marshall threw in. "*Be actin'*. Freelance, you're gonna get it." Marshall could easily tell his wife was really steaming when her use of proper English detoured.

"Maybe I can clear this up," Octavia suggested. She didn't know where to start so she plowed right in at the end. "Y'all, I'm really sorry to ruin your trip but Legacy's so upset that he can't even stand to look at me and I probably deserve that." Jasmine's stinging glare hadn't worn off when Octavia laid it out for their total consumption. Marshall was listening attentively and smacking on a cold muffin as she continued. "I was seeing someone when Legacy and I met. I wasn't ready to come clean about the other man, even though I knew it was over. That's something a woman needs to say in person, to be sure the man she's dumping understands that she's for real."

"That's right, girl. Don't worry about these menfolk," Jasmine said adamantly, encouraging her sister in need of moral support. "I'm on your side."

When the waiter stopped by to rattle off dinner specials, Marshall waved him off harshly. "Nah, man. We're not ready yet. This is getting good."

"Well, the brotha I decided to let go is not the kind of man who let's go until you make it real plain. Know what I mean?"

"I sure do, keep going." That was Jasmine again, lending her support and frowning Legacy into a corner.

"The man I was seeing had plans to come here for a concert and I agreed to interview him for the radio station I work for. It was an error in judgment, I see that now, but at the time it appeared to be an opportunity to kill two birds with one stone. I booked an in-depth interview from an entertainer who's been shunning the media after a couple of bad stories exposing his personal life and a chance to show him that I was moving on."

Marshall reached into that memory bank like he had earlier. "Jazz, isn't I. Rome in town for a concert?" He cast his eyes on Octavia for a response.

"You know him, too?" Octavia asked, not thinking it would have come to naming names. "I should have guessed it. UTC, right?"

"Yep, ol' boy's been getting around for a while." Marshall slammed his mouth closed when he heard his words imply that Octavia was simply another link in I. Rome's chain of fools. "Hey, I didn't mean . . ."

"Shut up, then," Jasmine barked, averting her ruffled attitude from Legacy toward him. "And we're not going to start discussing who did what." She'd learned through some difficult times that a man could mess up a wet dream if he had the notion to get ahead of himself. Marshall was solely a listener from that point on, having spread his wings a time or two when he and Jasmine were dating. "Anyway, what's done in the past should keep its place. Octavia said she told that scrub of a man where to get off and she moved on with her life. I've only just met her, but that's good enough for me. I say, good riddance to his trifling ass. That's right, I said ass." She rolled her neck when Marshall's mouth hung open almost as much as Legacy's. "I can't stand him. It wouldn't bother me in the least if he choked on a chicken bone." Legacy tried hard not to laugh but couldn't hold it in any longer. Jasmine was pissed. All the hostility she had for I. Rome came pouring out, just like the unbridled clamor that came from everyone else seated at the table.

"I don't see what's so funny. I don't like him. Never did. And he should want to write some lyrics that don't have anything to do with body parts slapping against one another. People should be way past tired of hearing that kind of mess."

After dinner, the waiter tipped back to see if he was welcomed. Marshall fought with Legacy over letting him pay the bill. With Jasmine on his side, it wasn't much of a battle. Octavia received a hug from Jasmine with the same intensity that she'd given Legacy. The ladies exchanged phone numbers and promised to keep in touch. The evening had been saved by Jasmine's relentlessness to help another woman in dire straits. Octavia had two new friends and a promising future that nearly skipped town courtesy of I. Rome and a thirty-six-month waste of time she'd rather forget.

During the ride back to what had been a promising future with Legacy, Octavia noticed that he had few words to say, which was understandable, but she hoped that he would find a way to forgive her deceitfulness, whether she deserved it or not. When she realized that she had never wanted anything so badly, she closed her eyes and offered a silent prayer to ask forgiveness for her shortcomings, misgivings, wrongdoing, and all of her misbehaving in general. She pleaded for a chance to keep what seemed to be slipping from her fingertips and silently begged Legacy to search his heart for that same forgiveness.

Octavia was still hoping when she used her key to enter the guest house while Legacy bedded the Lamborghini in the spacious three-car garage. She was alarmed when she found his small living quarters in disarray. "What happened here? Did you get robbed?"

"Almost," he replied sarcastically, stepping over extension cords and recording tapes. "I moved some things around earlier when I recorded the song I wrote. Well, I didn't actually write it because I can't read music. Anyway, I laid it down earlier . . . before you came." He almost felt stupid bringing it up again. " 'Maybe later we could go over to the house and listen to it?"

"Yesss, I would love to. I need you to know that I'm into any and everything you do. A woman's got to be there for her man. Jasmine told me that and made it clear that I understood how important it is."

"Oh, Jasmine told you that. What else did y'all discuss during that long trip to the powder room?"

"Wouldn't you like to know? Girl stuff." Jasmine had detailed how much it had pained Legacy when Kennedy died while he was out of the country and everything that led up to it, including his fear of AIDS and shying away from intimacy because of it. That explained why he backed off each time Octavia's passionate kisses found their mark.

"I'll bet," he said knowingly. "Whenever women talk about *girl stuff,* the topic of men is bound to come up so don't act like my name didn't get tossed around."

"It did, a little," Octavia admitted, with a wink. "That Jasmine loves her some Legacy Childs. You have a true friend in her."

"She has one in me, too." He leaned to the side, heavy hearted. "Yeah, she got it like that."

" 'Wouldn't have to guess that. You can believe she let me know it, too, and in no uncertain terms. I'm scared to mess up again. She might start cussing and I wouldn't want that on my conscience."

"Yeah, that's makes two of us," Legacy replied in a near whispered tone that trailed off at the end. Octavia picked up on it immediately.

"Legacy, honey, did I say something wrong?"

"It's not something you said exactly. It's just that I've been trying to get a handle on the whole you and I. Rome thing and every detail that has brought us to this point." Legacy cupped his hands around Octavia's waist, pulling her closer to him. Her eyes revealed a deep-seated uncertainty and reserved apprehension, so she inhaled nervously then looked at the floor while Legacy completed his summation. "I know that no one's perfect and love is easy to find but so much harder to maintain. I've also learned that the only mistakes worth regretting are the ones that a man . . . or a woman doesn't learn and grow from. It seems that we've gotten ourselves caught up in a pretty serious storm and there's no getting around it. So, I guess we'll just have to go through it instead. Despite my bruised ego, I still believe in love and I still believe in us."

As Octavia's eyes floated up to meet Legacy's, a tear streamed down into the crease of her lips. "Words can't tell you how sorry I am and how thankful to be given another chance to restore the trust you lost and show you that I can be the woman you need me to be."

"Oh, I'm counting on that, but you'll have to promise me one thing."

"Anything."

"That we never discuss any of the men in your past or the women from mine."

"I promise, baby," Octavia agreed from the depths of her soul. "I'm going to make you so happy, you'll see. I want to be so good to you, the same way you've been good for me. I never thought that a man could make me want to be a better woman, but—"

"Shhh," bade Legacy when he'd heard enough. "I know, and I understand."

Octavia threw her arms around him, nestling against his chest, kissing and squeezing all the apprehensions and uncertainty away. "Legacy, I'm so glad you found me when I had no idea I was lost. Thank you."

"Now don't go thinking that everything I do is just for you. I'm looking out for my own interest, too. Speaking of that, let me get a few things and I'll be right back." He disappeared behind the closed restroom door to slip out of his dress clothes. Octavia walked over to the window to gaze at the harvest moon. It was so bright and high in the sky that she decided to see what old Twinkle was up to. She peered through the telescope lens but the star was not in its usual place. She rose up, stared out of the window, then took another peek.

"Hey, what's going on?" asked Legacy when he returned.

"I think I changed the coordinates by mistake. I'm sorry, but I can't find Twinkle up there anywhere."

"Let me try." Octavia moved aside, looking out the window again. After he checked the triangular degrees, he searched the skies over and over. "What d'ya know. Twinkle *is* gone," he mouthed then scratched his head peculiarly.

"I'm sorry, baby. I know that star meant a lot to you." Octavia noted how he appeared perplexed but not as disturbed as she assumed he would have been. "It did mean a lot to you, didn't it?"

"Yeah, it sure did. But you're my star now, one that I can touch, feel, and hold. Wonder what I should call you?"

"Octavia!" she smarted back with attitude. "And, you could get it tattooed on your . . ." she added suggestively, allowing her eyes to drift downward to the front of his faded jeans.

"Oh, so you want your name on it?"

"When the time comes, but you've got me all geeked over hearing your song. Let's head over and listen to it together. You have a title for it yet?"

"I was thinking 'Octavia's Theme.' 'Bitch Better Have My Money' was already taken."

"And, I'm happy for it." She hit him in the chest with a playful love tap. 'Octavia's Theme', how sweet. You are such a sweetie."

Over the next hour, they listened to the song while sipping wine and kanoodling until Legacy had become burned out on it. "One more time," Octavia begged, "Please, baby, please. For me."

Legacy was eager to oblige, receiving more joy than he'd given as he watched her samba to his musical arrangement like a woman in love. He was transfixed by the way her hips swayed to the beat, nice and easy. "Octavia, can I paint you?" he asked when her sultry moves had taken a toll on him.

"Sure, I'm open for another sketch. As soon as the song is over."

"No, I mean paint you. Literally?"

Octavia stopped dancing, not aware of what he'd meant by that, so he pulled her by the hand and led her toward a room that seemed much too large to be in any residence. It was painted pure white from top to bottom. There wasn't a mark on the tiled floor or on the walls, making it difficult to clearly conceive just how big the room was unless she walked the walls. So, that's what she did.

"I've always wanted to paint in this room," he shouted across the barren floors.

"You would get in so much trouble if the rich guy who owns this house came home and caught you."

Once again he wanted to reveal who owned the home but the time didn't seem right. He wanted her to remain in the same state of mind, without clouding it and derailing his agenda. "Let me worry about that. Here, plug this in for me while I set up." He handed her a CD player. Wouldn't you know it, Etta James's voice wailed as soon as Octavia pushed the play button. "I had to get it after what you did at the Zanzibar. I've been listening to her all day."

Octavia started to sing along, moved by the music. The wine had a hold on her as well. Legacy hauled in several paint cans, set up a tall ladder and a camera tripod, and spread a humongous white canvas on the center of the floor. "So tell me, are you ready to be painted?"

"Yeah, how do you want me to pose?" She stuck her butt out, like many women do for a nightclub Polaroid shot. "Like this?"

"That's good, but not quite what I was going for."

"Then how do you want me?"

"In the nude," he answered plainly.

"You're kidding? You want me naked?"

"Naked is when you're about to get busy. I'm talking about getting down to business, that's nude." He handed her a fluffy right-out-of-the-box bathrobe. Here, put this on when you're ready."

"You are serious." She stood back on her heels, conjuring up the nerve. "What the hell, you're going to see it all sooner or later, anyway. But if you want to view my wares, you'll have to take my clothes off yourself."

"If that's the way you want it."

"That's the way it is, baby."

Legacy sipped from his glass of liquid courage and delved right in.

Octavia's heart fluttered when his fingers slid the mint green long-sleeved dress off her shoulders. She hadn't prepared for this. The way he touched her caused her body to shudder. It was so intimate. A subtle tremor followed when he unsnapped her lacey bra. She was glad to have worn matching underwear and made time for a fresh bikini wax. Legacy was glad that she was his, making it more pleasant when he maneuvered her panties down off her hips and past her long legs. It turned her on when she felt his warm breath brushing against her thighs before he awkwardly handed her the robe.

"Uh-uh," she refused. "I won't be needing that now."

His brow raised and his mouth watered, simultaneously. "Lay down, the canvas is Egyptian cotton. It's very soft." If she had known that she was about to press her skin against a two-thousand-dollar cloth, she would have been overly cautious, so he didn't mention it. "Please close your eyes and relax. I'll do the rest." That was a proposition worth considering.

"Okay, please be gentle. This is my first time . . . *being painted*."

"It won't be your last. Just try to keep as still as possible when I begin. The paint will be kind of cool, but you'll become infatuated with it eventually."

She took him at his word, closed her eyes, and let all inhibitions evaporate. She moaned after discovering that he was correct about the wet paint. As he traced her legs with the feather-soft brush, the coolness rocketed a sensation throughout her entire body. She quivered, apologized, then attempted to slow her exhilarated breathing. Legacy had to keep reminding himself that he was an artist, one who had to contain his desire of scrapping his project and moving to Plan B, the one that called for him to get naked, too.

Covered in ash-white paint, Octavia drifted, anticipating additional coats of cool wetness. When Legacy moved on to decorate the canvas on either side of her, she began to feel neglect but didn't complain. His brush skimmed over the cotton like it had over her welcoming skin. Shades of pastel greens, yellows, and blues were dabbled here and there until there was nothing left to paint. Legacy's "Beauty in Flight" was finished. Octavia was half asleep when the camera flashes began popping from every imaginable angle. She realized then what the ladder was for.

"We're done," he whispered in her ear, kneeling next to her. "Let's get you cleaned up."

Out of her semisedated state, she arose and stepped away from her mark on the floor. When she looked back to see what Legacy had spent two hours creating, it was an awesome site. Butterfly wings lay on either side of where she'd posed. She gazed down at her body. Strange markings ran across her torso and upper thighs. It was a surreal encounter to be immortalized on canvas the way Legacy had crafted it. She felt as if she'd made love instead of having had paint brushes make love to her.

The bath Legacy drew for her in the downstairs master suite was almost scalding hot, but the warmth of it engulfed Octavia. Legacy washed her hair and everything else his hands could reach as she soaked the paint away. Neither uttered what they were thinking; it wasn't necessary to mince words. After Octavia slipped into a fog of unconsciousness, Legacy wrapped her in a lavender beach towel and carried her limp frame into the master bedroom.

When she woke up the next morning, he was still sitting by the bedside in a cloth-covered redwood chair from the extravagant dinner table, where he had been all night. Octavia rubbed her eyes, looking around to get her bearings, and realized she was unclothed beneath the heavy tapestry-print comforter. Her eyes widened. "Did we uhhh . . . last night?"

"No, we didn't. I just watched you sleep."

"Wooo, I'd better get dressed before the man who owns this bed comes home to find a strange woman in it."

"Don't bother, you already spent the night with him. I knew he wouldn't mind."

"What are you talking about? I thought you were with me all night?" Then it hit her. "You? This is *your* house?"

"Yep, lock, stock, and barrel. The car is also mine, the laundromat, and the place where we met."

"Uh-uhhh. You do not own all this." She scanned the vast room from wall to wall. "Suds and Café Brew?"

"Yeah, I needed to make a few sound investments to move some change around."

Pleasantly bewildered, she sat up in the bed with the top sheet covering her breasts. "How . . . much change are we talking about?"

"A whole lotta zeros."

"If that is true, what's the deal with the guest house and the bicycle? What was all that about?"

"I like the guest house. It's cozy and this place is too big for a man to live in all alone. It would have only reminded me of that if I slept here. As for the bike, everyone needs exercise."

"Not that I'm so ready to believe all this, but why would you keep it secret? No, let me take a stab at it. When a woman learns that a man has wealth, he can't be sure whether she's falling for him or for his cheese?"

"Can't be too careful with the cheese. But you accepted me for me and that's what counts." Playfully he tried to peek beneath the sheets. "You know that you're the first person to sleep in this bed. How was it?"

"Play your cards right and you'll find out after we make an appointment to get tested."

"I don't think we need a compatibility test."

"No silly, an AIDS test. I don't want anything to come between us, nothing at all. You're mine now and I want to have a house full of kids, all looking just like *they* daddy. Now go'on and call the Café for some breakfast. And don't say they won't deliver 'cause I know they will.

Tell 'em that the owner's woman is hungry. I want fish and grits and hash browns and coffee, the good stuff and—" She noted that Legacy hadn't moved to comply with her wishes. "What are you waiting on? Just 'cause you happen to be rich doesn't mean I'ma let you skate on spoiling me. You've set a standard and I want you to keep right on treating me like you did when I thought you *was* broke. Had me ready to cosign on a used car for you. See, you play too much. Go on, time's a-wasting."

Legacy made his way over to the telephone. Octavia gawked at him to be sure he'd get her order right. "And get something for yourself," she insisted. "It's on me."

"Pushy, aren't we, this morning? You're beginning to sound so much like Jasmine."

"Good, then it'll be easy getting used to." She fluffed the pillows to get a bit more comfortable. "And go get mama her purse so I can give you a key to my place. Not that you'll be needing it, though, 'cause all this fits me like a size-six thong. Uh-huh, I said it."

Legacy chuckled while he was holding on the line, thinking just how much Octavia did remind him of Jasmine. If things stayed on course, perhaps he could start a family and have a little Deuce of his own calling him daddy and following in his every footstep.

"Hello. Good morning, Dorothy, this is Legacy. Let me talk to Javier."

29

All Said and Done

The Vicious Cuts beauty shop buzzed with customers discussing every subject under the sun. I. Rome's sold-out concert, which was scheduled for later that evening, received the most attention. Truest had grown weary of listening to a bevy of women chatter on about I. Rome's sex appeal and how he made them swoon while working thousands of fans into a screaming frenzy. The client in Truest's chair was the worst of the lot. It was I. Rome this and I. Rome that. She suffered from a severe case of I. Rome on the brain and Truest was about to lose it. If she never heard that name again, it would have been fine with her.

"I'm almost finished with you, Aliza," Truest told her, curling the back of her hair. "You need to stop letting people glue those micro braids in your head. So much of it has broken off that I was forced to cut more than I planned on."

"Girl, that's alright. I. Rome won't be looking at my hair when we hook up again tonight."

After enduring her client's constant babbling, she figured that she must have heard wrong. "What did you say about hooking up with I. Rome?"

"Well, I'm not supposed to say anything 'cause he's married and operates undercover. But if you can't tell your stylist, who can you tell?"

"So, you're saying that you've been getting with him often on the low-low?"

"No, just once, but he can't wait to come back for seconds. All that stuff you see him doing on those music videos, uh-uh, that ain't got nothing on the real thing. I ought to know. I can still smell the leather in that stretch Benz he had me bouncing up and down in. Good thing that wasn't my first rodeo. All that buckin' and bouncin', whew . . . I can't wait to climb back up on that horse for another ride."

That was the last straw. The rage that had come over Truest when she flattened Sylvia had returned, and it had mutated into a more monstrous version of its former self. Her blood boiled and her hand steadied as she lowed the curling iron to toward the back of Aliza's neck. When the scorching heat landed on her skin, a bellowing cry rang above the noise. "Ouuuuuch! Truest, you burned my neck! That hurts!"

"I should have done worse!" Truest hollered back. "Next time, learn to keep your big-ass mouth shut about who you' doin' the fool with." She backed away, disgusted. Every eye was trained on her. "Somebody finish this chick, so she can hurr'up and get the hell out of here."

Aliza stood in the middle of the salon, rubbing the back of her neck and steaming mad. "I don't know why you're trippin', Truest, but you'd want to watch your step!" She was still soothing her skin when Truest disappeared into the office and slammed the door. "Somebody get me some cocoa butter!"

When the office door closed behind Truest, Cee-Cee was asking Octavia how long she thought it would take her to move in with Legacy. Since both of them were well acquainted with Truest's tirades that heated up like a microwave and cooled off just as fast, they didn't break stride. "I'm doing this by the book," Octavia continued. "There will be no shacking up, no shacking."

"Seven bedrooms does not a shack make," Cee-Cee debated, smacking her lips. "I'm proud of you for dropping Isaiah and giving a worthy brotha the chance at making all of your dreams come true."

Truest calmed down when she heard Cee-Cee's update regarding Octavia's love life. "Whaaat? 'Tavia, you got yourself a real baller?" she butted in. "I thought you were so gone over some fine brotha living in a garage or something."

"You were right about him, Tru. He did call and we've been inseparable all week. I spent the night in his big ol' bed and did some things that some people get paid for." Octavia knew that Truest appreciated a good story better if she suspected hot sex was involved.

"Don't let her fool you, Truest," Cee-Cee warned quickly. She didn't want to get Truest revved up, only to have her dissatisfied after digesting the details. "'Tavia is saving it for the carats. Ain't giving it up this time until marriage."

"Damn 'Tavia, that . . . that's great. I'm happy for you." Truest's disappointment in another arena overshadowed the good news.

Just then, Octavia made a displeased expression. She wasn't about to let Truest steal her joy. "You could've fooled me. If I didn't know better, I might have mistaken you for a woman who just got her man took."

"It looks to me that falling in love has done wonders for your intuition. 'Tavia, listen, it's about time I tried to explain some things to you." Truest took a seat on the desk to harness too many thoughts zigzagging through her, all trying to come out at the same time. "You getting with that brotha you really like makes it easier for what I have to say, and believe me, I am excited for you." She closed her eyes briefly, hoping to muster the courage necessary to say the one thing that might bring an end to the friendship she cherished so much. "Uhhh, what I've been meaning to tell you is . . ."

"Ahhhhhhhhhh! It's him! It's him!" women screamed in the salon. High-powered pandemonium flowed freely on the other side of that office door. All three women rushed to it to see what had caused the commotion. Truest was the first one out of the small room. She knew what had transpired at first glance. Before she could double back and block Octavia's vision, her small window of opportunity was gone. Octavia stood next to Cee-Cee, both staring out into the salon area.

"I didn't tell Isaiah that I'd be here this afternoon," Octavia said, watching the women vying for his personal attention.

"Then why is he here?" Cee-Cee asked, watching the women making fools of them-selves. By the time she heard her own words she cringed at the implication.

Octavia's heart rate quickened. "I don't know, but I'm a few seconds from finding that out myself." When she started off on her fact-finding mission, Truest jumped in her path.

"Wait a minute, 'Tavia, before things get too broken to fix."

"Truest, it's not that serious. I just want to know why Isaiah is showing up where I get my hair done on the day after I made sure he understood it was over between us." Octavia tried to move Truest aside, but there was no pushing her off the determined stand she'd made. "Move, Truest!" she demanded.

"Uh-uh. Let's go back in the office and talk about it."

"You should listen to her, 'Tavia," Cee-Cee advised, the voice of reason. "There's something you should know and it won't do either of you any good to discuss it out here."

Moments before, Octavia couldn't understand why Truest had acted so peculiarly. Then suddenly it clicked. "Truest? Don't tell me you've been kicking it with Isaiah. Please tell me you haven't been screwing him behind my back all these years. Tell me, Tru!" Her accusations were loud, very loud. Unwittingly, all the attention in the salon had matriculated her way. I. Rome, surrounded by autograph hounds and sexually deprived fans, froze in his tracks after he noticed Octavia standing next to Truest.

"Not now, 'Tavia," Cee-Cee pleaded. "This is not the time for what you're thinking."

"Bump that, Cee-Cee. Ain't no time like the present to find out who your real friends are." She was staring Truest down as if they were longtime rivals. "I've been confiding in you and the entire time you've been using what I tell you to go tipping back for yourself. Uhh-huh, somebody's getting hurt over this and I won't be the last one!"

I. Rome backed away slowly. He signaled for Ty to make a break with him but the big fellow declined. "This time you're gonna face the music you groove to, homey," Ty informed him. He eclipsed the front door, daring his would-be passenger to try and make a mad dash to escape.

"Cee-Cee. Get your friend!" threatened Truest.

"'Tavia! This is getting way out of hand." Cee-Cee stood equidistance between them. "If you two are so determined to be mad at somebody, it should be him." She pointed out the culprit. Women started jumping off the I. Rome bandwagon like rats on a sinking ship.

"Uhhhhh-huh! I get sick and tired of sistahs fighting over a man that don't neither of 'em belong to," someone stated from the collection of spectators.

"I know that's right," another quipped. "Men have been pitting us against one another since I can remember, and I'm old."

"How about that, Isaiah?" Octavia confronted him with her teeth clenched. "Life's a bitch when your scandalous ways catch up with you, huh? What's the problem, playa? Some cat got your tongue?"

"Now that you've brought it up," Aliza interceded. She ripped off the smock, thinking it would serve her best to keep her hands free and accessible in the event that she needed them. "I won't even pretend to care who you are or what y'all had together. Romey and I ain't trying to let nobody mess up what we got going on now."

"Anika, or whatever your name is, I don't need you to speak for me and this ain't got nothing to do with you," barked I. Rome. "You need to shut the hell up!"

"The name is Aliza, and you didn't have no problem with my mouth being open when I was upside down and pulling stunts in the back of your limo."

There was a collection of "oooh's and ahh's" from the gallery.

Octavia was outdone. With innuendos flying from every direction, she knew it was only the beginning. "Sistah, you don't need to waste your time with this punk. He can't support the weight. As a matter of fact, you might want to lock your panty drawer when he slides by." She sauntered over to him and stuck her finger in his face. "The tabloid rumors about him getting busted in ladies' underwear . . . weren't rumors. Were they, Isaiah? And where in the hell is my favorite purse that suddenly came up missing when you stayed over for that long weekend?"

"Don't be running up in my face about no women's purses and none of that other bullshit y'all bringin' up in here!" he lashed back at her, and anyone else who wanted to be included in the argument. "I ain't to be stressed, so every last one of you silly bitches can kiss my double-platinum ass and anything else y'all find down there." He grabbed the front of his jeans with both hands, then shook two hands full of denim at the ladies. Some of them were appalled. The others went slap-off, screaming and shouting how he was a useless and poor excuse for a black man.

Octavia picked her jaw up off the floor. "Okay you just had to take it to the next level. I knew somebody was going to get hurt." She snatched up a hot curling iron from a nearby table and went after him with it while throwing whatever else she could grab with her other hand. The women cheered Octavia, hoping she'd catch him and teach him some manners. I. Rome stumbled over chairs and dodged all that she hurled his way.

"Hold on now, Baby girl," he pleaded. "Can't we talk about this? You' acting kinda crazy."

As he continued his retreat to escape Octavia's wrath, someone stuck her leg out and tripped him from behind. I. Rome landed hard against the tile floor on his tailbone. More embarrassed than injured, he huffed before further showing his true colors. His eyes floated up to rest on Octavia. "See, I knew I should have dicked and dumped you a long time ago. You wasn't nothing but a show piece and ain't never gonna be nothing more than some nigga's half-breed ho' piece."

Ty relinquished his post by the door and bolted for the car when the name-calling turned dangerous for all men who remained in the general vicinity. Octavia appeared virtually unscathed until tears started streaming down her cheeks. Then, as calmly as you please, she walked over to the nearest workstation. Truest was the first to see what she'd put in her hand. The florescent light glinted off a pair of pointed trimming sheers when Octavia pushed past the crowd of women to seek retribution for a number of his transgressions and swung wildly, barely missing her mark.

"'Tavia, don't!" Truest begged, bent over and breathless. "Please don't hurt him."

"Shut up, Truest!" Octavia exclaimed. "This is between me and Isaiah, and I'm gonna make sure I fix his ass once and for all."

Truest fell to her knees when Octavia shrugged off her wishes and continued her infuriated quest for blood. "Octavia, please, I'm pregnant! And . . . Isaiah's the daddy."

A hush fell over the salon. Pierced by those words, Octavia stopped swinging the sheers. It took a moment for the others to put two and two together, but eventually it occurred to everyone in the room who Truest was carrying a baby for.

"Awwe Truest," Octavia said, her heart broken. "How could you?"

"He's been after me to lose the baby but I wouldn't do it," Truest wailed. Her eyes swelled from tears pouring endlessly. "I did that when I was sixteen and I told him I'm not doing it again."

Cee-Cee helped Truest back into the office. Octavia's hand trembled as she dropped the sheers on the floor where she stood. She was numb when she staggered toward the shop's exit. As if it had been pre-arranged, Ty pulled the limo around. He proudly attended the back door, then escorted Octavia home and away from the scene of more heartache than one woman should have had to endure in one afternoon. She rode along in silence, knowing that she would get past the terrible incident with I. Rome, but she also knew that she'd carry a scar from the trauma that Truest inflicted. There was no way she could have seen that one coming. Some things couldn't be explained. No matter how many times she ran it through her head, she kept coming up short when trying to make sense out of nonsense. Truest had made a poor decision regarding I. Rome that she was willing to live with. Now, Octavia had her own decisions to make. Hers involved eliminating relationships with everyone who was capable of breaking her heart for no reason at all. That decision left her with one less friend than when the mess begun. Understandably, she'd miss Truest, but that was a decision she was willing to live with.

An entire year has passed since all that went down. It's kind of funny how much a person's life can change in twelve months. For starters, Truest had a healthy baby girl she named Chastity, praying the child would live up to her given name. Cee-Cee landed a job as a local reporter. Alphonzo continues to wow his listening audience with his philosophies on love and never misses Cee-Cee's TV news report. She's looking for a wedding proposal and he's looking for a perfect princess-cut three-carat diamond to present to the best thing that ever happened to him.

I. Rome is currently protesting charges of lewd contact with a minor. His new wife is dealing with it the best way she knows how, considering she didn't know what a publicist was when she checked him in at the Lexington Hotel. Tony Tune and Gwendolyn Tyme have not moved from their coveted number-one-spot at the top. They still remain king and queen of the morning airwaves. Surprisingly, Tony gave up his weekly sessions with Tyler and *the others* so that he could rekindle the flame with his second wife, Gladys.

Benny the white shadow intern hit the lotto, and the first thing he purchased was a small rural radio station south of Waco. If you happen to find yourself in central Texas, he'll be the one trying to push an innovative county-funk format. Ebony and Floreese left the radio biz after receiving their patent for an automatic CD-playing floor scrubber. J. C. Penny liked the idea so much they bought the product design from the fellas for 2.5 million dollars.

And, as for Octavia and Legacy, theirs was a romance made in heaven. She moved into the big house, then invited her man to join her there, after they were married of course. Legacy's photographs of *Beauty in Flight* went over big at Cachet last spring. Perhaps you received the catalog. Octavia will have to shed at least forty pounds before she's ready to try something like that again. Besides, she's taking a four-year break from the work-force to learn how to become a great mommy. That's right, she's expecting. Triplets. Legacy has a couple of hundred rhyming names already picked out for their biscuits in the oven. Unfortunately for him, none of the names he selected has made it onto Octavia's list.

Oh yeah, guess who's moving back to Texas? Marshall just signed a multimillion dollar contract with the Dallas Cowboys and Jasmine is already house-hunting. She has her sights set on buying the home two doors from her favorite couple. It's on the market.

READING GROUP GUIDE

1.   How accurate do you think this portrayal of radio life is? Is it less glamorous than you expected?

2.   There are a lot of pranks and paybacks in this novel. How do you feel about practical jokes? Do you think that everyone gets what they deserve?

3.   Many of the women in this book seem to regard other women's men as fair game. How do they justify themselves? Is Octavia two-faced for thinking it's okay for her to be with I. Rome even though he's married, and then blasting Truest for being with him as well? Is cheating with a married man alright if you don't know his wife or girlfriend?

4.   Octavia is frightened when she first realizes that Legacy is offering her everything she ever thought she wanted in a man. Why? Do you understand or sympathize with her fear?

5.   Do you think Octavia's decision to meet I. Rome one last time was the right one?

6.   Cee-Cee is an agent for change in a lot of lives—Octavia's, Truest's, Sylvia's, and Alphonzo's. How does she convince them to change? Do you think she's manipulative or caring or both? Does she manage to help herself in the end?

7.   Women's friendships are at the heart of this novel. How important are these women to one another? How do they express that importance? Do you think Cee-Cee was right to try and hide her knowledge of Truest and I. Rome's relationship from Octavia?

8.   What *does* every sistah want? What does Alphonzo think? Truest? Octavia? Who is right?

For more reading group suggestions visit
www.stmartins.com

St. Martin's Griffin